WORLD O

Nick Earls is the author of bestselling novels *Zigzag Street*, *Bachelor Kisses* and *Perfect Skin*, and the acclaimed short-story collection, *Headgames*. He has also written three novels featuring teenage central characters. *After January* and *48 Shades of Brown* were both award winners and have been adapted successfully into stage plays. His latest is *Making Laws for Clouds*.

Nick Earls' work has been published internationally in English and in translation. He has an honours degree in medicine from the University of Queensland. He has never fried chicken for money.

WORLD OF CHICKENS
NICK EARLS

PENGUIN BOOKS

For more on Nick Earls go to www.nickearls.com

Penguin Books

Published by the Penguin Group
Penguin Books Australia Ltd
250 Camberwell Road, Camberwell, Victoria 3124, Australia
Penguin Books Ltd
80 Strand, London WC2R 0RL, England
Penguin Putnam Inc.
375 Hudson Street, New York, New York 10014, USA
Penguin Books Canada Limited
10 Alcorn Avenue, Toronto, Ontario, Canada M4V 3B2
Penguin Books (NZ) Ltd
Cnr Rosedale and Airborne Roads, Albany, Auckland, New Zealand
Penguin Books (South Africa) (Pty) Ltd
24 Sturdee Avenue, Rosebank, Johannesburg 2196, South Africa
Penguin Books India (P) Ltd
11, Community Centre, Panchsheel Park, New Delhi 110 017, India

First published by Penguin Books Australia Ltd 2001
This edition published by Penguin Books Australia Ltd 2002

10 9 8 7 6 5 4 3 2 1

Copyright © Nick Earls 2001

The moral right of the author has been asserted

All rights reserved. Without limiting the rights under copyright reserved above, no part of this publication may be reproduced, stored in or introduced into a retrieval system, or transmitted, in any form or by any means (electronic, mechanical, photocopying, recording or otherwise), without the prior written permission of both the copyright owner and the above publisher of this book.

Design by Melissa Fraser, Penguin Design Studio
Cover photograph by Tim de Neefe
Typeset in Sabon by Post Pre-press Group, Brisbane, Queensland
Printed and bound in Australia by McPherson's Printing Group, Maryborough, Victoria

National Library of Australia
Cataloguing-in-Publication data:

Earls, Nick, 1963– .
 World of chickens.

 ISBN 0 14 300099 3.

 I. Title.

A823.3

www.penguin.com.au

1

Here goes: 'Shouldst thou perchance purchase this mighty fowl, all will be well, and well for all.'

Done with flourish, as it should be. With a flouncing and flapping of wings, and with the usual outcome. Taringa's most stylish fast-food selling, but not a word of the spruiking part reaching anyone beyond the moulded plastic chicken head it started in. To the traffic, it's all a big wasted mime.

The lights change and the Leyland P76 at the front drives by, with the children in the back clearly having been instructed not to look at the chicken.

Problem is, I'm the chicken. Me and seven tall feet of costume, from my orange rubber toes to my orange rubber comb, with my broad white rooster body in between. And, sure, it's the chicken they're ignoring, but it's hard not to take these things personally – at least to some degree.

'Sirrah, thou art nought but a beef-witted bum bailey,' I say rather too loudly, denouncing the driver, while giving an energetic flap of my right wing towards the World. Towards Ron Todd's World of Chickens. And anyone who thinks that, after weeks of this, I'm in some kind of rut out here should be aware that I saw it that way first, so that's why I turned things Elizabethan. I got in early, before all this bored me stupid and I gave it away and went looking for some other part-time job.

Not that this is exactly the job I thought I applied for. On the student union noticeboard it offered the anticipated shit pay, included meals and required 'some experience in the food-service industry' and 'good people skills'.

Now here I am, by the road – in the lonely world well beyond people skills – because I happen to fit the chicken costume, almost, and it's definitely one of those jobs when almost is more than good enough. If you almost fit the chicken costume you only spend half your time making burgers and the other half kerbside, attracting attention if not custom, swinging your arms around in mad-winged mime, saying whatever you want since they're all in their cars with the windows up.

But this time it turns out that Ron Todd is right next to me. This time, as I swivel enticingly – swivel and wave – there's a thump and my wing takes Ron in the chest.

'Whoa there,' he says, and takes a step backwards. 'Love the enthusiasm, Philip, but pedestrian traffic isn't out of the question. Remember that. We don't want to have me sued when one of you chickens decks someone.'

'Sorry. But there is a bit of a visibility issue when you're looking at the world through a chicken's beak.'

'Yes. I suppose we could open it a bit more, but then people'd be able to see you in there.'

'And that'd completely spoil the illusion, wouldn't it?'

'True, true.' Ron looks thoughtful, the cars cruise past. A chicken in conversation with a middle-aged man, maybe we should offer the traffic more of that – it's surreal enough that I'd look at it. 'Quite a brain for a chicken,' he says. 'I like that.'

'Thanks.'

'Now, what was that you were saying when I came out here?'

'When exactly did you come out here?' Okay, this is a

cause of at least some concern. I did most of Hamlet's soliloquy before the lights turned red and any self-respecting chicken where I come from would view that as, to say the least, a little passé.

'You were talking about beef. And we don't do beef.'

'No. Exactly. Beef-witted. That's what I was saying. As in, none too bright because they're passing up the pleasures of the World.'

'Beef-witted,' he says, trying it out for size.

'Yeah. It's Shakespearean. I do a bit of Shakespeare out here.' He gives me a look that says there has to be more to it. 'It helps,' I tell him, and I shrug the wings and turn them to him palms upwards. (Do wings have palms? Perhaps not.)

'Good, Philip. Good.' His look sidles from thoughtful to puzzled. 'You'd be up for a swap soon, wouldn't you? How about we see you inside in five, back on the counter with Frank, and we'll send Sophie out here?'

'Sure.'

He walks away. I resume my courting of the traffic.

And, all right, maybe he wasn't expecting Shakespeare, but what am I supposed to do? The chicken thing, certainly, but a person's brain does wander. Sometimes to old monologues or Elizabethan insults, sometimes to a list of the branches of the external carotid artery (superior thyroid, ascending pharyngeal, lingual, facial, occipital, posterior auricular, maxillary, superficial temporal), frequently to a catalogue of personal incidents that would be better off forgotten, sometimes to a few opening lines of autobiography, which might go like this:

> You know the sign of the neon chicken. You've driven past it countless times, heading west. As you come over that hill, the lights of Ron Todd's World of Chickens are like

a beacon on the western horizon. A complicated multi-coloured beacon, announcing chickens in large numbers. Indeed, a world of them. And now it's your world, too.

I think that's the most recent draft. In the film version it's prologue, with a hand-held shot from a car. It's voiceover, then there's something from INXS's *The Swing* and the opening credits.

But it's on hold. In film language, it's in turnaround. Very early turnaround, since it didn't move anywhere to start with. The draft script put me off. There wasn't a voice in which it sounded close to cool. Not even Bogart and, after all these years, that's still the ultimate test. Not that it doesn't have its limits (for example, Peter Brady and his attempt to go suave with pork chops and apple sauce), but I went out once with a girl last year and she took me to see *The Maltese Falcon*, and those things stick in your head. Bogart's voice makes a lot of mundane shit sound cool, but he met his match with my life.

I thought telling it in the second person would help, but it didn't help much. I thought it would at least sound better. I don't know if it would have been autobiography any more or not, but that's a technicality. I figured it'd make it a better story. It worked for Jay McInerney in *Bright Lights, Big City*.

I'd like to believe it's the chicken suit that's the problem with this job. I'd like to believe it's the problem with the second-person narrative of my life as well, but that's putting a lot down to a chicken suit.

The other problem with the job is that Ron Todd expects a lot from his chickens. We're his best and so far only promotional strategy, and he had the suit specially made. He said it took four attempts to get a moulded plastic chicken face you could trust – 'trust like a newsreader', was how he put it. Not that Frank and I could see the link between newsreaders and chicken burgers, but from day one we knew better than to ask. I knew better than to ask, and I told Frank that applied to both of us.

But Frank doesn't have to worry about that, anyway. Frank does not have the shoulders of a chicken, and spends the whole shift at the counter while Sophie and I alternate in the suit. Sophie's too small to fit it and I'm a little too tall, but if I crouch slightly and she walks with her feet well apart we can each chicken without falling over.

The three of us are often on together. Frank told Ron at the job interview that he and I were a package deal, and Ron said he usually did his own rostering but he'd bear that in mind.

'What Frank means is . . .' I remember saying.

And that's something I get to say quite a lot. In this case what Frank meant was that it'd be practical for us to work the same shifts. We'd be coming from the hospital together, and only Frank has a car. At least that was much easier to explain than most times when Frank says something and means something a little different (or more complicated, or more reasonable, or less annoying).

Frank's talk is content-driven, and there's not much thought given to conversational niceties. Actually, that's flattering him. Ideas trip out of Frank's mouth and pick fights when they don't even mean to. Frank calls any other approach to conversation 'pretty much bullshit'. Frank had his nose broken twice at school, and it didn't take me long to work out why when we met at uni.

And that's five minutes.

I head for the door and Ron comes out to meet me. No surprise. I'd expected that our conversation was only Part A of a two-parter.

'Is it the rhythm you're going for with the Shakespeare?' he asks me, in a way that's too earnest for anyone's good. 'Shakespeare lends himself to a bit of rhythm, doesn't he?'

'Sure.'

'Good. Rhythm's good. But I was wondering – and it's not a criticism, just an observation – I was wondering if it might be even better if you made it a bit more chickeny? I'm not sure.'

'It's a tough choice, that one. You're talking about getting into the chicken head space.'

'Hmmm.'

'And that means you've got to look at how to get there. It's a question of technique. It's not just *being* that chicken. It's *how* to be that chicken. It's System chicken versus Method chicken, Stanislavski chicken versus Strasberg chicken.'

'So, um, rhythm then,' he says after a long pause. 'Maybe we start with rhythm, work on that aspect first. So here's a thought. Now, don't get me wrong, Shakespeare's great. But I just thought I'd put another name in your head as well. Gene Kelly.'

'Gene Kelly.'

'When I think of rhythm, I tend to think of Gene Kelly. What do you reckon? I've always found him very . . .'

'Persuasive?'

'Yeah. Yeah, good word. Maybe you could talk that one through with Sophie when you're changing. Don't tell her this, but I'm not always sure her heart's in it and a new slant on it all couldn't hurt.'

He swings the door open for me, and Sophie comes out from behind the counter. She looks at Ron – in the way you can't help but look at parents when you're sure they've been boring people – she puts her tongs down, and we walk out the back to the toilet.

'Sorry,' she says, once we're in the corridor and I'm

walking along behind her, looking out through the beak slot at the back of her head. 'Bloody Dad.'

'It's fine. If he wants to pay me to chat, who am I to complain?'

'How were the surgery exams?'

'Don't know. Done, mainly. Okay, I think. The written was okay, then we had the clinical exam on Wednesday and you usually leave those feeling pretty strange about it all. Or maybe that's just me.'

'So, holidays now?'

'Yeah. Three glorious days, and one of them already gone. We start obstetrics on Monday.'

'Three days? Ripped off. You've got to love an arts degree,' she says as I walk into the toilet cubicle and start undoing the costume.

Sophie's doing a BA. Or, as Frank has been known to refer to it on days of overstudy or brutal timetabling, a BJA. Bachelor of Just Arts. A term I've persuaded him not to use in front of Sophie. He maintains he's never met an Arts student who had to get out of bed on a Monday or a Friday, and he's happy to tell them he thinks their lives are 'just one bloody Easter after another'.

I open the door and hand her the costume as she goes in.

'So, obstetrics,' she says as she's changing. 'What'll that be like?'

'I don't really know yet. There are parts of the term when we have to live in, I think. When we're on Labour Ward. That'll be different.'

'So you actually get to deliver babies?'

'That's the plan.'

'Well, that'll be interesting.' Then she's out again and now it's my turn to see her eyes in there, in the beak slot looking out at me. 'Here goes nothing.'

'Go, be that chicken. And tonight's theme, should you be struggling for motivation: *An American in Paris*. Imagine plummeting pretend rain, an umbrella, an amazing lightness of foot.'

'Dad. Bloody Dad. Gene Kelly. Is that really what he was talking to you about?'

'You mean Gene Kelly's come up before?'

'I'm chiiiicken in the rain,' she sings in a wobbly way that may or may not be put on. 'Just chiiiicken in the rain. What a glorious feeling to be chick-chick-chicken again.'

'Sure, but it's nothing without the footwork.'

She kicks the door open and swaggers into the food-service area with a gait that always suggests she might be in a shoot-out and about to draw. Sophie knows better than to try Gene Kelly out there, but Ron goes outside with her so I expect the topic will come up.

And that leaves me with Frank, and Frank has been in a shitty mood all day. I'm guessing it's down to something that didn't go well in his clinical exam yesterday, but with him you have to pick your time to bring it up.

'Thought he'd never fucking go,' Frank says as he scrapes some grungy bits off the cooking plate and watches Ron walk away into the darkness doing all the talking, one arm waving with each bit of good advice, the other trapping Sophie's shoulders so she won't miss a word.

Ron says it's all about the illusion. That's why we change out the back and use the toilet to do it. It's not as though you have to get anywhere close to nude to don the chicken, but Ron said at the start that we needed to get a routine going, and it should be about no-one ever seeing the chicken costume as a costume. So what they get to see instead is a big chicken that appears to have a bladder problem, and that's an image that's yet to ignite any kind of burger frenzy. Not that Ron isn't prepared to work at it. He told me a week or two ago that he used to call himself a battler but he'd recently upped that to self-made man.

Ron Todd wears a chunky gold bracelet, but he says he wears it for his rheumatism. He has a dark toupee, though the hair that grows at the back and sides of his head is grey. He wears a seemingly endless range of body shirts with yellow-brown armpits, but that's only because some of the synthetics from the seventies are proving to last a long time, even when they discolour early. And shorts. He wears semi-formal walk shorts every day, regardless of circumstances, and thick socks held just below the knee with the aid of the inevitable never-slip strategy of a couple of pieces of customised elastic. I haven't seen them, but I know they're there. I had maths teachers in the seventies who could have shared a wardrobe with Ron, and one of them used to sit twanging his home-made garters against his calf while we were doing geometry.

And a glass eye. Ron Todd also has a glass eye, courtesy of his Vietnam service as far as we know. A glass left eye with an iris that's a richer shade of brown than the right – a jersey-cow brown eye, and you'd think they could have done a better job than that. He limps as well, when his hip plays up, and we've assumed that that dates back to Vietnam too. And I always thought it was copper bracelets for rheumatism, not gold, but there never seems to be a good time to get into that.

We've been working here only five weeks and already we know far more than we need to about Ron Todd. But, as the sign says, it is his world here.

The Todds have the entrepreneurial spirit that runs in

some families but doesn't run in mine – the spirit that says there's no better way to be made than to be self-made, and to show it. Zel Todd – never Zelda, though I think that's what it's short for – is Ron's wife and Sophie's mother and one of her main jobs in the Todds' world is to take their success and show it. She wears lots of white, only white, always set off by the uncompromising whiteness of her thrashed-blonde hair, one of a range of gold fob chains and gold sandals. She carries herself in a way that, I think, tries to be statuesque, but ends up as an unearned kind of aloof at best.

While Ron and Sophie are inconspicuous shades of pale, Zel Todd is deeply tanned, but not in a kind way. Tanned like a saddle, not like a person. And her crow's feet look almost like crow's feet and her pastel lips almost shimmer. She has a background in hairdressing and, I'm sure, believes you never go out without looking your best.

But maybe I'm not being fair. I have a tendency to be silently critical of people. A girl once told me that, and it's not one of my better features. Perhaps I could be nicer about Zel, though it'd take some effort.

The way Frank sees it, Zel should 'produce daughters who are absolute spunks, but somehow she ended up with Sophie, and she's much more your type'.

There's so much there not to argue with, since every bit of it could do with several kinds of contradicting.

I'm out at the road again and, without Shakespeare, I'm losing focus. There's no Gene Kelly in me, and we're all simply going to have to accept that.

With Ron on his way home it's back to the three of us again and, when I turn around and look into the bright lights of the shop, I can see Frank with his lips set up for whistling. Behind the counter, I'm sure his foot is tapping away. Sophie is staring grimly into the distance, looking like someone trying not to think about a dental abscess. That pretty much confirms that Frank's making some attempt at music.

Frank thinks there's melody involved – he really does – but the tunes get lodged in his deep, troubled sinuses and the words come out with round about the same lilt as morse code. The last few shifts he seems to have slipped into a Jackson Browne phase. Sometimes, when Sophie's chickening and we're in one of those stretches between customers, he makes me do backing vocals to 'Running on Empty'. Mainly ooooos.

Frank's often said he wouldn't mind being in a band, and the only thing standing in the way is his singing. And the fact that he keeps forgetting to learn an instrument. He has the charisma angle covered, but a very narrow skill base. Plus, it's covers bands that get all the work and – Jackson Browne phase aside – Frank's more an originals man. He spends a lot of the time here gazing into the distance inventing song fragments with some poorly focused aim on glory. He gets pissed off when they all start sounding country. It could be the material. Frank's Greatest Hit: the mournful couplet, 'It's too late to fight and it's too late to run, I sold my ammo when I sold my gun'. He can make it sound quite heart-wrenching, while at the same time being almost meaningless. Narrative, Frank, I've told him. Give it some narrative. Make us care.

Sure enough, there's some sad tale unwinding under a big country sky when I walk in to change.

'One day,' I tell him, 'you've just got to take those Kenny Rogers albums and snap them over your knee.'

'I can't. They're my mother's.'

'You are so the coward of the county. She doesn't force you to play them, does she?'

'No, they're just . . . kind of contagious. You don't think they've sold millions by chance?'

Sophie and I head out to the toilet. 'It's good you came in,' she says. 'I was about ready to shoot him, and his fucking horse. Sorry, but I was.'

What Sophie never factors in is that Frank, contrary to appearances, has to carry the weight of being the family genius. That's a view held by four members of Frank's family, with his big brother probably the only exception. So, when it comes to things like medicine and songwriting, Frank admits he lacks benchmarks. 'We don't do creative, and we don't do tertiary,' he told me once when giving me his views on the differences in our backgrounds. 'I'm the first generation of my family that's come down from the trees, you know.' His family has a tree-lopping business, but they'd probably prefer him to find another way of putting it.

We call Sophie in when it's time to close. She goes out the back to take the costume off, and Frank and I start cleaning up.

Over the last couple of weeks, Frank has developed a routine for this. He gets most of the cleaning done before we shut and then, the moment ten o'clock comes around, he makes himself at least a couple of burgers. Which he justifies by saying we aren't doing enough business to turn the meat over effectively anyway, and a lot of it should really be chucked out.

'Chicken: the most dangerous meat in catering.' That's what he said when the plan first occurred to him. Said through a brave mouthful of burger, like a man sacrificing himself to save others from possible contagion. 'Remember micro? Never mix your cooked chicken with your raw. Never let your chicken get close to room temperature.

It's either in the fridge, or on the hotplate. Never keep your chicken a moment too long. Or Ron Todd's World of Salmonella is only one ugly blunder away.'

The best part of it is that he got me to talk it through with Ron — my job, since I got a significantly higher mark in microbiology — and Ron is therefore now grateful for Frank eating a lot of his food.

'We run a low-risk operation here,' Ron said, proud and totally sucked in at the one time. 'We've got to stand by our hygiene. I know I can trust you two. You're practically doctors. And I like that. I value your input,' he said, like a book.

But Frank couldn't leave it there. He turned the sudden availability of chicken into the challenge of making progressively bigger burgers and fitting them into his mouth in one go. And Frank's mouth, I have to say, is awesome.

Sophie comes back from hanging the costume on its hook in the stock room and she says, 'Dad left your pay cheques in there. Here you go.'

'Just in my pocket, thanks,' Frank says. 'I've got gunk on my hands.' Burger one is coming together.

Sophie looks suspicious, as though Frank's pockets aren't to be trusted, and she puts his envelope down next to him on the bench.

Mine goes directly into my gunk-free hand and she says, 'You guys right to lock up?'

'No problem. If you do the till business, we'll sort out the rest. Most of it's done, anyway. And Frank's snack won't take long.'

I put the lids on the tomatoes, lettuce and onion and carry them out the back. I can hear coins falling into the bag as I'm putting the containers away. Frank's whistling again, through his teeth this time. It's a different sound, but it's still not pretty. Kind of like wind passing through an old house.

'Walk me to my car, Phil?' Sophie says when I get back out there with a box for the sauce bottles. 'Keep the robbers at bay.'

'They'll never get past me.' It's a bold claim, but I think it was called for. Frank laughs into a mouthful of burger. 'Yeah, right. Go ahead and make a smart-arse remark. It won't be me we're laughing at when lettuce comes out your nose.'

I'm not the most obvious of unarmed guards. What would I use if someone went to rob Sophie? Negotiation? A good, shrill girly scream? A really tough sonnet? We'd give them the money. Walking Sophie to the car is procedure, something we've agreed to do. It simply didn't seem like a good idea to send her (or anyone) out alone into the night with a cash bag.

There's a train pushing past on the line behind the shops, accelerating out of Taringa station and heading west out of town, only three carriages lit and all of them mostly empty.

'So, you're another pay cheque closer to the video camera then?' Sophie says when the noise drops.

'Yeah. Still a few to go, though. But I'm really here for the love of it, of course. The money's just a bonus.'

She laughs, and our feet clang on the metal steps down to the car park. 'So what do you love most, do you reckon? Would it be the customers? Or do you just love chicken? The suit. I bet it's the suit.'

'The suit is liberating, I'll admit that. It's pretty special. I do love just about every minute I spend as the chicken. Plus, the counter part of the job lets me put in some quality time with Frank and that's a highlight.'

'Don't get me started.'

'How do you think it's going? The business side of it? I'm probably not supposed to ask, but I thought there'd be more customers. We seem to be doing a lot of flapping and not selling a whole lot of burgers.'

'Yeah, I know. I think dad thinks it's okay. For a new place. Quiet, but you have to expect that when a place is new, or when it's changed hands and had a totally new fit-out and got a new name.' She takes her keys from her pocket and opens her car door. 'I think it's okay.'

'Good.'

She gets into the car, shuts the door and winds the window down. 'All clear,' she says. 'Well escorted.' There's a pause that perhaps borders on awkward. 'Well, I'll see you. Monday, I think.'

'Yeah, Monday.'

She turns the key, starts the engine and the talking is done. She waves and drives the car up the concrete ramp, turns left into the traffic and she's gone.

The pause – or at least its borderline awkwardness – is a definitional thing, nothing more. It comes about because I am only there as some hopeless kind of protection, and neither of us has really adjusted to the concept. We can be workmates who share a chicken costume, I think we're becoming friends as well, but in those seconds out of the light and away from Frank and away from all that poultry we're more like two people saying goodbye at the end of an evening. I think that's what it is. I'm not used to being an escort, she's not used to having one.

Back upstairs, Frank is already slipping burger number two into his mouth, about a third at a time. I pull a couple of large cups out of the dispenser at the drink machine, and I ask him if he might be interested in a beverage.

'Please.'

'And would that be a regular Sprite, no ice?'

'Mmmm.' There's more burger in his mouth now. The

mmmm is a yes. Frank thinks ice is a waste of space in a bought beverage, and he can't break the habit when he isn't paying.

I squirt us each a Sprite and take Frank's over to the counter. I walk around drinking mine, checking that the front door's locked, turning the sign to 'closed'. Next on my list: the food preparation area.

'Benches?'

'Check.'

'Hotplate scraped and oiled?'

'Check.'

'Have you mopped the floor?'

'Check.'

'Are you lying to me?'

'Check.'

'You weren't even paying attention, were you?'

I fetch the mop and bucket and give the floor a cursory going over. It's only behind the counter, where I've shed my usual substantial amount of lettuce, that any real work is needed. Soon the job's done. The food is all away, the place is tidy and Frank is eating a handful of grated carrot and watching me do the unnecessary final walk around that I can't stop myself doing.

'Check already,' he says.

'Yeah, okay.' I join him at the counter and take my last mouthful of Sprite. He lets rip with a big gassy burp and goes back to chewing. 'With all the elegance of a cow at a fence . . .'

'No worries. Now let's get out of here. The last twenty-four hours have not been my finest.'

'This evening . . . ?' He doesn't mean this evening. 'Oh, last night. How was it?'

He swallows, raises his eyebrows. 'Patchy, to be honest. Pretty bloody patchy.'

'I did tell you that, without even seeing it, I was pretty sure *The Killing Fields* wasn't a going-out-type movie.'

'That was the least of my worries. She's, like, a talker, okay?'

'In movies? I hate that.'

'No, on the nest, mate. Stick with me here. This is back at her place after the movie. And I don't mind a talker, obviously, but then she starts going "Fuck me, fuck me . . . "'

'It's okay, you don't have to tell me all of it.'

'No, it's germane to the matter under discussion. Okay, she's going "Fuck me, fuck me," right? And I said, "I thought I was fucking you." Like, just for a second, I thought she was telling me I'd gone up the wrong way. You know . . . slipped it up the unintended orifice. And she thought I was taking the piss about her being a talker. And then it was on for young and old. It was like I'd never done a thing right in my whole life. She went on and on about me looking at other women all the time.'

'Which you do.'

'Looking. *Looking*.' There's indignation in the way he says it. 'What's the big deal? I'm only looking at bits of them anyway.' He starts to smirk. 'I mean, be fair. We live in a very visual world. What's a man to do? Obviously there was something wrong about it though, as far as she was concerned. In about five seconds I was out in the street with my clothes coming out the window. It turned out there was a bit she'd been bottling up.'

It's twenty minutes later, when we're halfway back to my place in Frank's purple Valiant, that we hit the usual blaming phase.

'Mate, I blew it,' he says. 'Blew it like a nose.'

'Self-loathing, Frank. They told us in psych it wasn't pretty.'

His grip on the wheel tightens. He brakes as the lights ahead of us change, and the two pine-tree air fresheners swinging from the rear-view mirror slap into the windscreen. Frank's proud of his car, with that pride taking a particular emphasis on odours and squeaks. His little sister, Vanessa, idolises him and he's not afraid to use that. He lets her clean the interior sometimes, to practise her car detailing skills, and she painted rally stripes down the sides for his last birthday. Because of them, Frank now refers to the car as 'a bit of a sports job'.

'Look,' he says, recovering some of that old fighting spirit, 'this isn't easy. Jesus, she was quite a package. And she spelt her name Cyndi too, like, with an "I" at the end. That's porn-star spelling. It kind of got my hopes up, you know? I know I've got to face it. I know it's a quandary. Shit, she had pink lipstick. Do you get what I'm saying?' He pauses, steadies. 'I know what people think about me, but I'm a relationship man at heart. I hate being single. I hated today.'

'Well, welcome to my 1985. Enjoy your stay.'

2

You've driven past it on the way to the coast, the sign of the neon mower. One by one, Ron Todd is claiming the city's arterial roads, putting some new world there, and the name Ron Todd in lights.

That was another line of bio, I think.

Ron Todd set up World of Chickens because Ron Todd's World of Mowers at Kedron was a success and he wanted to diversify.

In our early days, ambition got the better of him. We had four or five people on each shift, including some of the Mowers part-timers. Who never actually said it, but often gave the impression they were lowering themselves. They dealt with chicken like people doing the best they could with the wrong tools – they tried to get out of putting marg on the burger buns and they didn't even start to comprehend the importance of adequate refrigeration.

Now the standard staffing level is three: two at the counter and cooking, and one chicken. There's marg on every bun unless specifically requested otherwise, we treat the fillets with close to the respect you'd give a vaccine, and anything that might be past its prime we feed to Frank. We, the Chickens crowd, think things are much improved now that the Mowers crowd has gone.

Three hours into obstetrics, and already my attention

level isn't what it should be. We've had our introduction to the term, and the rest of the morning is a tutorial called 'Taking an Obstetric History'. It comes with an uncommonly good handout, so the usual frenzy of note-taking isn't necessary. Isn't allowed even. The tutor began by saying, 'I'd rather you listened and thought about this than had your heads down writing notes. So it's all in the handout.'

First day of term, Mater Mothers Hospital. We've turned up with our white coats in our bags, the free stethoscopes a drug company gave us last year and our yet-to-be-opened copies of Beischer and Mackay's *Obstetrics and the Newborn*. Those of us who have them, anyway. I've had mine since January. Frank, who denies most realities as long as he can, tends to hold off until scrounging each book from somewhere mid-term.

For me, the year begins and the summer holidays end when a parental credit card turns the book list into two box-loads of reality – a year of text books to be shelved and wait their turn.

We're already at least two thirds of a box into the year, now that we've put psychiatry and surgery behind us. Though not far behind us when it comes to surgery. At the end of 'Taking an Obstetric History', the tutor tells us that our long cases from last term are marked and can be picked up at the office.

'Some of us had been thinking coffee wouldn't go astray,' Franks says to me on the way to the door.

'It's a hospital. Don't think about the coffee. It'll only disappoint you.'

We leave as a group, and the curve of the drive leads us up the hill to the stately old Mater Private Hospital and the office of the Clinical Sub-Dean.

'I hate this bit. I just want to get it over with.' It's meant to be said in my head, but it comes out before I can stop it.

'It's only ten per cent.'

'Ten per cent where you've still got to get at least five or you do it again.'

'Yeah, whatever. It's just a case. As if you'll have any problem. As if any of us should have any problem. It's the other ninety per cent that's the big deal. This is the easy part – pick a patient, go through everything, write it up. You even know what happens to them in the end, before you hand it in.'

'It's O'Hare who's marking them,' one of the others says. 'Don't forget that.'

Charles O'Hare – apparently Charlie to his friends, not that we're aware of any – has been a surgical registrar at the Royal too long, and it's turned him mean. He keeps not quite passing his final exams and not quite making the consultants happy, but somehow he stays part of the system. This year, for the first time, his unit had a new consultant who was younger than him. We could have done without that.

'O'Hare and his bloody Tim Tams,' Frank says as we go up the steps. 'I'm so glad that's over. The bastard totally put me off chocolate biscuits.'

I'd rather not be reminded. O'Hare would sit on the edge of his desk eating biscuits in every tute, as though we were a waste of his time, a bunch of people who had turned up to annoy him while he was eating. But it was his learn-by-scorn approach that had least appeal. He'd sit there and fire badly-worded questions at his victim, he'd trick them into giving the wrong answer or freeze them into giving no answer, and then would come the scorn. The 'exactly what makes you think you might pass this term?' scorn.

My case report is near the top of the pile, which is starting to spread messily across the table outside the Sub-Dean's office. On other people's front pages I can see marks ranging between four and eight out of ten, maybe one eight and a half. I've got seven. I'll settle for that.

I walk back outside, into the clump of people who are flicking through their cases page by page. I've earned a few ticks, a few 'goods' and one 'unlikely'. On page five O'Hare has written 'An ultrasound would have been a cheap, quick and non-invasive way of getting the same information' and on page six, next to the last disease listed in my differential diagnosis, he's put 'maybe once in 100 years'. In tutes, that would have been one of his friendlier remarks. I've done pretty well. He even finishes with 'Good work overall. A bit too reliant on textbooks and not enough on judgement in parts.'

Frank's has no mark written on the front page.

'He must have put it somewhere,' he says. 'Maybe the thought of a ten embarrassed him, so he had to write it inside.'

Page one has a couple of ticks, pages two and three some circling and the next four pages have nothing. At the bottom of an otherwise untouched page eight it says, 'Mostly mindless copying of the patient's file. Do you even know what the abbreviations mean? I thought I'd made my dislike of them clear. RESUBMIT. Please see me.'

'Arsehole,' Frank says. He wasn't expecting a ten, but he wasn't expecting this. 'What an arsehole. Resubmit. Jesus.'

To O'Hare's credit, he was never anything but clear about his dislike of abbreviations. In our trial case write-ups we all used them, because that's what the residents did in the files in the wards. The afternoon he handed the write-ups back, he called abbreviations 'an evil kind of shorthand'. He even said they were 'festering'. And, if that wasn't clear enough, Greg Schmidt played into his hands when O'Hare went for the 'making an example of someone' part of the learn-by-scorn technique.

'SOBOE,' O'Hare said, one mean and dangerous letter after another. 'Is it a kind of musical instrument, and is it so important that you want to put it in capitals? Was the patient a very good soboe player? What are you saying when you put SOBOE?'

And the answer, we all knew, was shortness of breath on exertion. But that wasn't the point. We were about to get a lesson in thinking things through rather than copying, a lesson in spelling things out. A lesson in not being lazy.

Right up until Greg Schmidt said, with a tremor in his voice that we'd never heard before, 'Swelling of back on exertion.' Rising at the end like a sad lonely question and, even as we laughed, was all knew what we were up for. And that we'd never be using abbreviations again.

'He never liked me,' Frank's saying.

'He never liked anyone.'

'Yeah, he never liked anyone, but he knew my name. You kept a low profile. Smart bastard. "RESUBMIT. Please see me." I'm going to use that word Cyndi hated, and it starts with a C.'

'It's the Mater, Frank, and you're shouting. Use it quietly. It's not a nun-friendly word.'

'Mindless copying. Are you telling me you didn't copy from the patient's file? Are you telling me you made it up?'

'No. Not at all. You'd be mad to make it up. Copying's inevitable, it's the mindlessness he took offence to. The visible display of copying.'

'I've got to resubmit. Have you worked that out? At the end of this term, in the mid-year break, I've got to go to a hospital, attach myself to some poor sick bastard, write it all down and resubmit. And, even if I've passed the rest of the term, if it doesn't work out when I resubmit I get to do surgery again at the end of the year when you're all off doing an elective somewhere.'

'It won't happen that way. You'll pick a good case, and it won't be a patient of O'Hare's and you won't use abbreviations and you'll be fine.'

'Could I just copy yours, maybe?'

'Do you want to think that through? You might as well go and find a few nuns now and shout that word Cyndi didn't like right at them. And I could probably come along and do it with you, since I reckon O'Hare would be gunning for both of us. You could find a case that was like mine, and that might make it easier.'

'Ah, like yours,' he says, smiling, nodding, putting the emphasis on like. As if things are looking up, but now being conducted in code. 'I get it. So should I take yours with me now?'

'We'll talk in the mid-year break.'

Frank tosses me the keys when we get to his car at the end of the day.

'You take the wheel, Mister Seven out of Ten,' he says, and we drive.

Mister Seven out of Ten, as though it ranks me among the big over-achievers.

As we loop around onto the freeway from the Mater the sun is low in the west, easing down towards Mount Coot-tha, eye level and in front of us as we merge with the traffic. We're on our way to World of Chickens.

Frank opens the glove box. He takes out the jar of Staminade, sucks his finger and swirls it around among the clumps of crystals. He rubs the finger on his gums and works his tongue and saliva vigorously like 'Lancelot Link Secret

Chimp', that is, like a lower primate battling with a mouthful of toffee to create whimsical dubbing opportunities, and a kind of sixties TV I'm glad I can only vaguely remember.

Staminade, for Frank, isn't merely a green salty sports drink. It's become a habit, and not a simple one. If he's not driving, and if work is done for the day, he'll have a mouthful of vodka too. It's reminiscent of the best of his invented cocktails, the *brizgarita* – the hometown Brisbane version of a more famous salty cocktail from somewhere else. But the complex formula of Staminade means that the hard work's already done with the brizgarita, already in the jar. And all you have to do is mix yourself a strong, cold glass of it and toss in a shot of vodka and a shot of tequila. Perhaps with a slice of lemon and some Staminade powder crusting around the rim, if it's an occasion.

As Frank sees it, with that cunning electrolyte balance it's got its own built-in hangover cure. And if you don't get the ratios quite right you can always have a couple in the morning, with a raw egg and some B vitamins substituted for the vodka. The tequila, he says, isn't really negotiable.

'The brizgarita's day will come,' he claims, though it hasn't come yet. But right now, that kind of glory isn't on his mind. That's the ambitious Frank, the other Frank. This afternoon we have the Frank who is concentrating on being loudly shitty about his surgery long case mark and being dumped.

'Seems like he's got a lot of weekend jobs on at the moment,' he says, moving comfortably into item three of his catalogue of complaint, the fact that his father made him work most of the weekend. 'There's a lot of people who really want to be home when you come over to their place and drop a tree. It's lucky there were no heart murmurs today, since all I can hear is bloody chainsaws.'

He goes for some more Staminade, and he's talking again before the finger's out of his mouth.

I've known him long enough to know that this is one of those times when it's best to sit there and let him rant, and offer those things the psych people call 'minimal encouragers' in reply, since that's all he's looking for. It does make me wonder if they've also got things called minimal discouragers. I could use a few of those sometimes.

Where are we going? What are we doing? And the answers aren't: World of Chickens and making burgers. It's bigger answers I'm looking for. Day One of a new term – the usual first-day scare job and a few lectures. About to be followed by several hours in and out of a chicken costume, because it'll put me a few dollars closer to a video camera.

A few dollars closer to the video camera I didn't get when I turned twenty-one late last year. It was always too much to expect, even for a twenty-first. My parents gave me a regular still camera without zoom and a copy of Jay McInerney's *Bright Lights, Big City*. I know it's ungrateful to think of that as anything less than a good result. Good photography isn't about zoom and the novel was a hardback, and one I'd asked for. But it's ungrateful to think of it in 'result' terms at all. So, call me ungrateful.

Technically, I'm well aware it's the thought that counts. I also realise that, if parents get it close to right on birthdays, you're not doing badly. It's having the list that's the problem, but my parents encourage it so how can they feel blameless when I have it in mind when birthdays finally arrive? It's my mother who started it, her idea that a list cuts down the likelihood of unwanted presents while, if it's long enough, still allowing the gift-buyer choice. And so what if my father's list always goes no further than brandy and socks? It could, if he wanted it to.

Outside my family, choice was never a factor last year when it came to twenty-firsts. As far as the male members of the year went, it turned out by about April that it was your twenty-first that showed whether you were a pewter man or a crystal man. Frank was a pewter man. By my birthday in October, there was a new category: recycle man. I'm sure I ended up with some presents I'd seen earlier in the year, at the March–April twenty-firsts. Worse, I think I ended up with one or two I'd chipped in for the first time.

So, at my party I scored three mismatched pewter tankards, a set of tumblers etched with the university crest, cufflinks, a harshly ugly decanter, a cocktail shaker, six golf balls and a fart cushion. Plus, that butt of all bath-time jokes, soap on a rope.

And I have to admit, I don't get it. Pewter surely had its day in the ale houses of the seventeenth century, I don't understand cocktails, my cuffs – like absolutely everyone else's – have at least as many buttons as you could need, I don't play golf, and I've never in my life decanted. Where does that leave me? I suppose I shower, and I fart an average amount, but if that's the only personal connection with my twenty-first haul that I can muster, it's not good.

I remember looking over my collection at the end of the evening and thinking, since when did I become the man who has everything? The only thing missing was a ship in a bottle.

At least Frank's gift was original, even if deeply pornographic. It's the only hard-core wall clock I've ever seen. He said it was imported. 'Good lord,' my mother said, 'I think it's anatomically correct, Frank.' Then she turned to me and told me she thought it'd look lovely anywhere in my room that can't be seen from the door.

So, no video camera. My father offered me a deal, and

one I'm familiar with: dollar-for-dollar matching on video camera purchase if I was prepared to get a part-time job to earn my share. With the stipulation that my share was not to include money made from reselling any of last year's superfluous textbooks – since that's my parents' already – or unreasonable attempts to manipulate routine cost-of-living adjustments to my allowance.

My father's an accountant. It's not his fault.

My allowance stretches to fund the rudimentary lifestyle I seem to have fallen into – a reflection on the sadness of the lifestyle, rather than the abundance of the allowance – and it's given to me conditional on continuing to pass all my exams. Which was always my plan, anyway.

If I want anything more, one of my options is negotiation. If what I want is seen as part of a long-term serious plan and doesn't involve compromising my medical studies, I am occasionally awarded dollar-for-dollar matching.

Frank looks on these arrangements, complex though they are, with some envy. He gets no allowance and describes himself as 'self-funded'. Of course, it's not that simple and Frank can actually be quite a scam machine. It's not uncommon for jobs to come his way out of nowhere, and to pay cash. World of Chickens is now the job Frank calls his 'steady gig', and he always likes to have one of those. But it was me who, through my negotiating experience hard won at home, got us the meal-plus-bottomless-soft-drink part of our arrangements.

I'd wanted to read *Bright Lights, Big City* since I'd read about it when it came out in America. I put it on my list thinking it'd be an easy purchase, but it wasn't available here at the time so the book shop had to order it in.

I read it straight away, and told Frank to read it too. He didn't, so I eventually had to read bits to him to make the point. He told me to bring it in the car and we'd read it on the way to and from World of Chickens, which made me motion sick but I wanted him to get it.

Bright Lights, Big City showed me – made it clearer to me than before – what a slow, safe hole this place is. 'Don't you get it?' I said to him. 'In comparison we're living in Dim Lights, Big Town. Until about nine-thirty at night, when most of the dim lights go off. You see how far behind we are? How far off the pace? Even someone as old as Frank Sinatra gets to sing a song about New York as a city that doesn't sleep. Imagine one old person here staying up past nine, or even starting dinner after six. Do you think Frank Sinatra ends the day with meat and three veg in front of 'Wheel of Fortune' at five o'clock? Don't you get it?'

He didn't get it.

Frank has no idea of the outside world at all. Frank thinks the book is cool, and he thinks it in an uncomplicated way. He really got into the second-person style because, with me reading it aloud, it made it as though the story was about him. I told him it was not choose-your-own-adventure format, and that the expression 'insert your name here' wouldn't be occurring once in these pages.

I tried to explain what I thought second-person was about and he said, 'Yeah, yeah, I get it. You are obviously insufficiently acquainted with my literary masterpiece *Bright Lights, Big Chicken*. It's about this chicken-selling med-student guy who's a complete horn monger, but he's got this dull mate who holds him back a bit.' And he cleared his throat. 'You are changing gear,' he said as he changed gear. 'You are pulling away from the lights.'

I told him not to spoil it, but maybe he already had.

'You are, in the trouser, perhaps the largest and most gifted man in this town.' Definitely spoiled now. 'They want you, baby, they want you. Some of them will get you. It'll be excellent. They will call you the Love Master. Behind your back, they already do.'

Jay McInerney turns thirty this year, and already Frank's set him rolling in his grave.

The first reference to Bolivian Marching Powder occurs on page one, and it took us both a second to work out that it probably meant cocaine. At a better time than this, and during a better mood, Frank renamed Staminade Sunnybank Hills Marching Powder, after the suburb where he lives. And he did it without the aid of any irony at all.

We've talked more about New York since, enough that Frank now occasionally refers to Sunnybank as Brisbane's SoHo, since it's SOuth of HOlland Park. 'Don't you get it?' he said. 'Instead of SOuth of HOuston.'

'We are so not *Bright Lights, Big City*,' I remember telling him, to shut all this up. 'We're not even the fucking *Breakfast Club*.' A reference that only let Frank segue effortlessly into some very sleazy arrangement he'd like to discuss with Molly Ringwald, but had previously been decent enough to keep to himself.

Today he sits with the half-full jar of Staminade open between his thighs, loads his wet finger again and rubs more crystals on his gums. It's the dumping by Cyndi he's taking hardest.

'Is a bit of fucking respect too much to hope for?' he says, green crystals flirting with the gaps between his teeth in the late afternoon light.

'I'm sorry. When did it ever get round to respect?'

'Exactly. Exactly. I get taken for granted, you know. I'm not just sex-on-tap.'

'See, this is the problem. The emphasis there is on the "just". You are sex-on-tap, but you aren't *just* sex-on-tap.

You and I can make that distinction, but there'd be a lot of people out there who can't.'

'Shit. That's too subtle. Which means you're right. Subtlety's never worked for me. Subtlety's what you go for if you're the kind of loser who doesn't have anything better. Present company excepted, of course.'

'Of course.'

Okay, he's on the brink of annoying me, and I'm too subtle to tell him so he'll never know. Frank has now been single for almost four days. I've been single since September last year, or the preceding May, depending on how you look at it. I could be a whole lot more supportive if he could remember that sometimes.

I should've known he'd deal with *Bright Lights, Big City* the way he did. In first term this year we all started talking about the elective we have to do in December and January, between fifth year and sixth year. The faculty's intention is that we travel, and experience something we mightn't see here. I think it was in that context that I said something about really wanting to get out of Brisbane. Frank agreed. The next day he told me we could borrow his brother's panel van, since his brother had done his licence for the moment, and that we should go to the coast. Which wasn't exactly what I meant.

We drove north in the week between psych and surgery, Frank with his board shorts and his bare feet and his bad-boy attitude, singing along to his brother's Dusty Springfield tapes. 'Chick-pulling tapes,' he called them. 'AJ's too smart to have a stack of guy music in the van.' I was never too sure what 'guy music' meant, but I did admit I hadn't been expecting Dusty Springfield.

Inspired by our chick-pulling potential, Frank made up 'rules of the van', most of which were needlessly ambitious and relied on the prospect of a sexual encounter before coming into play. The relationship man may, or may not, have been single at the time.

In the hour and a half it took to reach the Sunshine Coast, I'd picked up most of the words to 'Son of a Preacher Man' and I thought I'd probably be having sex that night, or within the next couple of days at the outside. If Frank took up with a weird religion, or Amway, he'd be trouble.

We agreed the van was sacrosanct. Rule One: No rooting in the van. If you score, you score on the beach.

So how close did we get? All we scored was the meat tray at a seriously tough Caloundra pub. It wasn't even particularly near the beach.

We won the meat tray, and started playing pool with some locals. Which was fine while we were losing but then we hit a patch of form and, at the exact moment I was working out that winning mightn't be a good idea, Frank addressed one of our opponent's girlfriends as 'babe'. Things didn't go well from there.

'Frank's no good with names,' I had to tell them. 'And he's not used to this kind of luck with pool either. I'd be very surprised if that blue went down. Very surprised.'

And at that even Frank noticed their unnecessarily firm grip on the cues, and the way one of them had moved to cover the door. And I talked amiably about nothing much, and then about sport, and he duly fucked up the shot. Our form fell away in a rush, he left the girls alone and the door was open for us when they sunk the black.

'At least we've got something to eat,' Frank said in the car park, when he found the bright side. 'And you talked them out of hitting us. That was good.'

Then we had an argument about our meat and what to do with it, which became an argument about potato salad –

and what the white ingredient might be – followed by one about who should have brought cooking utensils, and finally one about matches for the barbecue.

'Why couldn't you have been a boy scout?' Frank said, the bright side now long gone. 'You're just the kind of person who should have been a boy scout. I should be able to hand you two sticks, and there should be nothing but friction between us and tea.'

We went to a takeaway place, and we asked the guy how much fish and chips he'd give us as a swap for the meat tray. We lay in the van that night, the wind picked up, the rain came in from the sea, we rooted nothing and the last thing Frank said was 'Do you want to go home in the morning?' and the last thing I said was 'Yep'.

So that's not what I mean by 'away'. I've been looking at the possibility of doing my elective in New York. Naturally, I've thought about it enough that it now goes like this:

> You are on your way again to Ron Todd's World of Chickens, but you have a plan. A plan that means you are now only months away from the real world. Give or take ten thousand miles. It's all a question of perspective. There's distance to travel, and the rest of the year to endure. A year of ward rounds and exams, of fried fillets of chicken breast with a choice of five sauces. A year in which female company has proven elusive and in which you know – inside, you know – that you have missed the John Bostock Medal for Psychiatry by the narrowest of margins.

Okay, hyperbole with the last bit, since half of the people in the year haven't even started psychiatry. But I still think I know.

There's a line in *Bright Lights, Big City* about the central character meeting Amanda and coming to New York and beginning to feel that he was no longer on the outside looking in. That, perhaps, is the bit I get most.

Sometimes it feels like I live in such a shit town. It meets all reasonable definitions of a shit town. There are still men who put on hats to drive on these roads, our only celebrities are sports stars and newsreaders, and everyone you meet already knows your mother.

Okay, in my case some of the responsibility for the last one rests squarely with my mother, rather than Brisbane. My mother: uni lecturer, occasional political activist, rose fancier, theatre buff, person entirely unable to understand where her business ends and another person's begins. Fluent in one language, shambolic in several but difficult to silence. Monty Python fan and, like most Monty Python fans, unable to understand people who don't think every conversation can be improved by a quick reference to the Spanish Inquisition, and surprise. Etcetera. Nightmare. Worse when she's excited. Otherwise far too British. Too bloody bloody British.

But I can't blame it all on her. If the world was a human body, Brisbane would be the last sphincter things pass through on the way out. Nothing happens here. I want to be a film maker, but every week here is another week without narrative and that can't be a good start. I'm not even on the outside looking in. I'm somewhere further away, and the people on the outside looking in seem pretty close to the action to me.

I'm out being the chicken, and all that's still in my mind. There's not as much Elizabethan material tonight, since

Ron's interest in exploring the chicken's Gene Kelly side seems to have done something to my confidence.

Tonight, the theme is mime. Marcel Marceau chicken. Chicken walking against the wind, chicken doing things with silly (invisible) hat. Chicken doing a Michael Jackson moonwalk would be good, but the feet are too big. That's the excuse. Chicken tripping up and falling to the pavement while failing to do a Michael Jackson moonwalk would be more embarrassment than I could handle.

It's changeover time, and Frank is moving his 'biggest burger in one bite' challenge up a notch. He says he's mastered the Chicken Little junior burger, and he's on his way to the big time.

'I've got a cut-down adult bun and two pec minor muscles, pickles and sauce,' he tells me. 'It's a PB.'

'Sure it is, if it goes in.'

'How is it a personal best though,' Sophie says, 'if it's not even an acknowledged product?'

'Good point.' I don't know what kind of point it is, but this'll be more interesting if I go with it. 'Would you call that competition standard, Frank?'

'No, I never said that. It's more like heavy training.'

'You've got two of the thin bits of chicken . . .' Sophie won't let it go.

'Pec minor muscles,' Frank says, trying to reclaim some ground using science. 'I know. Like two Chicken Littles, rather than the fully adult-burger pec major. Give me a break. I'll get there. And I know it's not the total complement of salad items, but I'm working up to it. And you've got to admit, it's pretty bloody big.'

'Yeah, okay. It's big,' Sophie says. 'It's a feat, even if it's not the one the crowd was hoping for.' She looks at me, as if I'm to speak for the crowd.

'I think it's all about creating a sense of anticipation. If he could just jam a whole burger in there right now, we wouldn't be calling this a challenge.'

'So, do it Frank,' she says.

And he does. He takes a deep breath, opens his mouth wide and holds the modified burger up to it. His lips work their way along the bun, measuring it out and preparing to draw it in. His jaw moves forward, his eyes bulge, his hand pushes and the burger goes. There's some very noisy nose breathing as he pauses between the engulf and the swallow, then he rolls his eyes back and tilts his head and takes it down his throat like a crocodile in a death roll.

He puts one hand onto the bench to steady himself, and raises the other in triumph. We applaud.

'Thank you,' he says. 'Thank you. It was a bastard, but I couldn't let you down.'

Once the two of us are out the door and in the corridor, Sophie says, 'How big a burger do you reckon we can get him to swallow? Do you reckon we can get him to black out?'

'Hey, on the first bad sinus day, anything's possible.'

Zel tells Frank, 'Just drizzle a little barbecue sauce across it,' and I don't like the way she says drizzle.

'And a bit of mayo on the bun, spread with a knife?'

'You remembered.' Said in way that I've seen described as cooing. Then she turns to me. 'Philip, is he this attentive to all the customers?'

'Sure. He's a professional.' I'm hitting Ron for nausea loading to my pay if I cop much more of this, dammit. 'Frank was born with great people skills, but I think he did invent the Big Chicken Little with you in mind.'

'Test drove the first one myself earlier,' he says, omitting to mention its ugly passage through his gullet.

She eats it in a way that's presumably supposed to resemble dainty, with a paper serviette in both hands and a dab at her lips after each mouthful. There's a gold trinkety rattle from her bracelets every time she does it, tiny horses and carriages and pineapples jangling into each other.

When a couple of students come in for burgers, I'm happy to take the work and leave Zel to Frank. The Todds, Sophie excepted, can be one of the downsides to working here. They turn up unannounced and need a lot of looking after. Sometimes Ron even tries to make a burger, but he treats it like celebrity day at McDonald's. He makes bad burgers slowly, he gets in the way and the whole time he's here he's hanging out for any opportunity to tell the customer he owns the place. 'I'm Ron Todd,' he says, and so emphatically I think everyone's expecting the next bit to go, 'and I'm an alcoholic'. But it's not his fault that everyone notices the big neon chicken and no-one notices his small neon name.

Sophie comes in to change and Zel stays talking to Frank when we go out the back.

'How's obstetrics?' she says from the toilet. 'I didn't ask you that yet.'

'It's fine. Not that we've done much so far.'

'Would you do it, do you think? Would you go into that?'

'Be an obstetrician, you mean? I don't think so. I've got no idea what I'm going to do, really. In medicine, at least. I keep hoping I'll work out how to be a film maker before I have to decide that.'

'So you're that serious about it?'

'Yeah. Have you seen how much video cameras cost? That's what I'm saving for. And I know it's not the same as film, but I think I could learn a lot from it. At least it'd be something to start with. And I've done some film work, so . . .'

'Really? What have you done?'

'Well, not much. I acted in a couple of alcohol-abuse films round about when I was finishing school. Educational films. I had a bit part in the first one and a bigger one in the second. It was the first time I ever got paid for anything.'

I don't tell her the obvious part. Those films are always 'cool crowd gone wrong' versus 'nerd made good', and I was never going to be one of the slick people who drank themselves stupid and fell from grace by throwing up tomato peel into the toilet. I was the nice guy who didn't drink and therefore, of course, got the girl. And that's just like life, isn't it?

'So it's a bit of a comedown to go from film actor to chicken then,' Sophie's saying, and sounding as though she's genuinely sorry for me, like I'm a Hollywood Where Are They Now? story.

'Yeah, it's not really like that, though. There's a few years in between. And I wasn't exactly co-starring with De Niro.'

She opens the door and hands me the costume. It's warm when I get into it. It always feels a little like sneaking into someone else's bed, putting on the chicken, particularly on a cool evening like this. And Sophie makes it smell like green apple shampoo. I always get a blast of green apple when I pull the head down, and I do wonder what kinds of smells I'm giving her in return.

Film actor. It sounds like a lot more than it is. I signed up with a casting agent after I did my two alcohol films, but all she was interested in was making fifty bucks out of the portfolio photos. But it looked easy. A film career looked there for the taking, for weeks at least.

'It's not much of a place for film-makers,' I say to Sophie

as she's zipping me up. 'Brisbane, I mean. So I figure I've got to get out of here and see more of what's going on out there, in the rest of the world. We get an elective at the end of fifth year. So I've been having a look at a few places in America. New York, New York, mainly. It'd be good to try New York. I've been reading some books lately, like *Bright Lights, Big City*. I've read it a couple of times. Have you read it?'

'No.'

'It's about New York. It's about this guy's life in New York.'

'Like a Simon and Garfunkel song. Did you see them at Lang Park last year? I went with Dad. Who would have preferred Neil Diamond, but you've got to take what's on offer. Not that he's New York. Well, I don't think he is. But *they* are.'

'Sure. Lots of New York references. "Whores on Seventh Avenue", "New Jersey Turnpike". Except that's a New Jersey reference, I suppose.'

'And what exactly is a turnpike? I've always wondered about that. Like, is there a pike there?'

'It's a good question. I don't know. Maybe I'll get to check it out at the end of the year. I'll send you a postcard. If there's a postcard of any kind of pike in New Jersey, I'll send it to you. Anyway, I got *Bright Lights, Big City* for my birthday late last year. I'd read about it somewhere. And I got a camera – a regular camera – since I figured I should learn about still photography too, if I'm looking at making films. Not that I've done much yet – my mother's birthday, and a few compositional things. And we started taking some photos for a uni revue sketch, Frank and me, but it kind of got canned. There was a difference of opinion. Well, Frank told the organisers some of their ideas were fucked, and that they had a real problem listening to constructive criticism. So they told us we didn't have to come back.'

'That doesn't sound like Frank,' she says. She knows him too well by now. 'Hey, Dad says you do Shakespeare when you're doing the chicken.'

'Sometimes. I thought that was between him and me.'

'We're a close family. Get used to it.'

'It's pretty boring out there. You've got to do something.'

'No kidding. I think Shakespeare's a good idea.'

'So what do you do?'

'Just wave my arms around a lot. Try to be like a chicken, I guess.'

'But what does your brain do?'

'Tries to stop me falling in front of the traffic. Don't you find the lights, like, hypnotic?'

'I think you're getting a bit too much into that chicken brain space.'

How did it become Shakespearean? I'm thinking when I'm back out there and realising I can't recall enough of 'Shall I compare thee to a summer's day?' to make it worth trying.

It was the chicken costume, and the comb on the head, which came as a separate piece of moulded plastic and had a bad lean to the left. It took a while to sort that out, so it was on my mind and led to cockscomb, and therefore to standing at the roadside mouthing faux-Elizabethan advertising slogans and insults at the unstopping traffic. And that led, irresistibly, to Henry V's speech before Agincourt (or was it Harfleur?) and eisteddfod flashbacks and Hamlet's soliloquy, which is so over-recited that practically no-one gets the emphasis right. No-one listens to it any more. No-one realises that the key word is 'be'. Except of course this seven-foot chicken at the Taringa lights on Moggill Road. The one whose brain is always elsewhere, the one at very little risk of being fatally mesmerised by the traffic.

Frank waves me back in early.

'Zel reckons we should pack up before ten if there's no-one around,' he says, having already tidied some leftover chicken into three burgers that he's now wrapping neatly and putting in a box for taking home.

I can remember, years ago, reading ads for bullworkers in American comics always featuring some bulky guy and a life-changing steel tube with handles. I was horrified when I worked out what their representative weakling weighed in kilograms. If only I'd left it in pounds and hadn't put myself through the maths, I would have had years of those blissful dreams of sea monkeys instead. I always wanted sea monkeys, even if they were just tiny translucent aquatic insects that came as a packet of eggs not much bigger than dust. And I wanted X-ray glasses and the famous Black Lite™ light bulb and peace patches for jeans. I must have been young. The peace symbol was everywhere on those pages.

But it wasn't peace I needed. My life has always had peace in abundance. What it lacked, clearly, was muscle. And perhaps the people who go to beaches are kinder here than in America but I knew that, when the time came to have sand kicked in my face – the characteristic way for shame to manifest itself in a bullworker ad – it'd be at the time of maximum embarrassment. It hadn't happened so far not because it wasn't going to happen, but because it wouldn't have meant enough. In the ads, the representative weakling was usually shamed in front of his girl. In the ads, the Charles Atlas way was the way of salvation. Charles Atlas never copped sand in the face, but nor did he kick it. He was above all that, oiled and buffed and able to shoulder the whole world. If Charles Atlas was on the beach, the sand kickers would look like scrawn and they'd have to run home and bullwork compulsively between now and next summer before daring to show themselves again.

It hadn't been my plan get a bullworker for my nineteenth birthday. It had been years since the comics and all I'd put on the list had been 'exercise equipment'. But that was too general so, when queried, I mentioned that I was thinking of something that'd bulk me up a bit, give me an all-over workout. Something that could do that in the privacy of my room. Something no-one outside the family would have to know about. It was my mother who was drawn in by the claims on the bullworker box in Kmart. She even got the shop assistant to take the booklet out and, as soon as she saw that it offered forty-two different ways to a total-body makeover, she knew she was on the money.

So far, the results have not been spectacular, and my commitment to the bullworker has been in the waning phase for nearly two years. We had a plan, my mother and I, a bullworker-plus-Sustagen plan that practically couldn't fail. It should have been very safely anabolic. It appears to be petering out into nothing. And that, dammit, is so very 1985 for me.

I'm in my sleeveless muscle shirt in my room realising that, on me, it's just a sleeveless shirt and all it's doing is putting my armpits on the outside. I'm pulling hard at the bullworker and trying not to grunt. Maybe there has been some progress. I grunt less than I once did and there are now only a couple of the forty-two bullworker moves where I get no compression at all, and they both involve holding the bullworker behind my back. As if I'm going to need those muscles out in the real world. Or, more to the point, as if I'm ever going to get a chance to display them. I am viewing muscles the way a peacock views tail feathers. I have been completely enslaved by those cruel sand-kicking ads. If only I'd put sea monkeys on the list instead. You got a whole damn country of sea monkeys, including a king and queen. They had a sketch of them in the ad.

That's it. I'm stopping.

I make myself a massive chocolate Sustagen milkshake, I turn on the TV and I watch my arm veins bulge in the dim blue light. In the relevant section of my second-person bio, that part will read 'muscles' not 'veins':

> You stop. You fix yourself a drink, you turn on the TV and your arm muscles bulge in the dim blue light. Not tonight, you tell her. Not again tonight. I'm spent.

Close to cool. Close indeed. Replacing 'veins' with 'muscles' and pretending my bullworker was a girlfriend certainly improved the look of my evening. That's a tactic I won't be sharing with Frank.

> Not tonight, you tell her. Not again tonight. I'm spent. Shagged stupid like the king of the sea monkeys, slumped low in his throne.

The awesome breeding power of sea monkeys was always a feature. First they'd hatch, then they'd breed and breed until you owned a nation of them. What was I doing, taking any interest in them? Surely they're just lice in a jar.

And what was it all about when Zel turned up tonight? I've had plenty of times when I've craved invisibility, but with this one I actually got there. I vanished, Frank went into autoflirt. I've told him that in less than twenty years all he'll be left with is autosleaze, but does he listen? Autosleaze won't be pretty.

I'm glad she picked Frank, and that he did his duty and

went with it. Made her a burger, schmoozed her like a prize customer. In the car I told him I was grateful, since I couldn't have done it, and he just said, 'No worries. I figure you handle Ron, so fair's fair. And you handle Sophie, too. Or you would, given the chance . . .'

I let that one go. Things didn't start out brilliantly with Sophie, but they've improved. I think, on our second or third shift together, I might have commented favourably on her earrings and she said something as fuck-right-off transparent as 'Yeah, my boyfriend Clinton really likes them too.' To which I said, My girlfriend likes it when I can be relaxed enough to compliment a person without having an agenda.

So, in an instant, I'd invented a girlfriend. Invented her and, in the following instant, called her Phoebe. Yes, my mother's name, and a present-tense girlfriend, even though it's practically been a year other than the second weekend of last September (a relationship that lasted all the way till the following Tuesday). Pretty sad. Sad enough that I couldn't stop myself going on to say, She's a bit older than I am.

Sophie asks about her quite often. She's like that. Annoyingly considerate.

Phoebe? Sure. I met her through my mother. She has brown plastic handles at both ends and an insanely strong spring in between, and she offers forty-two different ways to a total-body makeover. We've been together two and a half years. I don't need a human girlfriend. I've found the Phoebe Atlas way. She loves me, even sleeveless, and that's saying something. She makes my veins work, damn hard.

I can be excused, I think, for viewing myself as being in something of a rut.

In the week between psych and surgery, I wrote to six med schools in America. Two have rejected me, three haven't replied and UCLA was the surprise, offering me the possibility of a place in an exchange program for interstate and overseas final-year students planning to specialise in emergency medicine. I've read the documentation. It looks like hell. I'm waiting for the three who haven't replied, but it's two months since I sent the letters.

I can't imagine UCLA, LA or what it's really like in a US emergency room when things turn crazy. The letter has an embossed crest and says that the cheque for the thirty-five US dollar processing fee should be made out to the Regents of the University of California. All I know is that that tells me nothing about what it'd be like. I wouldn't be hanging out with the Regents, asking for someone to pass another sheet of embossed writing paper as a pierced femoral artery squirts blood across the lino floor.

What do I know? What do I know about America, really? Sure I watch every movie that comes to town, and a lot of TV. Sure there are bits of *Annie Hall*, and probably a few other Woody Allen films, that I can recite without ever having tried to learn them. And there are books, with *Bright Lights, Big City* only the latest. I ran my Dim Lights, Big Town idea past Sophie this evening, and she said she'd never thought about Brisbane that way but maybe she hasn't read enough books.

But the small flecks of knowledge I have only make the size of the gaps apparent. What's a Hostess Twinkie, for instance? The kids in the American comics I used to read ate them all the time. What's a turnpike? Okay, etymology: something ancient and British. Already I'm seeing a beefeater. A beefeater pointing and saying, 'No, go that way'. And I'm remembering my mother at the Tower of London when I was about eight, pointing to the beefeater's weapon and explaining the expression 'plain as a pikestaff'.

I'm guessing there isn't one beefeater in the whole state of New Jersey.

3

Frank's reward for all the driving is fondue. There's petrol money too, which comes out of my World of Chickens pay, but after day two of obstetrics the gratitude from my parents for Frank keeping me on the straight and narrow is expressed as fondue.

And that shits me. I am born to traverse the straight and narrow, and brought up to as well, but they've got it in their heads that it's only Frank's driving that keeps me at World of Chickens (possibly true) and that working there is somehow a worthwhile developmental experience (complete crap – it's a way of getting them to buy me half a video camera). My parents think I might develop awkward antisocial habits without someone like Frank in my life. Frank is himself a litany of antisocial habits, most of them at the more flamboyant end of the spectrum, plenty of which could see his nose broken for a third time if he didn't have someone like me in his life. But try telling that to them.

Before Frank, it was amateur theatre that was supposed to bring me out of myself. Before that, Boy Scouts. Frank was right that I had Scouts lurking somewhere in my past (but as if I'd tell him). Besides, I am out of myself. I might spend a lot of my home time in my room, but did they never stop to think that that might be partly about them? 'Spending time in your room is not a disease,' I told my mother once. 'Not when there's a TV in there. Even a small one, even black and white.'

I don't mind fondue. I just don't like to admit it. Frank thinks it's excellent, is happy to admit it, and regularly talks his way into being invited over with fondue in mind. My parents happen to like Frank and they've got no sense of boundaries, so he's here a lot. I've discussed it with them, I've said that petrol money is the prescribed payment, and I've told them they should think this through. They should realise Frank's parents will make me go over there for a barbecue. They're totally into payback. To which my mother said, 'They're not gangsters, Philby. And you know how Frank likes fondue.'

Since we have a guest tonight, we move into special-occasion drill. My mother has put the wine cask in the fridge.

She squirts some into a glass for Frank and he turns to me and says, 'Wine on a weeknight. Your family . . .' As if he couldn't be more impressed. 'This is like . . . France.'

'Oh, *Monsieur François*,' my mother says. '*Fondue pour vous ce soir, peut-être?*'

'Wow,' he says. 'Bugger me. Um . . . pretty much all the French I know is *voulez-vous coucher avec moi ce soir*.'

'Frank, this is my mother you're talking to.'

'Yeah, I know. I don't know what it means. *Ça plane pour moi?* That's the other bit I know.'

'Frank, *meaning*. When it comes to language, meaning is part of knowing.'

'Whatever.'

'No, not whatever. That's generally accepted. It's a rule. At least try to be aware when you're asking someone to go to bed with you.'

'Hey, sometimes that stuff just happens.'

'Well done Frank, then.' My mother raises her glass, and clinks it against his.

My father comes in the back door. 'Wine,' he says in mock surprise. 'I turn my back and we're entertaining. Evening, Frank. Phoebe. Philby. A good day had all round, then? I'll just get changed. Back in a tick.'

He stops to take his lunch box out of his briefcase, and he hums as he goes down the hall. He reappears in about a minute, his jacket swapped for his comfy green cardigan and his highly polished black leather shoes replaced by loafers.

'You could lose the tie, Allan,' my mother tells him, getting twitchy about the style crisis he's visiting upon us.

'Company,' he says, and nods Frank's way.

'And Frank does so love a chap in a tie.'

'Perhaps after the main. We'll see. No-one else has to wear one. Personal choice. That's what it's all about these days. Philby. Obstetrics. Like it?'

'Dunno. Day two. We'll see.'

No-one knows exactly what my father was like prior to his service with the British armed forces in India. He might have been just like this, but we don't think so. He's now an accountant for a cardboard-box manufacturer and he still, at times, speaks like a telegram. But it's something that hovers on the uneasy boundary between a past life's habits and self-parody, and I think that's the way he likes it. He's a military man, but then he's not. He takes a lunch box to work, he prefers cardigans after hours, he whitens his moustache to play Santa at the office family Christmas party. He's done that as long as I can remember, since his mixture of round-shouldered and avuncular, ready and willing means there could be no other choice.

Frank calls him Big Al, since the name's totally wrong for him, and my father likes it, since it makes him feel as though he's in with the young crowd. Frank provokes him into telling rambling bullshit stories – already the closest thing my father has to a hobby – and then he hangs on every word, as if it's Jesus and a parable. He can't be getting his full quota of tedious parental experiences at home.

We fondue, pronging our tiny pieces of meat and lowering them into the hot oil.

Our fondue cooker is burnt-orange and also burnt, owing to its circa-1970 origin and years of much use. It was originally burnt-orange with a chain of white flowers around it just below the handles, but they're now very off-white or yellowish or brown. Fondue, at our place, has never gone out of style. Frank says that the rest of the world doesn't know what they're missing and that, when fondue comes back, we'll have people like my mother to thank for keeping the art alive.

He and my father each lose a piece of meat at the same time, and end up fighting over one they both reprong at once. Frank likes fondue because it combines food and sport.

There's apple pie afterwards and my mother says, 'You'll notice you each get your own plate. So, no sword fighting.'

'Speaking of which,' my father says, 'how are you going with the script?'

'*Pirates of Penzance*,' she tells Frank. 'We're doing it at the Arts Theatre in June. Rehearsals start in a week.'

'*Pirates of Penzance*? I think they put it on at school once.'

'I did try to suggest it wasn't a very original choice, but I was shouted down. That's part of its charm, apparently.'

'And you get to do sword fighting?'

'No, wrong gender for that in G&S. Wouldn't it be much more interesting if we swapped the gender of all the characters around? I wouldn't mind some sword fighting.'

She closes one eye, swishes wildly in the air with her spoon and puts on a rather bad pirate voice, demanding doubloons.

'I could practically see the parrot on your shoulder,' my father says, giving me a look that suggests he's glad she's in a non-combatant role.

'From the way that voice sounded I thought it *was* the parrot on her shoulder.'

My mother drops the piracy and puts on her famous look of disdain. 'The artist is never appreciated in her own land.'

'I thought it was just at home you weren't appreciated, not the whole land. They quite like you at the Arts Theatre.'

'Well, where you work's a world apparently, and there's only ever three of you there at once. So this can be a land then, here at home. A three-person land. Harris Land.'

'Which leaves me with Greenland,' Frank says. 'So I'm looking pretty good.'

'Honestly,' my mother goes on, 'that Ron Todd of yours. Him and his Worlds. What's it about? What makes you have a world, rather than just a shop? And how do you pick what kind of world it is? Frank, if you had a world, what would it be?'

He gives it some thought. 'Well, the guy at the Royal who marked our long cases'd say Frank Green's World of Mindless Copying, but we're going to have a talk about that.'

'What would I have? What would I have?' my mother says, diving into her topic. 'Phoebe Harris's World of No Sword Fighting. Phoebe Harris's World of Scrawny Roses. Maybe that's too specific. Phoebe Harris's World of Scrawn. What else have I got that could fit in with that if it was a shop? I could always sell you, Philby.'

'Which begins to explain Phil Harris's World of Bullworkers and Low Self-Esteem, but don't worry about me.'

'Or you could go for lattice,' my father says to her, not worrying about me at all. 'There's an awful lot of lattice out there. You know your lattice, Phoebe.'

'And pots. I know them too. Phoebe Harris's World of Lattice and Pots. And what would you have, Allan?'

'Well . . .' He's part of the way through clearing the plates from the table but he stops to think about it, to think about the kind of world that might be his. 'Allan Harris's World of Cardboard, I suppose.' There's a pause, and he frowns. 'Some things really are just jobs, aren't they?' He takes my mother's plate, and mine, and carries everything into the kitchen. There's a whining and thumping from the pipes as he starts to run water into the sink. 'Ruddy airlock,' he says, and then there's some muttering that we can't make out.

'Go and tell your father you can't imagine a world without cardboard,' my mother says. 'Be a good son.'

'Blackberry Nip, anybody?' he calls out. 'I'm having one. Anyone join me?'

4

Friday gives us our first experience of large numbers of pregnant abdomens. It's our turn at Antenatal Clinic, our chance to put Monday's checklist into action and to take an obstetric history in earnest for the first time.

'Here's how we do it,' the charge sister tells us. 'All the patients are here by eight-thirty. You'll see a few of them as a group – all six of you, with Doctor Bellamy – if there are interesting findings. Then you'll sit in with the registrars or consultants for a couple of consultations, then we'll get you doing the assessments yourselves and you can present them to whichever doctor's due to see them.'

The word on Theo Bellamy is good. He's about my parents' age and scorn isn't part of his repertoire. His private practice is always overloaded, but he keeps up his regular public sessions at the Mater too.

'Mandy,' he says, introducing us to the first patient, 'is an example of things going very well.' We're in his room and Mandy is around our age, and lying with a drape over her lower abdomen. 'I thought some normal findings would be worth a look before moving on to other things.'

He talks us through the abdominal examination, and every move his hands make seems considered, a move you could trust to bring back information.

'Warm hands. That's the place to start. No-one'll thank you for cold hands. And with this examination, it's with the whole hand. Don't go jabbing in with your fingertips. Feel what's under your whole hand, then glide it across and feel again. Feel this,' he says, taking my hand. 'Tell me what you feel.'

'Okay, it's firm, it's quite firm, almost hard. It's rounded.'

'What do you think it might be?'

'A knee?'

'Think again about the size.'

'Yes, sorry. A head?'

'Good, a head. Now we'll acquaint ourselves quickly with the other main features, if it's all right with Mandy. Everyone watching. The others of you will be doing this after . . .' he turns his head from the abdomen to look at my name tag . . . 'Philip. So, Philip, first we have the head, as you've found, then a shoulder lying in the midline.' He moves my hand there. The shoulder is smaller than the head, I'm less sure I could find it myself. I'd find the lump, but I don't know that I'd be finding a shoulder. 'And limbs here. They're irregular and they might even move while you're doing the examination. And the limbs being here tells us that the shoulder we felt was the left shoulder. Which means that if you feel to the right of that . . .' I move my hand. There's almost an edge to what I'm feeling, a firm curved border of a baby. 'What do you think that'd be?'

'The back?'

'Exactly. And it's curved because it's flexed. So we've found a back here, and a shoulder here, and a head here,' he says, touching each lightly, this time with the tip of his finger. 'Do you want to have a shot at how we'd describe what we've found?'

'Okay. Is it longitudinal?'

'Yes, the lie is longitudinal. First do you want to tell me how many foetuses you think there are?'

'Um, one.'

'Good, always good to start with that.'

'So there is one? It sounded like a trick question.'

'No, there's one. It's just a good routine to get into. There's one, isn't there Mandy? It wasn't a trick question?'

'There'd better be one,' she says. 'Don't want to go finding another one at thirty-two weeks.'

'Which,' Doctor Bellamy says, 'brings us to our next point – what the examination suggests about the gestational age of the foetus. The first thing we look at is the height of the fundus which, in this case, is consistent with dates, at around thirty-two weeks. Then, as you said, we have a longitudinal lie. And the position? Remember, think about where the occiput and back are. And also remember where the shoulder is.'

'Okay. The occiput and back are over on the right and the shoulder is in the midline, so right occipitolateral.'

'Good. Now everyone else . . .'

I step aside and one by one the others check their hands are warm enough and put them on Mandy's abdomen. We're quite used to tumours now, used to all kinds of abdominal masses since we've just done surgery, so it's odd to feel a mass that's large and complicated and not a disease. Particularly odd to feel one with the parts of an undiscovered person and to be able to picture it in there, waiting its turn.

We're shown the Pinard obstetric stethoscope, and this time it's Frank's chance to go first. It's a simple device – a truncated plastic cone, with the wide end placed on the abdomen and the other end for listening, supposedly, to the foetal heart.

'It takes a bit of practice,' Doctor Bellamy says. 'What can you hear?'

Frank tells him 'the sea' and none of us, when our turn comes, can claim with any confidence that we're hearing more than that.

We're then shown how to use the Doppler machine and after some rustling of background noise we can all hear a heartbeat, blood whipping through the foetus at around 150 beats per minute.

Having bothered Mandy enough we move on to other patients, other abdomens, and without expert guidance it's just a bunch of lumps to me. 'It's all about practice,' the registrar tells me. 'And don't prod too much.'

'Okay, you've seen me out there,' Sophie says once we've done the changeover. 'How am I looking?'

'Good. Good. Would I be right in thinking there's a little more performance going on now?' It's night, around eight, and I'm sitting in the chicken suit on the back steps of the World again with Sophie, talking about whatever comes up as the evening trains fly by.

'I've gone for singing. That's the difference, mainly. I can do most of Cyndi Lauper's "Time After Time".'

'Good choice. It does work better than most things a cappella.'

'It's quite motivational, too. Not that I know it all. I have to make up some bits, so I put my name in it then. That's always motivational.'

'That sounds like a trick you might have got from your father.'

'Maybe. He's got a few. I got the performance angle from you, remember. But Dad's full of good ideas and, like he says, a good idea can come from anywhere, and then it's about having the vision to see what you can make of it.

It's about vision, and backing yourself. It's like what he did on the northside, when he took Lex Kellett's Lawn Land and turned it into Ron Todd's World of Mowers. You get the difference? The way Dad sees it, Lex was a good man, but he didn't have the vision. He had a grip on the whole northside mower scene but his hand was shaking. Dad had vision. He knew that if he pushed it to a World he might take it somewhere. And the Worlds won't end here. Just watch. He's got plenty of new ideas bubbling away. Who knows what it'll be next? When there's vision involved, you just can't tell. If you can pick where it'll take you every time, it's not really vision to start with. Just planning. You know what I mean?'

'Sure. It's not such a fine distinction as it first sounds.'

'Exactly. Clinton doesn't get that. Some people don't. Hey, do some of that chicken stuff you do. The Shakespeare stuff.'

'Well, I kind of make some of it up.'

'So do some.'

'It's like – I can't believe I'm telling you this – it's like insults and things. In Elizabethan language. Plus some Shakespeare and other stuff. Poetry and things.'

'So do some.'

'Okay.' She helps me stand, and I reverse my way up the two steps to the concrete. There's no turning on steps in these chicken feet. I strike a pose that's meant to be Elizabethan, feet apart, wings declamatory. 'Prithee cockscomb, wherefore dost thou trouble me with trifles when there's commerce to be had in fowl? There's fowl afoot tonight aplenty, so be instead nimble of foot, and get thee to thy servery.'

I manage a couple of shuffly dance steps, since the foot references seem to require it, and I bow.

She laughs. 'I suppose we should be getting back to it. Frank'll be getting lonely. Cockscomb's rude, isn't it?'

'Only in a friendly way, I think.'

'Dad really doesn't know who he's hired here, does he? You want to be doing other things, don't you?'

'I'm serious about getting into film, you know. I might be saying that out of a chicken's head, but I'm serious. I think it was when I saw Dustin Hoffman in *The Graduate* that I realised how amazing it can be – what film can be like when it's done really well. I really want to do it.'

'I know.'

'I don't want to be one of those people who talks about it but doesn't even try to do it. I want to do it like Woody Allen. He just does what he wants. He writes, he directs, he stars sometimes, and he doesn't even have to leave the island of Manhattan.'

'But wouldn't he want to? Wouldn't he want to see other things sometimes?'

'I don't know. Maybe he doesn't think he needs to.'

There's singing from inside, Meat Loaf's 'Paradise by the Dashboard Light'. I hope Frank's alone, and not turning it into some haphazard kind of charm.

'Hey,' Sophie says, 'Frank told me Phoebe Harris is your mother. Phoebe Harris the uni tutor. Is that right? She's my tutor in one of my media studies subjects.'

'That'd be her. Is this going to be embarrassing for me?'

'I don't know. Are a lot of things embarrassing for you?'

'Yes. Including almost everything to do with my parents. My parents, coloured drinks, exercise equipment, the present Frank gave me for my twenty-first – all of that's at least ninety-five per cent embarrassing. Other things less so.'

'She was telling us the other day about how she was injured in one of the right-to-march protests a few years ago, and how she's got a Special Branch file.'

'She assumes. They don't tell you. Lots of people have

got Special Branch files. That's one bunch of cops who take far more photos than they need to.'

Embarrassing? Sure it was, but Sophie won't have heard the story in its entirety. It all gets back to how my mother tells them, each time finding a way to step around the whole story while picking up a few of its better parts. And 'injured in one of the right-to-march protests' is certainly a good start when you're standing in front of a media studies class.

'What is it with you and Frank?' Sophie says through the toilet door on our next changeover.

'He's dangerous when he's understimulated. His mind wanders, and his mouth stays open. It's a bad combination.'

A bad combination – Frank was shitty about how long our last changeover was, so he decided to sing 'MacArthur Park' continuously to Sophie until customers came and interrupted. And when they went, he picked up from where he'd left off and kept singing.

'Yes, but, you're his friend and most of the time he's kind of, well . . . obnoxious.'

'Yeah. Tell me something I don't know. Next you'll be breaking it to me that he can't sing. But it's only pretend obnoxious, and it makes a surprising number of women want to have sex with him.'

'How many would you call surprising?'

'Well, one, but there are actually a few more than that. It's a little easier to take if you tell yourself it's bravado. A combination of bravado and simple directness. In cowboy movies those are both virtues and Frank could be either the sheriff or, more likely, the wronged outlaw with the good heart.'

'And in real life? Real life in the late-twentieth century?'

'Here and now he's more like the outlaw, and there are times when bravado and simple directness can be a lot to forgive. In real life his big issue is that he's been displaced from his natural genre. Sometimes I think he lives to shit people, but he's a good guy really. Frank is a low-rent rock star without a band. He plays life as if he's a connoisseur, but he thought cuisine in this town reached a new high when he found out that, with the aid of just one phone call, pizza would come to your home. It took a while to convince him that we don't all think the way he does, and that the world doesn't work for me in the same way that it works for him.'

'And how does the world work for you?'

It was my turn for 'MacArthur Park' after that but I was ready for him. I didn't care about his cake, I didn't care about how long it took him to bake it, I welcomed the rain.

How does the world work for me?

It's not fair that a conversation should be left hanging on such a question, that Frank should call out then, threatening to resume singing and immediately going through with it. I'm never sure how the world works for me. Most of the time, it's best not to think about it. Term Four is general practice. That's what the world has for me two months from now, and I know what happens next year and the year after that, or what's supposed to. But, in the end, that doesn't mean I know a lot.

I'm glad the evening's done and I'm away from the World and 'MacArthur Park', home in my room, watching TV with the volume down and sucking on a Sustagen milkshake. The bullworker is getting me nowhere, and I should accept that.

I should have had bikini babes lounging around every rippling muscle long before now. Do I want anything so shallow? It wouldn't hurt. Worse could happen, and has. For example, the past seven months have given me plenty of study time. Plenty.

Frank tells me I should keep putting myself out there, because sometimes something comes back. It's a matter of projecting confidence. Frank projects confidence to the point of projecting recklessness instead, and sometimes he scores. He says that there are people who find confidence persuasive, even if it's got no basis, and I think he might be right. He calls this kind of confidence 'pure confidence', as though it's a better kind by being untainted with content issues.

During psych I put it to him that it might, in a way, be the flip side to existential angst, so we should maybe think of it as 'existential confidence'. He told me he thought that was worth a shot. About a week later he said he'd tried it on a girl and found it had worked pretty well. 'Sometimes a reference like that can make you look kind of intellectual,' he said. 'And that can be good, depending on the girl. You should bear that in mind.'

Unfortunately, being pseudo-intellectual was already one of my better things, and hadn't been as persuasive as I'd hoped.

At least Sophie didn't seem to make the connection between Phoebe my girlfriend and Phoebe my mother. But why would she, I guess? It's not a common name but it's not exceptionally rare, either.

I shouldn't have let her talk me into doing the Elizabethan stuff for her. Pure confidence isn't easy but that's no excuse to project pure strangeness instead, even if her lack of availability meant that my guard was down. It would be smarter to remember that she's a girl, and to use her as practice.

The Elizabethan stuff is my mother's fault. Damn her and her insistence on eisteddfods. I can't even quote things in a cool way. I know people who can go, 'Well, Nietzsche did say . . .' as though they were just talking to him this morning. Doing slabs of Shakespeare that I've deliberately rote-learned, and doing them while chickening, is not the same.

I hated eisteddfods at the start. The worst part was being corralled into side rooms at City Hall before taking the stage to orate. Something always went very wrong with my hair and my mother would slick it down with water from a sink in the toilets.

Eisteddfods were an early attempt at finding the means to project confidence. And has the ability to recite sonnet thirty-one from Sir Philip Sidney's *Astrophel and Stella* (while water from your slicked-down hair trickles to your collar) improved anyone's confidence in the last four hundred years? I don't think so. For me, it was all nothing more than the bullworker and Sustagen equivalent of five years ago.

How is it that I'm much more confident reciting things as the chicken than as Phil Harris, confident enough that I'll make up Shakespeare and almost dance about it? The chicken is tall and broad and fearless, and a place to hide. The bigger dick I make of myself in there, the less chance there is that anyone driving past might know it's me. I play the chicken like I'm playing Frank in a good mood. Devil-may-care. I think it was even the chicken that paid Sophie the earring compliment.

I can't believe the things my mother says about her Special Branch file. She was destined to be involved in media studies.

The Joh Bjelke-Petersen state government banned

protest marches when I was at school. Perhaps they'd always been banned, but that's when it became a big issue. The biggest reason to march then was for the right to march. And, since there was no right to march, there were plenty of arrests.

My mother decided she couldn't stand by and let everyone else do the marching for her. She worked in town then, and she left work early to be part of the protest.

The police decided that the line for action would be the kerb. They made that very clear. One foot off the kerb and onto the road and you'd be arrested for marching.

My mother wasn't with the main group of marchers – she didn't know anyone else who was marching – and she was left behind, some distance away, when they surged onto the road. She stepped off the kerb but, because of her high-ish heel, turned her ankle and crumpled into the gutter. Two young police officers rushed over and, just as she was thinking of the great pictures she was creating for the next morning's papers – a forty-something well-dressed woman being carried off, arrested – they were totally polite.

They thought it was an accident, one of those things that can happen in a crowd, and they helped her over to the St John's Ambulance people, who strapped her ankle. She couldn't bring herself to say that she'd been setting out to march.

'I was born into a world of manners, Philby,' she told me later that day, her ankle strapped, iced and elevated, a cup of tea beside her. 'That was my downfall. I can't help but respond to manners. And they were so nice. I couldn't disappoint them.'

Then she said it was important that we all contribute, in our own way, and she settled for writing a stern letter to the *Courier-Mail*. I don't think it was ever published.

Sir Joh Bjelke-Petersen has been the Queensland premier the whole time we've been in Australia, and the state is a national joke for having a Deep North government that's said to resemble governments of a generation or more ago in some parts of the US Deep South – governments that always talk about getting things done and never talk about rights. Governments that send in the police to clear protesters before felling rainforest, or that set demolition crews onto old buildings in the hours before dawn. By morning it's too late. There's just rubble left, and pictures for the papers.

We're an easy target for remarks about crossing the border and turning the clock back fifteen years, or a hundred. We're a state that's known for pineapples and cane toads, old bad attitudes and the brain-addling heat that comes from the Tropic of Capricorn sitting right across our middle. We're that kind of state – hot and steamy, unlovely and unloved, far too much fodder here for metaphors about festering and putrefaction.

There are times when you get tired of it, tired of the easy bashing of the place. Sure, you'd like it to be different, but most days here are just like days in a lot of other places. They must be. You get on, you live your life, you try to vote them out when the chance comes.

Rigged electoral boundaries don't make it easy and, at the last state election eighteen months ago, Joh got back in without needing much of the vote. My parents were at a party that night. It hadn't started as an election party, but the topic couldn't be avoided. TVs were on and everyone was watching the tally room. There had been a split in the government coalition, and we really thought they might go down. My mother left for the party, anxious but hopeful, having campaigned during the day. As the results came in and Joh looked like clinging on to power, my parents sensed they were perhaps the only people at the party wanting a different result.

I'd turned the coverage off early and I was asleep in bed when they came home. I woke to hear my mother throwing up in the garden, having drunk too much for the only time I can remember, moaning about 'bloody fascists' as my father's voice murmured something supportive beside her.

Of course, the families of most of the people I'm doing medicine with probably voted for this government or for their ex-coalition partners. Not everyone's like my mother.

5

On Sunday I borrow my mother's car so that I can drive to the Greens.

'AJ'll be a while,' Frank says when I get there. 'A big night, apparently.'

'Work or play?'

'He didn't say. You want a beer?'

'Sure.'

AJ – Arthur Junior – is a couple of years older than us, and shares a flat at Paddington with a friend. He's an interior decorator, or something like that, but on weekends he DJs for weddings and twenty-firsts. It hasn't been long since he moved out and, when Big Artie decides there'll be a barbecue on the weekend, the decision's binding for the whole family, including his first-born namesake.

'Weekends,' Frank says, when we're out the back, 'there's nothing like 'em.'

He clinks his stubbie against mine, takes a mouthful of beer and keeps talking. He's straddling Fonzie, the Green family's pet sheep, and both of them seem particularly nonchalant about it. Frank's talking as though he isn't on the back of a sheep, even though he's patting Fonzie's head. Fonzie's pulling up mouthfuls of grass, occasionally looking at me as if I'm the strange one, this free-standing beer-drinking person. Surely I'm going to fall over any second, without a sheep under me.

Years ago, Big Artie – who loves nothing more than a fiercely irrational opinion – was mouthing off about butchers being a rip-off, so he went and bought a live lamb. But he couldn't kill it. Then Frank's little sister Vanessa called it Fonzie, so he definitely couldn't kill it. Now Fonzie's fully grown and Artie bullshits on about the savings on mower fuel instead. Once, in a cocksure moment about eight beers into a barbecue, he is said to have declared, 'No-one sticks it up bloody OPEC like the Fonz.'

I know that sometimes, when Frank gets bored during study, he puts David Lee Roth (their Yorkshire terrier) on Fonzie's back and tries to train them to do laps of the yard. 'Next,' he said to me once, 'there'll be a hoop to go through. Maybe even fire. That'd give us something I could tour.' But so far the excitable David Lee Roth and the dull-witted Fonzie haven't come to the party. The one that should stay still, can't stay still. The one that should be lapping, munches grass instead of moving. At its brief best it does look very silly, but you couldn't call it a show.

Today, while we're drinking beer and everyone's waiting for AJ, David Lee Roth is with Vanessa under the house. She's playing an Alice Cooper album, loud enough that Frank can't resist and takes a stab at the chorus of 'You and Me' (holds it down, takes a stab at it, leaves it for dead).

Vanessa is working on Frank's car. He tells me he does most of it himself, of course, but she's up on the electronics and he wouldn't want to stand in her way.

'I'm going to do something,' he says, turning purposeful. 'Something about that bastard O'Hare. I should have got eight out of ten for that case. I shouldn't have to cop his bullshit.'

'Yeah, but his bullshit is all about copping his bullshit. You cop it, you do what you've got to do and then you move on. He wants you to take him on. You do that and he'll get you.'

'I've got to go and see him. Tuesday. Between him and bloody Ron Todd . . . does that guy get to you? He gets to me.'

'Why? He's odd, but why does he get to you? What's the point?'

'Aren't you hanging out for a time when you don't have to deal with guys like that? When there's no-one who'll come up to you and put a hand on your shoulder and give you some patronising advice and a blast of halitosis? And you've got to cop it because he marks your cases or pays your wages or whatever. Not that Ron's like O'Hare. Okay, on one level I admire him – Ron, I mean. He's got some vision. I don't know how things are going at the World – I think they could be better – but he had an idea and he's seeing it through. I think I identify with that.'

'Yeah? Which bit?'

'I've got this idea for a franchise. I'd probably make some money from medicine first and then kick it off. It's a food thing. I thought of it the other night at the World. It's called "Eat of the Beast". I'm thinking it's a simple one-price-only all-you-can-eat meat restaurant.'

'A meat restaurant?'

'Yeah, total meat.'

'Even the salads?'

'Meat. Different cuts of meat. Salad cuts. It's a new concept. Thin cuts, marinated. The pastrami salad, for instance.'

'Which contains?'

'Pastrami.' Pause for effect. 'See what I mean? Simple. I reckon one day all those vegos are going to get wise. And when they come running for meat, I wouldn't mind at all if they came running for me.' He pauses again, nods this time. This one's a different kind of pause, like a pioneer cresting a hill in a covered wagon and pausing to take in the view. 'There'd be fondue,' he adds as an afterthought. 'Stacks of fondue. People'd go for that. Spike it, cook it, eat it. Nothing but meat and sauce.'

'Hey, Frank,' Vanessa shouts from under the house. 'I think I'm done.'

'Good on you, Ness,' Frank says when she comes out. 'Allow me to fetch you a tall, cold Diet Coke.'

She's wearing an old tie-dye T-shirt, baggy army shorts and a belt with battery-operated car signals – something that, I think, she won on an afternoon kids' TV show. Frank brings her the Diet Coke and swings his leg back over the Fonz, and Vanessa flops down onto a folding chair.

'Hey, Dad's pretty buggered after those Chinese elms yesterday,' she says, her right indicator flicking on and off.

'Yeah. It must be tiring, standing around giving all those instructions.' Frank's not much into tree talk.

She laughs. 'He's the expert. That's his job. It takes a lot of concentration.'

'Try being sixty foot up a tree with a chainsaw hanging from your belt.'

'Hey, that's only 'cause you've got what it takes, you know. That job's a privilege. You know what Dad says.' She puts on a serious look. 'You're a beaut young climber, Frankie. It's a bloody tragedy to waste a skill like that.'

'Well, we're all just going to have to live with it, aren't we?'

'No need for climbing when you're a surgeon,' she says. 'Unless you're a tree surgeon.'

Frank laughs. 'True enough.'

Big Artie hoped so much that Frank would be part of the family business that he even got him a personalised Green Loppers T-shirt, something formerly reserved for full-time employees. Frank had put in five years work on holidays and weekends by then. For the last two years he's been trying to stop, since he says it's not worth the hassle. All he has to do is climb one tree and Artie dreams about retirement. Plus, the way Frank sees it, he's not a flash payer. Which he admits is good business, but not if you're the employee.

Vanessa goes inside to get another Diet Coke. 'They should make even taller glasses,' she says.

'Another business that I don't think is going so well,' Frank says when she's gone. 'Green Loppers.'

'But does your father really think you'd stop doing medicine now to go into it?'

'No . . . I don't know. It'd be fine if he had a climber. I think if he had a climber we'd find that a lot of these weekend jobs could be done on weekdays. You only need one climber, really, if you've got the back-up. A couple of blokes cutting stuff on the ground and feeding it into the shredder and looking after ropes and shit. And one boss, who knows exactly how a tree'll fall. That's what the old man's good at. But the others? Nev. Nev's older than Dad and weedier than you, and he's famous for one thing and it's not tree lopping. Have I told you about this? I don't think so. There was this big philosophical bind he got into. There was one time when he paid twenty bucks for a blowie on Brunswick Street and then he found out he'd got it from a trannie.' He stops, raises his eyebrows in a how-about-that kind of way.

'I don't see the philosophical bind yet.'

'It was a blow job the like of which he'd never had before, the eye-roller to end all eye-rollers. So what's a man to do the next time he's got a lazy twenty in his back pocket? It's all right for the likes of you and me, who could practically audition the chicks if we had the inclination, hey, but Nev only gets it if he pays for it. And the story gets worse too.'

'That's hard to believe.'

'The trannie had lost his front teeth going over his handlebars when he was a kid, and for an extra five bucks he'd take his plate out.'

'Do you know how much I want you to be making this up? I want to stop thinking about it right now.'

'I reckon Ron Todd's got a plate.'

'And I don't want to think about that, either.'

Frank laughs, and I'll probably never know if the Nev story is true or a scavenged urban myth, or something Frank made up as he went along.

At the top of the steps, the screen door to the kitchen swings open and Big Artie's there with trays of meat and sausages.

'The boy's here,' he says, and Arthur junior follows him out.

AJ's hair is slicked back and he's wearing a white T-shirt that looks too small, and Ray-Bans sitting high on his head.

'Been working out?' Frank says, also noticing the new look.

'Oh, when I get the chance. How have you guys been?'

'Pretty good. We've finished surgery and we're onto obstetrics. You realise you can see your nipples through that shirt?'

'I've just got myself a tan, that's all. And moved to a non-bevan part of town where not everybody dresses like a tree lopper. Is that, um, girlfriend of yours coming over? Sorry, what was her name?'

'Hardly relevant now.'

'Really?' AJ looks at me, probably figuring I'm his best chance of an unbiased report.

'I don't think she's coming over. They had a misunderstanding a week or so ago.'

'A free man, hey?' he says to Frank.

'That's right. I was about ready for a change, anyway. She was a bit too immature for me.'

'Surely not.' AJ laughs.

Vanessa and their mother, Dorothy, come down the back steps with several large bowls of salad and at least a dozen bread rolls. As always, there's far more food than we can eat.

'Arthur made the potato salad,' Dorothy says. 'Didn't you?'

'Yeah.' AJ looks coy about it. 'I thought it'd be good to bring something.'

'It looks like a pretty flash potato salad too. What are the green bits, love?' Dorothy is calling his bluff. We all know AJ well enough to know that he's no food preparer.

He takes a look into the bowl and calls the green bits chives, but without much conviction. 'At least, they should be chives. We've got chives in a window box, and it's not as if anyone mowed the lawn today.' He knows he's blown it. 'Oh, all right, Rod made it. He's got lunch at his family's place today too, so I just got him to make twice as much.' Then he tries to reclaim some ground, pitch it as a positive. 'I mean, potato salad, it's one of your fussier salads, isn't it? So, if someone'll make it for you, why not?'

'He's a useful flatmate, that boy,' Dorothy says. 'I hope it's not all one-way traffic. I hope you're pulling your weight.'

'Yep, I iron his jocks, mum. I wash his sheets and I make his bed with hospital corners, just like you taught me.'

'Well, that's better. That's worth some potato salad now and then.'

AJ was first in line for Green Loppers, but he was never good with heights. Big Artie used to joke around to try to get him over it, but it never worked. He used to say that when AJ took over they could rename the company Theresa

Green's, since AJ was such a girl when it came to climbing. Heights, lopping and Sunnybank Hills were all wrong for AJ. They seemed wrong when he lived here and they seem more wrong now. Paddington's right for him – restaurants, a couple of nightclubs (the Underground and Cafe Neon), the city just five minutes away. That's his kind of world and now he comes back here, back to the burbs, dressed like a person from somewhere else.

Dorothy sends Vanessa back upstairs for cutlery, Frank fetches beers for the three of us and hands one to AJ.

'Hospital corners,' he says, and shakes his head.

'Never made a bed in my life,' AJ tells him, and he clinks his stubbie against Frank's as if he's toasting the declaration, making a commitment to it for the future.

'You're good, very good.' Frank's always admired people who have things done for them. 'You don't go anywhere without a slave, do you?'

'I don't go looking for them. They come to me.'

'Style wins out over substance yet again.'

'As it should. Substance is tedious. Style's the only thing that distinguishes us from apes.' For some reason, we all look around at Big Artie at that point, and he's hunched over the barbecue flipping steaks over, back hair poking out over his singlet, one hand swatting at flies. 'Like I said.' He raises his stubbie in another toast. 'You and me, brother. Down from the trees.'

Vanessa puts a handful of knives and forks down noisily on the table and walks over to us, clinks her Coke glass against AJ's beer and says, 'Welcome.'

'Thanks, Nessie. How have you been?'

'Pretty good.'

'And the flower business?'

'It's okay.'

'Just okay?'

'Okay is okay. It's not bad.'

'Maybe one day you'll be the actual florist rather than the helper, and that'll be better.'

'Yeah. There's a lot to know, though, to be a florist. Flowers, man,' she says, as if it's all a puzzle. 'What are they about? And what do I do if I don't do flowers? It's a bloody mystery.'

'Ness, it's a mystery for most of us,' AJ tells her, getting in just ahead of Frank. 'You're not even seventeen until next month. A lot of people who are years older than that don't know what they want to do.'

'Frank knows. Frank wants to be a surgeon. Phil probably knows too.'

'Not really.' Yep, another of those occasions when I can't say 'film maker', since it seems more like a dumb dream than a career option. 'And Frank's surgery plans are pretty recent too, as far as I know. In fact, I didn't even know that he wanted to do surgery.'

'Well, mainly I wanted Dad off my back,' he says. 'So I had to get specific. But, yeah, maybe. I think so.'

'Come on, all of you,' Dorothy calls out. 'Loads of food over here. Make sure you get plenty of Arthur's lovely potato salad.'

Frank looks at me as though his surgery ambitions are something I'm not supposed to know. 'Anyway, we'll see about all that, won't we? I've got O'Hare on Tuesday to get past first.'

'It should be okay. It's only the long case we've got back and, whatever happens, you should hopefully be able to bury last term's result when you're out there working.'

But Frank says nothing more than 'Hmmm,' and that's not like him.

'Eat,' I tell him. 'Get to that barbecue. Eat of the beast.'

6

I can't adjust to the idea that there's a medical career choice starting to become clear in Frank's head, but not in mine.

At World of Chickens the next night, we're at the counter and he's bored, fiddling around with a pencil while we wait for business.

'Did you know,' he says, having scrawled a few letters on the white laminate, 'that "happiness" is just an anagram of "penis pash"?'

'Hate being single, don't you, Frank?'

'What's not to hate? But I'm using it as a rebuilding phase.'

'Sure. That maturity thing, you mean? The maturity issue that seems to have emerged about the last one . . .'

'Yeah, pretty much. So I'm working on a new marketing plan. A few new lines . . .'

'Which I don't need to know.'

'As if I'd tell you.'

'You've always told me before.'

'Well, part of the new plan is not telling you. Don't wear your lines out on a guy, that's what I'm thinking. And there's a new look – black pants. I've taken blue jeans about as far as I can. Plus, a new fragrance for the vehicle, and a new fuck song.'

'That'll get them in.'

'No, you'll like it. "Eye of the Tiger".'

'But doesn't it only go for three minutes?'

'I don't start it till I've got my shoes off.'

'You *don't* start it, or you *won't* start it? If it's a post-Cyndi development you shouldn't have had the chance to use it yet, should you?'

'Hey, it's a matter of self-belief. Things mightn't have turned yet but, when they do, I'll be ready. I'll be out there, living life in the present tense. I'm a *now* kind of man.'

'A now kind of man? Do you know the difference between life and an aftershave ad?'

I have to admit, I've never been completely at ease with Frank's 'fuck song' concept. Call me a romantic, but it sounds rather calculated. Does he tell them? Does he say to them, 'I've got this new fuck song, babe, and I picked it with you in mind . . .'? Am I getting this all wrong, or would that fail to make a person feel special? At least it improves the timing. 'Eye of the Tiger' should buy them an extra two-and-a-half minutes, compared with the unaccompanied version of sex with Frank.

Another couple of customers, and then he decides it's time to resume his biggest-burger-in-one-bite challenge.

'We'll do it at the changeover,' he says. 'And tonight it gets serious. I've got this fillet that's a bit on the small side – but it's the real thing, pec major, not pec minor – and I'll go a bit light on the salad maybe, but it'll be an actual adult burger.'

Ron Todd arrives just as Sophie comes in from the traffic lights. He's looking energetic, tossing around a kind of contrived high enthusiasm, probably as something motivational since it wouldn't surprise me if we looked a little flat. I should tell him things are fine here, and he doesn't need to worry. Frank's going a PB with a burger again and he's got a new fuck song, and black pants. The World, clearly, is in capable hands. Plus, there's always that anagram. We're definitely the thinking customer's burger crew.

'How's the A Team?' Ron says, and rubs his hands together. 'Keeping you busy, are they?'

'Just sold a couple,' I tell him. 'A couple of burgers, large fries, bucket of coleslaw.'

Frank looks at me as though I'm engaged in some sad sucking up, just because I answered the question, but Ron seems pleased by the news that customers have at least been sighted in the recent past.

'Good lads. Good team. Good work the three of you. But don't let me get in the way of things. Keep at it.'

'No worries,' Frank says, so that something intrudes upon the potentially awkward silence that comes from three people keeping at nothing. 'The moment anyone comes in we'll ignore you completely.'

'Exactly. Focus,' Ron says, interpreting Frank's comment in an unduly positive way. 'You've got to focus. Give that customer a burger to remember. Good thought, Frank. Hold onto that. I'm just going to take a look at things out the back, make sure we're carrying all the stock we need.' He's about to go through the door when he stops and turns. 'Go A Team,' he says. And then he's gone.

'Go A Team,' Frank echoes. 'Nothing against you guys, but I'd hate to see how the bloody B Team stacks up.' He squirts barbecue sauce onto the chicken fillet and finishes making his burger. He presses down on it to flatten the bread, and tests the feel of it in his hand. 'Here goes nothing . . .'

Sophie flaps a wing and stops him. 'Wait a second. I didn't see gherkin, and you said this was serious. It's not serious if there's no gherkin.'

'A lot of people don't go for the gherkin.'

'Hey, they might turn it down, but it is standard. If they

say nothing, they get three slices. So there should be a penalty. You should have to have extra.' Until now, I hadn't realised how much I'd enjoy watching Frank being berated by a chicken. 'You should have to have a whole one, six slices or a whole one. Phil?'

'I think you're right. And I think there's a jar out the back with some whole ones in it. I could go and get one.'

'Yeah. That's fair isn't it, Frank? I mean, it's not that we don't think you can do it. I think we all just want to see it done properly.'

'What?' He's annoyed that his PB burger's ready but we've got him on a technicality. 'It's the full piece of bird. Oh, all right then, bugger you. I'll take the penalty, and I'll still do it.'

When I get out the back, Ron's not only in the same room as the gherkins, he happens to be right next to them, leaning on an empty part of the shelving and flicking through papers. Maybe I'll tell him I've come for a whole one because of a customer's request. Maybe I'll back out quietly and we'll go for six slices.

'Shit,' he says quietly before he realises I'm there. 'Shit, shit.' Then he looks up, just as I've decided six slices is the way to go. 'Oh, sorry, I . . .' He rolls the papers up in his hands. 'I was just, um, looking through a few figures. Cash register tallies, and things.'

'There's not a problem is there?'

'What? Oh, no, nothing like that. It's just . . . look, I think I can talk to you. Do you mind if I talk to you? Confidentially? I think you've got a good head for retail and you're here more of the time than I am.'

'Sure.'

'And you're practically a doctor.'

'Yeah, but practically a doctor is still not much.'

'Oh, sure, sure. Now, you kids, you're good kids, right? This is nothing to do with that. And you're working hard, I can see you're working hard.'

'But we're not selling a lot of chicken?'

'That's right. And I don't know why. I bought this place as a going concern and, between you and me, we haven't had one break-even week since we opened. I thought it might have been to do with overheads . . .'

'But it's actually to do with sales, isn't it?'

'Right again. Cutting the teams from five to three helped, but that's about as lean as we can have it if we want to keep a chicken on the road. Which we do, obviously.' His forehead furrows. 'But don't worry. It's not drastic, or anything. We'll get there. I think we'll get there, and we won't be cutting staffing any further. We'll get there. And I've got a few dental problems as well, to be honest. Do you do much of that in med?'

'No, not really.'

'I've had a partial plate at the front for a while, but now things are starting to go wrong with the other teeth. They reckon the whole lot's under threat.'

'That doesn't sound good.'

'No. Caries, they call them. They're like cavities. And I've got root problems, too. I don't know how it's going to go.'

'Well, if you've got a good dentist . . . are you happy with your dentist? If you've got a good dentist, you'll at least get the best outcome you can, whatever that turns out to be.'

'Yeah. Yeah, thanks. Just got to take it as it comes, I guess.' He nods, looks around the room as though any shelf in here might have the answers. 'I paid a packet for goodwill when I bought this place, and where is it?' He shrugs. 'But you don't need to know all that, do you? Sorry. My problem.'

'No, it's fine. Let's hope it . . .'

The door to the serving area swings open so hard it slams into the wall and Frank lurches past us, choking to death. I grab him from behind and heave into a Heimlich manoeuvre. An entire slimy burger flops out of his mouth and onto the floor.

'Good lord, Frank,' Ron says. 'What are you? A man or a bloody boa constrictor?'

'It was okay till it touched my uvula.' Frank leans against the wall, his cheeks still red, his short life still, perhaps, flashing before his bulging eyes.

'By all means, have a burger on your dinner break, but chew it Frank, chew it. God gave you teeth you know. And they're bloody useful.'

Frank nods. We're all now staring at the squished, partly disassembled burger, and I'm amazed that he got even close.

'And it's three slices of gherkin,' Ron says. 'Three slices. I can count at least five in that.'

'Six,' Sophie says quietly next to my shoulder. I turn around and I can see her eyes looking out at me through the beak slot. 'He just couldn't wait.'

When I finish my next go at chickening, I get into a discussion with Sophie on the back steps. And this time we don't need to hurry and there won't be bad singing.

She's come up with the idea that there should be chicken-free intervals to give us maximum impact when we're out at the road, she's put it to Frank and he didn't complain. He's more passive than usual, and describing the burger incident as 'heavy at the very least, if not a near-death experience.' The only flicker of the regular Frank that's broken through was his assertion to me that Ron's comment about the boa constrictor confirmed his status as a patronising prick.

'I'm so sick of being Libra,' I tell Sophie, since that's the way the conversation seems to have turned.

'There's a lot of good things to Libra. Librans are balanced, nice. Aren't they? Or are they looking for balance? I'm never sure.'

'I don't know about balance, but I'm sick of being the nice guy of the zodiac. That's exactly my problem. It's the eighties now – nice is baggage. Not that I want to be mean – not at all – but it's a fine distinction. I've got to get edgier. I want to have the potential to break hearts, but to choose not to. I want to be known to hang out with bands, even if I don't. I want to have at least one friend named after a day of the week, preferably Wednesday. I want to be trouble of the "Phil, he's trouble" kind, but I'm beginning to think that trouble isn't in me.'

'Trouble?' she says. 'Trouble is trouble. It can look good from a distance, but close up it sucks.'

'But it looks good from a distance. It's that long-range stuff that gets you the chance. Look at Frank.'

'Not a Libran.'

'Definitely not a Libran. Taurus, or some shit like that. Frank's a funny kind of trouble from a long way off, but it gets noticed and he'll be going out with someone in minutes. That's his style. And he'll only do them harm. Can't they see that?'

'It's not like he hides it.' She shrugs. 'But anyway, you're with Phoebe. What's the problem? *Nice* must have got you somewhere.'

'Oh, yeah.' I had completely forgotten the Phoebe lie. I'd forgotten it's Sophie I'm talking to. 'I was talking theoretically. About Libra. And I do get some pretty long stretches of in-between time, so maybe that's where I think Libra is. I must have got a lucky break with Phoebe. I'm talking generally. Like, supposing Frank and I were both available at the same time, I'd be backing him to change his luck first.'

'Can't see why.'

'Plenty of reasons. Confidence, bravado, how it all looks from a distance. You should see him dance. Most of us, we're not good dancers. A lot of guys look bad out there. A lot of guys know they look bad out there and they stiffen up, and things get worse. Not Frank. Frank says he chooses not to carry the white man's burden, which he defines as the burden of trying to dance and trying not to dance at the same time.'

'Does he think girls find lines like that clever?'

'I don't know. I don't know if that's part of what he tells them or just part of what he tells me. But, I have to say, I know what he means.'

Suddenly, the lack of time pressure isn't enough reason for me to stay on the steps. I don't want to talk about Frank and me and girls and dancing. Sophie keeps it up a while longer, mainly the Frank part, while I take the costume off and then while she puts it on.

'Done,' she says, and she kicks the toilet door wide open with her big orange foot and bounces out. She turns her back to me. 'Pray, sirrah, there's many a slip with an undone zip.'

'Verily, we wouldn't want our chicken skinned before its time.'

Frank, when we get to the serving area, is eating coleslaw out of the tub with a spoon.

'Hey,' he says, 'how good is this coleslaw? I hadn't tried it before. Why are we not selling heaps of this stuff? We should give it a big push in the next half hour, while Sophie's out at the road. And we should have a slogan, like, "how good is slaw?"'

'I hope you're going to eat the whole thing, now that you're dunking a spoon in there.'

'For sure.' And that's when I see that he's not only eating the coleslaw, he's also wearing the lid around his neck on a piece of string. 'Hey, if we're the A Team,' he says, 'I figured I'm probably Mister T. Yeah?'

On the next chicken changeover, Sophie says she doesn't want to spoil it for Frank, but the A Team stuff's a management strategy, really. Not that we aren't the A Team, but she's pretty sure Ron got that from a course he did. He does a lot of courses. Sometimes management, sometimes copper enamelling. He's right and left brain, she tells me, and he didn't used to be. He's a big self-improver and he reckons you'll never know what's going to improve you until you try, so you've got to think laterally. But it's a complicated state of affairs. Books have also identified him as a people person and a hands-on manager, both of which can be good but they also have an association with a tendency to take things to heart, and boundary problems.

'There was a while when some of the Mowers crowd came round for darts in our downstairs bar every Friday,' she says, 'and that was a boundary problem as far as I was concerned. But it kind of died out. Anyway, I think tonight was from a course he did that said you should look enthusiastic when you turn up, and tell every shift they're the A Team. I filled in for Barb last night, and we were the A Team then, too. Even though they're not much fun and, to be honest, their approach to chickening leaves a lot to be desired. They just stand out there and point.'

'And where's the magic in that?' There's an instinctive shrug of my wings when I say it, and I'm sure the other team doesn't inhabit the big bird the way we do. 'Where's the chicken in it, even?'

I'm on my way out to the road when Frank calls me over, shows me slaw.

'See the carrot?' he says, pointing to the bottom of the now almost-empty tub. 'The bits of carrot? Do you think they look like Jesus?'

'What?'

'Just a passing resemblance. Not exactly, or anything. It was just a question. Hey, I'm not the one who looks like a fucking chicken, all right?'

I've always been the kind of person people tell things to and tonight, courtesy of something that might be a minor boundary problem, I got to learn that all is not well at World of Chickens or in Ron Todd's mouth. But as long as Ron's got a good dentist and the boundary problem doesn't push me to darts in the downstairs bar with the Mowers crowd, we should be okay.

Frank should have been part of the conversation with Ron. Maybe that way he wouldn't have been mouthing off about him being a 'smug bastard' in the car on the way back to my place. But perhaps that was more to do with the lopping business, and the fact that its trajectory seems so earth-bound. That got talked about too. I don't understand how the Greens can work the way they do – how there's still pressure on Frank to take the business on, at the same time as there's genuine family pride in him being at uni studying medicine. Don't they get it?

I've got none of that pressure and not much of the

pride. Uni was always part of my plan, and it didn't break new family ground to get there. My mother even works there, tutoring while she does her PhD. Frank's the one who broke the mould. And he's serious about surgery. I can tell. I'd wondered why he'd been so annoyed about the long-case assessment, and that's it.

Perhaps surgery, for him, is like film-making for me – an ambition that came to him years ago and seemed implausibly out of reach. The difference is, he's reaching for it. If I'd started in Frank's position it's likely I'd be up trees by now, a beaut young climber and learning the ropes of the business as well.

But film-making's not the same. There was no course in it that I could see, nothing that would actually get you anywhere. I'm working on it, working towards it at least, saving for a video camera. It's a long-term plan, and I'm doing what I can.

7

Frank's late getting to the Mater the next morning. He's been at Royal Brisbane, talking to Charlie O'Hare about his long-case assessment.

'The arsehole. He could have passed me. He said he'd never liked my attitude, so he looked more closely at the write-up when I handed it in. The patient had only just been discharged, so it was easy for him to get the file. And he sat there eating bloody Tim Tams the whole time. The way he used to in tutes. He couldn't even stop eating to talk to me. Him and his "mindless copying". Mindless bloody biscuit eating . . .'

'So what happens now?'

'Do it in the holidays. Like you said. He's actually taking holidays then too, so someone else'll probably mark it.'

'Well, that's good. Hard to believe anyone'd want to take a holiday with him.'

'He's got kids, you know. And that's even harder to believe. How would it be, your dad getting stuck into you at the beach because you'd built a shit sandcastle?'

'Or, worse, copied someone else's sandcastle.'

'And he sat there, the whole time I was explaining what I'd done and that I thought the no-abbreviations rule was for tutes and that the write-up actually had to show that we knew what a hospital file looked like, and he just smiled. Smiled like "you ignorant, dumb bastard", tapping biscuit crumbs onto my case write-up.'

'Well, you're out of there now. You'll do the case, someone else'll pass it and O'Hare'll be some other tute group's arsehole next term.'

'Yeah.' It sounds like he's agreeing, but he's still thinking about O'Hare, not wanting to let all the anger go just yet. 'Did I miss much with the eight-thirty lecture?'

'No. Bleeding in early pregnancy. There was no handout but I took a lot of notes. There's a chapter on it in the book, too.'

'Well, I should see about getting myself a copy then, shouldn't I? I might go through your notes at lunchtime.' He takes a look at the first couple of pages. 'Jesus, could you please learn to write legibly? People other than you can end up depending on these, you know.'

'I can translate at lunchtime. I'll tell myself it's revision.'

'That'd be good.' He puts the notes in his bag. 'Hey, I've lined up a job for us, this Saturday night. It's cash, and it's a better rate than Ron Todd pays. We'd be working the bar on the *Paradise*.'

'The *Paradise*? As in, the barge with the plastic palms that goes up and down the river while people sink as much beer as they can manage?'

'That's the one. Except I thought the palms were real. And it's a theme night – Viva España. I don't know exactly what that'll mean, but I guess there'll be sangria and cocktails. And a lot of regular dull girls pretending to be hot-blooded Spaniards for the night. That should be okay.'

'I thought you were looking for maturity, not regular dull girls.'

'I was thinking of you, mate. You're always up for a crack at a regular dull girl, aren't you? Anyway, I've accepted. It's a white-shirt black-pants job, so you've got the gear for it. There might be funny hats, or something, but they'd give us those.'

'Hey, I don't do hats. You know I don't do hats. You should never have . . .'

'I was kidding. There's no hats. Funny hats'd be Mexico, not Spain. Get real. Anyway, it's organised. AJ heard they needed a couple of guys and he thought we'd fit the bill. And I thought it could be good for some more camera money for you.'

'Well, that's true.'

'And it'll get you talking to girls other than Sophie Todd, and that's not a bad idea.'

'What's wrong with talking to Sophie Todd?' No, not indignation, stupid choice. He just gives me a look. 'You expect us to get changed in silence? Is she silent when she's working at the counter with you?'

'Close to it.'

'She's got a boyfriend.'

'You know that's the kind that's trouble for you. You know that's the kind you fall for. No performance anxiety because she's got a boyfriend, and then your little heart gets all knotted up and you have to hate the boyfriend and you don't even know him.'

'We're friends, dickhead. And it's actually because she's in a relationship that it's easy for us to be friends. So don't make out . . .'

'Would you turn her down if she made a move?'

'It's not happening.'

'So that'd be a No then.'

'It's an N/A. Not applicable.'

'You're going the spoil aren't you? You're out the back being Mister Sensitive Chicken and quietly white-anting Clinton. Next you'll be telling her stories about your childhood and you'll be all vulnerable and engaging.' He says it as though vulnerable and engaging are two of the least desirable things to be, a bad act that's close to making him throw up and laugh at the same time. 'You'll be listening to whatever guff she comes out with about star signs and bad dates she's been on, and you'll be doing funny voices and poetry and shit. I've seen your routine, fancy man. I've never seen it work, but I've seen your routine.'

Okay, I don't have to cop that. Vulnerable and engaging aren't bad at all, and they're not necessarily a tactic. Frank says they're a tactic, but he calls them a 'just good friends' tactic, which means they're inherently flawed. You put in the hard work, you put yourself on the line, and how does it end up? If it misfires you've got nothing. If it succeeds, you've got yourself another just good friend.

'If you want to be the guy with the shoulder to cry on – the guy they go to for guy advice – go for vulnerable and engaging. Really, they're pretty much like being gay.' That's what he said. 'You've got to get a bit of mongrel about you to get noticed.'

And he's got it all wrong when it comes to Sophie. She's with Clinton. We share a chicken costume, some conversation and the occasional hint of green-apple shampoo, and anything else is not applicable. Completely N/A.

It's well into the evening. My mother's at her first *Pirates of Penzance* rehearsal, my father's working in his study and I'm on my bed listening to one of my many artfully compiled compilation tapes and trying to read Beischer and Mackay, chapter eighteen, 'Bleeding in Early Pregnancy'.

And vulnerable and engaging is not a tactic. As it is, I'm not particularly vulnerable, I'm not trying to look that way and what's wrong with engaging? That's a part of interacting with people. I like getting on with people, and that's something Frank could actually be better at.

It's only now, looking up at the old model planes hanging from my ceiling – at the 1:72 scale Battle of Britain being fought up there – that I realise I've never even thought it possible that there might be a girl in this room some day. I can imagine myself being vulnerable and engaging and how well it'd go, how much I'd impress her with the way I'd downplay my clever hot-skewer work to the fuselage of several of the German planes where my Hurricanes and early model Spitfires have been savaging them.

It's a winning combination, an irresistible package, this room and the guy in it – the planes, the bullworker, the porn clock above the door and me. At least there's a TV. And the what's-not-to-love 'Steam Engines of Great Britain' bedsheets which, to their credit, have lasted a lot of years now. So long that most of the time they're just sheets to me, but then I suddenly glimpse the unmistakable elegant cylindrical flank of the Flying Scotsman and it's 'oh my god there are steam engines of Great Britain on my bed'.

Naturally, my mother's involved. I'm sure she could give me other sheets, but she says the steam engine ones are so colourful it'd be a shame to waste them in the spare room. I think she's trying to wear me down. It's a tactic. She keeps giving me kiddie sheets, so that if I want grown-up sheets I have to behave like a grown-up and get them myself – make my own bed. She has no idea how small a risk I face, having these sheets in my room.

'Vulnerable' and 'engaging' are longer words for nice, and that's their problem. There's a group of girls I get cards from at Christmas. Four girls who don't know each other, so it's not as though they've conferred. I met them one at a time, wanted them, pursued them in the previously described futile manner, slept with none of them and now it's cards every Christmas. So I have to send cards back every Christmas, because it's rude if you don't. Which means I'm in this big fat Christmas-card rut, and I probably will be all my life.

What amazes me is how many awful Christmas cards there are out there that thank a person for friendship, often with the aid of a cheesy rhyming couplet or two. That's what they send me, and it's not like I give them much friendship. Two of them I don't even see during the year.

For the sake of those girls – to free them from the rhyming couplets, if nothing else – they should print cards that say:

Thank you for last year's card
And for putting up such a poor effort to get me into bed
That I feel compelled to do this every year

And they should also print one for me that says:

Thank you for last year's card
Allow me to correct a misunderstanding
I have never wanted to be your friend
A while back I wanted to sleep with you
And then you turned out to be the kind of person who sends
Friendship Christmas cards with cheesy rhyming couplets
Are you unable to understand
The meanings of the following words
platitude
vomit
But supposing you want to have sex with me
You have my number

Enough Beischer and Mackay for now. It's time to change my luck. Will it be The Cars' 'Let's Go' or Heart's 'Magic Man'? They'd have to be the two best choices on the tape.

If only Fleetwood Mac's 'Second Hand News' wasn't called 'Second Hand News'. It'd be just right otherwise, with that line that keeps coming up about doing my stuff in the tall grass. 'Magic Man' – that's the one to go with. It has the edge when it comes to passion, in a slinky sort of way, it's got that storyline about sheer irresistibility and, most subtle of all, it's a chick song. Like Dusty Springfield in AJ's car, I'm swerving the cliché of guy rock, I'm looking sensitive, and surely geniune desirability is only one small step away. It's decided. 'Magic Man' is to be my new (and first) fuck song, and that's all there is to it. It won't give me mongrel quality, but it's a start.

I can record tape-to-tape in the lounge room, so I find a blank ninety-minute cassette and set out to make forty-five minutes of fuck song. This is where I'll outdo Frank. I'll not only be ready when my chance comes, I won't have to try to cram it into three minutes.

I'll have a full three-quarters of an hour of hot, passionate Heart fuck song, and surely that's a timeframe that's considerate to all concerned. I can see it like a movie sequence, time slipping into something more comfortable, the song playing and playing, the physical attraction inevitable, all-powerful. Fans circling above, curtains billowing, majestic halls. Probably not doves – that'd be overkill.

Actually, it'd be the Bonnie Tyler 'Total Eclipse of the Heart' film clip. I'm going to have to be careful about that.

I'm taping the song for the fourth time when my father comes in.

'Oh, Philby, you're in here. I thought something must have become stuck.'

'I thought you were working.'

'Well, yes, but I'm not deaf. I thought there was a problem.'

'I'm just doing a tape.'

'Really?'

'It's a film soundtrack thing. An experiment. For a film idea I had.'

'Oh. And you have that song going over and over?'

'Yes.'

'What's it about?'

'It's just a song. It's got the right sound.'

'No, what's the film about?'

'What's the film about?' He's expecting an answer. He's expecting it to be about something. Doves, fans, curtains, irresistible physical impulses involving me and a person yet to be located? What am I supposed to say? 'Well, the music's a big part of it. The film's more a montage. There's not really much narrative, so it's hard to put into words what it's about. It's a montage of images, with the meaning inferred by their, um, artful juxtaposition.'

'Quite passionate, though,' he says, ignoring my ugly over-faking and noticing more Heart than I'd like him to. 'You know, in that lock-up-your-daughters kind of way. He sounds like he's that kind of fellow.'

'What?'

'The magic man. "Sorry, mother, but he's got magic in his hands and that's all there is to it. I was powerless to resist," and so on. Listen.' He stops us talking, for the length of an entire chorus and some of a verse. Yep, there's passion. Just like there was supposed to be. 'When I was your age there was a particular Glenn Miller number that I . . . um . . . doesn't matter. It's to do with girls. It would have been handy to be able to make a tape like that though. The song only went for about three minutes. Anyway, now I know what you're doing I'll leave you to it.'

He goes back to his study, whistling 'In the Mood'. There are some things about your parents that you don't need to know. Did he take his shoes off before starting his Glenn Miller record, I wonder? No, I don't wonder. I don't wonder at all. Did he take his tie off?

What I decide to wonder about, once I shake that thought, is the prospect of meeting a girl on the *Paradise*. And I don't mean a dull regular girl pretending to be Spanish. I mean one who might be worthy of my now very extended mix of Heart's 'Magic Man'.

I can see her when it plays for the first time – her acknowledgment of the good taste it shows, and perhaps a hint of arousal. It's an unseasonably warm afternoon for May – but they happen, it's not impossible – and she takes the initiative. She's amazed I'm single, pleased but not completely surprised that of all the women on the *Paradise* I ended up with her. She calls me 'irresistible' when the song plays a second time, and she laughs at herself for saying it. For saying something so corny, and/or so self-evident. When it plays a third time, she kicks her shoes onto the floor and makes her move. During the first chorus of the fourth she stands, takes my hand and says, 'Maybe we'd be more comfortable in another room'. By about the twelfth time through it turns out that, as well as being irresistible, I'm the best she's ever had.

Okay, there are a few outstanding technical issues to deal with before that's reality. I could start by getting some new sheets, and taking down the 'Catweazle' poster and a couple of the planes.

What am I thinking? This room is comprehensively bad, and I've never made a move to change that. It's like I've decided that, however many poker holes the Messerschmitts near the ceiling have suffered, the Battle of the

Bedroom is already lost. Life will be conducted outside these walls, this place is beyond saving. And the bullfighter poster featuring the matador in his 'suit of lights', with my name the middle one of the three below and the only one that's faded? Should I keep that, to help us recall the few early tender moments we shared cruising under Victoria Bridge on the memorable night of Viva España?

What would my mother think if I put 'new sheets, non-steam engine, etc.' top of my next birthday-present list? She'd know, wouldn't she? I need to pick a girl who has already moved out of home, then find some way of making it seem normal when I pull the tape out of my pocket at her place.

Pick a girl. I've been hanging around Frank too long – Frank, who doesn't see that I live in a world that exists in a crack somewhere between his chick auditions and the lazy twenty bucks in Nev's back pocket. A contemplative, bull-working world with a 1:72 scale war on the ceiling and a 1:1 scale real-life diorama of nothing in most of the rest of the room.

How can I go to America when I can't even change my sheets?

I told Sophie about the UCLA offer, and she said, 'So that's where you're going, then?'

I wanted to stop her right there and go, 'Soph, in life, nothing's that straightforward.' I did tell her the positions were for people with an interest in emergency medicine, and I wasn't sure that was me.

It didn't stop her.

'But the medicine's not really what it's about,' she said. 'You want to go, don't you? It's LA. You want to go to America. I know New York might be your first choice, but LA's even better from the movie point of view, isn't it? Even if that's not what you'd be doing in work time. That's the reason you're going, isn't it? And you wouldn't be working all the time.'

'But . . . but emergency medicine in LA,' I wanted to say to her. 'Don't you watch TV? It won't be like the Mater. It won't even be like the Royal.'

But I didn't say that. I agreed with her, because there seemed to be no alternative. But I told her there were a few things to straighten out first. It wasn't just a matter of sending a cheque to the Regents of the University of California and turning up at the airport at the end of November. There was the visa application, the price of the ticket, a lot of things I didn't have time to think about right now. I didn't mention that the ticket would probably be seen as an educational expense, and that parental support was therefore likely to be substantial.

The whole US thing was easier earlier in the year, when it was just talk. I assumed they'd reject me, or not reply. And five times out of six I was right, but the scariest one of all said they'd take me for a thirty-five US-dollar processing fee.

I want to go, don't I? I want to go to America. Why can't I even think that in a confident voice?

8

Some Wednesdays we finish early, but this Wednesday is Frank's first twenty-four-hour shift in Labour Ward, so he stays on at the Mater when I go home and try to convince myself to study. By four-thirty, I'm reading the newspaper on the back patio.

My mother is working in the garden, being maddened by her roses in the way that some people are maddened by their misbehaving hair. Her roses make their own decisions, and wind and grow whichever way they like. My grandmother, who still lives in England, once said she would quite like to come to Australia, but she didn't want to leave her roses. And my mother called it 'not much of a reason', but she's been working on her rose bed ever since. Today she's weeding with her tape recorder beside her, and singing one song from *Pirates of Penzance* over and over. I'm glad I made my 'Magic Man' tape before this afternoon.

She stands up, still singing, and looks over the work she's done.

'Better,' she says. 'Better.' She hits her gloves together to loosen any dirt, and takes them off. 'Enough,' she tells the tape recorder, and stops the music. She walks over to the patio and sits down facing me, folding her gloves over the arm of her chair. 'I so prefer Chekhov. Chekhov never needed songs. But sometimes you've got to play to the popular tastes. You never lose money on G&S.'

'I've never quite understood that.'

'You and me both, Philby. It's a funny old world. A funny old world that loves a good tune. Look at all that Andrew Lloyd Webber nonsense. Give me Pinter any day, or Beckett or Tennessee Williams or David Williamson. The big moments in life don't come with a soundtrack, or people bursting forth into song. They creep up behind you and then, whack. That's what theatre should be.'

'The bit that goes whack?'

'Well, yes. It should draw you in and then surprise you, show you something you haven't seen before. Don't you think? Film too. I know why you want to do it, you know. It's just a question of getting the chance to, isn't it? And not being distracted from things like obstetrics in the meantime.'

'Yes. Are you suggesting that chapter eighteen, 'Bleeding in Early Pregnancy', is waiting for me on the coffee table in the lounge room and wondering what I'm doing out here?'

'Well, it's hardly my place to do that, is it?'

When we're back inside, she starts to chop vegetables for dinner and I make another move on chapter eighteen, this time in front of the TV news and then 'Perfect Match'.

I do like it when she fights G&S every step of the way but takes it on despite that and bides her time, waiting for Beckett or Chekhov. She earns her Chekhov by doing that, by staying part of the team when they're putting on things she doesn't particularly like. But the mood at home varies distinctly. The roses got no attention at all during rehearsals for *The Cherry Orchard*.

About two minutes after I've succumbed fully to my motivational lapse, put the book down and decided it's late enough in the day for me to devote my undivided attention to a 'M*A*S*H' repeat, my father arrives home and says,

'It's good to see you lounging around doing nothing for a change.'

'He's been working,' my mother calls out from the kitchen, always in favour of credit being given where it's due, and sometimes even where it isn't. 'He's been reading something about bleeding.'

'Let's not get into that. Dinner's not far off.' My father's not good with bleeding. 'I meant that it's good to see you having a bit of a break. You've been at World of Chickens quite a few evenings recently.'

'Yes, but it's not intellectually taxing work. And I'm saving up for that video camera, remember.'

'Don't worry, I remember.' He sits down and looks under the papers for the TV remote. 'There's no hurry, is there? They'll still be around after the mid-year break. This is a repeat, isn't it? Isn't this the one where Hawkeye and Hotlips get trapped behind enemy lines?'

My father is philosophically opposed to repeats, which is why I have the remote tucked down the side of my seat. He has some issue with them, and the closest he can get to articulating it is, 'Well, they've shown them already.'

'Dinner soon, I suppose,' he says, giving up the search. 'How's obstetrics treating you then?'

'Like everything else. I've got Labour Ward this Friday, and that's a twenty-four hour shift starting at 8 a.m. Frank's on tonight, so we've swapped at the World and we're doing it tomorrow. And I've got a different job on Saturday night. Just a one-off thing, bar-tending on the *Paradise*. You know the *Paradise*? The barge with the palm trees that goes up and down the river at night with a lot of loud music and drinking?'

'Not really my bag.'

'Come and get it,' my mother calls out, using a rough-hewn western accent I haven't heard since *Oklahoma!*.

'Musicals,' my father says, but only to me. 'She's got that musicals bit of her brain going again. Suppose we should humour her.'

'Mighty fine chow, Miss Phoebe,' he says as he ambles into the kitchen, a round-shouldered green-cardiganed cowpoke after a tough day on the range doing balance sheets for cardboard box sales.

From there it gets worse, both the accent and the corn level, which is definitely elephant-eye height at the very least. My mother plays accents for maximum comedy, my father tags along. My mother steals scenes with accents, my father abducts accents and then roughs them up in a nearby alley. The one thing in his favour is that he has the decency to confine it to home. He's completely aware of his own shortcomings – those relating to theatre, anyway – but his amazement at my mother's modest gift for performance seems only to grow with time.

Once we're at the table, the two of them get over it and start talking like displaced British people again. But displaced British people who, in the distant past, invented the ritual that says dinner is the TV-off time when we each have to report on our days. It's rare that anyone has anything worthy of reporting but it's still what we do, usually for two courses. Tonight: beef stroganoff followed by Sara Lee Chocolate Bavarian. My father's summary: 'a veritable feast'.

'Did you see they're going ahead with that honorary doctorate for Joh?' my mother says to me during course two. 'There are posters up about it on campus.'

'Joh? As in, Joh Bjelke-Petersen, the premier? Renowned hater of universities and all connected with them?'

'Yes, that's the one. Doctor Joh. Doctor Sir Ruddy Joh.'

'But that's ridiculous.'

'Of course it's ridiculous. It's worse than ridiculous.

I'm going to end up with a doctorate from the same institution. Apparently it's a tradition, for the seventy-fifth anniversary. The premier of the day got an honorary doctorate at the twenty-fifth and fiftieth anniversaries, too. That's where it comes from.'

'But that's no argument at all. Tradition's no reason to keep doing anything. If it was, we'd all wear neck-to-knee bathers and you wouldn't vote.'

'I couldn't agree more. So you're going to be protesting then? That's what the posters are about. They're planning a big rally on campus to coincide with the degree ceremony on Friday week. It's in the afternoon, starting at two.'

'That could be a bit early for me.' Me? Protest? Well, in principle, sure . . . 'I think I've got a clinic on at the Mater, and they usually go until about four-thirty.'

'That's all right. The protest starts at two, but the ceremony isn't till six. Plenty of time.'

'I'll check my timetable.'

Somehow I've railroaded myself into political activism. But, thinking about it, perhaps it's where I should be. It's a senseless tradition for a start. Maybe there were particular reasons to do it the other two times, but to hand an honorary doctorate to an anti-intellectual whose entire cabinet boasts one Ag Science degree doesn't seem right.

My father starts clearing the plates.

'Ah, a family dinner,' my mother says as the uneaten third of the Chocolate Bavarian is carried away. 'We haven't had enough of those lately, what with you doing all that work and now me starting rehearsals.'

'You only had your first rehearsal last night, didn't you? You don't need to get weird about family dinners just yet.' Particularly when, most evenings, they're just an obligation standing between me and television.

'Philby, you have family dinners to make sure things don't get weird. That's why you have them.'

My father stops on his way back into the room, unsure of what he's missed and where it's now going. 'I wouldn't mind a Blackberry Nip. Anybody?'

'I'd love one,' I tell him. 'Blackberry Nip's always been good for stopping things getting weird.'

Our pay cheques are waiting for us the next night at World of Chickens. I'm closing in on the video camera.

Frank's bored. I walk inside from the street to change and he's there by himself, staring into the distance. 'Mate,' he says, 'what is it that's so close to perfect about college girls in their underwear having a pillow fight? Is it simply the combination of underwear and squealing?'

'If it was just underwear and squealing, you could put pants on a pig.'

As the door swings shut behind me, I can sense I'm leaving the room while there's serious thought going on, and I'm quite glad I'm not there to catch the detail.

Frank and I don't think about films the same way, but I guess that's no surprise. He once said *National Lampoon's Animal House* was the kind of film that he knew was destined to be a permanent fixture in his all-time top ten. He told me that sometimes you just know that kind of thing. *Citizen Kane* was his reference point. He said that there are plenty of people a generation older than us who have had it at the top of their top tens for decades, so long that it's now not negotiable. It will always be their favourite film, the best film they've ever seen.

I didn't know where to begin in countering that. I put it to him that it might be more a matter of content than film making, as far as he was concerned, and that *Citizen Kane* wasn't set up to deliver his kind of content. We had to reach a compromise. I had to concede that *Animal House* was at least the finest example of its genre yet made — better even than *Porky's* — and Frank, in return, said he was prepared to go as far as admitting that his favourite of the cinematic techniques used in the film was the combination of college girls, underwear and violence featuring bedding. 'That pretty much always works for me in a movie,' he said, 'but it reached a new zenith in *Animal House*, and I doubt it'll be surpassed in my lifetime. Five stars.'

I put it to him that there was a little more to it than that, that the full combination is college girls, underwear, vigorous squealy pillow work and a student desperado up a ladder at the window. And he said, 'Oh, sure, there's always a desperado. Where would the frat-house comedy be without the desperado? That's where you get the dramatic tension. It's the perennial question of how much gear'll come off before they notice him or the ladder topples backwards.'

Sophie's putting in some Frank-free time out the back. She's got a large Diet Coke in one hand and she's leaning on the railing, looking intently up at the windows of the blocks of units on Swann Road.

'Much happening up there?' Through the beak I can take the view in only a piece at a time. With my head tilted I must look like a chicken yawning at the hillside, or bracing myself to crow at it and wake the suburb up.

'Yeah,' she says, without looking round. 'But all the usual things. People in kitchens making dinner, TVs on. Nothing really dramatic, not that I can see. But you don't know, do you? You don't know what it means from this distance. Some of those dinners might be people's first together, or their last, and from here it all just looks really . . .'

'Mundane? It's like that photo – that series of photos – put together by Robert Doisneau to represent . . .' starting to feel like a wanker, pushing on regardless . . . 'a building in Paris in 1963. With the guy on the top floor having a smoke next to a girlie poster and someone on another floor trying to touch her toes and the old guy downstairs having a blast on his tuba.'

'Except, when it's black-and-white photos from Paris, it's like there's more . . .'

'Dignity?'

'Maybe, but do you always finish people's . . .'

'Sentences? No, not usually. I don't know what's got into me. It's being the chicken. It makes me kind of pushy. I'll have to watch that.'

'I might have just been going to say "smoking".' Now she's looking right into the beak slot, as if my interruptions should be firmly put in their place. 'There's more *smoking* in Paris.'

'And maybe there is, but that's not what you were going to say, so don't suddenly make out that I was being pretentious. You were going to say "style", maybe even "art". In Paris there's more art to it, living some cheap shitty life in a flat.'

'More berets. I bet there's more berets. I don't know about art, though. I'm not sure how that'd work.'

'Well, Sartre would have been in one of those places in Paris in 1963. In some cheap shitty flat writing something.'

'That's one guy. I bet there were plenty more guys with dirty posters on their walls, and hundreds of people happy just to touch their toes, and not many of him at all. Most evenings in Paris I'm sure people just eat dinner and watch TV. You can't go out every night. Even Sartre. Don't tell me Sartre never had TV.'

'Don't spoil Sartre for me.'

'I can't spoil Sartre for you. I'm only guessing, so I can't spoil anything. It's not like I even really know who he is. I know the name, obviously, but I don't think I've read anything he's written and I wouldn't have seen more than a couple of his movies. I'm doing media studies, remember, not . . .' She laughs, as if she's got nowhere to go . . . 'Sartre studies.'

'And I'm doing obstetrics at the moment, so as if I can . . .'

'And, by the way, you're a chicken.'

'So it's not like I'm an expert. I'm sure he had a TV. How could you not have a TV? How could you make any relevant comment about contemporary society if you didn't have a TV?'

'Exactly. So maybe there are people up there on Swann Road living the Sartre life and not even knowing it.'

'Anguish and sitcoms and supreme pizza.'

'Family size with free garlic bread and a bottle of Coke.'

'That Sartre knew how to impress chicks.'

'Hey, I've had far worse than a pizza deal. What's your worst? What's the biggest disaster you've ever had when you've gone out with someone?'

'Disaster? I've had some that have been bad, but I've tried to avoid disaster.' Disaster. Should I tell her that usually they just peter out into awkward silences and after that my calls don't get returned? Or, even more often, don't get made? 'We should probably do the changeover. You know Frank can be trouble if he's left unattended.'

'Nice change of topic. You must have had a few bad nights out.'

'Hey, I haven't had a bad night out for months. Many months.'

'A year?' She's smiling, figuring she's got me on the run and that a disaster story might be about to be prised out of me. 'How about a year?'

'Let's not get bogged down in details.' She has no idea of the key to my recent perfect record, and that's how it's going to stay. 'Let's just say there have been no complaints for some time about what I've got to offer.'

'Ha. You're hiding something. But you'll keep. For now I'll settle for a poem, an Elizabethan poem. You were doing some of that stuff out at the lights. I could tell.'

'Okay. The one I did at the lights?' That'd be Martha and the Muffins' 'Echo Beach', as far as I can recall. 'Okay. John Donne's Meditation Seventeen.' I strike the pose, and deliver:

'No man is an island, entire of itself; every man is a piece of the Continent, a part of the main. If a clod be washed away by the sea, Europe is the less, as well as if a promontory were, as well as if a manor of thy friends or of thine own were. Any man's death diminishes me, because I am involved in Mankind; And therefore never send to know for whom the bell tolls; It tolls for thee.'

I do it once in a version that sounds as olde English as I can make it and then, while I'm taking the costume off, I find myself trying it as Brando, then as a race call.

'Was that a poem?' she says when I come out.

'You're tough. I'm not even sure it's Elizabethan, but it seemed like a good idea at the time. Would you settle for Jacobean? There's something very wise about it, though, don't you think?'

'What if you don't live in Europe?'

'Good point. You should talk to him about that.'

I hand her the costume, and she goes in to change.

'Hey,' she says, 'I was talking to Frank earlier and . . .' There's a clunk as the beak hits the inside of the door. Her voice becomes muffled as she pulls the chicken head on. '. . . and he said he thought we should all go to the Underground after work tonight. He said you guys are going.'

'I don't know where he got that idea from. I've got a twenty-four hour shift in Labour Ward starting at eight in the morning. Plus, we wouldn't get there before ten. We'd have to pay the cover charge. There's no way I'll be going to the Underground.'

On the way to the Underground, Frank turns the radio up and sings loud sinusy words that are all his own, and that he thinks might be comical. Sophie's lucky that she gets to go there in her own car.

'I just did a shift in Labour Ward,' he said back at the World. 'That's no excuse for anything. You should be out all night deliberately, to get your body clock ready for tomorrow. I'm doing this as a favour to you, you know.'

So, I'm in his car with his burger box on my knees. He had all the answers. Today's takings could go under Sophie's seat, because we take practically nothing anyway. He's right. Most day's takings could go in a standard business envelope if you left enough coins for the next day's change. And he said it didn't matter if his burgers got cold – they're always cold by the time he gets home. And it doesn't matter that the cover charge kicks in at ten. He'll do the talking and get us in for nothing, then I can buy the first round of drinks to pay him back. That's the deal.

It was easier just to go with it. Besides, why not?

I can feel the warmth from the burgers on my thighs. I only hope the grease isn't getting through as well. Frank's mood is the best it's been all week. He's told me he reckons people have a problem if they can't turn boredom into something a lot more optimistic. Personally, I've always found 'morose' and 'introspective' far easier than 'optimistic', but they're hardly attractive. Frank does morose too, but he plummets there rather than wallows, so that means he bounces back faster.

Frank, Sophie, me and the Underground – there's nothing bad about it (with the possible exception of Frank), so I should go with some of that optimism.

When we're stopped at a red light, he pulls a handful of fries out of the box and eats them loudly, with his mouth open. For the first time I notice exactly how much he's taken tonight.

'Do you really need six burgers and two big buckets of slaw?'

'Have you seen what we're getting paid?' All said through a wad of chomped potato. 'I'm assuming this is part of the package. And I don't think you can complain. You seem to be spending a lot of time out the back. It's like you're being paid to go out with the boss's daughter.'

'We were only talking. I think we've established that.'

'Isn't that what it's like when you go out with someone? Only talk? Wouldn't that be one of your better attempts? Or has something changed?'

'Hey, I'm a contender. I'm going to the Underground, aren't I?'

'Sure. But I don't want to see you wasting all your time sitting there talking to Sophie. Particularly if you aren't getting paid to. Spread your charm around a bit. Get up and get a few moves happening. Imagine how they'll be when they find out you're a talker as well, not just a dance machine.'

'I'm not fucking remedial, you know.'

'Sure. I'm just saying, give it a shot.'

'I've done okay in the Underground before.'

'Sure,' he says, far from sure. 'Sure you have. You could have some of those fries if you wanted.'

'Thanks.'

'You're a contender.'

'Yep.'

I eat a couple of fries and look out at the dark hills slipping by us, wooden houses mostly with their lights out, closed shops, the Night Owl convenience store (open for business twenty-four hours). Sophie sticks close behind us all the way to the Underground and we park in the street, not far from the entrance. It isn't looking like a busy night.

'Just go with me on this one,' Frank says as we walk up to the head of the short queue. 'Look happy and go with me.'

There's dance music coming out of the doorway, and the smell of cigarette smoke and spilt drinks, like always. People pushing in and out, showing the stamps on their wrists, a clump of girls who are too young and overdressed and waiting to try their luck. The last word I hear Frank say is 'Mate' as he approaches the guy on the door, using his best one-bouncer-to-another voice.

Sophie looks at me, as if I'd know what's going on.

'There's a plan,' I tell her. 'Apparently. I think we just have to hang back and look interested but not too needy.'

'At least we don't look like we're going to the school formal. Do you think they'll let me in without babies' breath in my hair?'

Frank's pointing back to the two of us and the door guy's looking. I nod and smile, but in a way that's appropriately measured. He's smiling too, more than I am, and he waves us to come in.

He takes hold of my arm on the way past and he says,

'Congratulations, you two,' like someone in on a new secret. 'You have a good night.'

I thank him, and I tell him I'm sure we will. We go through the open door and we don't stop until we're several steps into the darkness of the corridor beyond.

'Told you,' Frank says to me. 'Looks like you're buying.'

'Sure. What were we being congratulated for?'

'Getting in for free, I suppose. There's a knack to it, and I have to say the two of you carried it off pretty nicely. Now, drinks. I could go a couple of rum and Cokes.'

'A couple?'

'I've got two hands. Might as well give 'em both something to do. Soph, Philby's buying. It's a rare thing. What are you up for?'

'Oh, maybe just a lemonade. I've got to drive to Carindale later.'

'Oh, come on, one drink. Hit his wallet a bit harder than that.'

'Okay, let's have some vodka in it then,' she says, as though it's a wild act for a Thursday.

She tells us she has to go to the Ladies. Frank says we'll meet her inside, in the side bar since it's smaller and we'll be easier to find.

The corridor is lined with people, heads together in what might be conversation. The music's louder when we turn the corner, and the dance-floor lights make it down this far too, patches of light moving across drinks and hands and faces, the occasional chambray-shirted rugby legend, blonde private-school girls who managed to sneak by the bouncer and are standing against the wall, wide-eyed and in taffeta and wondering what happens next.

I got talking to a girl like that once at Cafe Neon and, when her friends started referring to me as 'the doctor', I knew I'd erred. It turned out that she was sixteen, though she looked far older (now, there's an observation that never stacks up in court).

Frank cruises down the corridor with the pure confidence that owns nights like this, and this whole world. But I own it now almost as much as him. It's not a bad feeling. We're not the desperate kids at the door who won't get in without a lot of luck.

'So what did you tell the door guy?' I shout out to him as I'm pushing up to the side bar with a twenty dollar note in my hand.

'That you two had just got engaged. And I said you met here, round about last September when you were down on your luck.'

I shout the drink order across the bar and Frank leans in closer to tell me more.

'I said you'd got engaged tonight, and that I thought it'd be good if you could stop in here for a drink on the way home.'

'And he believed that?'

The guy at the bar checks that I want two of each and I give him an exaggerated nod to make it clear.

'Sure. Why not?' Frank shouts, practically in my ear. 'It's a level of bullshit above the usual, and that's all it takes. Have you heard what people say to that guy to scam their way in? Mostly it's just pissed chicks, crying and going "but my friend's already inside" or "but the other guy said". It's not hard to pitch it a level above that. You just need enough story.'

'That's surprisingly complicated.'

'Hey, I'm full of surprises. It's just that some of them are less obvious surprises than others.'

I pass him his two rum and Cokes, then take the other

two drinks and my change. He leads the way to a table in the far corner.

Engaged. I make him agree not to tell that to Sophie when she turns up. I don't think I've got too close to getting engaged to anyone I've met at the Underground (not that that's ever been the aim). Usually you just end up in a corner of the dance floor at the edge of a big clump of people you already at least half know, squeezing out some pretty average moves to Duran Duran, wishing you had better clothes and limbs. Or maybe that's just me.

I managed to pash a foreign girl in an alcove once, but she wasn't behaving like a person with a lot of judgement. She was spilling drinks all over herself and, when she started dropping the glasses too, the bouncers pulled her out and put her in a cab. I tried to talk them out of it, of course.

'Mate,' one of them said to me. 'Once they start smashing glass there are issues of public safety.'

Which made a lot of sense, since he was built like a bouncer and I'm built like me.

We only come here because there's nowhere else to go. The music's the same every week, but there's a certain comfort in that. And Frank tends to try a lot harder than I do, but he usually strikes out as well. So I don't mind this place.

Frank waves when Sophie walks in, but she doesn't see us straight away. She pushes past the bar crowd, checking out the tables, then she notices his flailing arms and waves back. I push her drink across to her on a coaster when she sits down.

Frank tells us he's up for a dance, but Sophie shakes her head and says she hasn't even tasted her drink yet. He finishes his first rum and Coke, puts a couple of ice cubes in his mouth and shimmies off among the tables.

'I think,' Sophie says to me, 'that you were about to tell me the story of your worst night out before work rudely interrupted.'

'And I think we remember the conversation a little differently.'

'This is going to be good.' She's treating me the way you treat a person who's hiding something, someone who's clutching onto a story they want to have weedled out of them, but don't want to give up too easily.

'No, it's not. It's not going to be anything, because there's nothing much to say. All it could be now is anti-climactic.'

'Go on, give it a shot.'

'Really, there's . . .'

'Okay, we'll do a trade. You go first, then I go. And, trust me, mine's pretty bad.' She curls up her hand and looks through it at my face, winding the other hand in circles beside the first in a mime of an old-time movie camera. 'You're the movie man. We'll do it like a movie if that's easier. Using that technique when they cut from the main story just to a head talking to the camera.'

'That's a pretty sophisticated technique, even though it looks easy.'

'I know. Pretend I'm Woody Allen,' she says, still winding away.

Pretend she's Woody Allen. Winding, winding with the hand. Four girls I've gone out with since I started uni, maybe five, and not one of them's mentioned Woody Allen. Stop, I want to tell her. I want to pull her camera hands apart and say, 'Does Clinton appreciate this? This Woody Allen stuff? I hope so.'

'Go for most excruciating,' she says. 'If there were no actual disasters, I'd settle for most excruciating. The time when you most knew it was going wrong.'

And then I can't say No any more. It's not much of a story, but I have to tell it, and it's excruciating enough.

She puts her camera hands down when I get started. She drinks her vodka and lemonade, she listens and she laughs when I know she will, she blows on the palm of her hand when it's appropriate and she calls me an idiot when I explain the physics. Then, as promised, she pays me back with her scene, staring down at the table in front of me while she tells it.

```
INT.    NIGHTCLUB.    SOME TIME AFTER TEN
PHIL sits in almost complete darkness, cradling
a vodka and lemonade in his hand, as though he
needs the support. He is about to divulge the
story of his most excruciating night out with a
girl. And he's about to divulge it to a girl, of
all people. This is best done if he imagines it
as an aside in a Woody Allen film. In his mind,
he even changes font.


     PHIL
Okay, there was this time when I was out with a
girl. We went to a movie and then we had coffee
afterwards. Things hadn't been going brilliant-
ly with the conversation, and maybe I was
starting to sense that. She said something about
'life's mysteries' and then she said, 'like the
way, when you blow air onto your hand, it's
colder than you'd expect'. Well, anyway, I know
now that I should be much more tolerant of
life's mysteries, if I'm in the company of some-
one who finds such a thing mysterious. (He
pauses, but is urged to continue.) Okay, but
```

this is just an example of where I won't be
going next time that kind of thing comes up.
I can't really explain it. It was a kind of rush
of physics to the head . . . you know the way
people talk about a rush of blood? Well, this
was a rush of physics. And as it happens it's
Bernoulli's principle that explains why the air
is cold when you blow it on your hand. Not so
mysterious. As this girl now knows. (Another
pause, as if he's waiting for the signal that
his turn is done.) You want me to? Really?
Really? She made me do it, too. (He shrugs, as
though the detail of physics is usually the
beginning of the end for him.) Okay, well, the
theory is that the total energy of the air is
constant, but that the energy can be manifested
as temperature, pressure and velocity.
Therefore, if you increase the pressure and
velocity, you necessarily decrease temperature.
And the girl said something like, 'Right. Well,
it's not one of life's mysteries at all then.
Bad example.' And that was pretty much it. As
you'd expect. I'm not always good with silences,
and we'd had a few leading up to that point. We
had more after, though. But I'd stopped trying
to make the running by then. Some of those
silences, they just went on and on.

INT.   NIGHTCLUB.   SOME TIME A LITTLE MORE
AFTER TEN
SOPHIE sits in almost complete darkness,
fiddling with the straw in her vodka and lemonade. She was the one who came up with the idea

of doing a piece to camera, but of course
that's not what she'll do. No, she'll look at
the table instead. Phil looked at the camera,
or at least at Sophie, so is it fair that she
does things differently? Probably not, but
that's the world he lives in, and he knows it.
He suspects she knows it, too.

SOPHIE
My worst night out was the night with the *Star
Trek* drinking game. It was a Tuesday, the student discount night, at a Mexican restaurant
down the road from the World. The guy turned up
with a cask of red wine, a couple of bottles of
lemonade, and a bag of chopped oranges. And
mint - there was a bunch of mint, too. That was
all for sangria. Which, I guess, was okay. But
he also had an old airline carry bag and
between the nachos and whatever we had next, he
pulled out all these pages of computer printout. He said we'd play this game where, just
for fun, you know, we'd have to drink any time
we said something from *Star Trek*. These were
the complete scripts, as it turned out. And he
knew them well, really well. So no way was he
going to be caught out. Me, on the other hand -
it turns out I speak more *Star Trek* on a regular
basis than Captain bloody Kirk. Any time I
spoke this guy would flip through pages and
show me something like it. If it was even just
a couple of words, I still had to drink sometimes. I started feeling kind of hazy, and I
said maybe we could stop. So he said I was no

> fun. Which, since I hadn't gone out with anyone
> for a while . . . it had already occurred to
> me that I might not be. And I didn't want to be
> no fun. Once that sort of thing starts being
> said about you, it gets around. Even later,
> when I was throwing up out the window of his
> car, I wondered if maybe this was just the
> going-out world and I'd have to get used to it.
> But I checked with a few friends later and they
> said I was in the clear. No normal definition
> of fun actually requires the *Star Trek* drink-
> ing game. I haven't felt the same about sangria
> since. Or airline carry bags. If a guy turned
> up with one of them, I'd be out of there. I
> wouldn't wait for the trekkie stuff. He'd
> seemed normal in lectures. He probably had all
> the models hanging from his ceiling at home.

She raises her eyebrows, like someone who came out of it wiser for the experience, and she lifts her drink up to her mouth.

'Boldly going where only World War Two fighter planes had gone before,' I say in my best voiceover voice, though it's probably not a clever move.

Frank is still dancing. We can see him through a glass panel beside the bar, and it's hard not to watch. Like a plastic bag in an updraft, Frank's dancing is unpredictable but hypnotic. I explain to Sophie that his sinuses can affect how he hears things, so he tries not to dwell too much on issues like rhythm. But it frees him up to make other choices. That's how he sees it. Plus, he's very supple, and he uses that to advantage. Frank says no-one should be afraid of their limitations. It's what you do with what you've got that counts.

I should stop now. Always leave them wanting more, my mother once said (often says), and it applies to social situations, as well as going out with someone, and public speaking. I should stop dumping on Frank to look smart. But only because it doesn't make me look smart.

'There was one time tonight,' Sophie says, 'when you were out at the road and there was a fly in the serving area. It was buzzing his head, so he stood there with his mouth open. For about fifteen minutes. He wondered why it was totally prepared to keep landing on the edge of his mouth, but it never went right in. One of life's mysteries, maybe. They're everywhere, and who can tell when it's a genuine mystery or just stupid?'

'This might sound harsh, but over time I've found that Frank's mysteries tend to be easier to classify than most. They're usually things like, "Why did Musical Youth never pass the dutchie to the right-hand side?"' No, stop, no more gratuitous dumping on Frank. 'The big issue for me is failing to work out when it'd be stupid to step in and dispel the mystery. But that's my parents' fault. They used to be proud of me for knowing dumb things from physics. They'd tell people. Any time I start going out with someone and take them home, my mother practically puts on a show. She is so goddamn embarrassing. She's got this thing on the wall that I wrote when I was about six. It's framed. It's a medical report and it says "Phoebe Harris's report: pulse good, knees good, blood warm." Things like that.'

'That is so sweet.'

'It's goddamn embarrassing. And where does *sweet* get you? On the desirability scale, sweet people are even below nice people. And, you know, it meant that there I was, at the age of six, set up to be the family's first doctor. And, having got so excited about it fifteen years ago, I'm pretty much over it now.'

What am I doing? Do I leave anyone wanting more? No boring people. In the world of my mother's good advice, it's the worst thing you can do.

But that's as far as it goes. I don't tell her about all the other notes I wrote to my mother. For the first couple of years after I learned how to write, notes were big for us and they covered everything – demands for particular toys, suggestions about food, questions about her day, comments when things didn't go my way. For example, the note I stuck in her bag that said, 'I hate you more than a rat. My life is terrible.' I'd never even seen a rat, of course, but it was the principle that counted.

'Don't be so hard on sweet,' Sophie says, while I'm still fighting off the temptation to go the rat story. 'It must be working for you at the moment.'

'Really? Oh, Phoebe, yeah.'

'So don't go and be "Phil, he's trouble". Clinton can be trouble, and sometimes trouble can border on too much trouble.'

'But you still go out with him, which proves my point.'

'And Phoebe still goes out with you, so there you go. Okay, question. Do you and Phoebe have names for each other? Like, funny little names.'

'Clinton has a funny little name for you?'

'Maybe.' Said in a voice that means she's not supposed to tell me, but . . .

'And does he have funny little words for things?'

She gives an exaggerated sigh, as if I'm stumbling onto it all by myself. 'Maybe.'

'Oh no, you might have entered the shmoopy phase.'

'The *shmoopy* phase?'

'The phase when suddenly the names the rest of the world gives things aren't enough any more and the shmoopifier's using one crazy made-up word after another and you've got fifty special names you never knew about.'

'That's a phase?'

'Sure it is, Shmoopy. It's not a phase I do, but it's out there. Even Frank does it. He'll go a "cupcake" occasionally if he thinks it'll be the clincher. Me? I don't get it. It's, like, the last people to talk to me that way were my parents, when I was an infant in a high chair with a bowl full of mush in front of me and they were trying to convince me that there'd be an excellent picture of a train to take a look at if I ate it all up. Once people can feed themselves, I've pretty much got a no-shmoopy rule. There are some things you don't want to sexualise. But maybe I'm the one who's got it wrong. Do you think I should be doing that stuff? If I found myself at the beginning phase of something, some time in the future? Is it a problem if I don't do it at all?'

'A problem, Shmoopy? Are you kidding-widding wid me Shmoopy-woopy? Vomit, vomit. No . . . Not that that's Clinton. Well, not totally. I'm just with you on the no-shmoopy rule, you know?'

'Yack bloody yack bloody yack,' Frank says, his head suddenly inserted into the middle of the conversation. 'Don't you get enough of that out the back at work?'

He drinks his second rum and Coke in one go and tells us it's no longer optional. We have to dance now, or what's the point in being here?

The place is starting to fill up, I notice when we get into the corridor. Some more of the overdressed teenagers have made it inside, and now the kind rugby boys are buying them a lot of drinks. The music is suddenly louder when we're through the doorway, too loud to think about talking, then louder still when we tun the corner and head for the dance floor.

There's not much room up there now, but Frank makes space for himself anyway. His limbs demand it and he moves until he finds a girl to dance in front of.

So, Clinton's gone shmoopy. That can't be good. He's got a funny little name for her, and he's working on their own funny little language. She can't find that endearing, surely.

Sophie dances small, moving her arms from her elbows down and her feet hardly at all, staring into the distance as though she's somewhere else. I can relate to that.

There must be other girls like her. Single girls like her.

I could do better than the guy who went the *Star Trek* drinking game. I'm confident that the next time I'm eating Mexican with a girl I won't whip out the complete scripts and try to compromise her judgement using DIY sangria. My mother tells me I'm quite a catch. Compared to that guy, she's right.

'She's still with Clinton, you know,' Frank says in the car on the way back to my place. 'I asked her at work.'

'I know. There's never been any doubt about that. He gets talked about. It's fine.'

'Yeah, just . . . I know where you're heading, that's all. And don't head there.'

'I'm not heading there. I'm not heading anywhere. It doesn't hurt to put in some practice sometimes. The *Paradise* is only two days away, remember?'

'That's more like it,' he says. 'That's my boy.'

9

Nothing's close to happening when I arrive at Labour Ward at 8 a.m. so I go to Antenatal Clinic, as I'm supposed to. A few patients into the morning I'm not sure if I'm fooling myself, but I'm beginning to hear a sound that might be a foetal heart and starting to be able to tell heads from backs and knees and elbows.

The only difference between what Sophie had to say about Sartre and what I had to say was not that she thinks she's seen two of his movies. It's that I'm a better fake. For example, Simone de Beauvoir and her American circumstance. I didn't even know she'd had one until the new Lloyd Cole and the Commotions song, and now I'd fake knowledge of her on the strength of that alone.

'Yes, but have you read her,' I could say, 'in her American circumstance?'

I shouldn't get attached to this. This Sophie talk. If it becomes a reason to look forward to work, I'm in trouble. But I usually have to go to Woody Allen films alone, and maybe we could go together some time. That's all I'm thinking. Sophie and me. And Clinton.

Or, alternatively, I could never bring it up. I do have some dignity, and I'm not going to blow it on an ill-conceived move on Sophie Todd. I have learned a thing or two these past few years.

Halfway through the clinic, my new-found examination

confidence is tested by a patient whose abdomen baffles me. It turns out she's having twins.

'That's why it feels like there are bits everywhere,' she says, laughing at the little sense I can make of it all. 'That's how it's supposed to be.'

How should I look at last night and our time at the Underground? I wrap the cuff around the patient's arm to take her blood pressure. I was probably supposed to do that before the rest of the examination. Between the systolic and diastolic, there's the thump of moving blood:

> It's a beat you're familiar with, a room you know well. You are at the scene of several of your previous triumphs, particularly the one with the foreign girl in the alcove. Tonight, you're swapping stories. You could turn on the charm now, and perhaps you should, just for the sport of it. But, no, that wouldn't be fair. Not to her, not to him. He's not even here, and it'd all be too easy. And you agreed with yourself to be a better man than that, some time ago.

Her blood pressure is fine, about the same as it was on her last visit.

Around lunchtime I have a false alarm in Labour Ward, an apparent labour that doesn't progress. By early evening I feel like I'm jinxing every uterus on the floor, switching off labours and only hanging round to get whipped at Scrabble by the charge sister. She sends me to dinner and, while I'm away, one labour in my bit of the ward takes them by surprise. A student midwife is delivering the baby when I walk back in.

I pick a new patient and sit with her until, around ten o'clock, she says, 'I'm starting to think it's a false alarm,' and the objective evidence agrees.

By midnight I'm discovering that the charge sister is very good at Scrabble. I haven't won once, but she's kept me playing somehow. I'm not sure if it's because of her convincing compliments when I score more than ten or her well-feigned surprise each time she scores more than twenty, or if I can't say no simply because she's in charge of the ward and I've never been good at challenging authority figures.

'So, who have we had the last few nights?' she says, as if conversation needs to be made to keep us both going. 'We had Vince last night, and he seemed very keen. We had Frank the night before – the one with the interest in older women. That was entertaining. And we had Therese on Tuesday night. She got a couple of deliveries and then assisted on a caesar at about three in the morning. A busy night for her. So, you'd all know each other pretty well by now?'

'Yeah. Some better than others. I know Frank best, probably. We were out at the Underground last night, actually. After work. We've got part-time jobs at the same place.'

'At a chicken place, isn't it?'

'Yeah. So what happened that was entertaining? What did he tell you about him and older women?'

'Nothing, really,' she says, as I'm wondering if this might be a mistake. 'He was a funny guy, and maybe it was one of the things he talked about. What's there to know about him and older women?'

'With Frank it's hard to tell sometimes. He keeps a lot in.'

He keeps a lot in . . . He keeps nothing in, but the charge sister's in her early thirties, certainly not unattractive and Frank's an acknowledged sucker for a uniform. I have no idea what he's been trying up here, and it's definitely best to keep it that way.

She dumps XYLONITE on a triple-word score, and the game is over.

'Not your night,' she says, 'from the look of it. We can call you if anything's likely to happen. It's just another word for celluloid, by the way. In case you were wondering.'

'Thanks. I'm sure that'll be useful.'

I never was a Scrabble player, never will be. If I ever had the letters for xylonite on my letter rack, I'd never notice they spell xylonite.

I retire to one of the on-call rooms. The whole corridor is silent. So much for the cheap formula fantasy that says it should be one big romp up here. Or maybe that's an idea Frank's put in my head — an idea that makes far more than it should of brown rooms that smell inoffensively sterile and have harshly starched sheets on the beds. Friction from these sheets could cause abrasions and, everywhere you turn, you have either Jesus looking down at you from the cross in one of his more foresaken moments or Mary looking up from prayer. You don't rest easy here.

We ran through a list of favourites at the Underground last night. Sophie had read an article in a magazine that said you could tell a lot about people based on their favourites in particular categories. She couldn't remember what the categories were, so we made them up.

She suggested book first, for which she said I'd pick *Bright Lights, Big City* and she'd pick a good thesaurus any day. Not a bad start. We made it through the first few unscathed, then I said band and she said, 'Huey Lewis and the News'. I said drink, she said, 'Cooler'. And she thought they were two great answers. She had me even more concerned when I went for ideal job and she said, 'Copperart. Sales assistant, Copperart. I mean, the combination of copper and art — how could you not want it?'

Then she said that was irony and I said, 'Like coolers?' and she said, 'What's ironic about coolers?'

She made up for it with favourite superhero power. Mine was invisibility – useful, but very run-of-the-mill. Hers was the ability to detach both arms before going to bed. She couldn't name a single superhero with that power, but she said she was sure there must be one. At least one. How many superheroes do you see going to bed anyway?

'Think about it. You've got to admit they get in the way,' she said. 'You've got to admit arms are a big mistake when it comes to sleeping.'

So I agreed. 'Very much a daytime body part, the arms,' I said. 'You've got me with that one.'

I've got to watch this. If I apply the Frank Green Spoiler Checklist:

Sensitive childhood stories: tick

Funny voices: tick

Poetry: big fat tick

How's Clinton looking?

She made me do the poetry. And the Underground was simply a chance to talk without the pressure to jump into or out of a chicken suit, a chance to have a conversation that could run for an hour or so instead of being segmented across an evening. We are friends. So just friends that we talk about Clinton pretty regularly, and Phoebe sometimes too. Phoebe exists specifically so that we can talk, so that there are no doubts. No, Phoebe exists because of a bumbling accident on my part. It's fine to convince myself I'm not out to white-ant Clinton, but there's no rationalising Phoebe the imaginary girlfriend.

And the worst-date stories? It's taken me twenty-four hours to work it out. Mine was worst because I was such a Bernoulli dweeb. Hers was worst because the guy was psycho.

I was the only one of us who ever caused a worst date. What makes me think I could white-ant Clinton if I tried?

I've learned something, though. Sophie's Sartre comment, her liking for coolers, probably also her liking for Huey Lewis and the News – those are things that could put me off a person (meaning, girl). With Sophie they don't. There's too much to like. On the *Paradise* tomorrow, I'm going to remember that. If the prospect of any interest arises, I won't be put off in the usual way. I won't be there with my usual mental checklist and my impulse to judge early comments harshly.

The more I think about it, the more I realise how indefensible my position is. I've been looking for a girl who knows exactly the right amount about exactly the right topics. I've been looking for someone very like me but, if I found them, I wouldn't even know it because they'd be faking something smarter and putting me off. And probably judging me harshly because of one accidental slip: Psychedelic Furs' 'Love My Way'? No, that'd be the second-best song of 1983, not the best song. What kind of completely perfect girl do I think I deserve, with this fascinating repertoire of sensitive childhood stories, funny voices and poetry?

Part of John Donne's 'Meditation Seventeen' is on my wall at home, a very brief quote out of context on an old environmental poster: 'No man is an island, entire of itself; every man is a piece of the continent, a part of the main. If a clod be washed away by the sea, Europe is the less, as well as if a promontory were . . .'

Next to that I have a certificate saying that for five dollars I became the guardian of an endangered Little Bent Wing Bat at the Mount Etna Caves. Maybe I was more involved in my mother's causes then. Not that it was five dollars of my own money. We didn't even go halves on that one. I kept pressuring my parents to let me visit my bat, since I felt responsible for its upbringing, but they said that wasn't how it worked.

Sensitive childhood story: tick. Rehearsed and ready to go. Realistically, it's probably not more than two shifts away from coming up in conversation at the World.

Tomorrow, on board the *Paradise*, I break this cycle.

I'm at the front door in my waiterly black-and-white when Frank's Valiant pulls up outside.

'Are you ready for this?' he says when I get in.

'Ready as I'll ever be.'

'Are you carrying?'

'Always.'

We drive off, men in uniform on a mission. Am I carrying? It sounds like he's talking about a concealable weapon, but he means condoms. And I always say Yes because that way we avoid the talk about how this might be the night when my luck changes. 'People have got lots of names for these babies,' Frank said once in a profound moment, showing me the condom in his wallet, 'but I call them hope.'

Tonight he spares me the profundity, and moves straight to, 'How was Labour Ward?'

'Uneventful. The gravid uterus takes no encouragement from my presence. I close cervixes. I don't think obstetrics is my future. It and pro Scrabble probably got struck off my list of possible careers last night. Particularly the Scrabble. I thought I knew a lot of words, you know? But that charge sister . . .'

'Yeah, she's good.'

'Hey, she said something about you and older women.'

'What do you mean? You're talking about the one who's thirty-ish, bottle-blonde?'

'Yeah.'

'Wants me, obviously, and she's sounding you out.'

'It's not that you were sounding her out?'

'Not intentionally. But am I supposed to stop it when it happens?' He shrugs, as though it's a gift he can't control. 'Don't forget it's you we're chick-spotting for tonight. Remember the plan – cash for both of us, a chick for Philby?'

'There'll be none of that on the *Paradise*. None of that Philby talk. And we've got to be subtle. Remember that booking agent and the row you got into with him about using DJing as a way of meeting girls at parties?'

'I was pretty much over it, anyway. The main issue when that went wrong was to make sure it didn't stop AJ getting work. Remember, I only ever got into it through him, and I used his records and he took them when he moved out, so I couldn't have kept it up. No more "Tainted Love", no more Plastique Bertrand, no more Bronski Beat, no more Wham, no more Frankie Goes to Hollywood. Where's the act? I would've had to recapitalise if I'd wanted to strike out on my own. But I was over it. Vanessa reckoned she could have helped me rig a few lights but, mate, if I hear that fucking "Nutbush City Limits" one more time . . .'

'Come on, it's one of the classic school-dance songs.'

'You private school boys and your school dances . . .'

School dances were all we had. A sanctioned opportunity to meet girls and be continually monitored in their company by teachers and parents with strong torches. I'm sure some of the girls' schools were only ever one wrong turn at a P&C meeting away from bringing in pheromone-sniffing dogs and putting up guard towers.

How could it ever prepare us for Queensland Uni, where the socialists ran the student union, the Hare Krishnas chanted for peace, there were always battles to be won and rights under threat and every cartoon in the campus newspaper was about the fascist state government or marijuana, or both? Even the ones in which every human character was a circumcised penis (now, there was a cartoonist with no secrets).

Imagine trying to raise a rights argument at school. The right not to be tracked by searchlight when outside at school dances, for instance. Try it and you'd be told what you were always told – school dances were a privilege, not a right. And the next one would always be hanging on a thread, waiting for 'one person to spoil it for everyone'. That was something that happened often at school. I think we lost the privilege of inviting St Margaret's girls for a while, because one person had spoiled it for everyone by getting the DJ to play the Dead Kennedys' 'Too Drunk to Fuck' when parents were turning up to take their daughters home.

It was referred to at the following school assembly as 'that song' and, no, it wasn't anything to laugh about. We were told that, too.

Frank is humming as we drive through town, and it's only when he starts thumping the wheel and nodding his head in time that I work out it's 'Eye of the Tiger'. Like a punch-drunk prize fighter, he can't help psyching himself up.

'Remember, it's me who's scoring tonight,' I tell him. 'So you can put that fuck song of yours away.'

'Yeah, righto. Don't be afraid to borrow it if you need it.'

'Thanks. I think I'll be okay.'

Okay? I've got forty-five minutes of Heart's 'Magic Man' waiting at home, but that's best kept to myself for now. Its day will come, and maybe it'll come sooner after tonight. Here, in a better world, is how it might be:

It's night again. You're over this scene already, but Frank keeps it coming. A man has needs, he tells you. He rolls his finger round in the powder, but that's not the need he means. There'll be girls, he says. Girls whacked on green drinks, and Spanish, for one night only. But you've had enough of that talk. For once, you would like not to see dawn or you would like to see it from your own bed and by accident, the noise of a garbage truck stealing just a minute of your long deep sleep. But in this town, the girls are relentless. It's as if they don't sleep at all. It's as if every last one of them knows about your 'Magic Man' tape and is lining up for her turn. Don't worry, you tell Frank, whose lean streak has strung along a while. Tonight, luck will change. Tonight, my friend, the music might be playing for you.

'They're going to want you tonight,' Frank says. 'That's what I'm thinking. You? You should be bracing yourself.'

'I'm braced. They're going to want me.'

When we park, I step out of the car with a demeanour that's as braced as I get. A kind of seafaring, drink-mixing, girl-talking demeanour that holds together until the food and beverage manager says, 'I'm assuming you've both got a lot of experience with cocktails.'

'Sure,' Frank tells him. 'Lennon's Hibiscus Room, but we're free agents now.' This is the kind of lie that I think is called a bald-faced lie. It's utterly confident, and it couldn't be less true. Unless he's leading a double life, neither of us has ever been to Lennon's Hibiscus Room. 'Plus, we put in a few nights at the Underground with the easy stuff, of course. So, have you got anything special on for tonight? Anything Spanish we should know?'

'Well, there's margaritas, so that'll be no problem for you.

There's sangria, obviously, but we won't be needing you guys to mix that. That can be done behind the scenes and we'll put it out there in some big punch bowls.' The food and beverage manager has droopy eyelids to match his droopy roll-your-own cigarette, a long-ago-broken nose and a quiet sense that he's done this a million times and he's not to be messed with. 'There's another cocktail we got from somewhere, mojitos they're called. They're Spanish or Cuban, one of those.'

'Don't know it.' Frank again, coming straight out and saying it.

'Yeah, it's not one of your big ones. The recipe's behind the bar. It's mint and Bacardi and lime. Just make sure you use the lime cordial for most of it, and only juice the actual lime as a finishing touch. Other than those two, it's in your hands.'

'No worries,' Frank says, not even trying to disguise the smugness on his face as we walk on board, leaving the food and beverage manager to put the cocktail question to the next new black-and-white arrival. 'Well, I reckon we're set.'

'What were you doing with that Lennon's Hibiscus Room remark?'

'I had to say something. It was the best I could think of. Can I help it if we aren't part of the cocktail crowd? Dad took Mum there for their twenty-fifth anniversary in seventy-eight and she had a fluffy duck.'

'That's what you were relying on?'

'It's a cocktail. Apparently lots of people were having them. It's that kind of joint. They've got a piano up there, you know. But don't worry about it. We're in. We look the part.'

'Look the part? We aren't the part. We couldn't be less the part . . .'

'How hard can it be? After the first few they won't care how they're put together, anyway.'

'After the first few I might actually be able to do them.

It's the first few I'm worried about. This is just like when you lied to get us those ice-cream stall jobs and I had no idea which way to coil a soft-serve.'

'And it worked out fine. It's like uni. It's like suturing, or delivering a baby. See one, do one, teach one. And hold the lid on good and tight.'

'I'm assuming the last part's cocktail-specific. You know, I thought we'd just be picking up glasses, or something. Something I can do. Me buying a round of drinks at the Underground the other night doesn't exactly qualify us to make cocktails.'

'Do you talk about every dollar that gets out of your wallet?'

We meet the rest of the bar team, and only one person's made mojitos before, so he shows all of us how to do it. It's not hard then to ask if the *Paradise* has a particular way it likes its margaritas made, as though the two of us have made them everywhere and all that island-to-island variation in the Caribbean, for example, means it's always better to check which way a venue prefers. This time, since I'm the detail man and we've had a chance to think it through, it's me who does the asking and Frank stands back with his 'that's my boy' look on his face.

'Why is it only me,' he says afterwards, 'who has every confidence in you?'

'Because it's better that way. Because, if I had your level of confidence, I'd take it just that one step too far and I'd say something like, Ah, Aruba style, and we'd be gone.'

As if to show how right I am, that's when Frank pulls the big bag of powder out of his pocket and says, 'I've got a couple of these. It's time.'

'What do you mean?'

'Brizgarita time.'

'You idiot. Can't you show any judgement at all? What are our priorities here tonight? One: money. Two: get me a girl. Where is three: launch brizgarita on unsuspecting public?'

'You should have brought a change of underpants. As if you're ready for a girl to come your way. We should get a bag for you to breathe into, I reckon. You're looking dizzy.'

'If they catch you, you're on your own.'

So, we started with a plan and before we leave North Quay we already have discord. I decide, if pushed by anyone who matters, to describe Frank as 'a guy who got here at the same time as me'. I don't care if it's only a kilo of Staminade that Frank's carrying. I can do without looking like an idiot. The DJ tests the sound system using 'Nutbush City Limits', and I'm glad. Frank'll hate that.

Tina Turner's voice screeches across the empty deck and the beats ricochet heavily around. It's going to be a dark cruise out here tonight, with everything painted black and illumination limited to the swirls of soft pink and blue light swinging across the scuffed dancefloor from two mountings high on the walls. Other than that and the strings of coloured fairy lights draped among the web of streamers, there's only the fluoro spilling from beer fridges, and signs marking the toilets and emergency exits. Those Spanish, I figure, must like their anonymity. How could you have any idea who you're bumping into on the dance floor?

The first people on board, naturally, rush the bar. They've worked out that that might let them drink forty-two cocktails tonight instead of only forty-one. My early margaritas are crap, but I work out it's easy to compensate by offering an extra shot of tequila. There's plenty of repeat business, and no complaints.

'Nutbush City Limits' starts up properly, the serious noise begins and the *Paradise* shrugs away from the wharf.

They keep us busy, demanding cocktails by the handful and slopping them across the deck. I can't believe I was worried that even one of these people might be picky. They're not here for drink-mixing precision. Those kinds of people have probably all gone to Lennon's Hibiscus Room to drink fluffy ducks with tiny paper parasols in them, while they listen to some guy croon 'Strangers in the Night'. The *Paradise* crowd is jumping up and down to the B-52s' 'Rock Lobster' and getting whatever they can for their twenty-five dollars all-inclusive. They're here for the drinks, the dance floor, the dark, an incidental river, and all we have to do is keep it coming.

I can hear Frank next to me talking to his latest (female) customer and telling her, in a sly way, 'It's more Bolivian than Spanish, if you get what I mean.'

But he's almost got to shout for her to hear him over the music and that does the slyness no good. She's looking intrigued – intrigued or confused. He says something about adding 'a bit of crystal' to the mixture and she asks if it'd be safe to have two.

'Get back to me on that one, babe,' he says, even louder than before. 'Have one, get out there, have a bit of a jiggle and work up a bit of a sweat and see how you go, hey?'

She dances off into the crowd with her glass. He's telling girls to sweat and they seem to be going along with it. He catches me watching. I try to look bored.

I start mixing the drinks in beer jugs, lining up half-a-dozen glasses along the bar and pouring them in a row. 'Nice touch,' the food and beverage manager says, taking it for theatre. 'Just don't pour it directly into their mouths. They'll ask you for it, but they can pass bugs around that way and that only causes trouble.'

Carnage takes hold in forty-five minutes. In the distance, against the railing, I can just make out the outlines of people who may be engaged in acts that involve passing bugs around. Paper streamers are pulverised, paper plates are pulverised. This is last year's Med Ball revisited. That was the night we learned that if you blend a wide range of expensive and pulverised things together and spill a lot of alcohol, you can't tell it from any other kind of mud. But it is great for bedpan races. Most of us went home looking like we'd rolled with pigs. Maybe we had.

I go to the storeroom to get more tequila and I ask the food and beverage manager if it's always like this. 'Like what?' he says, and he sucks on his cigarette, bored with it all.

It's my turn for a break. I pour myself an orange juice and then, maybe because I'm in the habit of adding it to everything tonight, I toss in some vodka. I decide to get away from the crowd – if that's possible – maybe get to the railing somewhere right down the back and work out where we are. We headed upstream and we haven't turned yet, but I'm not sure how far we go.

I skirt the dance floor. Fail to skirt the dance floor. A yellow glow-in-the-dark feather boa loops around my neck and almost takes my head off, and I'm dancing. A girl puts her hand on my shoulder and shouts into my ear something like, 'Your cocktails are fantastic'. I'm pulled by the neck into the middle of a hens' night crowd, and it's the bride-to-be who has pulled me there. She's wearing a condom pendant and waving a large glow-in-the-dark drink-bottle penis, into which someone has poured a lot of cocktail. She's gripping her boa with both hands and working it round my neck like a fanbelt. The penis, in her right hand, keeps thrusting forward, spurting cocktail. I know I'll dream about this. Her friends are around us, clapping. They pick up the pace, she picks up the pace. I'm trying to break free before she breaks skin, but I think my struggle might look like dancing, almost like real non-white-man dancing. It hurts, but I'm good.

That's when Frank turns up and I shout, 'Thank god, the cavalry.'

No-one hears. Frank pushes in, they push him away. He pushes forward again, they move to repel boarders. No-one's getting aboard this hens' night, with the exception of the hens and their close-enough-to-virginal human sacrifice. Frank reappears, dancing in an overtly suggestive way, with his shirt knotted around his waist and a pineapple held on his head. It's confusing as hell, but I give him a thumbs up for this valiant attempt to distract them. They move in closer to me, dancing right up against me. Frank's gone again. The pineapple bobs around the circle like a trophy, like the head of an enemy taken in battle. One of them holds a brizgarita up to my mouth and it pours down my chin. The song ends.

I duck, push under the bride's flailing penis, and I'm out of there, catching a spurt of cocktail in the hair as I go.

That's enough time off for me, and I escape to the safety of the bar. Frank's there already, tucking his shirt back in.

I'm about to thank him when he says, 'I hope you feel cheap, flirty boy.'

'What?'

'You could have shared them around.'

'What?'

'Not cute. Don't play cute with me. You were an animal out there.'

'No, I . . .'

It's no good. There's too much noise to explain, so I just have to shrug my shoulders as if it happens all the time. Me? Animal? Sure. The lion auditioning the lionesses, that's what it was. So Frank has come at me with a mixture of admiration and jealousy, and I'm not used to either of those.

Nothing I'm used to was happening out there. My neck feels like it's copped a carpet burn but, for a moment, I stopped trying not to dance. I set down the white man's burden. And I became flirty boy. That's Flirty Boy. It's a superhero's sidekick's name – Love Master and Flirty Boy, by Mattel. Comes with cape, mask and special Flirt Power Boa™. Detachable arms sold separately for daytime use.

I mix drinks with new enthusiasm. I watch flashes of glow-in-the-dark yellow over on the dance floor – the boa, the penis – and this could be looking pretty positive. I can pour, perhaps I can dance. These people don't know me at all, and I've started well. My cocktails are fantastic, and it wasn't even the bride who said that. It might have been someone single.

Even Frank's treating me differently now. We're working like a team at the bar, both pouring drinks by the row. He's the only one spooning powder out of his pocket for girls but, other than that, we're a team.

Victoria Bridge passes overhead. We've turned somewhere upstream and come back. We're halfway through the cruise.

A woman leans over the bar, shouting. I hold up a drink, but she shakes her head. She says something about med students, and a friend who's sick. It's help she wants. I signal for her to come around to my side, and she follows me down the corridor to the storeroom.

'What are you after?' the guy there says.

'Someone's sick. I'm a fifth-year med student. It's too loud to talk out there.'

'No worries.'

It turns out I've been followed by two women and, in the storeroom lights, they both look drunk but not sick. We shut the door and the volume drops.

'You're the one we danced with,' the one who spoke at

the bar says. 'Our friend's throwing up over the side. The bride, Belle. Someone said you guys are med students, and that maybe it was something you'd cooked up in biochem.'

'What was something we cooked up in biochem?'

'The um . . .' she looks at her friend.

'Brizgarita.'

'Oh, okay. I wouldn't worry. We always had to cheat at biochem. The stuff in the brizgarita's more an upper in the post-sport sense. Nothing too dangerous.'

'But you guys are med students?' the first girl says.

'Yeah.' And it seems as though that's newsworthy in itself so I add, as if I'm channelling Frank's wanker side, 'But biochem was years ago. We're practically finished now. I've just come off a twenty-four hour shift in Labour Ward at the Mater.'

UCLA comes to mind, I fight it off. Get back, you big lying Love Master, get back. Leave this one to Flirty Boy.

'I'm Jacinta,' she says. 'In case you were wondering.'

'Phil. Hi.'

Played cool. Very cool. Her friend is more attractive, so I don't get her name and she doesn't talk. That's a tribal law we established back in the school-dance days, and we all know it. At least, it's always looked like some kind of law as far as I've been concerned – the really attractive girls stand back and have a less attractive emissary do the talking for them. Jacinta has dark curly hair and slightly buggy eyes, but in a way that's far from unattractive itself. Her mute friend is of the type often described, I think, as willowy. Tonight, though, the willow is swaying and has a few small greenish bubbles clustering at the corner of its mouth. She's looking risky, and maybe conversation isn't an option.

They take me to their friend, the bride, who is clinging onto the railing at one of the less noisy parts of the boat.

She's still clutching a plastic cup in one hand, and I take a look at it to see what she's been drinking.

'I didn't know there was punch.'

'Um, no, there's no punch,' Jacinta says. 'There's sangria, but Belle's been drinking brizgaritas.' She takes a close look at the contents of the cup. 'That's just, well, backwash. She's a bit of a mess. Stuff goes down, stuff comes up, you know. And she's never been good with seafood.'

'I don't feel good,' Belle says, sounding angry and sad and sick and showing me her cup of prawn swill. 'And I've totally lost the penis.'

'Belle,' Jacinta says firmly, 'don't worry about the penis. We've got a doctor here instead, and that's what you need right now.' Belle looks no happier. Jacinta turns to me.

'I always wanted to be a substitute for a penis. Thank you.'

'I'm sure you can be a real penis if you try,' she says, and laughs. 'Or maybe that only happens when you graduate.'

We take Belle to the storeroom and clear the bottom shelf so that she can lie on it. We find a bucket she can throw up into, I pour her some water and I tell the others to keep her on her side while I go to check with the manager.

It turns out he's more than happy with how it's all being handled. In fact, he's impressed. He asks if they've got our contact details, and how we feel about weeknights.

By the time I get back, Frank's in the storeroom and turning on the charm, despite days of telling me he's not interested at the moment. Straight away, I feel like the substitute penis, and Frank's definitely behaving like the real thing.

He sees me and says, 'The man. I've just been telling these ladies about that time you saved that guy with the ruptured triple A.' What is it with this lying? I don't think I've ever even seen a man with an aortic aneurysm. Frank's turning on the charm on my behalf. Suddenly, the situation's slipping out of control, and I don't think I like it. 'Cool Hand Phil, they call him. He always downplays things. Don't be fooled by that. He's a man of action – a man of total action – when it counts.'

'Yep.' What can I say? I can't come up with a second syllable and that makes me completely Cool Hand Phil by default, just when I was starting to grow into Flirty Boy.

'Anyway, we should be getting back to business. You know where we are, girls, if you need us.' Frank leads me out the storeroom door, and it shuts behind us. He claps his arm around my shoulders. 'Man, you're looking good with that chick with the eyes. Hope you didn't mind the triple A story. I just figured a little help wouldn't go astray.'

'No, that was great. In fact, I think you've helped me so much – so much – that I should really try to take the next step alone. There comes a point when you've got to fly solo.'

He looks at me with something that might be a glint in his eye, but it's hopefully just a trick of the light. I'm willing him not to say he's proud of me, and somehow the message gets through.

'Hey, the brizgarita,' he says. 'It's working.'

'Working? What do you mean?'

'They love it. Like, *love* it. And people keep hitting on me for drugs, all the time now. All the time.'

'What? I can't believe it. Are you trying to screw up the plan? Objective number one: money. Objective number two: get me a girl. And somehow, just when that's starting to work nicely, you're like the big drug baron around here, and all you've got is a family-size jar of Staminade in your pants.'

'Yeah, well, you put Bolivia into my head and now I'm stuck with it. Do you reckon there's any way I could actually make money out of this?'

'Out of selling Staminade? Yeah. You could get a job in a supermarket. Don't even try it. If that goes up one nostril while we're still on this boat, you're a dead man. And I'm not going down with you.'

I'm annoyed with him again. Typical Frank. The moment he gets in anyone's good books, he rips out the pages.

I'm still annoyed when I claim a toilet break twenty minutes later. There are too many people talking about whatever it is Frank's got, and I'm sure the evening is now only going to end in trouble. I pour myself a stiff vodka and orange, and drink it on my way to the bow. The toilets at the stern are too close to the dance floor, and so busy it'll be a cesspool in there by now.

One of the lights is out near the bow, but it's not so dark that I can't find the door handle. I need some Frank-free time to think, so I go straight for a cubicle.

I've made the right choice of facility. It's clean and there's no-one around, and Patrick Hernandez's 'Born to be Alive' is a dull noise at a party somewhere far away. There's a blast of it when the door to the corridor opens, then the door closes again and there's only the sound of feet on the floor, the click click of heels.

The click click of heels?

A woman speaks. I'm in a cubicle in the forward female toilet.

Of course. There were no troughs, and it's way too clean. How did I not notice that?

They talk about guys, and not spewing. One of them goes into a cubicle but leaves the door open so they can keep talking. Has no-one told her sound travels over the top?

'Have you had one of those drinks with the marching powder?' one of them says. 'They've got a bit of zing to 'em.'

'Yeah, I had a couple, but they were a bit salty for me.'

'That's the *garita* part, apparently. It's garita if you add salt. Brizgarita, margarita.'

'Yeah, well, I reckon it tasted pretty much like tequila and Staminade.'

'And what would you know about how tequila and Staminade tasted?'

'Yeah, I s'pose.'

Someone else comes in and, for the next ten minutes, the traffic is heavy enough to trap me. Should I shout 'Maintenance' and make a run for it?

More feet. Never a crowd but a steady stream in and out. More conversations. Most of the men on board aren't being ranked too highly, including the men on the bar.

'That med student Frank's a bit of a wanker,' one voice says, and I think it might be Jacinta, the one with the eyes. I shouldn't keep thinking of her that way. 'But I don't mind his friend.'

Suddenly, pay dirt. Go, Flirty Boy, go.

'What, the one with the chin?' her friend says, and there's a pause. I think lipstick's being reapplied, something like that.

'Yeah, Phil.'

Go, Chin Man, go. What's that about? I check my chin right away, and it feels no different to usual.

'Oh, yeah,' the non-Jacinta one says. 'I wouldn't say No.'

I wondered if she was the willowy one. Now I know she isn't. That's not the way life goes. The willowy ones? No is their best word, if they bother to talk at all.

'Hey, I've met him,' Jacinta says. 'I'm halfway there.'

'Yeah? You reckon?'

'Yeah. Okay then.' She laughs. 'Five bucks says I pash him before you do.'

'All right. Five bucks? All right. I'm up for that.'

Okay, I felt weird about the chin remark, but now I know I can get past it. There's a price on my head tonight.

'Well,' the friend says. 'Let's hunt him down.'

The door swings open, and shuts. They're gone.

Women come, women go. 'Hunt him down.' I'm quarry. That's something that'd work so well for Frank's outlaw self. I feel more like a pheasant. I talk myself round. Flee, be hunted. Be caught, and give them the full five bucks worth. Use all your special powers, Flirty Boy.

A cubicle door swings shut. Otherwise it's silent in here. I make a run for it.

Back to the bar, I decide. Stay cool. Plus, I'm being paid to serve drinks. I have to remember that. Objective one.

After only a couple more jugs, I hear someone call out, 'There you are,' and it's Jacinta. 'The second I start looking for you, you're nowhere to be found.'

'Oh, I've been around.'

'Well, it must be time for a break.'

'Um. I just sort of had one, but maybe . . .'

'You should check on Belle. Come with me and we'll check on Belle. Come on.'

I turn to Frank and he shouts, 'Go. Just go. It's totally covered. Check on Belle.'

Jacinta takes my hand and pulls me along the corridor. 'Belle's fine,' she says. 'I just checked her.' She takes me past the storeroom and around the corner and she shepherds me back into a fire-hose recess.

'It's quieter here,' she says.

'Yeah.'

'Have you bumped into any of my friends lately?'

'Don't think so.'

'I was beginning to wonder if I'd ever find you.' She's smiling. I hope it's not just the five bucks she's smiling about. What the hell, I win either way. 'I kept bumping into your friend, though. In the end I had to give him my phone number to give to you, just to make it clear to him that I wasn't interested. In him. I hope that's okay. I hope you don't mind that I'm not interested in your friend.'

'No, he can be a bit of a wanker sometimes.'

'Well, I wouldn't know about that . . . You though, I'm sure that's a different story.' She reaches her hand up to my face, runs it along my chin. 'There's something decisive about you, and I don't mind that. Not one bit.'

I've never been on surer ground than this. She's even telling me to be decisive. I play it the way Frank might, without a single word. I make a move. I put my hands on her hips, I tilt my head a little and I make the move. My open mouth meets hers and I taste the zing of Staminade. Her hand moves around to the back of my head and she spreads her fingers in my hair. Her tongue writhes around in my mouth, and last September was a cruel long time ago.

I spin it out as much as I can and I give it everything, but finally our heads separate. She gives a lopsided smile, takes a breath, and moves in for more. The five dollars is indisputably hers, and there's no sign this is ending.

She runs her fingernails up and down my back outside my shirt, then inside my shirt. She pulls my shirt out at the front and starts swirling her hands around on my abdomen. She pulls herself closer to me and moves us deeper into the fire-hose recess. My back's against the wall and her pelvis is pushing against mine, pushing and pushing. I move my hands down low on her back, then lower, down to her buttocks and I'm pushing back against her.

She pulls her mouth away, then bites my neck all the way up to my ear. Her breathing's different now. Her mouth is cool when it meets mine again. She pulls herself up on the fire hose, higher than me, and I feel her thighs move around me. Oh god, it's been ages.

We're both breathing heavily and she moves one hand down my front, slides it down to my belt and over it, rubbing the front of my pants, rubbing and rubbing. I'm gasping for breath now, gasping for breath with my head back against the steel wall of the fire-hose recess. She's rubbing faster and faster, my hands are clenched round her thighs. Suddenly, I can't breathe any more. It's all . . .

In one breath out, I let it go.

One breath, and it turns into more of a moan but it's far too late to stop things now.

I grab the front of my pants and she staggers back, away from me. I plunge the other hand down inside to catch what I can and limit the damage. I move the first hand in there to join it, cupping the two of them there, as though it might be any use.

'Shit, sorry,' she says, and she tries not to laugh.

'Toilet paper,' I tell her. 'You have to get me toilet paper now. Lots of it.'

'Okay. Don't run away.'

'Just get me the toilet paper.'

She goes, leaving me to stay as still as I can and watch the lights of New Farm and contemplate the ruins of the evening. Here I am on the *Paradise*, hiding in a fire-hose recess, cupping my own semen in my hands, hoping there's not too much of it on my clothes and sending a girl off for toilet paper.

And that's when the food and beverage manager appears, with a torch.

The beam hits me in the eyes, and he says, 'Oh, g'day. We're not far out from docking, so I was just giving the place a once over. You on a break?'

'Yeah.'

'Listen, you've been a big help tonight, what with the sick chick and all. Thanks a lot, mate.'

'No problem.' He reaches out to shake my hand. I pretend I don't notice. 'I'd better be . . . better be . . .'

He wants me to notice, and he shines the torch lower. The light flares from my white sleeves and wrists. His hand casts a bunny-rabbit kind of shadow on the front of my pants. The huge bulging two-handed front of my pants.

'What the fuck . . . ?'

'No. No, it's not like it looks. It's . . . an accident. Medical . . .'

'Listen, mate, I know what I'm looking at, and it's not bloody medical and we don't do it on this ship.' There's a pause, a very ugly pause and it's not filled by any good excuse of mine. 'Here's what we're going to do,' he says, in a tone that includes no room at all for negotiation. 'You've been helpful tonight with the sick chick, you've been pretty good on the bar. This is the kind of bullshit that could get you into a lot of trouble. And I mean a lot of trouble.'

What do I say to him? I really, really hate trouble. I'm so not 'Phil, he's trouble'.

'So here's what we're going to do. You're going to get your pants into a fit state for bar work, you're going to get your arse back out there, and my guess is you're not going to expect to be paid at the end of the evening.'

'That's fine,' I tell him, in a whiny voice I could do without. 'More than fair. If that's as far as this goes I'd have to call that more than fair. If we could not tell Frank, though . . .'

'Frank? Who's Frank? Is he one of the other bar guys? They've all worked bloody hard tonight, and they're no trouble at all.'

'Yeah, sorry. He's just a guy who got here at the same

time as me, really.' Still whiny, dammit. 'Well, we might have done a couple of shifts together at Lennons, but . . .'

'Okay, got some,' Jacinta's voice calls out, as if she's gone to borrow sugar from a neighbour. She stops, caught by the torchlight, and she stands there, half a roll of toilet paper hanging from her hands and glowing in the beam. 'Hi.'

She laughs nervously, rolls the paper up as though she's tidying it. The food and beverage manager looks at her, looks at me, shakes his head.

'Shit, bloody fraternising as well. I thought you were just working off a bit of steam. Pal, you are trouble. Capital fucking T, right? I don't know what this is all about, and I don't want to. You're not coming back here, not even as a paying customer. Life ban, right? Life ban. There's a list at the gangplank, we've got your name, and it's on it for all time.'

'Sure.'

There's something sticky on the back of my knuckles, and that's the wrong side. Not that there's a right side, but . . .

'I don't want to see your face again tonight. Not for the rest of this trip. Not ever. Understood?'

'Understood.'

'Good,' he says. 'Good. Bloody students. You give 'em a bloody job . . .' And he strides off.

'Sorry,' Jacinta says. 'Bad timing?' She laughs. 'Sorry, I meant me coming round the corner, not the other . . . timing problem.'

She offers me the toilet paper, then realises the situation's complicated by my inability to move my hands. She turns her head away, and starts pushing the paper between my wrists and down into my pants. Suddenly the whole region that, minutes ago, was so good for rubbing has become distasteful. She laughs again.

'I just wasn't expecting the hand,' I tell her. 'At that point of . . .'

'I thought you'd like it.'

'Well, obviously I didn't hate it. It was just a surprise. Not a bad surprise, just a surprise.'

'For both of us.'

'Please.'

'Sorry, Speedy.'

I groan, she keeps laughing. She stands guard while I clean up, as best I can. My hands were quicker getting in there than I thought, but I still couldn't call it tidy. I rub and rub, but there's a limit to how much good it'll do.

The DJ's voice announces the last song. Survivor, 'Eye of the Tiger'.

I roll the toilet paper into a ball, and toss it out into the river.

'I'd better go and meet my friends,' she says.

'Yeah.'

'Sorry about the job.'

'It's not a big deal. And thanks for the help with the, um, paper.'

I give her a few seconds to get ahead of me, then I walk round to the bar.

Frank's waiting and, from his face alone, I know he wants a progress report, a hint of some success at the very least. He gives me a thumbs up and it's clear he's expecting confirmation.

'Like you wouldn't believe,' I tell him, and he claps his arm around my shoulders again.

'I knew it. I knew we'd turn you around.'

He's so pleased for me, he practically dances. Which jiggles me up and down, and I hate the way movement feels in my pants.

The *Paradise* docks, and Jacinta and her friends pass us on their way off. She gives a polite wave, and one of her friends goes '*Arriba arriba*'.

'Good on you,' Frank says, when they're too far away to hear. 'Bloody good on you, Speedy. Hey, I got her number for you, you know. Just in case you never had the chance.'

10

Flirty Boy: comes with patented push-button Quick Trigger Genitals and twelve pairs of highly absorbent Wonder Pants™. Where were my goddamn Wonder Pants last night?

Dawn comes to Sunnybank Hills, and I can't say I've slept well.

I can't wait to get back to World of Chickens. I've now got myself a much better horror date story than any slack reference to Bernoulli. Not that I was even going out with Jacinta last night, but the magnitude of the disaster makes that irrelevant. Cool Hand Phil, the man of total action. Definitely not, when the big questions came to be asked, a substitute penis. Definitely the real thing.

This can never be spoken of, I can never see her again. And Frank's going to try to make me, I just know it.

The day begins, and the dark shapes in the Greens' lounge room take on colours and clear outlines – the timber-finish TV near my head, the two-tone brown armchairs, the red of painted hunting jackets in the glass-fronted display cabinets. The Greens are collectors, with a particular emphasis on Franklin Mint plates. Dorothy probably started it and her collection goes way back, beginning with English hunting scenes. Vanessa specialises in the 'Woodland Creatures' series, AJ collected 'Legends' (featuring James Dean, Marilyn Monroe, Judy Garland and more) and Big Artie's 'Vintage Cars' plates are in the far corner.

The full tour of the room for the first-time visitor involves some explanation of each piece (purchase history at the very least). It's also important to have it pointed out to you that the three ducks flying up the wall are a set, not merely three ducks put together at random, and indeed they're one of those rare sets in which you find the first duck turning to look back at the other two. 'Now,' Dorothy told me once, tonguing a tissue and lifting a fleck of dust from the duck's head, 'you don't see that everyday'.

The large butterfly on the outside wall near the front door, however, is merely decoration, but it's easy for the non-expert to become confused. 'You can tell it's decoration and not a collectible,' Frank said, 'because it's pink like the house, with brown spots like the gutters. That's not like a real butterfly.'

'Thanks, Frank. So, it's the colour scheme that gives it away? As opposed to the one-metre wingspan, you mean?'

Frank's a collector too. I happen to know that he's got a few plates stashed away in his bedroom. But only as an investment, he tells me, and 'only if they feature Lady Di. No recent plate's appreciated in value like the Shy Di plate (1981). I can't believe I only picked up one of them. I'm a fool sometimes.'

Frank's room is on the other side of the wall from the sofa. I can hear him roll over in bed and he starts humming, a snuffly early-morning version of 'Eye of the Tiger'. At least in his dreams he's getting some action. And at least he'll be getting paid for his work last night.

Last night. Much as I'd like to focus on the Green family's plate-collecting habits, the twin peaks of last night's disaster keep coming back into view. First Jacinta going way beyond five dollars' worth, then the food and beverage manager, his torch and his interest in closing a successful evening with a handshake. Some nights could do with a lot more rewriting than others.

> Enough. That's what you've told them, but the music's back. A hum only, but an intrusive hum. And some of your thoughts return to the night before and the speed things sometimes move, mainly hands. Another strange bed, another improbable night now done. There was dancing, seduction, a kind of alcove. Then . . . the song sucks you into its whirlpool and parts of you – parts of you for which you'd had far higher hopes – are suddenly as hypnotisable as a snake in a basket. It's a simpler life for the woodland creatures. That's what you'd rather think about. Badgers and foxes, rabbits and dormice. A simpler life, and guaranteed only forty-five firing days.

Next, I'm woken by sawing from a dream made up of bits of a clumsy weekend last year, but featuring the food and beverage manager from the *Paradise* more than I'd like. Except in the dream he's a weasel, I'm a vole and the whole thing's like A.A. Milne gone to porn. There's a handsaw working beneath me, under the house. There's a yelp in a voice that sounds like Vanessa's, then Vanessa telling herself to be more careful, followed by sawing again.

I get myself a glass of water from the kitchen and, once I'm convinced after a quick inspection in real daylight that there are no external signs of the catastrophe, I go outside and down the back steps.

Vanessa looks up from marking a piece of wood and says, 'Hi.'

'Hi. What are you doing?'

'Bird house. Hope I didn't wake you.'

'I wasn't really asleep.'

'We've got this rule. I can't saw before seven. Well, I can't make things before seven, but this'd be the first time there's been sawing involved so I'm only assuming it's the same rule. And I make it seven-oh-five, pretty much on the dot.'

'I'm sure you're right.'

'How do you think it's going?'

'It looks good. Not that I'm an expert on bird houses, but it looks good to me.'

'Hey, you're a chicken sometimes.'

'So, I guess I'm qualified after all. I'm sure, at my more chickeny times, I'd be happy to call it home.'

'Good. Good to hear. And it's still only pieces. Wait till it's all put together and painted. Hey, what colours do you reckon I should do it? We've got house leftovers around, but do you think I should get something different?'

'Well, if you did the bird house with the same colour scheme, it'd be like a kind of model of the house. That could be nice.'

'Yeah. Yeah, like, deliberate? That'd look good out the front, wouldn't it? Like, a feature.'

'A feature, good thinking.'

'See, that's the kind of thing I've learned from work, florist work. Features. If you're putting a bunch together for someone, you've got your leaves, you've got your babies' breath, you've got your regulars and you've got your features. Like, you know, bird of paradise.'

'So how's work going?'

'That, my friend,' she says, measuring another line on the timber, 'is the sixty-four-thousand-dollar question.' She looks up, pushes some hair away from her face and tucks her pencil behind her ear. 'I've learned a thing or two, there's no denying that, but do you ever get those times where the things you learn are the things that let you know you maybe want to be doing something else?'

'Sure. Obstetrics might just be shaping up that way. But I'll be on to something else in a couple of months.'

She puts the wood down and opens a couple of fold-out chairs. 'Smoko,' she says, and points me to mine. She sits, pulls the pencil from her hair and taps it on the plastic arm of the chair. 'Right. The flower caper? I'm not sure it's for me. I can't say that to . . .' she points up to the floor-boards and the world upstairs . . . 'but I can say it to you. You want to get into the film game, and maybe I've got a few wild ideas myself. Right?'

'Right.'

'Good.' She picks up a glass of Diet Coke from the floor and takes a drink. There's noise upstairs now, footsteps in the kitchen, a jug boiling. She looks down at her rainbow-coloured handpainted sandshoes. 'I've got a plan. I want to finish this bird house for a start, and maybe do more in that line. So do you really think it's going okay?'

'Let me take a proper look.' I pick up the pieces she's cut, and she leans over to fit them together so that I can see how they're supposed to be. 'I can confidently say that this is a better job than I could ever do. You've got these edges joining perfectly. I could never do that at school.'

'Really?'

'Really. I'm not bullshitting you. For a lot of us, this kind of thing isn't as easy as you might think. You, I think, might just be one of those people who can do it. A lot of us are pretty bad with our hands. So, interestingly, some of us'll get to do surgery instead. I couldn't make a bird house, but I'll be operating on human skin some time in the next year or so. Figure that out.'

'Okay, next question. This is medical. If you wanted to bulk up a bit, add some muscle, what would you do? What would you take?'

'Well, some people go for Sustagen, and stuff, but it doesn't always have the desired effect. Some people are good at adding muscle bulk and some aren't. But I don't think I really need a lot more muscle bulk for what I do.'

'So, Sustagen, good. And upper body work – what would you do there?'

'For what exactly?' She sounds like someone who knows far too much about my bedroom. But no way am I going to be the first to say the word bullworker.

'Just work for your upper body, you know? I've got some weights down here. They're AJ's, but he left them 'cause there's a gym near where he lives now.'

'Well, coincidentally, I happened to have a tutorial or two in the uni gym on upper-body weights. Back when we were studying anatomy.'

Back when we were studying anatomy and about to start taking off our outer layers for surface anatomy tutes. I had weeks of slinking off to the gym in its quieter hours, working away at creating at least some muscle definition.

She takes me over to AJ's weights bench and I pick up two of the smaller dumb-bells and show her some of what I learned. She draws stick figures of the exercises on a spare piece of wood and makes me check that they're correct.

'And what about balance?' she says. 'Dad's got this thing with his ears, or something, that affects his balance. Like, whenever he looks up, he gets really dizzy.'

'I don't think you have to worry about that. You want to do things to avoid it, is that what you mean?'

'Yeah.'

'I don't think it works like that with balance. You

should be okay. But this is pretty impressive, trying to do all these healthy things now.'

'Well, Dad can't climb because of his balance problem, so it really gets in the way. And Nev's not much of a climber either. He's a demon on the ground, but he's a dud up a tree. So, you get to thinking about these things. Your back and your balance, Dad reckons you don't miss them till they're gone.'

'I think you'll be okay. But it's good to look after yourself.'

'Hey,' Frank's voice says from the doorway. 'If it isn't the last of the red-hot lovers. You should have seen him, Nessie.'

'Seen what? He didn't tell me about any lover stuff.'

'Cool Hand Phil, they call him,' Frank says, his words getting a kind of swagger to them. 'Who would've thought? The guy waits months for some action, and then he scores and he hardly says a thing about it in the car on the way home. If I'd been waiting so long I'd be busting.'

'Some of us,' I lie, 'have more restraint.'

'Restraint.' He laughs. 'And don't the ladies fancy that? He was firing last night. They were calling him Speedy, those girls.'

'Really?' Ness says. 'Like Gonzalez, you mean? Cool.'

'Last night,' Frank goes on, like a man about to flourish the final card in a trick, 'he was such a bad boy they figured they couldn't even pay him.'

Ness looks at me with bug-eyed admiration. I could do without anything bug-eyed too close by at the moment. She has no real idea what we're talking about but, then, neither does Frank. And from my point of view it's just another conversation I'm going to have to live through, and then it'll be done. I preferred it down here when it was me, Ness, her obscure health concerns and the beginnings of a bird house.

'What a night,' Frank's saying. 'What a night. I got the cash, Philby got the chicks. Who would have guessed? And they were mad about the powder, weren't they? Mad about the brizgarita. We've got ourselves a hit.'

'I think we were lucky to get away with that.'

'Yeah, it was probably your smokescreen that helped. Hey, remember how you said that thing about it going up people's noses?'

'You didn't . . .'

'No, no. Well, only mine, but you put the idea in my head. I only did it to see what it was like. To see if it did something I could sell. Shit it stung, and then it started to fizz and I was down the back of the boat and these chicks turned up and it was coming out my nose. This green foam, like I was possessed. So I shouted out, Ah fuck, my septum's going, and they ran away.'

He laughs, and I wish I'd been there. I could have done with something like that in my night. Vanessa's laughing too, looking at Frank and imagining him foaming.

'Your septum's the bit in the middle of your nose,' he says to her, 'and some drugs wreck it.'

'Oh, right,' she says, and thinks about it. 'What are they doing up your nose? Why don't they come in tablets?'

'Good question. It didn't do a lot for me with the Staminade. I was sneezing crystal for the rest of the night while Phil was off . . .' He pauses and looks at me, searching for the right word . . . 'gallivanting around'. It's a dad word if ever there was one, a dad word used to rebuke rebellion with pride.

'I'm sure you taught me everything I know.'

'Yeah. I expect I did. But don't use it all at once. Remember, use your powers wisely. There were times early on when you were dancing that I thought it might get the better of you.'

'Good advice, Love Master. Hey, how would you describe my chin?'

'Your chin?' I show it to him side on, and he gives it some thought. 'Decisive. What do you reckon, Ness? Decisive?'

'Yep.'

'You know,' he says, nodding his head as if the change might have come from my much-needed gallivanting, 'I'm not certain I noticed that before.'

Of course, the morning ended the way I'd expected.

'I assume there'll be a call going in,' Frank said in the car once he'd given me the phone number. 'Say, tomorrow evening? That'd be two days, generally taken to be the right balance between desperate and not interested.'

I made some evasive remark about preferring her friend, but it didn't get me too far. So I told him I'd think about it and he threatened to dial the number for me.

'I'm going to put it to you,' he said, 'that you're afraid you can't live up to last night. And, can I just say, if you did it once you can do it again. You were the man last night, and I'm doing my best to adjust to that. Give me a break and do the follow-up.'

So, now calling Jacinta seems to be a favour to Frank.

I'm glad when I'm back in my room, lying on my bed and listening to him gun the Valiant up the street and over the hill. My mother's at rehearsals, my father's gone into work and there's plenty of time completely alone to launder things that need it.

You wouldn't have believed the mess on the *Paradise*, I'll tell my mother. Not even I could leave clothes around in that state for someone else to wash. French onion dip everywhere, and you know how it goes off if you don't get to it.

I pick up my bullworker. I put it down again.

The images of last night stagger before me like pictures in a home movie. Pictures in a home movie no home should make and that I know I don't want to watch, but I also know I can't walk out on it. The lurching moment of abandon as control switched to autonomic and there was nothing I could do to save it. The tousled silhouette of the food and beverage manager against the city lights. The torchlight, flaring and flaring from my cuffs, my hands darting around in my pants like surprised hamsters, trying to vanish, to bolt away from the light. Only looking more like masturbation in action.

There's also pressure from my mother, growing by midweek, to be part of the protest at the campus on Friday, the day Joh gets his honorary doctorate. She tells me she'll be protesting, but there's a limit to what she can do since she's on staff. I ask her what that means and she says, 'Peaceful protest,' which makes it sound as if she's urging the violence on me. She tries to explain, but blithely tosses in the expression 'front line', waves her hands in the air and says, 'Oh, Philby, that's all rhetoric. You know what I mean. It'll be rowdy, nothing worse.'

The other topic that came up after Saturday night was my neck. Early Sunday evening, when I was watching TV and the room was becoming dark, my neck apparently gave out a yellow glow from behind. We talked about it at dinner. I explained it was from a feather boa, a glow-in-the-dark boa, but that didn't seem to dispel concern in quite the way I'd wanted it to. I told them it was nothing more than one of those spur-of-the-moment dance-floor things, an incident involving a little playful lassoing. I said it as if playful lassoing was something we'd do most family dinners between courses. Anyway, it put me fifty bucks closer to the video camera. That's what the *Paradise* was about.

'You should be pleased for me,' I told my mother. 'I'm sticking with my plan and there was interest in me last night. Not interest that'll go any further, but interest nonetheless.'

There was no need to complicate the story with the admission that I came home not a cent richer.

Frank doesn't let up, but I knew he wouldn't. On Monday I got encouragement, on Tuesday questions, on Wednesday in the car on the way to World of Chickens it's deteriorated to, 'I don't get it. What's your problem? She's slipping through your fingers.'

'I'm not like you,' I said, but it did no good. 'I don't call them all.'

How should I have put it? 'Frank, I took things a step further on the *Paradise* than I might have admitted. But I took that step alone . . .'

I'd call her. I would, and that's what annoys me about it. I'd call if Saturday hadn't ended the way it did. But there's no changing it now, and it's good to get back to World of Chickens, to normal conversations with Sophie and the life that preceded my *Paradise*-pants madness.

'Pray, sirrah,' she says the first time I come out of the toilet in costume, 'give me something poetical.'

'Out, out, brief candle!' I jump into delivery position and stand, legs braced, the way I hope Olivier might. 'Life's but a walking shadow, a poor player, That struts and frets his hour upon the stage, And then is heard no more; it is a tale Told by an idiot, full of sound and fury, Signifying nothing.'

'God, tough piece,' she says, back in the language of the century of our birth.

'Sure. *Macbeth*, Act Five, Scene Five. It's a tough part of the play. He is within the castle at Dunsinane, and he is indeed buggered. Now, as Churchill, circa Battle of Britain 1940. Note change in intonation.'

I run through it again, and she says the change is more subtle than she'd expected. I put it down to Olivier, drawing on Churchill at that moment. Back when Olivier did Macbeth, I'm sure Churchill's phrasing was still recent and compelling. So, next, I decide to go for the same speech in the voice of Peter Brady as Bogart. Degree of difficulty: 2.8.

'Pork chops and apple sauce,' I'm saying as my warm-up, 'pork chops and apple sauce,' when the sound of humming, and shoes on the steps, comes up from below.

That stops me. It turns out to be Zel and, from the way she looks at me when she gets to the top, I know she heard. So I tell her it was a vocal warm-up, since it's my turn out at the road. Deep inside the chicken head, I can feel my face go red.

The three of us walk through to the front and Frank, when he sees Zel, immediately looks more focused and says, 'Burger, madam?'

'Why, yes, Frank, how nice of you.' She walks round to the customers' side and puts one proprietorial arm up on the counter, her trinkets settling noisily, like a handful of loose change. 'How have you all been this evening? Good?'

She's more contained than usual, more business-like. Frank, I expect, will take it personally. His interaction default setting is 'flirt', it's worked with Zel before and business-like isn't an easy shift from there. In the car, I'll explain to him that the change in Zel's style of presentation is actually a good idea.

When I'm back at the roadside, I work out pretty quickly that *Macbeth* Act Five, Scene Five sets up a miserable mood for chickening. I resort to a few old favourites. I throw in some Heart, once I've done a quick scan through the beak and I'm sure there's no-one around to hear it. Then Heart done by Peter Brady as Bogart. 'Magic Man' followed by 'Barracuda'. Now, that's tough. That's talent. Actually, when it's echoing around in the chicken head, it feels like I'm not alone in the suit and the other guy's pretty creepy. So I stop.

I start humming 'Eye of the Tiger'. That song's pursuing me. More than I thought – it might even have been what Zel was humming on the steps. It must be three years old now. It's getting far too much airplay. It always has, and I've never liked it.

Antepartum haemorrhage, I tell myself. Think instead of antepartum haemorrhage. Think of the causes, common and uncommon, and come up with a flowchart that could differentiate between them.

Something beeps as I go back inside. For a second I wonder if I've triggered it, then Zel pulls a pager from her bag and says, 'It's me, don't worry,' as she presses buttons to read the message. Frank shows her where the phone is while Sophie and I go out to change.

'I wonder who it is,' Sophie says. 'She's been getting a few calls lately.'

'I didn't know she had a pager.'

'It's for home hairdressing, mainly. Dad pages her sometimes, but she's got it for work. She does hair, make-up and style consultancy part-time,' Sophie says, as if reading it to me from a business card. 'She says the big word in hair right now is "volume". Have you noticed she's got volume?'

'I've never been one for volume really, or for noticing hair. But, yeah, I think I might have noticed hers.'

'Some of us don't even have the option of volume. Me, for instance. Dad doesn't even have all his own hair and he looks kind of two-tone, but Mum reckons it's different for guys. She says my hair comes in just this side of "lank". Lank, for hair people, is a bad word, and I don't think that's going to change. Whatever anyone's tried with my hair – even Mum – it just falls right out. Even perms. And I don't mean just some stupid home perm. Mum used to have her own salon, but she sold it a few years ago. She was good, you know. Respected. She was the first person on the south-side who could do every style from 'Charlie's Angels' and match it properly with the customer's needs. As far as the salon business goes, she went out on a high. Round about when Dad's World ideas started taking off.'

The back door swings open and Zel's there, voluminous of hair in her white and gold as she sweeps by. 'Just your father,' she says to Sophie. 'Worried where I'd got to.'

Her heels clang down the stairs, click across the concrete and into the dark.

'Hey,' Sophie says once she's gone, 'I read this article. Automatic turn-ons and turn-offs.'

'Yeah? You read a lot of magazines.'

'I'm doing media studies. So what do you reckon? Automatic turn-ons first. What would you rate as an automatic turn-on.'

'Quirky observation,' I tell her and I'm quite proud of myself. It sounds so much more sophisticated than 'sizeable shapely breasts', for example, or 'fast trouser hand'.

'Yeah, I'd go for that,' she says. 'I'd rate that pretty high. Okay, turn-offs.'

'Turn-offs . . . A lack of appreciation of the finer points

of physics? No. A genuine attachment to extreme right-wing political beliefs. It'd be very hard to come back from there.'

'So, Phoebe's not a Joh fan then?'

'No.' Yet again, a Phoebe reference catches me unawares. Why am I never ready? 'She's going to the protest on Friday.' And why do I always end up appropriating a small amount of Phoebe my mother to play Phoebe my girlfriend? If I don't stop doing this, I'm destined for some kind of therapy. 'So, what's your automatic turn-off then?'

'The named penis. If a guy drops his pants and goes, "say hello to Charlie," I'm out of there.'

'And if he drops his pants and doesn't ask you to say hello to Charlie?' 'Depends on the guy, I suppose. Hey, I had a friend once who went out with a guy who was a big *2001: A Space Odyssey* fan and he called it Hal.'

'And was that friend called Sophie?'

There's a pause, as if she honestly hadn't expected to be caught out. 'Maybe.'

'You've spent far too much time with the sci-fi crowd. But here's what I don't get. How do the Hal-penis guys even get that far? Nothing personal, but surely it's not the first signal that there's something wrong. Surely things aren't going along swimmingly, then all of a sudden it's Howdy Hal that gets you wondering for the first time.'

'Depends, I suppose. That's why it's the automatic turn-off. There are plenty of turn-offs out there, but a lot get you a second chance. Howdy Hal gets you a definite nothing, at least as far as I'm concerned.'

Her hair's not really lank. That's what I'm thinking, sitting in Frank's car with his burger box on my lap. Thin and straight, yes, but lank's a bit harsh. Not an observation a parent should make, particularly a full-haired parent. But they do, don't they, they do. And they never mean it badly. It's been two weeks since my mother classified me as scrawn, she's not forgiven yet and she doesn't even know it.

The named penis. Sophie had had time to think about it, but it was still good material. It's reassuring that that's a turn-off. Frank's penis, from what I've heard, has many names. Not that that's made it any kind of master of disguise.

We pass within a block of the Underground on the way to my place. We should have gone there tonight, the three of us. I put it to Frank after Zel left, but he said he'd told his parents he'd come straight home after work to 'move a sofa, or some shit. You know how it goes. And it's always got to be done today.' So the idea never even made it to Sophie.

'I'll do you a deal tomorrow,' he says.

'Yeah?'

'Your parents won't be home till about six, right?'

'Round about. My mother's usually home around then, my father some time later.'

'I'll give you a lift home from the Mater if you'll help me out with a photo or two. I've got a plan for O'Hare.'

'The surgery tutor? Do you really think that's a good idea?'

'You haven't heard the plan yet.'

'The last plan I heard was keeping a low profile and doing another case in the holidays.'

'Yeah, this is a new plan. On top of that plan. That's still happening too. It's just a couple of photos.'

'Okay.' Said in that 'against my better judgement' way, but that'd never bother Frank. 'Hey, Sophie said this thing about photos tonight.' Which I can't believe I'm about to quote, but . . . 'I can't remember what we were talking about but she said, "Do you get that thing where, when you look at old photos of yourself in public places, you wonder what's happened to all those people in the background that you've never met?"'

'You sick bastard.' He shakes his head. 'You total lost cause.'

'What?'

'You know what. Your sly little plan to get me to ask her to the Underground. And then that photo shit – that's just the kind of stuff you like.'

'What kind of stuff?'

'You know . . .'

'No, I don't know.' Yes, I do know, but the two words that come to mind I keep to myself: quirky, observation. 'The Underground just seemed like a good idea. You made us go there last week. And the photo story just seemed topical.'

'Topical,' he says, and laughs. 'Well, that's all right then.'

11

Frank's got me wrong – wrong in two ways. I know exactly where the boundaries lie with Sophie, and of course I'd be calling Jacinta if things were different.

But Frank's got a lot wrong. His tactics for his surgery long case, for a start.

'You'll like it,' he says, pulling his bag over from the back of the car when we get to my place on Thursday afternoon.

It turns out I don't like it much. First, he makes us confirm that there's no-one home. Then, when we go into my room to get the camera, he shuts the door and starts to undo his belt.

'Is there any bit of your wall that you don't have English-boy posters on?' he says, as though that's the problem with what's happening. 'I'm going to have to squat in the corner. It's the only bit that could pass for the Royal.'

'And, you know, I'm okay with that.'

'Whatever. "Catweazle" and bullfighting don't fit with the plan.' He pulls a packet of Tim Tams from his bag, tells me, with clinical detachment, 'Just arse and biscuit,' and crouches down on the floor. 'Here's the idea. We get ourselves a good photo . . .'

'Singular, Frank. You get yourself a good photo. I was never here.'

'I get myself a good photo, I get into his office at the Royal, I give a couple of his Tim Tams a bit of a suck, put them back in the packet and slip the photo in there for him to find just when he's taken a bite.' He sticks his buttocks in the air, pulls his tiger-print hipster underpants down and lifts a biscuit from the tray. He reaches it around, then stops. 'I don't have a mirror. You might have to . . .'

'Hey, I might be going to take the photo just to get this over with, but I'm not loading the biscuit into your arse.'

'Come on. It can't just be jammed in there. It's got to be . . . aesthetic.'

'You really aren't standing where I am. Have you seen your arse? It's not particularly pleasing to the eye. Just stick it in.'

He reaches round behind himself again, like a child struggling with a slot toy, trying to poke the square peg into the . . . it doesn't bear thinking about. The sooner the photos are taken, the sooner this is over. That's what should be on my mind. He manoeuvres the Tim Tam into position, but it keeps slipping and it's starting to melt, sliding over his buttocks and marking them like a brown crayon. Brown crayon, I tell myself, since that's the better thought to fix in my head right now.

'Shit,' he says. 'We'll have to eat this one if I lose any more chocolate.'

'Hurry up.'

'Okay, cut. Take two.' He pulls a new biscuit from the pack. 'How's it looking?'

'Messy, to be honest. But that might even be adding to the effect.'

'Ooh, cold,' he says, having plunged the new biscuit right in. It drops out and he picks it up again. 'I'm assuming this floor gets cleaned regularly.'

A car turns in from the street, revs up the driveway and slides in under the house.

'Your mother?'

'Yes. So clench, will you? I want to get this over with as quickly as possible.'

I take a photo as soon as his hand's away from the Tim Tam and he says, 'Jesus, that was all face. Don't you get this? No identification. Just arse and biscuit, remember. And closer. Close enough to recognise that it's arse and biscuit. I've got a point to make here.'

A car door shuts beneath us. I fire off a few in quick succession and it seems to satisfy him. By the time my mother's coming up the back stairs, I'm in the kitchen and he's in the toilet attending to the skids of chocolate across his buttocks.

She opens the screen door and says, 'Hello,' and I come back at her with, 'Hi, you're early. Frank dropped me home today. He's in the toilet,' before realising that's a lot more information than usual. 'We had some notes to swap.'

'Good,' she says carefully, like someone who plans to get the whole story later. The toilet flushes. 'Good for you.'

'Hi,' Frank says, coming out of the bathroom. 'I had to visit my grandmother and she lives over this way. Thought I might as well drop Philby home.'

'Good. Two reasons to do it then. Your grandmother and the notes,' my mother says. 'It's quite a way to come, so it's handy to have two reasons.' There's a pause. At least a couple of us have decided to say nothing more. 'Cup of tea?'

'Thanks,' Frank says, 'but I'd better go. Nan, you know. She'll have had tea already and she'll be off to bed soon. I'd better just get the notes.' He turns to me. 'The ones in your room.'

'Yeah, come on.'

We go into my room and he whispers, 'Photos . . .'

'What? It's not instant.'

'What?'

'It's not an instant camera. They've got to be developed.'

'I thought it was instant.'

'That's so like you.'

'Shit. Okay, let's go to the car. We can work out a new plan.'

The kettle's boiling as we go via the kitchen, choosing the back door so that he can say goodbye to my mother and make a show of carrying a bag, a bag that might have notes in it.

'Well, I suppose we'll have to wait until the end of the roll to develop them,' I tell him when we're outside. 'That could be a while.'

'I'll pay. I'll pay to do them now.'

'I don't think they'll develop them. They'll probably think they're porn. And with some justification.'

'Well, give them to me. I'll get them done. Let's go back into the house and I'll take the film. We can call it more notes.'

'No, it's better if I do it.'

'And you'll do it now? I was sure it was instant. Isn't that what people do on modelling shoots to check it's all okay before doing the real things? That's what I thought you had. I thought you'd be going to do the same thing when you got the video camera.'

'Remember the revue photos? When we were shooting things for the med revue and you never got to see the pictures? They're still in there.'

'Oh, yeah. I forgot about that. It must be getting on to the end of the roll by now then.'

'Yeah.'

'I'll pay. For all of it.'

'Okay. But just for the blank ones and the biscuit ones. I'll pay for mine. But they'll take a week to come back. We've got no chance of getting them through a one-hour lab, since they're really tough on porn, so I'll send them to a place at Tweed Heads. I think they sometimes develop those kinds of photos in New South Wales.'

'Now you're thinking,' he says, but what I'm thinking is that I've at least bought myself a week to talk him out of it. He opens his car door, tosses his bag onto the passenger seat and gets in. 'How's that call going?' he says, back on the topic of the week. 'Had a word with the *Paradise* girl yet? Got to keep those man bits working or they atrophy, mate.'

'Yeah, thanks. I think they're still okay. I might call her tonight.'

'Go on. Surprise me.' He starts the car, gives a honk of the horn and pulls out from the kerb with a wave.

As if this afternoon needs one more surprise.

My mother hands me a mug of tea when I walk into the kitchen, and she says, 'What are you boys cooking up?'

'What do you mean?'

'All that secrecy.'

'Oh, that. I'm not sure . . . Okay, it's for the protest at uni tomorrow.'

'Oh, really?'

'Yeah. I can't tell you what it is though, obviously. I wouldn't want to compromise you. Since you're on staff . . .'

'Of course. I'm intrigued. Biscuit with your tea? Tim Tam perhaps?'

'Might just have a piece of fruit after. You can never have too much fruit.'

On the bus on the way to the Mater on Friday morning, I realise that Frank's misunderstanding of what I'm doing is simple. He thinks I prefer Sophie to Jacinta. He thinks I'm pointlessly choosing the unavailable Sophie over the possibly available Jacinta, when I've actually got no choice either way.

I'm expecting questions about the phone call I still haven't made, but he's not at Antenatal Clinic. I keep assuming he's in one of the other rooms, but he's not there at all. I hope he's not off doing something dumb involving Charlie O'Hare's room at the Royal, but why would he be? That's not scheduled till at least next week, and the film's in my bag.

Whatever he's doing, I live up to my part of the bargain. I leave the Mater at lunchtime, and I mail the film on the way to the bus stop.

I catch one bus into town, then another out to the campus at Saint Lucia. I don't know what this'll be like. I think I'm learning that I'm cut out to complain, but perhaps not to protest. They're not the same thing. I wish my mother hadn't used expressions like 'front line' and 'barricades'. Did she say 'barricades'? Maybe not.

But I have the right to protest, and there's no need to do more than that – stand up, be counted, lie low, get home in time for dinner. Add my body to the crowd of complaint about this degree, this government. With the ideal performance involving making noise, not looking scared and avoiding arrest. I'm sure there'll be lots of people doing just that this afternoon.

'Fascist,' one of the other passengers bellows venomously out of the bus and into the traffic. And then he says, 'Oh, shit,' in a completely different voice as he takes a second look. 'It's just a big black car. I thought that was him. Sorry mate,' he calls out to the puzzled driver. 'Love your work.'

His friends laugh, and so does he. 'Save a bit for when we're out there,' one of them says, and they seem more like fans on the way to a game than protesters. They don't seem like people taking a risk. They're keyed-up, ready to go but, from the look of them, ready to surge at a concert rather than a barricade.

I have to get barricades out of my head. It's most likely to be a few hundred people standing around shouting 'fascist' while a cordon of bored unarmed police marks the way in for the dignitaries.

The campus is busy when we get there, but it's probably always busy. There are posters about the demonstration all over the bus shelters, more people getting off the buses than on and I don't imagine that's usual for Friday afternoon. In the distance, from somewhere beyond the sandstone buildings of the Great Court and over near Mayne Hall, I can hear an amplified voice but I can't make out the words.

I stand near the bus stop, listening, trying to get a sense of what's going on. I'm tapped on the arm and it's only when I turn it sinks in that, far closer than any protest, someone almost beside me has been saying, 'Hey, Speedy.'

Jacinta's grinning, laughing at me again. She's standing there holding a basket of books and looking totally different to Saturday night. But those eyes and that laugh are things I'd recognise anywhere. There are parts of Saturday night indelibly inked into my brain, and her laughing is involved.

'I thought it was you,' she says.

It's the first time I've seen her properly, in day clothes, in real light. The *Paradise* wasn't big on visibility. Somehow, in daylight, Saturday's incident seems even more exposed, as though she's going to start shouting out, 'This is the guy, the one I told you all about,' and then hundreds of people and a loud hailer will be clustered around me chanting 'Speedy, Speedy,' and I'll never go out with a girl in this town again. Which is how it looks some nights, anyway.

'I thought you were at the Mater,' she's saying. 'Didn't you tell me that?'

'Yeah.'

'So what are you doing out on campus? You're not going to tell me you made up the fifth-year med-student story?'

'No. That much on Saturday night I got right.'

'You're not out here for that silly protest are you?'

'What? What silly protest?'

'The degree ceremony.'

'No, no, I . . .' I can take a hint. The word silly is usually a hint. 'That kind of thing doesn't have much bearing on us in the clinical years. Campus politics, I mean. I'm just out here to look up a few things in the Biol Sciences Library. For a case report I'm writing.'

'Well, you'll never get near it because of the silly protest.'

'Oh, right . . .'

'You'd be better off not even trying.'

'What, just catching the bus and going home? That seems like a bit of a waste.'

'You could always have a drink at the Rec Club, or something. Make it worth the trip. We could have a drink at the Rec Club.'

'Yeah. If you're not doing anything . . .'

The protest fails to re-enter my mind most of the way across campus. I can get to it later, when Jacinta has gone wherever she has to be next. I'm not looking very protesty anyway in my hospital clothes – even with the tie off – so I'd look out of place near the front. Middle, and towards the back – that'll do me.

Jacinta doesn't look like a protester, either. I don't know what she's studying, but it might be law. The book basket has become a sign of a certain kind of law student in the last year or so. I'm connected enough with the campus to know that, and to know that a check sleeveless top and a big denim skirt and court shoes doesn't constitute protester uniform.

She swings the basket as we walk and it's like walking

with Gidget, but I don't mind it at all. This could be a second chance I'm getting, in which case her list of automatic turn-offs is surely more generous than most. And tonight the phone call goes like this: 'Hey Frank, I talked to her, like I said I would. We had a drink this afternoon. So will you stop hassling me now?'

It sounds good and, if I word it that way, it's not even a lie.

On the stairs going down to the Rec Club, I tell her I'm buying and she says she'll have any kind of cooler. We find a table out on the balcony and away from the pool games and the noise. And then she laughs at me again.

'Sorry,' she says. 'I just hadn't expected to be here, you know? Drinking with you, Speedy.'

'I know. Don't worry, I know. Is there any chance we could . . .' There's nowhere to go from there, other than to pause and let her laugh again. 'You're enjoying this too much. You can't begin to imagine how embarrassed I am.'

'It's all right.'

'All right? It couldn't be much further from all right. Last Saturday . . . I was kind of unprepared. I didn't realise the turn events would take.'

'Obviously.'

'Obviously, or I'd go around wearing plastic pants. Yes, thank you. No, I mean, I didn't know how things would . . . proceed. You know what I mean. So, enough about me. Enough about that. Tell me about you.'

She seems reluctant, as though we're already skirting the edge of a better topic, but she relents and lets me off the hook for now.

She's third-year Arts/Law, with the Arts major in French because she did it at school (though that stopped looking like a good reason at least a couple of semesters ago).

She doesn't mind French films, but she still has to read

the subtitles. She'd like more to happen in some of them, and less attitude. I mention Sartre and she tells me, 'We don't do him. It's not that kind of French.' She doesn't have a part-time job. Her parents don't like her to. Her father's a solicitor. Her mother doesn't come up in conversation. She has a brother, but they don't really get on. 'And Saturday wasn't all bad,' she says. 'You mix a pretty good jug of cocktail, and what would Belle have done without you?'

She buys the next round of drinks, another cooler and another beer.

I'd like a photo to show Frank, just as proof. That's what I'm thinking while she's standing at the bar. What a waste sending the film off with three or four blanks at the end. But Frank will still hassle me, and a photo wouldn't change that. I'll tell him about this later, and he'll still hassle me if I haven't got follow-up organised.

And so he should, dammit. Jacinta, with her lively eyes and an Alice band holding back her wavy hair, telling me about herself and being interesting enough and not running away. Interesting enough and not taking flight: two major desirable girl features in my world. Somewhere in the distance, the shouting of silly protest is rising. I need to get over there, but I can't yet.

There's a drink coming my way, and perhaps a chance I couldn't possibly have expected. She hands me the beer, takes her seat and gives a Friday afternoon kind of sigh, paying attention not to the shouting but to the lorikeets flying by, the people with bags on their shoulders crossing the playing field below us to head for home, and me. And she says it's my turn – time for my life story, the part prior to last Saturday.

I tell her about my parents and their strange ways – material that could make anyone look like a raconteur. My mother's flair for accents and my father's for coloured drinks and old cardigans. How much better fifth-year medicine is than the other years, but I'm still not sure what I'll do in the long run. How I've done Labour Ward once, but my time there hasn't amounted to much so far. How I might travel at the end of the year, I suppose, since we have to do a term somewhere out of Brisbane. America looks good. Which leads me to World of Chickens and Ron Todd, his two-tone hair, his rank beige teeth and his seventies body shirts gone bad in the armpits.

And I'm not boring her, whatever my mother says. I'm on a roll, particularly with the Ron Todd stuff. So I keep going, making this big move on Jacinta mainly at Ron's expense, long past the point where I feel guilty about it and forgive myself on his behalf, since chances like this don't come along every day.

Then I realise I need to convert. I need to stop now while things are going really well and convert this opportunity into something, this talking into an arrangement.

'Maybe we could do something some time.' In my head the line sounds casual but, when it comes out and interrupts the conversation, it's more like someone holding up play to take a kick at goal.

'We're doing something at the moment, aren't we?'

'Yes, but maybe we could go out, or something.'

'You had my number, as far as I know.'

'Yes, but . . . circumstances. What about the circumstances? As if I could have called. What would I have said? If your father had answered the phone, what would I have said? Tell her it's the guy who . . . ?'

She laughs. 'Chicken.'

'That's hardly fair. But we're past that now. Aren't we?'

'Maybe.'

'So let's do something.'

'I'm busy over the weekend.'

'Okay, next week. Or the following weekend.'

'What kind of thing?'

'A movie? Something to eat? Whatever. How about next Tuesday night?' I'm plunging right into it now, fearlessly wading knee-deep into this asking out.

'How about Wednesday? That's probably my best night.'

'I think I'm working at the World on Wednesday. Lunchtime Friday? A week from today?'

'Hmmm. Okay.'

'So that's a yes?' I'm playing it almost like Frank. Right at this second the *Paradise* is practically a plus because it means I've got nothing to lose. She's seen the worst of me, and we're still here talking.

'Yes.'

'Okay. Um, so, lunch . . . How about I make you lunch? You can come to my house. We don't live far away from each other. And I'll make lunch.'

'That sounds nice,' she says, and lunch it is.

I write my address and phone number on a beer coaster, and she puts it in her bag.

But I don't cook. All that pride about wading, and now I'm stupidly out of my depth. Okay, I do burgers and other simple chicken products, but there's nothing resembling a good lunch in my repertoire. I needed to anchor a timeslot, and I overshot.

I'll deal with it, somehow.

There's a roar of voices from the direction of Mayne Hall, like the roar of a crowd acclaiming my heroic comeback from a tragic last game.

Jacinta shakes her head, in a very tut-tutting way. 'Why don't they just grow up?'

'Who?'

'The demonstrators. They're such a cliché. They'll shout about anything. Rent-a-crowd. Most of them are just socialists who turn up everywhere. They're not even students at all.'

'I think there were students on the bus that I caught to get here.'

'Well, if they were students they were probably going to lectures. Nothing to do with the demonstration. Joh's done a lot for Queensland. My father was in the Liberal Party, and then he moved to the Nationals after the last election. But I'm still in the Young Liberals. It's a tough choice, now we're not in coalition any more. We'd be in the same electorate, wouldn't we? How did your family handle the election?'

'We're not very political.' Actually, some of us find the very mention of politics depressing.

'Really? I think everyone should be political. That's what democracy's about. It's not about all that protest rubbish. They're just getting in the way. Getting in the way of people who are actually doing things. It's like unions.'

'Don't get me started on unions.' By which I mean, please don't get started on unions.

'Yeah,' she says. 'Yeah.' More animated than she's been all afternoon. 'Don't get me started, either. And what is it with hippies? What's wrong with progress? What about all that rainforest in north Queensland? It's completely under-utilised, and there's so much of it. Think of the tourism potential if you just cleared some of the coastal bits and put in marinas and theme parks and things.'

'Hey, Phil.'

The voice doesn't stop Jacinta, but it catches my attention. I turn around, and it's Sophie.

'I thought it was you,' she says, as Jacinta talks up the virtues of Japanese tourists landing big marlin off the reef. 'I wondered if I'd see you out here. Oh, sorry, am I interrupting?'

'No, not at all.'

A minute or so earlier would have been perfect, but I can't complain. Jacinta stops telling me where this state's future lies, and she turns her head towards Sophie with the expression of someone who feels quite interrupted. Sophie looks from me to her, then back to me again. Jacinta appraises Sophie vertically, from head to foot – her lack of make-up, her sleeveless top, her khaki shorts, her boots – and she does it openly, as though it's what happens to intruders.

'Phoebe?' Sophie says tentatively. 'Would I be right in thinking you're the Phoebe I've heard so much about?'

'Um, no, this is Jacinta, actually.' I manage to say it in a way that makes it sound as if I'm hiding something from both of them. 'Jacinta, this is Sophie. She's one of the people I work with at the takeaway place. A friend I met at the takeaway place.'

'Oh, right.' The context helps, and Jacinta smiles. 'Hi. It sounds like quite a place. How about that awful guy Ron with the bad rug and the bad . . .'

'Sophie's father. Ron is Sophie's father. You're thinking of, um, of that guy from the Mater. The obstetrician. Ron the obstetrician. Ron Bellamy.'

'Oh.' Jacinta still has the smile, though it's stiffened up a little. 'Oh, yes. Sorry, I've heard about so many people this afternoon. Anyway, I wouldn't worry. Your teeth are really very nice, Sophie. And dental care's come a long way.' She laughs, but it gets us nowhere. 'On the other hand, your hair could do with a bit of work.' She grins, Sophie gives her nothing back. 'I'm kidding.' She puts her hand on my forearm, as if to reassure me that we're all just playing. 'Your hair is . . . I'm kidding.'

'I thought it was Theo Bellamy, the obstetrician at the Mater,' Sophie says to me, in a tone that could easily be described as terse.

'Oh, sure, Theo's there too. Ron's the kind of less high-profile of the Bellamy brothers. The quiet achiever of the family. Not a bad guy, though. Doesn't go out a lot, so he doesn't go in for the same level of grooming. You should see . . . yeah, well.'

'Yeah.' She looks down at my arm, still with Jacinta's hand on it. 'So are you coming over to Mayne Hall then? For the demonstration.'

'Um, yeah. I thought I'd get over there soon.' Jacinta's hand lets go of my arm and moves back to her drink. 'Why don't you go and I'll see you there?'

'Okay.' Said in a way that means, okay, you've done nothing but lie this whole conversation, so I expect I'll see you some time next week instead. 'I'll see you there. Just follow the noise.' Then she turns to Jacinta and says, 'I'm sorry about my hair, but it's a bit of a lost cause.'

And all Jacinta can say is, 'Right . . .' as Sophie turns and walks to the door. She walks quickly and she doesn't look back. 'Sorry,' Jacinta says, 'I think I might have upset your friend. I really was only kidding.'

'Of course. She's a bit sensitive about her hair, but you couldn't know that. It's a long story. I wouldn't worry.'

'So, are you really going to the demonstration? What was that about?'

'Oh, another long story. A misunderstanding. I think I mentioned at work that I was probably coming out here today. And I decided not to bore her with the detail of what I was going to do in the Biol Sciences Library. I didn't know she'd got the wrong idea. And when she started talking about it just then . . . you know, politics. Sometimes it's a lot easier not to get into it, and to just let it go.'

'She's not the best at taking a joke, is she? The two of you don't have some kind of . . .'

'No, we just work together.'

'And Phoebe? Who's Phoebe?'

'An ex. That's a situation that was over a while back. I don't know why Sophie brought it up. I can't have mentioned the name more than once or twice.'

It was a time for succinct answers then. I'd already been wondering if we should wrap it up before Sophie arrived and then, once she'd left, all I could think about was that I'll have some explaining to do next week. Or, as far as the Ron part goes, probably no explaining at all. If I'm lucky, we'll both pretend it never happened.

It feels like Sophie stood on the edge of the conversation, and Jacinta and I sat at our table and made her stand there. That's what her face was saying, too. Perhaps in a few weeks I could have introduced them in more ready circumstances. These worlds weren't meant to collide yet. It's as simple as that.

No it's not. I could have chosen some way other than dumping on Ron to try to impress Jacinta, if I'm going to be honest about it. If only it hadn't worked so well. But then we got to politics, and things worked less well.

By early Saturday morning, I've decided to think of her simply as misinformed, and I've decided that it's not fair to view her political position as an automatic turn-off. She's giving me a second chance following my *Paradise* performance, after all.

The afternoon nearly ended so well. We'd talked just

enough, we were finishing our second drinks, an arrangement had been made.

'Always leave them wanting more. Never outstay your welcome.' My mother's advice again, and perhaps this time she could have offered it to Jacinta too, and said 'particularly when it comes to politics'.

My mother means to help, but outstaying my welcome is now one of the main things in my mind when I'm talking to a girl. Along with 'be anything you like, but don't be dull' and the various other pieces of misinformation that have lodged in the advice part of my brain over the years.

All this gives me no credit for the progress since my early days at uni, when I lost myself in biochem and bad clothes and ponderous uneventful silences. It's a long way back from there, but I made it, linking by chance with Frank when he was the big man on campus, and finding myself with a long-term spot at the fringes of the in-crowd.

Since settling into that – definitely as good an outcome as I could hope for – and since getting rid of both my pairs of brown board shorts, things have been better. Learning to order beer with confidence, bullshit till all hours on cheap port and play at least mediocre pool was a big help, too. I'm a much, much slicker package than I used to be.

So, I left Jacinta wanting more. Or, at least, agreeing to more. And I mightn't quite have had mystique, but she was wondering about Sophie and asking about Phoebe, so I look like a contender.

We parted at the door of the Rec Club. It was starting to get busy with the late Friday afternoon crowd, and the first-year law students putting money in the jukebox had a thing for the Violent Femmes' 'Blister in the Sun'. It wasn't an atmosphere for hanging around.

'Well,' I said, 'I'll see you next week then.'

And she said, 'Yeah, see you,' and walked off into the evening swinging her basket of books as the protest, not far away from us, turned louder still.

And that was Friday.

It's about 7 a.m. when the front door opens, and I'm never ready for Saturday this early.

There are feet on the steps, down and then up, and the door shuts again. My mother's feet, and they walk this way and stop outside my room. She knocks.

'I've got the paper,' she says. 'Come and we'll see if we can find you.'

'I'll be out in a few minutes.' What else can I say? I can't go telling her I'll only be in there if they included Rec Club photos, and I'll be the guy sitting next to the Young Liberal.

We didn't see me on the late news last night, but I did say that I hadn't seen TV cameras where I was, so I wasn't expecting to appear. There were two thousand people. A degree was burned, and a swastika. When the invited guests arrived, the crowd surged and broke three panes of glass and drowned out the speakers. Joh Bjelke-Petersen wasn't even there. He was ill and didn't make it. Apparently there had been announcements on Thursday, but word didn't seem to travel too far. Either that or the organisers hadn't believed it.

In the dining room, my mother has spread the *Courier-Mail* out over most of the table. She's scrutinising the coverage like a general studying the map of a battlefield. Eventually, after close inspection of the biggest photo, I convince her that the haircut somewhere in the third ragged row of protesters squished against the window is mine, with the scuffle making a mess of it. I push my hair around, tilt my head.

'See?'

'Yes. Yes, it does look like you,' she says, suddenly proud and wanting to believe. 'You wouldn't want to go out with that hair, though.'

'No. Combed hair, clean underpants. That's how I always start off at a protest.'

'I'm never sure that it's a good thing to flout the law, of course . . .'

'The law of hair? Or do you mean the law of combining combed hair and clean underpants?'

'The law of the land, Philby. But I am proud of you for standing up for what you believe in. I'd bail you out. You know I would . . . Oh Philby, you're just too thin to get arrested. It'd be very cruel television.'

It's not till later, when I'm sitting reading the article, that I realise that the head next to the one I claimed is probably Sophie's. Most of her is blocked out by the person in front, but it looks like her hair and, near it, her shoulder and the top she was wearing yesterday.

I should have been there. Standing up, being counted. Standing next to Sophie instead of giving tacit approval to turning the northern coastal rainforest into marinas, and all of that.

But in this state you can be political just about any time. A drink with a willing girl doesn't come along so readily. The rainforests understand that. Don't they?

Frank calls mid-afternoon and says there's a group of people going to the Underground later, so by midnight we're sitting in the side room again and I've had a few drinks and invented a better version of yesterday. The version in which I caught up with Jacinta (pre-arrangement implied but not stated) and it's all going just as I'd like it to. But I'm trying to pace it, and we're getting together again next week.

Sophie gets a mention, as someone we happened to bump into because she was on campus at the time. I describe their meeting as uneventful, and brief. And how was Sophie with Jacinta? Fine. Why would she not be fine? But I have to admit that, okay, it probably felt a little odd for both of us – worlds colliding when, but for one visit to this room, my life and Sophie's have overlapped only to the extent of a chicken suit three nights a week.

'Yes, there are firm plans. No, you can't have the detail. With detail comes hassle.'

'I thought I did the hassle, anyway,' Frank says. 'I thought I was supposed to do the hassle regardless.'

'Yes, and you will. But I get a much better kind of hassle this way. You'll hassle me for information about the plans. That's way better than all that hassling about making the call, or psyching me up for the day. You know that doesn't work for me.'

Tonight, I don't have to impress. I can dance like someone trying not to dance at the same time, and it doesn't matter. Tonight, my arrangement with Jacinta is a good thing. An unqualified good thing and I'll think it all through later, some time between now and Friday.

'She might hold certain views,' I tell Frank, 'but I wouldn't want to be more specific just yet. There's a lot I don't know. She does Law, Arts/Law. That much I know. She's got a car. I sensed an ambivalence about subtitled films. She's not bad in daylight, I'll say that for her.'

Frank nods and clinks his stubbie against mine in a toast. 'Daylight doesn't do anyone any favours,' he says. 'And you're about due one with a car.'

I go back to the dance floor when they play the

Psychedelic Furs' 'Love My Way', and I dance for a full two minutes with a girl with tight leather pants, big hair and eyes made up as blue and vivid as fireworks. She mouths the words of the chorus at me when it comes round the second time, and then her boyfriend starts looking territorial and taps her on the shoulder.

'I'm already going out with someone,' I want to tell him. 'I've already lined up lunch with someone else next week. You don't have to worry that your bad girl's fooling around with me.'

'I think you made a drink for me,' she says when the song ends. 'On the *Paradise* not so long ago, a foul green cocktail.'

The next song's crap and we end up beside each other at the bar, her wary boyfriend still in attendance. She fiddles with the clasp on her nice-girl purse while the bar staff ignore us, and I tell her the *Paradise* is just a part-time job, but it's hard to get started as a film maker.

'That's interesting,' she says. 'Interesting that you want to do that, because I want to get into publishing.'

And that's when her boyfriend decides he's had enough. He steps in again and tells her that if she goes and finds a table, he'll buy the drinks, even though it isn't his turn.

'The beer's on me,' he says once she's gone. 'Assuming you're going to give me a break and leave the little lady alone.'

12

I looked for Sophie on Friday, but I couldn't find her.

That's my story for Monday. And there were two thousand people there. I could have looked a long time and still not found her. And I've got more background on Ron Bellamy, too. By Monday night I know what car he drives and the name of at least one of his kids. Plus, there was that brief but amusing conversation while we stood in the queue in the hospital dining room at lunchtime.

All right, maybe that's overkill. But it'll only come up if it's in context.

There's no context. Not even a chance for context. We walk into World of Chickens and Sophie isn't there. Instead, holding the costume and ready to go, we have the alternate Sophie – Barb. After a full day of obstetrics, I can do without Barb.

'I just got a phone call,' she says when I ask about the roster change. 'I don't know why Sophie couldn't make it.'

I do my best to make things work the way they usually do, but am I expecting too much? If I start to talk about something non-work-related, she gives me a look that says, 'Get real – we don't do that on the A team,' and she starts agitating for the costume. I can't guess how she'd deal with it if I tossed in something Elizabethan or asked her to speculate on Jean-Paul Sartre's all-time top-five American daytime dramas.

Out at the lights, I try to fix the evening by doing the Village People's 'YMCA' dance, but the wings won't bend enough for M. This job, in the wrong company, sucks. I wish Friday had gone better with Sophie. Not that her absence tonight is anything to do with that – rosters do change sometimes – but I should have handled it differently. Some bits of Friday caught me off-guard, though.

I never clarified what I meant by 'extreme right-wing political beliefs' in my stated exclusion criterion and, the more I think about it, the more I realise I can't recall anything definitely extreme in what Jacinta said. Okay, she was right of centre, and maybe strongly, but in a mainstream way. A way that's mainstream for Queensland, at least.

Ron's visiting when I go back inside.

'You,' he says. 'You are bloody good out there.'

'Thanks. I don't feel like I'm in top form tonight, so it's good to hear that.'

He follows the two of us out the back for our mute and very businesslike changing process.

'Right,' Barb says, her eyes blinking deep inside the beak when we're done. 'Right.'

And I want to say, 'Wrong, dammit, wrong. Take some more responsibility for the quality of my day, will you?' She turns to walk back in and waddles ahead of us with what looks like the friendly gait of a theme-park character. But it's just how she walks, costume or not.

'You get on out there, Barb,' Ron says. 'We've got a couple of things to check back here.' The chicken head wobbles, which I know is a nod, and Ron shuts the door behind her. He looks at me, raises his eyebrows. 'Morale. I look at some of the folk here and the word that comes to mind is *morale*. You're an example to these people, you know that? You didn't get to be a chicken just because you fit the costume.'

'That's good to hear.'

'I hoped you'd give Barb a bit of a boost tonight, but . . .' He shakes his head. 'Just do your best. You've got Sophie thinking the right way, and that's good. Or, at least, she was thinking the right way before this assignment deadline came along. I gave her my stress-management tapes, but does she let them go to work? We're not the best with stress, the Todds. But she'll be okay. Now, listen, I can trust you. I know I can trust you. And I know you see things the way I do, and I think you've got a pretty good head for business.' What's he going to do? Promote me? Where do I go from being best chicken? 'Just between you and me, back when this was Max's Snax, did you ever come here?'

'No.'

'Did anyone ever come here?'

'What do you mean?'

'Did you drive past?'

'Sometimes, I guess. It's a main road.'

'Was it ever busy? Did it ever look busy?'

'Not that I noticed.'

'Okay.' He takes a big breath in and blows it out again, like someone lifting something heavy. 'Again, for the sake of morale and a lot of other things, this is just between you and me. I've got a three-year lease on this place, with options. I bought Max out based on a certain set of figures and there's not one day we've been trading that's lived up to them. And Max hasn't been returning my calls, and today whoever answered the phone said he's not in Australia at the moment, and she's not sure when he'll be back. And I went to the dentist and he says the whole lot has to go. Clearance.' He waves one arm, as though summarily dismissing his teeth. 'I don't know what I'm going to do.'

'About which? The teeth, or . . .'

'About the lot of it. The teeth, the World. Mate, I was so sure this was the right move, you know? There I was thinking how well things were going with the mowers and thinking, don't put all your eggs in one basket, Ron, so of course it was chickens that came into my mind. Now it's bloody all on the line.'

'Well . . .'

'Bloody all of it.'

'It's not over yet. We've got customers. Not a lot, but more than when we started. A few more. We've even got some regulars. Frank attracts a certain kind of crowd, and we work on being a friendly crew. Friendly, hygienic and prompt.'

'Good, good. Of course you do. I should say that to myself more often. Friendly, hygienic and prompt. You are, aren't you? You're a good crew.'

'We do our best. And we've got a good product, and parking. I mean, I don't know this business, but we must be doing a few things right. And Sophie's an asset, of course. We've got a good team thing happening here, and I think we've got to keep that going.'

'Yeah, you're right. I'm letting you down. That's the problem.'

'I'm not saying that. That's not it at all.'

'No, I'm not showing enough belief in you.'

'It's not about you and it's not about us. We've just got to keep plugging away.'

'Yes. Yes, we have. With our "friendly, hygienic and prompt".' He's fighting to come around. 'And pretty keen prices too, I might add.'

'Absolutely.'

'Oh, these teeth. Do you do much on teeth?'

'No. We sort of leave that to dentists.'

'I'm on Panadeine and some antibiotics for an abscess. What do you think of that?'

'Sounds sensible if you've got an abscess. Of course, if you've got an abscess, you wouldn't be feeling too good at the moment, and that wouldn't be helping. You could be feeling tired and listless, and getting headaches and things.'

'Yeah, yeah. I am.' Finally, he starts to brighten up. 'I feel . . . like crud.'

'Okay. Well, at least some of that might be down to the abscess. So, you and the dentist work on that, and we'll all work on the World.'

'Good. Good idea. Full clearance, hey? Do you reckon I should go ahead with the full clearance?'

'Well, I'm no dentist.'

'I've already got a plate,' he says, and takes hold of his front teeth, about to pull it out to demonstrate.

'No, it's okay, you don't have to . . . Sometimes, I think, if you get a problem with the teeth the plate's relying on, your options can be pretty limited.'

'That's it. That's what I'm looking at,' he says, reality sinking heavily back into him.

'It could be the end of abscesses, though. It's not all bad news.'

'No. True. It's not all bad news. So, um, keep up the Panadeine for now, and the antibiotics?'

'I think so. If that's what your dentist says.'

'Right,' he says. 'Right. Better sell some of that chicken for me before it goes off, hey? We'll just keep plugging away. We all have days like this, I guess. Don't you reckon?'

'Sure. I have them myself. I've got all my own teeth and it doesn't seem to stop them.'

The big question in Wednesday morning's lecture: when did I become Ron Todd's dad? I don't know. But Ron 'acted in good faith' when he bought Max's Snax. I think that's how the expression goes. He deserves better.

Okay, that's not the big question. The really big question is Friday. Friday, and how to play it. What got into me at the Rec Club? I disowned the protest first chance I got, came up with some story about a library and two minutes later I was buying Jacinta a drink, then milking Ron's imperfections for laughs and grappling for a place in her diary. And I'm the one he trusts, comes to with morale problems, looks to for advice. Advice, Ron? Don't change a thing. Not even the old shirts. What would I do for material?

'You could do worse than learn a thing or two in the kitchen, Philby,' my mother once said while whipping up a jam-and-buttercream cake. 'You see a whole new side of a man when you see that he can cook.'

And I needed Jacinta to see a whole new side of me, so lunch didn't seem like a bad idea. It'd seem like a much better idea if I'd taken the trouble to learn the thing or two in the kitchen first.

After the lecture, six of us have a session in the Special Care Nursery. We put on gowns and caps and it's the kind of place that makes us automatically quiet. From the viewing windows it's the machines that you can see, surrounding and towering over the tiny new babies in humidicribs as they lie there, splayed out like small beached sea creatures, each with their own history of a rescue in progress.

Some are closer to routine cases than others, simply born very early and making the kind of progress that's expected. One or two aren't making much progress at all yet.

We're farmed out individually to nurses in the unit and we have twenty minutes to learn what we can, then we'll present our cases. My nurse is Brian, whose beard is held in something like a neat surgical chaff bag and it makes his face look almost bottomless.

He leads me over to his corner of the unit and he tells me, 'This is baby Neil Armstrong.' He's already looking down and flicking a switch so I don't see his face when he says it. 'What we've got here, just to give you an idea of what you're looking at, is a monitor for skin temperature – which should be in the low thirty-sixes – a cardiac monitor and an IVAC with an infusion going in through an umbilical vessel.'

We talk through the machines first, then the baby – how he came to be here and how he is now. He seems fragile and very outnumbered, even though every machine is on his side. He doesn't look fully human yet. He was born two days ago at twenty-six weeks and he looks like he's still fighting to stop being something else and to emerge as a land-ready person. I can see, almost, where he's come from, as though he's a model of an earlier internal more aquatic life form.

I make some notes about the fluids, and everything that has to be measured. Plus his mother's history of recurrent miscarriages, no other live births and a damaged uterus. I wonder if his name is in the family, the Neil a grandfather's first name maybe, or if it's some hope that he'll move beyond this rugged start and fly, make history. It's so different to the fourteen- and fifteen-year olds in Antenatal Clinic six floors below, making babies because they haven't learned how not to and carrying them for forty standard weeks.

We reconvene outside the viewing window to present our cases. Frank goes first, and begins with, 'Well, little Natasha should end up okay . . .'

'Natasha whoever... was born whenever...' the tutor says drearily, trying to pull him onto a more orthodox track, 'at however many weeks...'

I'm going through the figures in my head while I'm out at the lights in the chicken suit. One more pay day and I think I can buy my half of the video camera. I could leave then. It is why I started working here. But it'd be bad timing for Ron, and I don't think he'd take it well. His teeth, and Max, have already let him down. I guess I'm staying for now.

Sophie's putting a chicken in a bag for a customer when I go inside. 'Family fries, large slaw,' she says, verbally ticking off the order. 'There you go.'

The door swings shut, and it's just the three of us again. It's been five days since I saw Sophie at the Rec Club, and so far tonight it hasn't rated a mention. She's been swamped by her assignment ever since. I asked her about it when we arrived and she said, 'I thought it looked easy and then it blew up in my face. But it's done now. It's crap, but it's done.'

Frank stops halfway through eating a spare burger. 'You know, whatever way I look at it, I still find Marcia Brady hair really attractive. Do you reckon that any chick could get that kind of thing happening if they brushed it two hundred times a night?'

'In a word, no,' Sophie says, like someone who knows it to be true, someone who has counted to two hundred with a brush in her hand, perhaps.

'And in more words?'

'Marcia, Marcia, Marcia.' She goes with a Brady quote, though I know the word she's fighting back is 'lank'. 'Another of life's mysteries,' she says on the way to changing.

'How is it that I have no sisters at all, and still it's the Jan Brady issues I end up identifying with?'

'You know, I think that was something the producers planned. I think there's a little Jan Brady in all of us.'

'What about Frank?'

'Almost all of us. Maybe even in Frank. But some of us deny our inner Jan Brady, and that's not healthy.'

'You did get that high mark in psych, didn't you?'

'And four hours a day of TV was pretty much the minimum to get me there. It's your Jan Brady issues that are your identity issues. Greg's the big man on campus and Frank tried to play that role, but not with absolute conviction. Frank's more complex than that, he just keeps his Jan below the surface most of the time. He's actually got plenty of issues. Marcia's the prom queen, Peter's as woolly as his haircut in the big hair episodes, the kids are just kids – with the exception of Cindy's lisp, but that's a can of worms and we're not opening it tonight. It's our Jan Brady issues that go right to the big stuff – our place in the world, that kind of thing. We're all in Marcia's shadow, every one of us.'

'She's out there, isn't she? Marcia and her bloody hair . . .'

'Jan's the question mark. What's she going to make of her life? Greg? He becomes a high-school teacher and gets sacked for having an affair with a student. Too easy. His life peaked early, and he couldn't let go of the glory. Marcia?'

'Has kids with great hair – long straight blonde hair – and she brushes it for them, two hundred times a night.'

'That's it. It's a prison, but she can't see it. More kids, more brushing as the years go by. Condemned to brush a thousand times a night.'

'Sounds only fair. Peter?'

'He'll be okay. He'll be some happy-go-lucky guy with

tools on his belt. Jan? Mystery. What happens to Jan is up to all of us.'

'You know what I think's good?' she says. 'Jan's got all that turmoil when Greg and Marcia look like they've got everything, but they're just having their best years early. For Marcia, getting Davy Jones to the prom is the best thing she'll ever do. And she'll tell her kids about it forever, and she'll say things like, "I was Miss Maroubra 1962 and that's because I put some effort into my hair. If I'd left it like that I wouldn't have made third runner-up". Or things about getting Davy Jones to the prom. Or whatever. At least you've got your life together. You've got hardly any Jan Brady issues at all, as far as I can see. You're most of the way through a medical degree, you're juggling two girls . . .'

'Well, I wouldn't say juggling. It's . . . the situation's a bit more complicated than that. And I might be most of the way through a medical degree, but I want to make films, remember? And I'm spending my time either as a med student or dressed as a chicken on the roadside at Taringa. Do I sound close yet?'

'Okay, maybe one or two Jan Brady issues. As well as the girl-juggling, which is more a Greg Brady issue. But at least you've got an idea of what you want to do with your life. I'm not so sure. I think I'd like to be one of those people with acumen. Business or media maybe. I'd like my dad to be proud of me. Is that dumb?'

'No, it's good.'

'He's a sort of self-made man. He's done really well. He's not always like everyone else's dad, I know that, but everyone's parents are kind of weird, aren't they?'

'If you ever doubt that, come round to my place. But it's all part of their charm, right? How interesting would they be if they were normal?'

'Yeah. Well, I don't know what I'm going to do, but I have to end up doing more than wearing a chicken costume and making burgers. Speaking of which, it's probably my turn. So, a poem, then we change.'

'Okay.' I assume the position. 'One of my finer eisteddfod pieces. It's by Andrew Marvell. "To His Coy Mistress":

'Had we but world enough, and time,
This coyness, Lady, were no crime.
We would sit down, and think which way
To walk, and pass our long love's day.

'That's how it starts, anyway. And then there's some line about the Ganges, or something. The poem's more about time, really. It's just got this funny start that's designed to make you think . . . something else.'

'Well, you'll have to remember the Ganges bit for next time, otherwise people could think it was all about some mistress.'

'I was never so good with the Ganges bit. I mean, why the Ganges? Had he ever been there?'

I go into the toilet to take the costume off. Why, when I read through the poem last night, did the Ganges bit not sink in? I happened to find my old eisteddfod folder, I happened to take a look. It made sense. I was starting to run out of material, and it gets dull out at the road. But, without the Ganges bit, the poem really does sound as though it might mean something else.

'You know,' Sophie says, when I pass her the costume, 'if we both weren't the right height to fit into this thing, we might have found each other in the crowd on Friday. There were way too many tall people with a lot to say about that honorary doctorate.' She goes in and shuts the toilet door.

'It's all a bit depressing, really. I don't know if it got us anywhere. All that shouting, and I copped an elbow in the face. And for what? Do you ever have those times when nothing is really going right? You probably don't. Anyway, back to it I guess.'

She bounds out of the toilet, in case she can fake her way to real enthusiasm. I zip her up and she strides for the door, like a superhero. Requiring theme music, I decide – since I can't think of one useful word to say – and I begin to do percussion and horn noises.

She starts to punch the air in slow motion with her wing tips and then stops and says, 'Is everyone singing that at the moment?'

'What?'

'"Eye of the Tiger".'

'Oh. I didn't realise it was "Eye of the Tiger".'

'You. Frank, my mother, me. I'm singing it now, it's so contagious. At least Frank says he's got the album.'

'Yeah. I've got no excuse. I don't even like it.'

'It's everywhere. Everywhere.'

'Well, I tried "YMCA" out at the road the other night, but the wings don't bend enough to do M. Don't go thinking "Eye of the Tiger" was even close to top of my list.'

13

Friday, the plan: confirm I'll have the house to myself, go to Toombul Shoppingtown, pick up . . . something. Enticing pre-prepared food?

Friday comes along too early, before there's much of a plan at all.

'It's lunch, just lunch,' I said to Frank when I explained why I wouldn't be at Antenatal Clinic. 'It's nothing big. So, no advice. I think I can put together a simple lunch myself.'

He asked me if I still had any condoms left after our night on the *Paradise* and he said that that was a health issue, which was exempt from the no-advice rule. 'Cuisine and conversation,' I told him. 'Lunch. And I'll tell you how it goes afterwards.'

So, I'm flying solo on this one. If my mother leaves the goddamn house. She's not usually home on Fridays. What's going on? I'm out on the back patio with Beischer and Mackay's chapter sixty-four, 'Immaturity and Disorders of Growth', in front of me, and she's hovering not far away, being very annoying.

'Three more to go,' she says.

She's marking assignments in batches and allowing herself time away from the table after every third or fourth one. She could do that on campus, couldn't she?

'So, what have you got planned for the rest of the day?' I ask her in a transparently agenda-laden way.

'Why?'

'Just asking.'

'You don't usually.'

'Maybe I'm . . . Okay, I've got plans. Frank'll be coming over to study. Antenatal Clinic's cancelled for today. We're going to be going through some notes. I wanted to make sure we wouldn't be in your way. You'll be gone before lunch, won't you?'

'Perhaps.'

'I didn't think you were going to be home at all today, and we've got a lot of study . . .'

She laughs. 'No, really. Stop pretending you're in the company of the village idiot and tell me what it is you're scheming about.'

'Um . . . right. You're not usually that blunt about it.'

'You aren't usually this evasive. You've got my interest, Philby. I could stay for lunch if you'd like.'

'All right. I'll tell you if you promise to go.'

'I'm all ears.' She sits down at the table.

'You're going then?' She'll hear nothing until I know we've cut a deal.

'If I have to.'

'You have to. I have someone coming over. Nothing special, just someone coming over. You know how it . . .'

'What kind of someone?'

'A not-Frank kind of someone.'

'Mmmm.'

'A female kind of someone.'

She nods. She's had years of instruction that there should be no visible excitement if I mention a girl, and she's starting to get the hang of it. For that, she gets a little more.

'We met on the *Paradise* a couple of weeks ago. I had to

help a friend of hers who got sick. Then we bumped into each other again at Saint Lucia last Friday.'

'At the protest?'

'Yes.'

'I like her already,' she says, with an enthusiasm that's quite out of bounds. 'Sorry, shouldn't have said that.' She erases any sign of it from her expression. 'So, um, what are you doing, the two of you?'

'Lunch. I've invited her for lunch.'

'Lunch? Have you been practising behind my back?'

'It was a spur-of-the-moment choice. Don't make me feel bad about it now.'

'No, no. Don't feel bad. What have you got planned? And that's just general interest of course, an interest in lunch, not maternal nosiness.'

'Of course. I don't know yet. Something pre-prepared from Toombul.'

'Right. Good. Well, you're not asking for my advice, I know that, but let me just say that if I'd known you were planning to entertain, I would have bought party pies. Just in case they might have come in handy.'

'Party pies.'

'Yes. Your chance to serve hot food with minimum risk. A rather nice daytime choice, some people say. And very good for autumn. Into the oven straight from the shop. Nothing to think about.'

'Good idea.'

'And I'll put the riesling cask in the fridge, shall I?'

'Remember, we're not making a big deal of this.'

'No, no. It just might be nice to offer her a glass of wine, that's all. Civil. And she could have it straight, or with a dash of soda water as a spritzer. Just a thought. Nice for lunchtime.' Her good-advice look fades. I must be glaring at her. 'Too much? Too much like a big deal? Surely not. Oh dear. Well, barbecue sauce, not tomato,' she says, as though in passing, 'Or as well, so there's a choice. We've got both. And that's it. Over to you. Not my business. I'll be gone by the time you get back from Coles. I could make a salad in the meantime. Or not. Not a salad? Right.'

I take the bus to Toombul, and by the time I get home the only sign of her is a note on the kitchen bench saying, 'Be bold! M.' So that goes in the bin pretty quickly.

Bold. Be bold. I invited her round here, didn't I? I went out for party pies, dammit.

Party pies. What can go wrong with party pies? Hot food, but casual. Festive, yet satisfying. Party pies and a glass of wine on the patio. A glass or two of wine. This is going to be good. It's going to work.

This might work. Who knows how well it might work, and I haven't got the planes down yet. I could at least have changed the sheets on my bed. Party pies, a glass or two of wine, and who knows what? Nice crispy, flaky party pies, wine, a warm autumn afternoon, birds in the trees. It's still a goddamn Bonnie Tyler film clip in the making, and I never took the plan beyond the catering.

I've got to be ready for anything. I've got to be ready to play my 'Magic Man' tape, and go wherever it takes us. We'll sit with a cushion between us – no pressure – and take it from there.

First time through, she acknowledges the good taste the song shows, and perhaps there's a hint of arousal. It's an unseasonably warm afternoon for May, you've eaten your fill of party pies, and she takes the initiative. She's amazed you're single, pleased but not completely surprised that of all the women on the *Paradise* you ended up with her. She calls you 'irresistible' when the song plays a second time, and she laughs at herself for saying it, as though her secret's out. When it plays a third time, she kicks her shoes onto the floor and makes her move. During the first chorus of the fourth she stands, takes your hand and says, 'Maybe we'd be more comfortable in another room.'

And then I'll be history, because that line doesn't go, 'Maybe we'd be more comfortable in another room with steam-engines-of-Great Britain sheets on the bed.'

Is there anywhere – anywhere at all – to go with it in that goddamn room? 'No, Jacinta, they're not kids' sheets. You haven't heard of this one? Okay, here's how it goes. I'm the Fat Conductor and you're a very naughty . . .'

Fuck. What am I going to do? We can't go in there. So what are my choices? Can I possibly have sex in my parents' bed, with its totally non-descript but also non-mood-killing sheets? Sex beside that pile of Robert Ludlum library books, then laundry afterwards, as if they'll never notice? Sex in the spare room on a bare mattress next to the ironing board and among piles of clothes?

There's still time to make a bed up in there. That's my best bet. No planes, no Robert Ludlum and, once the ironing board and clothes are moved, it doesn't look like such a bad choice. I might even bring a few textbooks in, make it look as though it's my room.

It's just lunch. I shouldn't forget that. I know that's all it'll be, almost certainly, but I'll feel better if I'm prepared for anything. There are sheets in the cupboard in the spare room, and I pick a set that's understated and not too old – lots of little pale flowers. I stretch the bottom sheet over the corners. We might end up here. It's at least possible.

I unfurl the top sheet over the bed and start tucking it in. Jacinta and me, riesling and this warm afternoon, Heart. The *Paradise*, that hand of hers. I could do it again, just like that. Simply making the bed is putting me close enough.

Frank had a theory a year or two ago: masturbate beforehand, since it sets you up for a bit of longevity when it's called for. It's only stuck in my head because of the number of times he's picked me up to go out somewhere, and we've driven off from my place with Frank reciting his wild plans for the night and I'm wondering, Did you? Half an hour ago in Sunnybank, did you fit one in somewhere between the shave and the shower?

I don't know how serious he was, but it's altogether too Frank an idea. Even if he did argue that it was 'considerate', knowing the number of times I'd accused him of never taking anyone else's interests into account.

It's a bad idea. I can see it now, me masturbating beforehand to minimise the risk, like a crippled bomber dropping its load before coming in for a landing. Jacinta turning up really early, or me getting the time wrong, or some other circumstance that leads her to look in the very worst window at the very worst moment. No, there'll be no third chance.

I test the two pillows in the spare room, I pick the one that isn't a hundred years old and I fold the top sheet over it and back, and tuck it in at the sides. It's just a bed. No pressure.

Time is starting to run short, and I should get back on track and shave. The party pies are defrosting on the counter, the riesling cask is in the fridge, 'Magic Man' is in the stereo ready for playing. I'm going to shave, this'll all go well.

The phone rings.

The phone rings, and it'll be her. She's cancelling. We can reschedule maybe, and that's not necessarily a bad thing. Today's a rehearsal, and that's been useful. And if she's cancelling completely, it's a rehearsal for someone else, some other time (month, whenever). And that's fine, too. It's okay that she can't make it.

But it's Ron Todd.

'Mate, the other night,' he says. 'Bit of a low point.'

'That's fine, Ron. We all have them. Say no more about it.' Like, say absolutely no more and get off the phone.

'Thanks. I know I can talk to you, mate, that's the thing. And now we've just got to see if there's a way through this.'

'Yes. I'm sure there will be. And the teeth . . .' I know the conversation will turn to them and I want to get there as quickly as possible. 'Have you thought any more . . .' Finally I'm flaccid. So that's the secret. Why couldn't I have got Ron's stinking beige teeth in my mind on the *Paradise*?

'I reckon there's no avoiding it,' he says. 'But sometimes you only see these things clearly when you talk them through with someone else. The teeth, World of Chickens . . . Hey, how about coffee?'

'Well, maybe, but I'd be thinking we should consolidate the chicken side of things first before we get into hot drinks.'

'No, mate, you and me. A cup of coffee some time.'

'Oh, sure.'

'Some time next week?'

'Yeah, I . . .'

'Okay, how about Monday? How's Monday for you?'

'Yeah, Monday, right. Look . . .'

'So what's your timetable like?'

'On Monday?'

'Yeah.'

'I think I've got a break in the middle of the day.' Get

off the phone. Get off the phone. 'A couple of hours in the middle of the day, I think.'

'Starting?'

'Twelve.'

'All right, I'll pick you up then. At the Mater? We could . . .'

'Um, okay. Listen, I'm sorry, but I've really got to go. I've got my study group arriving here any minute.'

'Monday at twelve.'

'At the main entrance to the Mater. I'll see you there.'

Coffee with Ron Todd. I'm bordering on late, I'm far from safe in the pants and now I'm lined up to have coffee with Ron Todd.

I run the water, lather my face, fail to find my razor. So, this is where things become unstuck. I worked out the bedding issue in time (however irrelevant it might be), I've got the music, I've got the party pies, I'm running round the bathroom with a foamed-up Santa face and nothing to shave with. I'm running out of time. I find a packet of new razors under the sink, and I get to work.

I stand there shaving, thinking through music, mood, masturbating. So I hack my face to bits. Why does Frank put ideas like that in my head? He knows they aren't helpful. I'm never a great shaver, but I'm so much worse when I don't concentrate. And there's nothing that can draw blood like a brand new razor. By the time I notice, I look like I've either got a death wish or I'm short a clotting factor or two. I dab and dab. I apply pressure. I have one bad moment when I seriously think clumps of tissue on the face would be better, and I wonder if there's some kind of tissue in the house that'd be the right shade to let me get away with it. Peach perhaps?

I go to the fridge and I wrap some ice in a Chux and

hold it against my face in the right places. I press it hard against my silently haemorrhaging neck, but there's still active bleeding whenever I take it off. There's no time for a shower now, so I have to resort to the Old Spice someone once gave my father for Christmas instead.

Calm, this would be a good time for calm. There's still ten minutes or more before she gets here.

She's early. The doorbell rings, and I'm dressing with one hand while the other holds my ice mask to my face.

I throw the ice into the kitchen sink, and shout out to let her know I'm on my way. I turn the oven on high and toss in the full packet of pies. The aroma of baking, that's what I need. People always respond to the aroma of baking. And then buy your house. It's a real-estate strategy – what am I thinking?

I pull on the clothes I dumped on the floor before I went to the bathroom. This will be a casual look, I tell myself, and a casual look can be good sometimes. I check in the hall mirror and I look pale and wet – artistic perhaps. Maybe we can talk film-making. There is no evidence of major facial bleeding.

It's only lunch, I tell myself, only lunch. Cuisine and conversation. Study, obstetrics, Ron Todd. Think anti-arousal.

I reach the door. And there's an opened packet of photos on the table just inside.

The mail arrived while I was at Toombul. It's the photos from the film I sent away. It must be. And my mother has looked at them.

'Arse and biscuit', I'm thinking as the door opens. I'm swinging it open thinking 'just arse and biscuit.' I want to check the photos. Need to check the photos. As I'm opening the door all I want to do is shut it, take a look at the packet and see if they developed those ones or not. But I can't.

Imagine if they did, and she saw them. What would it say? 'Hi, welcome to my house. What do you think of these? I've got some party pies warming out the back. Are you feeling photogenic?'

'Hi,' she says, standing there with her basket, expecting something very normal.

'Hi.'

'I should have brought something, but I didn't know what to bring. So I brought books.' She holds up the basket as a joke. 'I thought I'd bring this in, since I didn't want to leave it all in the car.'

'Good move. Can't be too careful.' Shut up. 'The library'd give you hell if someone lifted them all.' No, really, shut up. 'Come on through.'

We walk down the hall to the kitchen, and the first hint of a baking aroma is there waiting for us.

'Hmmm,' she says, in a way that sounds prepared to be appreciative.

'It's getting on to the time of year when hot food doesn't seem out of the question.' I wish I hadn't said that. My part of the conversation is being overrun by platitudes. What's going on? 'Wine? Wine and soda?'

'Just the wine'd be good, thanks.'

'No problem.'

I squirt us each some riesling and I still want to check those photos. Just once. I need to know.

She takes her glass and says, 'Thank you. Um, do you have any ice? I know most people don't, in wine, but . . .'

'No, that's fine.' Or, not fine. All the ice in the house has been pressed against my bleeding face, and is now in the sink. 'Why don't you take a seat and I'll bring it over with the ice in?'

'Oh, okay.'

'I thought we might eat outside, so take a seat on the patio and I'll check how lunch is going and get you some ice.'

She smiles. 'You're nervous about your cooking, aren't you?'

'No, no. Well, a bit. And it's not really cooking, but . . .'

She nods, says, 'I'll see you outside,' in an understanding way, still with the smile, and she walks towards the glass doors.

She turns around precisely when my hand is in the act of scooping ice from the sink and dropping it into her glass.

'Ice,' I say redundantly. 'You wanted ice?'

'Yes . . . that seemed to come from the sink.'

'Yes . . . overfilled tray. It was all clumped. One big piece. So I thought I'd break it in the sink. Before you got here. In the tray, which . . .'

She's nodding. She'd like to understand.

I toss a couple of cubes into my drink as well, as a sign that it's safe, that everything's normal. There's blood on my hand, a smear of blood from the ice. I check the pies, and that gives me a chance to wipe my hand on the tea towel.

'They'll be a little while longer,' I tell her. 'Why don't we take a seat in the lounge in here until they're done?'

'Sure.'

Okay. So far, not exactly so good, but all still workable. She sits on the sofa and puts her basket on the floor by her feet. She picks up a cushion, sets it down on her lap, picks it up again and puts it back on the sofa next to her.

'So . . .' she says, as if I'm to make conversation, or take the next step. I hand her her wine, and she sips it and says, 'Mmmm.'

It's warm in here so I turn the ceiling fan on and, while I'm there, I release the pause button on the stereo. I sit down, and there's only the cushion between us. 'Magic Man' starts playing, at just the right volume.

The first time through, nothing happens. Five minutes of hot, passionate Heart fuck song, and I'm pretty sure she doesn't even notice. She keeps smiling, but it's a smile that's starting to look for somewhere to go by the time the song's ending. That's not the same as arousal. She asks me how long we've lived here, questions like that. We drink our wine.

'It's Phoebe, isn't it?' she says. 'You're not really over her, are you?'

Time two for Heart, and she looks as though something unexpected has just happened when the song starts again. And it's not that she's suddenly twigged to my irresistibility.

'No, no the Phoebe situation . . . it's hard to describe, but . . .'

'It's okay. Was it recent?'

'Yes. Well, not really.'

'She got to you, didn't she? You're not over Phoebe at all. You can tell me.'

Nothing plausible about Phoebe crosses my mind, and we have ourselves a pause that could take on its own strange meaning. I drink a mouthful of wine.

'So, what, um, what books have you got in there that people were going to steal from the car?'

'Oh, uni stuff.' She looks down at her basket. 'That's Simone de Beauvoir's *The Second Sex* on top.'

Which reminds me of our conversation of last week, so that gives me somewhere to go. 'Do you think she had her own TV, or did she just watch Sartre's?' Except that wasn't our conversation. That was Sophie. 'You didn't see that, um, article in the *National Times*?' Liar, liar.

'We don't get the *National Times*.' The song finishes,

and starts again. 'What was it about?' She moves back further into the corner of the sofa, pulls another cushion out from behind her and pushes that between us as well.

'Her, um . . . their, um, American circumstance . . . So naturally TV came up, since it'd pretty much have to. I didn't read the whole thing. It's not really my area. Not that I'm not interested. It's just that I've got exams coming up.'

'Can I just ask – and don't take this the wrong way – how did it end with Phoebe? Did she really hurt you?'

When the now relentless bass line of 'Magic Man' kicks in for the fourth time – and, guess what, there's not one suffocating garment loosened, even though it's definitely warm for the time of year – she starts looking twitchily around and saying, 'What's going on? Is something stuck?' Her forehead turns puzzled. 'What were you saying about TV?' She clutches her glass, looks down into her drink.

'I just really like the song,' I tell her.

And the comment was supposed to be low-key but, bugger it, I've somehow picked psycho instead and made 'I just really like the song' sound about as thoughtful and normal and non-threatening as 'Have you checked the children?'

'I think there's something in my wine,' she says. 'Something . . . coming off the ice cubes.'

'Probably just turbulence. There's a temperature difference . . .' Turbulence? I'm about to go for Bernoulli again. Have I learned nothing? 'The riesling's warmer than the ice cubes, so . . .'

'No, no I think it's the ice cubes themselves. I might go and get a couple of fresh ones.'

No, not the sink. But she's already standing, as though getting a couple of fresh ones is mainly a chance to put some distance between us, step away from this fractured conversation and its mesmerising 'Magic Man' soundtrack.

'I'll help you,' I tell her, as she walks around the far side of the coffee table. 'I might check on the pies, too.'

'No, no it's fine,' she says a little sternly. 'Stay where you are.'

'I'd really rather . . . you're the guest.'

I stand, but she's already up to the breakfast bar. The song's up to the chorus. Jacinta's up to the sink.

'I'd really . . . There's some things I should explain.'

She stops, just as she's about to reach down for ice. 'Phoebe things, would that be? You haven't been entirely honest with me about Phoebe, have you? And you've been creeping me out a bit with this music, I have to say that. I don't know what you were thinking with this tape.'

'I'm not sure where to begin.'

'Blood,' she says in a voice that's oddly deadpan. 'There's blood in the sink.' She looks up at me, as though not a thing makes sense any more. 'That's what's in my wine, isn't it?'

'Phoebe's my mother,' I tell her, and straight away I know it's not how I should have put it.

'Oh, Jesus,' she says, same voice as before. 'Your mother.'

'I can explain.'

'You just have. Um, I have to go now.'

'No, no it's not like that.'

'I'm really sorry, okay? Really sorry. But I've got to go. I don't think I can . . . I just have to go. You should get help. You, and especially your mother. But you too.'

'No, it's complicated.'

The song moves from languid guitar solo to sensual synthesizer, plus wailing.

'These things are never simple. The blood, for example.

I can't guess . . . Could you step away from the basket? I have to go right now, and I'd be much more comfortable if you'd step away from the basket.'

'No, you have to let me . . .'

'Okay, let me put it another way,' she says, every syllable louder than anything before. 'I'm likely to scream if you don't step away from the basket.'

I step away, three slow backward steps towards the French doors. A gust of air blows in from the garden, the curtains billow.

She moves forward, watching me all the time, even when she's picked up the basket and she's feeling around in it for car keys, backing away past the coffee table.

'We'll talk later, though,' I say to her, in a way that sounds somewhere between a question and completely stupid.

'No, no we won't. I'm sorry. I can't be the person to get you through this.' And then, in the ultra-firm voice again, 'I don't even know what the blood's about.'

She gets to the pantry and the kitchen door, checks the hall, and runs. She's at the front door in seconds and it slams behind her and her feet clatter down the wooden steps outside.

'Magic Man' starts for the fifth time. The enticing aroma of party pies fills the air. Outside, a car engine roars into life and rubber scorches into bitumen as Jacinta leaves the scene.

I hit the stop button on the stereo, walk into the kitchen and turn off the oven. My appetite's gone. Won't be back for some time.

There was a better way of saying that. Sure, there was also an ice-cube management issue, but there was a better way of explaining Phoebe. There were probably many better ways, but I would have settled for any that didn't imply I was fucked-up because my last relationship was with my mother. Someone once told me that when you try to explain things you should get right to the point. Now I know that's not always the best approach.

I go into the spare room and I pull the sheets off the bed, fold them and put them back in the cupboard.

The only lucky break that comes my way is that the lab didn't develop Frank's photos. The packet couldn't be more innocuous – straggly roses, people at a party doing nothing special, compositional exercises showing that I still have a thing or two to learn about perspective and framing. These photos – that's where my life is. My life is made up of dull backyard things, and I shouldn't try to be so bold with party pies, and shaving at the last minute and some song about a man with a kind of chick magnetism that can't be explained by science and has to be put down to magic.

I should have masturbated. At least it would have put a couple of minutes pleasure in my day.

A while later, Frank calls. 'If it's a bad time . . .'

'No, we've done the bad time.'

'I just thought I'd see how it was going.'

'Thanks. It's sort of gone. She's gone. It's a long story.'

'It's never a short one.'

'Oh, look, it's nothing major. Just a misunderstanding. She got some funny ideas in her head about my relationship with my mother, and I kind of cut myself shaving and some of the blood got in her drink.'

'What?' He's laughing. 'You bled in her drink?'

'In her wine, yeah. But not directly . . .' A pager goes off in the background. There's a muffled voice somewhere but it's drowned out by Frank, still laughing. 'Where are you?'

'Um, still at the Mater.'

'Yeah, the pager was a hint, but we're not rostered on this afternoon are we? I thought it was only the morning I was missing. Has anyone noticed I'm not there?'

'No. I was working for Dad last Friday, remember? So I missed Antenatal Clinic and I thought I'd do double today. After what happened in surgery I'm taking no chances. So I've stayed on for the afternoon one. But forget that. You served a girl a drink with your blood in it. Have you hooked up with a vampire and not told me?'

'If she was a vampire she'd still be here. You should have seen her. She didn't so much leave as flee.'

'You've got to call her and straighten it out, before she gets any strange ideas.'

'She's got them. Trust me.'

'No, call her. I know you don't want to but it'll only be worse if you don't. Call her and explain. What have you got to lose? You don't want her going round saying you put blood in drinks.'

'Yeah, I . . .'

'I've got to go. I've got to call the next patient in. You have to call her, right? Don't stress. She'll never go out with you again. It's fine. It's just damage control, and you're very good at damage control. Yeah? Pretend I've got myself in some situation and you're bailing me out. It gets down to explaining. You're good at explaining.'

'Yeah.'

He's gone before I get to mention that his photos weren't developed. Maybe he's right. Maybe I should call her. I don't want the wrong version of the story getting round. I'll probably call later.

I should tell him about the photos. I'm sure he'd want to know. I give him twenty minutes to see the next patient, then I call the Mater back. The switchboard puts me through to Antenatal Clinic, but there's only a clerk there. He tells me the morning clinic finished well over an hour ago, and there isn't an afternoon clinic on Fridays. Frank must be somewhere else at the Mater, even though it was an Antenatal Clinic he missed. But I don't know where to try next. I'll talk to him later.

I plan my Jacinta conversation most of the afternoon, sitting at the table making notes about the directions it might take and what I might say. This time I'm leaving nothing to chance.

I revisit lunch from all kinds of bad angles. I blame my mother, I blame Frank, I blame Ann and Nancy Wilson and anyone else connected with Heart. Each for different things but, ultimately, I know where the buck stops. For a while, I wonder if it might have been better if I'd gone with the moderately sensual 'Let's Go' by The Cars rather than the story of a man with an allure so compelling no girl's mother could understand it. But, let's face it, that's not the issue. The way things panned out, I might as well have picked Warren Zevon's 'Excitable Boy' and sung along to the bit where he killed her and filled the cave with her bones.

My mother arrives home, making a lot of noise as she gets to the door.

'It's okay,' I call out to her. 'She's gone. I'm back doing obstetrics.'

'Oh, right,' she says as she comes along the hall. 'I wasn't going to ask.' She stands in the doorway to the kitchen, holding shopping bags and looking around, as if hoping to catch some lingering interesting sign of the visit before it fades away forever.

'You can ask. And the answer is I don't think she's for me. You know how, sometimes, you just know that? So, I'm moving on. There'll be other possibilities.'

'What? What other possibilities?' she says with a speed that gets the words out before her usual tone of measured curiosity manages to catch up with them. 'None of my business. Sorry.'

'That's fine. It was a general observation. Not specific.'

She looks at me, trying to work out how fine it really is. 'If you want to talk about this, or anything we could. We could talk, couldn't we?'

'I'm sure we could. If there was anything to talk about. Are you after salacious details or do you just think I need therapy because lunch didn't work out?'

'Oh, nothing like that. It's just . . . well, you bought party pies. You probably got your hopes up. Or maybe not.'

'Well, it's all irrelevant now, whether I did or I didn't. She's not for me. Back to obstetrics, I think.'

And she navigates herself so cautiously through her well-intentioned concern that I don't even have the go at her that I was planning to about opening my photos. My photos. Does anyone open anyone else's mail around here? Definitely not. That's definitely a rule. Even if there might be photos of their roses in there.

So the photos stay in my room, and we don't discuss them. She's making dinner by the time I tell her I'm about to use the phone in the study. I explain that I've got to talk through a lot of uni things with Frank – lecture notes and case studies – and I need to do it with everything spread out in front of me. I take my conversation outline and a large irrelevant pile of paper in there, and I shut the door.

Just go with the plan, I tell myself. The necessary outcome's simple, and it's not like lunchtime. Damage control, that's all.

It still takes a lot of pacing before I pick up the phone, and it gets put down again twice before I dial one digit. Do it. Just do it.

I call. It rings. Three times, four.

'Hello.' A female voice, and familiar.

'Hi, Jacinta?'

'Yes.' The voice toughens up already.

'It's Phil.'

'Yes.'

'I just wanted to have a chance to explain a few things. About today.'

'I'd really rather not do this.'

'No, it wasn't the way it seemed. Things got a bit jumbled. Some of them came out all wrong.' New tactic: start peripheral, move towards the point. 'I was fighting off a migraine. I get them sometimes, and they affect my speech and I can say odd things. About relationships. That aren't true. They're just a jumble. And they affect my vision – the migraines – so that made me shave very badly and made me quite clumsy with the ice and it might have made me seem a bit strange. Did I seem a bit strange?'

'Have you still got the migraine?'

'No, I'm fine . . . yes, I have, just a bit. And it was a new razor, and they're sharp and they can slice through just about anything without you feeling it. When you're shaving. And the tape, that strange tape that we played, I don't know how it got into the machine. It's my brother's.'

'Yeah? What's his name?'

'Name?' It's the pause that does me in. That and the tragically tentative way I invent my brother Peter.

She hangs up.

I call back.

'Okay, this time I'll tell you exactly what happened.'

Having gone with Plan A, the migraine, and less successfully with Plan B, my brother's tape, I move to another sheet of paper and Plan C, the jokey explanation of the photos, to explain how my mood was completely thrown exactly when I got to the door.

'So there they were,' I tell her, 'and my mother had opened them. And they weren't just any photos. My friend Frank – you met Frank, I think – has a problem with a surgery tutor, so he'd got me to take some photos in my room of him with a Tim Tam between his buttocks, and I was worried that my mother . . .'

'Naked buttocks?'

'Hard to get the Tim Tam in there otherwise.'

'Don't call me again.'

She hangs up.

I call back. She's kidding, surely. Anyone can recognise a prank. At least I have to finish Plan C before giving up.

The phone rings and rings. This time a man answers. It's her father. His tone isn't friendly.

'Are you the guy who stuck the biscuit up that other guy's arse?'

'Me? No. He did it himself. I just took the photos.'

'Listen, that's exactly the kind of thing I've heard about you. I know you've got a very disturbed personal life, and I'm sorry about your family background, but let me be clear. I don't know why you're calling my daughter but, put it this way, I've got your name, Phil Harris, I've got your number and I've got friends in Special Branch. So there's plenty of stuff a lot bigger and uglier than a biscuit that could find its way up your arse quick smart if I made one phone call. You won't be calling here again, will you?'

'I think there's been a misunderstanding.'

'You won't be calling here again, will you?'

'But there was this cruel surgery tutor . . .'
'Listen, mate, get help.'
'I never had sex with my mother.'
There's a click, a loud click. He's hung up on me.

It's enough that someone in the family claims to have had their photo taken by Special Branch. My mother's political cred will not be enhanced if Special Branch is persuaded to insert plenty of stuff in my arse quick smart because I made a dick of myself with some guy's daughter.

My parents, spared the details, know me well enough to work out that it hasn't been one of my better days. During dinner, my father tries his hardest to stimulate a conversation about current events or obstetrics or the mysterious eternal appeal of Gilbert and Sullivan.

Afterwards he pours two glasses of one of his better brandies and says, 'Fancy a film? *The Bridge on the River Kwai*, perhaps?'

He lopes off to the study, to the shelves of taped-from-TV videos he euphemistically refers to as a library. Soon the two of us are in the darkened lounge room in our recliner seats, sipping our brandies and watching Alec Guinness do his best work, my father murmuring 'watch out, sir' and 'chin up' as the mood takes him. This is not the evening I had planned.

The phone rings and my mother answers it. From her tone, I know it's Frank. My father hits the pause button, but I tell him to keep watching while I'm out of the room. I should be able to fill in any gaps by now.

'So,' Frank says. 'What are you doing?'
'Drinking the good brandy and watching *The Bridge on the River Kwai* again.'

'You fucked up the phone call as well then, hey?'

'Correct. You know the score. You don't get the good brandy and *The Bridge on the River Kwai* around here if you've had one of your better days.'

'We should go out. We should have a drink now.'

'I don't want to go out. And I *am* having a drink now.'

'I'll pick you up at nine-thirty. The video should be finished then.'

'Okay.'

'Usual plan,' he says in the car. 'The Underground. Cruise in at five-to-ten, beat the cover charge. Vince and Greg are meeting us there. There might be a few others, too.'

He's playing Springsteen tonight on the car stereo, early Springsteen, *Born to Run*. We went to the concert a few months ago, us and fifty thousand others in pounding rain at the end of a hot day. I've never been to anything quite like it – spectacle and steam and mud, with the Clarence Clemons sax solos soaring all the way to the low clouds. Until that night, I thought the best thing about Springsteen was the girl in the 'Dancing in the Dark' film clip.

I can't believe the mess I made of this afternoon.

'The photos,' I tell him. 'They came back today. No butt shots. Sorry.'

'Bugger.'

'We always thought that might happen.'

'Yeah. Yeah, the more I thought about it . . . we should take it as a sign. I think you were right about how to handle this. The more I thought about the particular film genre I got the idea from, the more I realised it wasn't the butt pranks I had the affinity with anyway. It was the sorority pillow fights.'

'I didn't realise we were working in that kind of paradigm.'

'Well, you're always working in some kind of paradigm, aren't you? Why fight it? So, do you want to tell me some more about the phone call this afternoon?'

'Not really. I've kind of gone off Jacinta, anyway.'

'Surprise me. Elaborate.'

'When it really came down to it, we fell out over politics.'

'Politics.' He lets out a laugh that goes 'hur hur hur hur', like an engine turning over, but stalling short of starting. 'What did you say in that phone call?'

'I think the only common ground we found was that, by the end – by which I mean the end of the third call, after the two hang-ups – she and her father and I were all of the understanding that I wouldn't be calling again. Her family tends to be quite right of centre, politically, and I think we had very different views on the role of Special Branch.'

'God, you really go all the way when you talk things through, don't you? I thought you were kidding with the politics. But, whatever does it for you, I guess.'

'Yes. So, moving on, a different topic . . . where were you this afternoon?'

'What? What do you mean? At the Mater.'

'Yeah, obviously, but not at Antenatal Clinic. I called. There was no Antenatal Clinic this afternoon. What were you doing?'

'I don't know why they couldn't find me. That's where I was, down in Clinics.'

'Doing what? Straightening up the piles of out-of-date copies of *National Geographic*?'

'No, no. Work. Kind of. You know the way they've got the portable ultrasound up the back? Well, there was a patient who was being admitted after the clinic this morning and she'd gone home to get her stuff. She was being admitted through the clinic so that the registrar could take a look at things on ultrasound on the way in. She's got polyhydramnios for investigation. So I was there for that.'

'Acute or chronic polyhydramnios?'

'Um, acute.'

'So she's got twins?'

'Is she supposed to?'

'Doesn't it almost always occur in association with twins? Acute polyhydramnios?'

'Um, yeah. Maybe this wasn't quite so acute. I don't remember all the detail. I was mainly there to have a look at the ultrasound. I didn't see her when she came in this morning.'

'Right. Sounds like you learned a lot.'

'Yeah. Not as much as I thought at the time, maybe.' The idea seems to make him edgy, as if obstetrics might go the same way as surgery without more careful attention.

'Look, we've still got weeks to get it together.'

We turn off the street and into the car park opposite the Underground. There's already a queue outside, waiting to be let in for nothing when it opens at ten. I can't see anyone I know.

'Yeah,' he says. 'Yeah. I've, um . . . hmmm. It's just there's pressure from home to do more lopping work. But I'll keep it to weekends as much as I can. Anyway, you totally crashed and burned with Jacinta, then?'

'Yeah. We're calling it "fell out over politics", remember?'

'Yeah, sorry. I do that all the time. I think there's a possibility Sophie and Clinton might be falling out over politics at the moment.'

'Really? I wouldn't be so sure.'

'Should I go and ask her if she's up for some action, now that you're back on the market?'

'No, don't.'

'Well, you won't cut through the bullshit yourself.'

'Okay, it's not happening, right? You keep bringing things back to Sophie, and it's not happening. And if it was, she wouldn't tell you. And if it was and she tried to tell you – which it isn't and she wouldn't – she wouldn't say it in a way that you'd understand. No-one's quite as direct as you. And that's not a bad thing, it's just a thing. And there are times when it needs to be factored in. Some of us don't cut through bullshit. We navigate carefully around it, and that's how it is and you don't get it. So if she told you, she'd tell you in a way that meant you wouldn't or couldn't tell me.'

'But you're not touchy about the subject or anything, are you?'

We park down the back, next to the fence.

'With minutes to spare,' Frank says, looking at his watch as we get out of the car. 'It's amazing that you live in such a complicated world, and yet practically nothing happens there. You realise – and I'm speaking strictly theoretically – that if it turns out she's available and you're off wandering somewhere near Outer Bullshit, someone else might make a move.'

'That's a chance I'm completely prepared to take. Now, let's go in. You've got us here on time. You've saved us the cover charge, so that's two more drinks each. Tonight, I'm going to dance badly with girls I don't care about and will never see again. I'm going to get the taste of my father's brandy out of my mouth and Alec Guinness out of my head and I'm going to have a better time.'

'Listen, your Dad, he really means it when he plays *The Bridge on the River Kwai*, you know.'

'I know. He's a good man. A strange man, but a good man. I realise that.'

14

By Sunday, I'm definitely going with 'political differences'. Irreconcilable political differences, and her father's Special Branch contacts confirmed it. We fitted together no better than a Montague and a Capulet, and those kids would have done well to work it out much earlier.

'The planned date's never been your strongest option, has it?' Frank said on the way home on Friday night. 'Never great for either of us, really. Which is a shit, since it seems to be a mainstay of the contemporary courtship ritual.'

And I wanted to say to him, 'Look, I'm so much better than I used to be. If it hadn't been for that lapse in concentration on the *Paradise* . . .'

I'm right about acute polyhydramnios (Sunday's task: read Beischer and Mackay, chapter twenty-one, 'Amniotic Fluid'). It's much rarer than chronic polyhydramnios and almost always associated with uniovular twins. Frank must have got them confused. But at least he's now got his own second-hand copy of the book so, if he can find some time away from tree-lopping, he should be okay when the exams come around. And they can't be far away, if Frank owns the text book and has been sighted in the hospital outside minimum rostered hours.

I don't know what he was doing on Friday, though. I'm sure it's just Doppler gear down the back of the clinics, and the nearest scanning ultrasound's on a different floor.

There's too much wrong with his story. It's almost like it was made up from scratch, as if he wasn't there at all. Maybe he was working for his father, and he didn't want to get into talking about all that again. No, there was a pager. A pager went off in the background during the call. So it was the hospital because, apart from hospital staff, the only person we ever see with a pager is Zel Todd. He was at the Mater, somewhere.

Enough of chapter twenty-one. I go into the kitchen, get myself a drink of water and a couple of biscuits, turn on the radio. 'Eye of the Tiger'.

Like Sophie said, it's everywhere. It mightn't be getting any action as Frank's fuck song, but it's everywhere. He's singing it, I'm singing it, Zel's singing it.

Zel's singing it, or at least humming it. How has she crossed my mind twice in the one minute? Zel Todd, humming 'Eye of the Tiger'. Zel Todd, pager owner. Coincidence. No, reclassify that as 'ugly coincidence'.

But Frank's Mater story was odd. The more I think about it, the more he seems to have come up with something that couldn't have happened at the hospital. His story doesn't work, and he hasn't been there enough – or studied enough – to make it up convincingly. Over the last few weeks, he's missed at least one whole day and bits of others. I thought that was just him, and maybe it is. He was there for his whole Labour Ward shift. I remember the charge sister talking about him – him and his interest in older women. Which Frank put down to her having an interest in him.

Older women, a big lie about Friday (and a pager involved), a series of absences and none of the usual libido madness that's around when Frank's single.

I tell myself this isn't evidence. It's supposition, with some sketchy circumstantial evidence to help it out. Frank is not having an affair with Zel Todd. That's it said, and the very idea that he might be is insane. In fact, amusing. An affair – the word sounds so out of date but, with Zel married, I guess that's what it'd be. Maybe I should call and tell him Beischer and Mackay's got to me so much that this is how my brain's working today.

Frank and Zel. Ludicrous. Look at how they are when she comes to World of Chickens. Early on she was foul and flirty with him – something Frank would love from just about anyone female, and play up to – lately it's been much more contained. A lot more reasonable. So . . .

So that's exactly how it would be, isn't it? They'd be very careful not to show any signs. Based on how they were before, if they were having an affair, they'd actually be less flirty now. Which is how they are.

The Monday morning Antenatal Clinic is starting to look busy when I divert from my usual walk to our tutorial room from the bus stop. I put on my white coat and badge outside the door, and I go past the desk and past the growing crowd and down to the consultation rooms at the back.

It's ten past eight, and the doctors aren't here yet. I take a look around. There's no sign of any ultrasound equipment.

'Morning,' one of the RNs says. 'I think you're the first one here.'

'I'm actually just meeting someone. I'm with the Friday group, but I'd arranged to meet one of the registrars either here or in Ultrasound this morning. I can't remember which. Is there anywhere down here that he could be doing an ultrasound?'

'No. Ultrasound's on three.'

'So there's no unit here at all? Not even a portable?'

'No. He'll be on three if he said anything about an ultrasound.'

'Thanks. I'd better get up there then. Don't want to miss it.'

So, whatever Frank was doing on Friday, it didn't involve an ultrasound in the clinics. And if he was at the Mater at all, why did he bother making that up? There's nothing that he could have been doing at the Mater on Friday afternoon that he couldn't have told me at the time or, at the latest, that evening. Which suggests he wasn't at the Mater. Which suggests he must have something interesting to hide – a Friday afternoon, somewhere, with only a pager going off in the background and not a chainsaw anywhere nearby.

He turns up to our eight-thirty tutorial a few minutes late, and he sits across the room.

He comes over when it's finished and says, 'Mondays, hate 'em. Do you want to go for coffee?'

'I thought I might take a look in the wards. Why don't we go and drop in on that patient you saw on Friday with polyhydramnios? I've never seen it before and it's a fair bet for the exam.'

'Yeah, um, good idea, but there's probably a lot of other stuff worth looking at too. She wasn't that interesting. And I don't know if I can remember her name. It was a few days ago.'

'Why don't we call the registrar you saw her with?'

'Yeah, right. It was that kind of medium-height guy with the brown hair. Short to medium height. I don't think I'd actually seen him before Friday.'

'And you don't remember his name either, do you?'

'No.'

'Probably couldn't even pick him out of a line-up.' He

says nothing. 'And you don't remember the consultant the patient was admitted under?'

'No. I was concentrating on the polyhydramnios.'

'I hope you've got name tags sewn into your clothes in case you wander. Otherwise who knows where you might end up these Friday afternoons when you think you're in Antenatal Clinic. You could find yourself roaming the outer suburbs of the southside being taken in for cups of tea by kindly middle-aged ladies.'

He looks at me, as if he's waiting for more, waiting for some definitive sign. I'm smiling, like someone who might have made a joke out of nothing, or might not.

'It got busy,' he says. 'I was all over the place here. I think I'm a bit behind, so I was trying to pack a lot in. So I'm not likely to remember the people's names. I was seeing whatever I could, making the most of it. Which is probably what we should do now, like you said. We should go to the wards.'

'Okay. Lead on.'

'I don't think I've been to the fourth floor yet. We might give that a try.'

'Sounds good to me.'

Our ten-thirty session is supposed to go for an hour and a half, but it finishes fifteen minutes early.

'I can't believe you're having lunch with Ron Todd,' Frank says, laughing, when I tell him why I won't be in the dining room. 'You are such a loser. Lunch with Ron Todd.'

'Ron's not such a bad guy. And it's only coffee, anyway. Just a quick cup of coffee, then I'll be back here for lunch.'

'You've got such a middle-of-the-day social life happening all of a sudden. Jacinta on Friday, Ron today. Just don't get talking about politics, that's my advice.'

'I don't think it'll come up. Ron's already got things to talk about, stresses going on in his life, you know? The business, the teeth, maybe even stuff I don't know about. Who knows what I'm going to hear today?'

'Yeah, the business could be doing better. Let me know how that bit of the conversation goes. I'm kind of relying on the job.'

'Okay. I'll tell him he's got to keep it going for your sake. I'm sure that'll do it. The two of you have always been so close, after all.'

'Oh, Ron's okay, I suppose. He just aggravates me sometimes.'

'And you'd be putting that all down to him, wouldn't you? It's not like you'd ever do anything that might add to his stress.'

'No, I wouldn't . . .' It's not said with the usual pure confidence. Pure confidence would have come back at me with an emphatic denial, and not one that tailed off into something uncommonly like doubt.

'So, um, on a different topic, are you getting much use for "Eye of the Tiger" at the moment?'

'Eye of the Tiger?'

'That song gets around, you know. You'd be surprised who I hear humming it.'

He stares at me, gives me a stare that's as impassive as he can manufacture, shrugs his shoulders. 'Really?'

'Yeah. Sophie tells me Zel hums it a lot of the time. And that'd have to make you think, surely. That wouldn't be what you'd want for your fuck song.'

'Yeah, well . . .'

'I wouldn't have thought they'd play it much on whatever Easy Listening format gets a run in her car, but there you go. Don't know where she can have picked it up.

I would have seen her as more your "Sweet Caroline" or "Delilah" fan, or maybe even one of your cheatin'-heart ballad types. I could see her going for that kind of stuff. Couldn't you? All those songs about women and men and reckless affairs with bad consequences . . .'

That's as far as I can push it. It's marginally short of an open accusation. I can backtrack from here if necessary, and I'll just look like I've taken the conversation a little further down Zel's possible play list than I needed to. Perhaps I'm simply telling him his fuck song's not special enough to do the job, if everyone's out there humming it.

Or maybe not. He gives a heavy forced smile. 'Actually, she prefers talkback.'

He confesses.

'Look, I don't know what you know . . .' he says. 'It's not like it's been going on a long time, okay? But, mate, when she . . .'

'I don't think that the details are any of my business, okay?'

I tell him I'd wanted to be wrong, that it was supposed to be a stupid idea that I'd got in my head, and that the plan was for him to deny it and come up with a much better explanation for last Friday. Something frat-house, a nurse in one of the on-call rooms.

'I'd settle for cliché with this one,' I tell him. 'Every time.'

'Come on,' he says. 'Give me a break. It's frat-house enough. With the right interpretation. She's playing the role of the wife of the dean of the college. They always get sexually frustrated and sleep with a student.'

'I can't believe . . .'

'It's not that simple. Obviously.'

'Oh, and because it's complex it's okay?'

It turns out it's been going on for more than two weeks, but probably less than three. It started when Zel said she could find more work for him, if he needed it, and she slipped her pager number into his pocket.

'And I knew,' he says. 'I knew what she was on about. There'd been . . . it was pretty clear there was some kind of interest when she turned up at the World. And, you know, she walks into that place and it changes. You can't deny that lady has an impact when she walks into a room. I hadn't expected . . . anyway, I gave her a call. We only talked the first couple of times.'

'It's okay, you don't have to . . .'

'No, no, I do have to. There's a lot of stuff you don't know. There's a lot of stuff I still don't know, because she doesn't really want to talk about it. But you want to know how it all adds up to me? I'm pretty sure he hasn't had external genitalia since an incident in Vietnam.'

'What? Ron?'

A Merc pulls up at the kerb not far away. The horn sounds. Ron's in the driver's seat, waving to me.

'How can you tell me that when I'm just about to have coffee with the guy?'

'You're not having coffee with his external genitalia. Or is there something you're not telling me?' He gives that hur-hur-hur-hur laugh another go and says, 'If you get a pay rise because of it, remember to tell him it has to apply to both of us.'

'You . . . I don't believe you sometimes.' That's all I can say, and it sounds weak. Ron hits the horn again, in case I haven't seen him. 'We'll talk later.'

My head's spinning on the way to the car, and it keeps spinning all the way into town.

'Mate, I've done it,' Ron says. 'I've booked myself in

for the extractions tomorrow afternoon. So instead of coffee we're going to a flash place in town for a bite on me. Lunch at Michael's.'

'Good. That's good . . . I mean, that'll be great. A big improvement on the hospital dining room.'

'Well, it's practically my last meal with my own choppers, you know? Fourth last, actually. So I'm trying to make the most of them.'

That's how it begins, and we talk teeth most of the way into town, Ron working on a stoicism that I think he's been practising, me offering one generic piece of reassurance after another. 'You'll probably be a lot better off when they're gone.' Etcetera.

But it's still the Frank stuff that's playing through in my head, though it now really has become Frank and Zel stuff. To think I was worried about the vigour of my pursuit. He didn't even try to deny it. He actually tried to justify it. I wasn't ready for that, not even from Frank. And Ron . . . I look straight ahead. If Ron has problems we're to talk about over lunch, they're to do with teeth and business. Not war wounds.

How did I get to be in this car, anyway? How am I in this Merc on a uni day, looping off the freeway and into Margaret Street, lunching in town at Michael's with the husband of Frank's older woman? Why did I chase Frank about it? Why did I choose ten minutes ago to remove all doubt? Why am I not in the hospital dining room right now with a plateful of subsidised ravioli in front of me, complaining about all the usual things?

I've never been to Michael's. I've only heard about it or, actually, read about it. I don't know anyone who's been here, so there's no-one to hear things from. We go up a burgundy carpeted staircase, and there's a man in a dinner suit waiting for us at the top, holding menus.

'Mister Todd,' he says when Ron identifies himself. 'Of course. Please come this way.'

And maybe he's just doing his job, pretending to remember Ron, but maybe he's not. The lighting is low in here. It's all dark wood and richly patterned upholstery and almost-noiseless carpeted footsteps, with a small candle set in the middle of each stiff white linen tablecloth.

'Let's eat,' Ron says, folding back his menu and scouring the entree page.

When my family goes out to eat, it's most often at a Bonanza steakhouse, but my father says that's because it combines good service and good value. On rare special occasions, we've gone to a suburban restaurant of the à-la-carte variety. We've never been anywhere quite like here. There's too much French on this menu. Possibly even creatures that I don't know.

'What are you thinking?' he says. 'Remember, we're here to eat up big.'

'Um, I don't know yet . . .' What am I thinking? I'm thinking that if I could go for a couple of serves of garlic bread and take the balance in cash, I'd practically have my half of the video-camera money.

'No. It's a bugger of a choice at this place,' he says, misreading what the menu's doing to my head. 'You could do worse than open with the lobster bisque. If you want to know what I'm thinking.'

'Sounds good.'

Ron, somehow, is still able to be Ron in here, while I can't stop wondering if I'm sitting up straight enough.

He closes his menu and says, 'Done,' and he asks about my day.

I find myself burbling about some fictitious woman with acute polyhydramnios. I go on and on, staring at the candle and then at the pattern woven into the table cloth, talking about how they're thinking of getting a portable ultrasound for the clinics area, but they don't have one yet, about the way people sometimes get acute and chronic polyhydramnios confused and that could really cost them in the exam. Burble, burble. All the time thinking Frank's getting it on with Zel. This place spins me out. You might not have external genitalia. This was supposed to be coffee.

He listens intently, like someone with a deep but unsatisfied urge to unravel a parable. And I want to say to him, don't be absurd, it's not a parable, it means nothing but I have to keep going because if I talk about polyhydramnios I won't tell you Frank's having an affair with Zel. An affair — it's such a stupidly deceitful grown-up 'Days of Our Lives' kind of idea.

I like life so much better when Frank is sleeping with young single women I don't much care for.

But what about you, Ron, I'm thinking. That's what we're here for. Open-ended question, open-ended question. So, how are you feeling about the teeth? It shouldn't be as bad as getting your genitals blown off. Or Frank doing the wild thing with the missus.

'How did you get your start in business?'

That's the question I go for, and it's a glorious choice. It compels Ron to bore me and bore me, and I couldn't be happier. I knew he had it in him, and it's just like the back room at the World again, pre-affair, pre-all this.

He orders lobster bisque for two with pepper steak to follow, and a bottle of Queen Adelaide riesling. And he tells me about his life. The self-making of the man who is Ron Todd, from passing the public-service exam at fifteen, to his mission of progressive betterment. He tells me how he really thought self-help books would have helped him more. How some days he thinks he's ended up winning only a couple of friends and influencing practically no-one. And is that enough? Is that enough to have done in the world?

'I've only mastered two of the seven habits of highly effective people,' he says. 'Imagine what I could do with, say, four of them . . .' And on he goes, roaming from one topic to another, grazing at each before moving on, talking and talking but proving very hard to listen to. 'You'd be surprised at the prospects I had before 'Nam . . . Mowers? Mate, I could tell you a thing or two about mowers . . . I wanted that Merc and I wanted it bad. There have been a few ups and downs, but I've got no regrets. You can't afford to live with regrets in this life.'

The bisque bowls go, the mains come, he pours me a second glass of riesling.

'Mate, World of Chickens,' he says, and shakes his head. 'Some days I don't know if I've got the guts for this. I don't know if I've got the balls. I don't know what's going to happen. I don't know if throwing money at it'll get us out of the hole or not. We really need to freshen the place up, but I can't even afford new signs.'

Signs, I tell myself. Think signs. Don't think balls. 'New signs could be good. Maybe we could do a few things without it costing a lot. I don't know. Maybe there's a bit we can do ourselves. It should work, the place should work. I keep thinking it should. It's just got to build from a much lower base than you thought.'

'Yeah, that's it, isn't it? I've got to keep telling myself that. The problem's not with the World. Max's Snax wasn't all it was cracked up to be. We've got prime position, we've got a good product, we've got no direct competitors, we've got a top-notch hygiene record, we've got a big bloody chicken out front. Yeah. We're doing a lot right. We're doing a lot right, aren't we?'

'Yes, we are. We're doing all those things right. They're not the problem, so changing them's not the answer. We've got the chicken side covered. We just need to be selling more. It's about vision. That's what Sophie said to me a while back. And you had the vision to put a chicken on the street, and we've now got to tap back into that vision and get creative again.'

'To us,' he says, and raises his riesling glass. 'To the World. To chickens on the streets.' We clink our glasses together, and he takes a mouthful. 'To the finer things. How's that pepper steak going?'

'Couldn't be better.'

'Mine too. Steak.' He shakes his head. 'It's the last time these teeth'll get to deal with a steak.'

'Yeah, but if you kept the teeth they wouldn't be able to deal with steak for a lot longer, anyway. You'll get things fixed up. You'll be surprised how much better it gets.'

'Yeah. Another thing I've got to keep telling myself, hey? We'll push through, I guess. Solid stuff'll be off the agenda for a while till the mouth settles down, I suppose, but we'll push through.'

'There are plenty of things to do that don't involve eating. Like, movies.'

'Yeah, good idea. Great idea.' From nowhere, enthusiasm. That wasn't . . . 'We should take in a movie some time.'

'Um, yeah . . .'

'Oh, don't worry, I'll see you right. We could call it some kind of consultancy fee. Your time's money.'

'That's very . . .'

'Unnecessary? Not at all. It's how it's going to be. You're a student. Students are always needing money. I've got one at home, remember. You, me and the movies – I'm looking forward to it already.'

'Yeah. Me too.'

'You're going to be picking them, by the way. That's part of the adventure for me. I've tended to give a lot of my attention to musicals and it's about time I developed an interest in serious motion pictures. I mean, you've got to love *Grease*, which might have been the last movie I saw, but you can narrow your scope unnecessarily. Sophie tells me that film-making – you know, the actual making of films – is a big interest of yours, so it'll be good to get your take on things when we watch them together.'

I'm late back to the Mater and I sneak in to the ultrasound tute, full of three gourmet courses and smelling of riesling. The lights are down so that we can see the swirly moonscape images on the monitor, and every so often over the next hour my chin bounces onto my chest and wakes me. As far as I know, I manage not to snore.

The others go off in the direction of the wards afterwards and I tell Frank it'd be a good time for that coffee he mentioned earlier.

We don't get coffee. There are people in the kiosk and the coffee's always awful there. We sit on a bench in a nearby small square of garden, and the loosened corner of a memorial plaque catches on my sleeve. I've eaten too much, had too much to drink. My head's fuzzy. I'm not ready for this, but I already wasn't ready.

'So, go on,' I tell him, wondering where the hell it's supposed to take us.

'Look, it's just one of those things.'

'I don't know what those things are. And I thought neither did you.'

'Zel has needs,' he says. 'It's not like it could have

happened otherwise. And Ron's got problems, remember? That 'Nam stuff, or whatever. There's also his attitude. She's a great woman, and he's totally neglecting her. That was obvious from the start.'

'What do you mean? How much time have you spent with these people?'

'You can tell. Particularly once you know.'

'What made you think . . .'

'I didn't do all the thinking, remember. I might have picked her up on my radar, but she noticed me, too. And she made the move.'

'And, like your Dad says, you're such a beaut young climber, Frankie. It's a bloody tragedy to waste a skill like that.'

'Fuck . . . Look, what's it to you, anyway? Just because you were off having lunch with your mate Mister No Nuts. Since when are you the moral guardian of the World? Or is that part of your new job description as a pay-off for all that brown-nosing? I might have to take you aside for a talking to, if you and Ron take things any further. Who knows what the two of you'll be doing next? And is that wine I smell or are you going to tell me you've been grappling with a difficult case of acute polyhydramnios?'

'He took me to Michael's. The restaurant. The one up the back of the clinics, next to the portable ultrasound. He wanted to have three courses and something to drink. He's having all his teeth out tomorrow. It was his fourth last meal with his own teeth, and he happens to want to make the most of them all.'

'For his teeth you get lunch at Michael's? And what? For a gall bladder you'd root him?'

'I think it's just that he doesn't have a lot of friends. And we'd agreed last week to have coffee today anyway, to talk about a few things.'

'Next he's going to be . . .'

'Don't say taking me to the movies. Because there's nothing wrong with going to a movie occasionally. But this is about you and Zel, so don't try to drag it off somewhere else. It's about you and Zel. And what I'm saying is: does she ever take you to Michael's? Because watch out, it's our turf.'

He laughs. 'We tend to stay at her place more. We eat in. But don't think she's cheap. She does slip me a twenty now and then.'

'She slips you a twenty?' I'm now laughing at his joke, except . . . except a couple of things. First, it wasn't so long ago that Ron told me he'd pay me to go to the movies with him. Second, it appears that it's not a joke.

'Yeah for, like, offering it up. Twenty bucks. And you should be able to open any bloody dictionary in the land and find that as the definition of a win–win situation.'

'There's a name for that job, though. You're aware of that? I can see it now, the next enterprise, Zel Todd's World of Boys.'

'It's a gift. It's appreciation. And there's nothing wrong with being appreciated.'

'It's twenty dollars. It sounds like it's a set fee. It's hooker money. You know what you're getting into now, don't you? Don't try to tell me this doesn't have bad telemovie written all over it. You've gone from frat-party comedy and ended up somewhere next to the policewoman-centrefold genre.'

'And what a conflicted genre it is,' he says. 'They always shoot them to go straight to TV, so you never get to see the hot stuff anyway. Just bubbles and meaningful looks and shit. Side-on nork occasionally.'

'And you, you my friend, are the policewoman centrefold. You're the schoolteacher stripper. You're the med-student hooker.'

'Come on, they're just a user-pays kind of family. That's all. It's how she shows she's happy. There's no harm in it. And, anyway, they're loaded. They've got heaps of cash, even if Ron is whingeing about the World.'

'Right, so this is political now? A kind of redistribution of wealth? You're some kind of sexual Robin Hood?'

'That's not how it works. She's a very sophisticated woman. You don't . . .' He shakes his head, as though I'm annoying him. Me and my lack of sophistication. 'I always knew I was the kind of guy who'd have an older woman phase.'

'How do you get to know that?'

'It's been apparent for weeks. And she's pretty stylish, you've got admit it. She might even be about to start a column on style for their suburban newspaper. Style File, she's going to call it. Except she doesn't know whether it should be Stile File with Is, or Style Fyle with Ys.'

'Well, stile with an I is a means of getting over a fence. A couple of bits of wood.'

'There you go then. Y it is.'

'Isn't rhyme enough? Don't the two of you know when to stop?'

'Hey, how's this for cool – Style Fyle cool – sometimes, if she sees a white top she really likes, she'll buy two of them, but she'll change the buttons on one so that it works for a different set of occasions.'

15

Some days I think there's a whole world in Frank's head to which I don't have a visa. And it's a place med students could go to do psych on their electives, but they might never come back.

I give up running a morals argument, since it doesn't counter much of Frank's reasoning, anyway. I tell him about the Todds – the important parts of how I see them – and at least he listens, but I don't think it'll change much. Not immediately. They're a family, that's the thing. He's messing with a family now. It's not one of those times when he inserts himself into someone else's month-long relationship, figuring that if it breaks up that's where it was heading anyway.

Maybe there are some problems between Ron and Zel. Maybe that's how Ron ends up talking to me. Or maybe there aren't any of the problems Frank thinks there are, and there's a lot of Ron invested in his self-made-man status. He doesn't want the World to let him down, he doesn't want to be toothless. He wants to keep Zel in her endless wardrobe of white clothes and her gold jewellery and her tan so deep it looks like it took medical intervention rather than mere sun exposure. He wants to keep Sophie admiring him the way she does, and wanting to be a success in business because he is. He doesn't say that, and he doesn't need to.

I don't quite know how I end up being a part of it, but someone has to be on his side right now. And the food's not bad. I shouldn't have mentioned Michael's to Frank. It's the best restaurant I've ever been to – the only restaurant like that I've ever been to, and maybe the best in town. I decide not to tell him about the brush that was brought over to sweep the table between courses, or the prices, or any of the other mad fanciness of the place. Frank'd love all that. I think it's the lure of proximity to that kind of life that might be partly what draws him to Zel. Something must.

The other reason I don't tell him too many details about lunch is because I watched Ron put his teeth into their last pepper steak, and it only made me realise that the problems won't be fixed by a place like Michael's. Not the teeth, not anything else. All the money spent today hardly bought him a diversion. And, since money's one of the problems, I understand today's spending of it even less. I felt guilty about eating, matching him course for course all the way to the profiteroles, but there's no doubt that it's what I was expected to do.

So instead of telling Frank what Ron spent to buy his teeth their second-last lunch, I tell him he should be fairer to that family. But he doesn't see that he's being unfair. He doesn't see that fairness has anything to do with it.

If this gets out, Ron will fall apart. That's my prediction. Ron will fall apart, Zel might openly be with Frank until that falls apart, World of Chickens will fall apart and I can't imagine how Sophie would struggle through it all.

But that doesn't occur to me until later, when I'm in my bedroom in the dark. Lying here, not sleeping, having eaten far too much today. Lying here, being quietly angry with Frank for saying things like: 'Look, it's not such a big issue. Shit like this happens all the time.'

Low moonlight comes in through the window and glints from the black plastic underside of a Wellington bomber on a night raid to Bremen. Clearly, my mission has at least two objectives, and must remain covert. Ron is freaking out about the teeth, and it's up to me to give him some support. At the same time, I have to work on Frank. I have to chisel away at his affair with Zel until he sees it's not right, and ends it. I am the moral guardian of the World after all, dammit.

First, Ron. I go to the pay phone in the kiosk at lunchtime on Tuesday and I give him a call to wish him luck with the teeth. It doesn't go so well.

I tell him if he keeps breathing like that he should sit down and put his head between his knees. He writes that on a piece of paper as a two-step process. He asks if he can have a contact number in case of emergencies and I tell him I'll be home by four-thirty.

At four twenty-eight I'm walking in the door and my mother's on the phone. She's scribbling something on a piece of paper. An address, other details.

'Hold on a moment,' she says. 'He's here now.' She puts her hand over the mouthpiece. 'Mister Todd. Not so good after his dental procedure. This is the receptionist I'm talking to. They're wondering if you could catch a cab into town and drive him home in his car. He says he'll pay for the cab there, and the cab home later, after dinner. Is that . . . ?'

'That's fine.'

'Fine? Really?'

'Yeah.'

She lifts her hand and says, 'Tell Mister Todd he's on his way . . . Yes . . . Yes. Thank you.' She nods at the phone, and hangs up. 'Philby . . .'

'Sorry. I should have told you this might happen. Ron's having a full dental clearance today. He's going to end up with dentures. He's been having a lot of problems with his teeth.'

'And you're . . . he's calling you?'

'I said he could call if he needed any help. It seemed to be a pretty foul thing to be going through, that's all.'

'Oh. Well, that's . . . very nice of you.'

'Don't look so surprised. I can be nice sometimes.'

She offers me a lift but I tell her it's okay, we'll stick with the plan. There's no need for her to put herself out.

My mother has a nose for a story, and I have to keep this one from her. I can't let her lure me into her car for twenty minutes, and then crack under questioning and tell her I'm putting in an effort with Ron because Frank's sleeping with Zel. It's the people with story noses who are the worst with secrets, and I have to take the no-risk position on this one.

In the cab on the way to the city, I know I'm right.

When I get to the dentist, Ron's lying across three seats in the waiting room with a towel on his face. The receptionist says, 'Mister Todd,' and he sits bolt upright, like a vampire from his coffin in an old silent movie. The lazy dribble of blood from the corner of his mouth doesn't help. She dabs it away with a tissue, and he blinks his heavy-lidded eyes at her, not sure what's going on.

'Numb,' he says on the way to the car, squeezing his mouth. He slumps into the passenger seat and struggles distractedly with the seatbelt until I sort it out. His lips move, he's working at saying something. In the end he gets there, precisely and slowly. 'I've been very heavily medicated.'

Then his head swings to the side and clunks against the window, and I don't hear much more from him.

'Anything I should know before I drive the car?' No response. 'Any tricks? I've never driven a Merc before.'

There's a loud spluttery snoring noise and he half lifts his head, quarter opens his eyes and says something that sounds like 'incoming' and clunks his head against the window again. From then on, it's up to me. I check mirrors, I check the seat position, I check where everything is. I do all the checking I possibly can and then there's nothing to do but drive. Ron slips into fidgety drug-addled flashback dreams beside me as we pull out of the parking station and into the evening traffic.

The Merc, it turns out, isn't hard to handle.

'So, Ron, are you up to giving me directions?'

Apparently not.

At the first red light, I take a look in the glove box and find registration papers with his address, and a street directory which I open in his lap. I wedge his fingers around the edges to hold it to the right page, and I discover that there's a special passenger-seat lap light for navigating. That's the kind of car this is.

The traffic moves slowly, bumper-to-bumper as we make our way to George Street. There are tapes in the glove box too, and – having never been a big Mantovani or Herb Alpert fan – I go for The Animals, some kind of 'best of' album. I push the tape in, turn the volume up a little and wind my window down. From outside this must look like me and my coma buddy on a road trip. At the very least, it's my turn for a scene from a frat-house comedy, so I decide to play it the way any reasonable free-spirited frat-houser would and I'm singing along to 'We Gotta Get Out of This Place' as the Merc cruises down the freeway and the wind blows into my face.

In your hands, the Merc positively glides around the freeway's curves. Night sets in. You glimpse the city, the light-stacks of its buildings, in the rear-view mirror. Sometimes you take lunch there, three courses with bottled wine.

Sometimes it's you and the Merc and this endless open road. You wonder what drugs your coma buddy is on, what he could possibly have taken that could shut his brain down so completely. When you laugh, he can't even hear you. When you sing to the music, you sing well. Where would the road take you if you were not to leave it now? What is there, past the lights of the suburbs? Where does the world begin? Somewhere, probably, beyond Mount Gravatt.

In my psych term, I would have called this denial. The meeting at the Rec Club last Friday week was a lesson about keeping the parts of my life separate. Soon tonight it'll be me and all the Todds at once – three of my worlds colliding. My drugged-out toothless new pal Ron, my back-stairs chicken-sharer friend Sophie and the white-clad Zel with the dark secret she doesn't even know I know. Carindale, though it's quite a way out of the city, arrives long before I'm ready for it.

Ron stirs as we turn off the main road and into the recently-planned winding streets with their very English names and oversized brick houses.

'Number seventeen,' he says, pointing to a nearby chateau. 'That one over there.'

We park in the driveway, and the front door opens. Zel's hair volume is silhouetted by the hall light in a very 'Charlie's Angels'-at-fifty way and her harem pants are back-lit like the Lady Di kindergarten shot. I don't even notice at first that Sophie's following her out.

'Oh, you poor thing,' Zel says to Ron as he clambers out of the car. 'I've got a big packet of Kool Pops like you asked me to. Now, come on in.' She takes his arm, and then half turns to me. 'Thanks so much for driving him home, Philip. Sophie, why don't you give Philip a tour of the house while I get your father settled.'

'Hasn't he been here before?'

'I don't think so. When would he have been here before? You haven't, have you, Philip.'

'No. Hi Sophie.'

'Don't forget downstairs, Soph,' Ron mumbles as he's led away. 'He'll want to see it.'

'Sorry about this,' Sophie says. 'But it's my job. Everyone gets the tour. It used to be a display home. It was one of the first houses in this bit of Carindale.'

Sophie, here in bright light and in her own home, isn't the same as she is out the back of World of Chickens. She's more subdued, and she sticks to the script most of the time. It's odd for both of us, walking through these rooms. Things feel much more normal at the top of the back steps of the World, between the storeroom and the train line. Much more normal when one of us is dressed like a chicken, peering out of a beak to do poetry or speculate about whatever comes to mind.

The house is everything it should be – sunken lounge, exposed beams painted mission brown, a feature wall. Why is it that the 'feature' aspect of feature walls never seems to amount to more than a simple absence of plaster? If anyone doubts how smart decorators are, they should talk to the person who came up with that concept.

The place has been built only a few years, and Sophie says, 'Mum's still pretty houseproud,' as an explanation for the plastic runners marking out where it's okay to walk across the shag-pile carpet. 'Of course, she does have a couple of toy poodles that shit on the carpet more than you'd expect, but humans don't get to walk on it. Figure that out.'

'See? Life even has mysteries in your own home.'

Zel, as Frank said yesterday, is 'a true lady of the Dale'. I'd hoped it was sarcasm, but why would it have been? Zel and her home are ready and waiting for *Vogue Living* to ring the chimes at the front door, and it'd seem very unfair if she was left doing nothing more than dispensing a few hundred words of advice a week as the writer of a southside suburban paper's style file (sorry, Style Fyle).

Sophie saves downstairs till last, and it's everything in a room that my parents would never understand – the wet bar with jokey bottle openers and souvenir cork coasters from Tweed Heads, the tall Galliano bottle on a stand, a king's head dartboard (featuring Henry VIII), a series of dogs-playing-pool pictures. She tells me that Ron knows the pictures aren't quite a substitute for a table, but it came down to a question of size.

'It'd be a squeeze even for a six-by-three,' she says. 'This'd be their dream home, if this room was as big as Dad had wanted. But that's rock back there, so they didn't go any further. It's his territory down here, in case you hadn't guessed. It's Party Central when the Mowers crowd comes over.' Two poodles run out from behind the bar and start jumping around her ankles. 'And, to finish the tour, welcome to the world's worst-behaved dogs.'

The dogs yelp and scratch and bite at the heels of her shoes. She says 'sit', several times and firmly, but it's not a word or a tone that they recognise. She tells me she wanted to called them Ralph and Malph, but they were a present from her father to her mother so they ended up being Beau and Hope. She'd suggested Mork and Mindy as a compromise, but Zel hadn't gone for it.

'Dinner's ready you two,' Zel calls from upstairs.

Ron is sitting at the table when we get there, and he's still managing to look like a propped-up dead guy.

'Mate,' he says, with a friendly wink to show that he's picking up.

When he talks, we all try very hard not to look at his mouth and to pretend we can understand what he's saying. Zel serves a casserole, which she'd hoped would be soft enough for Ron but it doesn't work out that way. Ron dines only on Kool Pops and moselle. Quite a lot of moselle, and he rapidly becomes even less coherent. He starts rambling in a way that seems to be advice, mainly to me, or perhaps gratitude. Advice, winking, grinning, slurping at the moselle that's slopping from the still-numb right side of his mouth. He sidesteps whatever he's saying, moves into an analogy involving cattle on a hillside, moves somewhere else and gets lost in a conversation he's never been to before.

'Dad,' Sophie says. 'You're home now. You could take it easy. You've had a big day.'

Ron pulls himself to his feet, calling out, 'Speech, speech,' and tapping his eyeball with his fork to get attention.

'Dad,' Sophie says sharply. 'Hit the glass one, not the good one.'

He blinks, and gives his eye a rub. It starts to water.

'Sorry,' Sophie says to me. 'He does that. It's like tapping on a glass, you know? Usually he . . . it doesn't matter.'

'Hits the other one?'

'Yep.'

'He's a good lad, this one,' Ron begins. 'A good lad when a fellow's down. Like Atlas, with the weight of . . . history . . . repeating, repeating. Get it? And there's the matter of . . . teeth . . . more on that . . .' The pharmacology of moselle and medication and the chemistry of stress sweep across his brain like the waves of an incoming tide. He sits down, but still thinks he has the floor. 'And you,' he says, 'my ladies . . . thick and thin, richer poorer . . . sickness teeth . . . well done all of you. Bloody well done.'

He starts to become tearful, but then falls asleep in his

chair, the tip of his Kool-Pop-blue tongue slipping out of his mouth as his head lolls forward.

There's no unravelling that, I decide later in the cab on the way home. But the teeth are gone now, and that's progress. Next, we have to make World of Chickens work, and I'm not sure how we're going to do that. And I have to pass obstetrics. It's lucky that Jacinta and I discovered those political differences, or I'd never get any study done.

For the moment, Frank and I settle on something that could be described as an uneasy truce. I've told him what I think, I haven't backed down and he hasn't said what he's going to do. It's his idea that we go back to my place between our Wednesday early finish and our shift at World of Chickens.

'We could take a look at antepartum haemorrhage,' he says. 'That'd be good.'

I assume he means we'll be talking about bigger issues but, Frank being Frank, it turns out there's no code involved and it really is obstetrics he wants to look at.

We sit at the kitchen table with Beischer and Mackay, my notes, two cups of tea and Frank's half-baked ideas. We start to draw up lists of clinical features associated with particular causes of antepartum haemorrhage. Frank gets bored and develops an unhelpful liking for the term 'Couvelaire uterus' instead. He plays around with a biscuit until it starts to crumble on the table. He slurps his tea and hums. I can't believe there's any room in his life for this kind of boredom at the moment.

He experiments with the word 'Couvelaire' in an accent he probably thinks is French, and the list we draw up of clinical features is just about all mine. I tell him he won't get far, throwing names around with abandon because they sound good, and we have an argument about it.

'Well, we're going to have to agree to disagree,' he says eventually.

'That depends on how much you want to pass.'

'What's that about? Ever since surgery . . .'

'It's not about surgery.'

We move on, to the degrees of placenta praevia and their implications.

Ron Todd calls before we're too far into it, before we've found anything new to fight about. My mother hands me the phone and the first thing he says is, 'Mate, you champion. Couldn't have done it without you yesterday.'

'No problem.'

'The old mouth feels a bit funny today – a bit bloody roomy – but we'll get there.'

'Yeah.'

'Listen, I've been thinking. It's like you said. It's not about chickens. We've got that covered. It's about buzz. It's about the customers feeling attached, like they belong. It's about love.'

'It's about love?'

My mother looks up from her book.

'That's right, mate, we want them to love the World.'

'Okay, well, we'll work on it.'

And that undertaking – nebulous as it is – seems enough for now. Sometimes I get lucky.

'Just thought I'd put it to you,' he says. 'Just that one big broad brush stroke. We can get to the details later.'

And then he's gone, a busy man in pursuit of something about love.

My mother's still looking at me over her reading glasses. She's never good when she hears half a conversation. I knew I was right to let her know nothing about what's going on.

'It's just work,' I tell her, and she maintains her look of unease.

She lifts her book up again and goes back to reading. 'Me too,' she says, as if she's got plenty of stories she's not telling. 'Just starting work on a new module for next semester.'

A train pulls into Taringa station on its way into town. Sophie flaps a wing at the passengers, but they never see us up here in the half-dark. The carriages are too bright. It's physics again, but I don't go Bernoulli on her with the detail so she still waves sometimes.

'Your mother,' she says. 'She's working me hard.'

'Are you doing her thing next semester too?'

'The rise of the tabloid, or whatever?'

'No, the thing about adolescence – adolescents in the media.'

'I haven't heard of that one.'

'She was reading books for it at home before we came here. *Your Child in Trouble*, that kind of thing. About adolescence and how the media portrays it, and the new set of problems that creates.'

'What? Why don't I ever get told? I was sure it was something to do with tabloids. I've put my name down for it already.' I can see her eyes in there, deep in the beak, imploring me to take my mother aside and talk some sense into her. 'This is too hard. I'm going crazy.'

'It's next semester. Don't worry about it. It's nearly two months away.'

'Why is nothing normal any more?'

'Um, I didn't mean . . .'

'No. It's okay.'

'It doesn't sound like it's okay.'

She leans on the railing and the big chicken head slumps down. 'Did you think last night at my place was normal?'

'Well, that downstairs bar . . . was fine, obviously. But your father had just had his teeth taken out. There was medication involved. He wasn't going to be at his best.'

'Yeah, it's more than that. I don't know though. I don't know what. There's this place here. He's pretty keyed up about it, turning it into something.'

'And it's a great opportunity, but that doesn't mean it's all easy. But given some time . . .'

'Yeah. He's big on family as well, though. He's been big on family lately. You know what I think? Just between you and me?' She turns to face me again. 'I think he might want another baby while mum still has time.'

'What? I didn't think that'd be possible after the incident in 'Nam.' Okay, big trouble. She's caught me completely by surprise, and I've blown it badly.

'What? He was just a clerk in the Defence Department in Canberra.'

'I think I've misunderstood something. A couple of things. He said I'd be surprised at the prospects he had before 'Nam. There was an idea I got that something had gone badly wrong there.'

'Oh, right. No, that's not it. He had no prospects before 'Nam. That's what he means. You'd be surprised because of what he's made of himself since. They worked some pretty awesome hours back then, you know. So the overtime he got paid was what let him get started in business. And he got to put through the paperwork to get himself a medal. They all did, his unit at work at the Defence Department, the four of them. P Force, they called themselves. The 'P' was for the paperwork. But don't tell anyone. He's pretty proud of what he did in the 'Nam campaign. It wasn't easy over there, remember? And they got a really bad time when they came home. P Force stood by its own when not a lot of people were there for them. And Dad might not have been part of the actual Vietnamese end, but he copped the stigma pretty much full on. There was a long time when it wasn't easy being a Vietnam veteran, and that's only starting to change now.'

'But what about his glass eye and his hip problem?'

'I think the eye got put out by a stick when he was a kid. He was giving some other kid in the neighbourhood the shits. And the hip was something to do with an inter-departmental touch-football match in the public service. He fell over. He's well into his forties you know. He's taken a few knocks. Anyway, why would his eye and his hip get in the way of having another baby?'

'Well, they wouldn't, obviously. It's just the way it all added up. Or, really, the way rumours circulate. I think it was something one of the Mowers people said when they were doing shifts here early on. You know, if there's a glass eye, it gets talked about. And if it's the guy who owns the place, and he's got a Vietnam medal and a limp as well, the story gets a lot more interesting and gets totally blown out of proportion.'

'Really? That's what they said? They said my Dad's damaged down there? That's just the kind of bullshit they'd come out with. Those Mowers people really piss me off.'

This only gets harder. I took it to the brink of calamity, perhaps over the brink, and somehow I might have pulled it back. And what am I left with? More secrets. Sophie's baby theory, the real story of Ron's Vietnam non-service, my lie about the talk circulating in the Mowers crowd concerning his external genitalia. Only the lie seems really plausible, and it's the part I definitely made up.

I'm outside, being a really distracted chicken while I think it through. Does Ron want a baby, or is that just a theory? Where did the genital story begin? Is it Zel's? Is it Frank's? Did it start as a misunderstanding between Zel and Frank? A misunderstanding between Frank and me? What did he actually say?

It's not as though I can fix it tonight. I can't raise it with Frank in the car later, tell him I ran the idea past Sophie and she seemed to think Ron's intact in the pants and what does he have to say about that? I've talked too much already. I'm going to listen. I'm going to be much more careful. I fixed it with Sophie this time, but only just.

Zel's there when I turn to look back inside. Zel, Frank and Sophie are talking at the counter. I'm fearful that, even through the glass, I'll see it all fall apart. There'll be a revelation that I can't hear – Zel or Frank will slip up and something will come out – Sophie will realise and everything will collapse. I go in a few minutes early, determined to make it as normal as possible and to steer us clear of risk for now.

'Hello, Philip,' Zel says. 'It is Philip in there, isn't it?'

'Who else would it be?' Sophie says, in a tone that could be more friendly. But she's lifting buckets of coleslaw, so perhaps it's the effort.

'Philip was wonderful last night you know, Frank. Ron had a shocking experience at the dentist and Philip thought nothing of catching a cab into town and driving him home.'

The strange week I'm having, in one move from Zel, gets stranger. She's trying to treat us all normally, I'm trying to treat her normally, Frank's pretending to be taciturn – his version of a low-risk approach to group conversation – and I'm pretending not to notice. I'm hiding in the costume like some kid peeping out at a badly behaved grown-up world, trying to remember how I'd handle this back in the old days. Back last week.

'Now, you're not on on Friday, are you?' Zel says, apparently to all three of us. 'I don't think you are because I've checked the roster. Are you boys free?'

'Free? On Friday?' Frank's still working on taciturn, so the question's left to me. 'You want us to work?'

'No, no, something quite different. Anyway, you two, you're always working, here or at that hospital. This is Friday night I'm talking about. A bit of a jaunt.'

She looks at Frank, looks back at me. I'm not sure what to say. The sentence 'Are you completely insane?' comes to mind as a good starting point, though. Instead, I try to hide a little deeper in the costume. That superhero power of invisibility? I could really use it now. Also the superhero power of being at home in my room with the door shut. I often think that one's highly underrated.

'You're probably aware that I'm on some committees,' Zel's saying, like a woman whose abundant leisure time is known to be spent importantly. 'There's a fundraiser on Friday for the Little Kings' Movement for the Handicapped. I took a few tickets weeks ago and Ron's still resting up after his dental work. So I thought, the four of us . . .'

'Like, you and me . . .' Sophie's trying to come to grips with the suggestion . . . 'and him and him?'

'Count 'em, babe,' Frank says. 'That'd be four.'

'But it won't just be the four of us. There'll be lots of people. You can bring guests if you'd like. We can get more tickets. It's a boat cruise. A late afternoon and early evening cruise up the river to look at the bats. Quite novel. They take you up to the bat islands just as they're waking up, and you get to feed them. Apparently there are thousands of them, hundreds of thousands. It could be a bit of fun,

I thought. And it's for a good cause, of course. Plus, wine and cheese.'

'Um, sounds good.' It sounds ridiculous but she's looking right at me again and what else can I say? Another reason to wish things had stayed the way they were – she never once felt the need to look my way before she started sleeping with Frank. 'I should probably check something though – it's not on the *Paradise*, is it?'

'I don't think so. Why?'

'No reason.'

'Girl trouble,' Frank says. 'He put a bit too much effort into entertaining the passengers last time, or so they say.'

'Thanks, Frank.' I preferred him silent. 'Sophie and I have to change, I think. Friday would be great thanks, Zel, but we should keep moving now. We've got to get a chicken out to that road.'

I walk past her to the back door, and cop another compliment on the way. I'm glad to get outside.

'Okay,' Sophie says as she's unzipping me, 'what happened on the *Paradise*?'

'Oh, nothing. Weeks ago, when we were working on the bar there, one of the passengers got pretty sick and I helped out. Frank's got these wild ideas. You know Frank.'

We go through the changeover briskly, since I've made an issue of getting a chicken back out to the road. But it doesn't seem like much of a night for poetry, anyway. With Zel around, the atmosphere's different. Maybe it was different already. It doesn't feel the same for me, working here and knowing some of what's happening behind the scenes. I'm on edge now, all the time thinking that Frank will let something slip.

Zel leaves once we've changed. Some customers have turned up, enough that Frank goes, 'Hey, is that line of people the thing they call a queue?' when we're tossing chicken breasts onto the hotplate. We sell a whole chicken, two half-chicken dinner deals and five burgers before the store is empty again. We even have to make two people wait for fries, since we can't fit enough in the oil at once.

'Phew,' he says when it's just the two of us. 'Wouldn't want it to get like that too often.'

'I think we're safe enough.'

'Yeah, back to normal now.'

'Normal? Two words – bat cruise.'

He shrugs. 'Buggered if I know. It wasn't my idea. She thinks you're a good guy. She thought the four of us could have a good night.'

'Are you mad? What kind of a foursome . . .'

'Hold on. There might be more. There might be Clinton, there might be Mowers people. Who knows? She said it's a work thing. She gets a bunch of tickets to events all the time, and takes work people. Her and Ron and a few other people. Different people each time. Share it around, you know? It's the corporate world. It's how it works. She's connected.'

'It's a bat cruise. It's Friday night, and it's a charity bat cruise for sick kids.'

'Yeah, right, this time it's a bat cruise, but it could be anything.'

'You mean we could be going head-to-head for fanciest hat at some racecourse on Melbourne Cup day?'

'Exactly, and with that head of yours I'd be worried.'

'At least it's raising money for something, I suppose. And it's not darts in their downstairs bar.'

He laughs. 'I've never seen that part of the house.'

He straightens up the tomato slices with his tongs and the laugh stays on as one of his bad-boy smirks, but I won't be provoked. He sets the tongs down and walks over to the hotplate and starts scraping.

I tidy up some fallen coleslaw and I tell him, 'You make a hell of a mess when you cook things, you know.'

'I've always got you there to clean it up for me, so why not? Anyway, I think that coleslaw's yours. You were stressing out with the dinner deals.'

'Yeah, maybe. It's splitting the chickens exactly in two. It's quite a responsibility.'

'I'm sure you're up to it.'

'Yeah. Just one thing about the Couvelaire uterus . . .'

'Yeah?' This time he's smiling because he knows I can never let go. He knows I don't work well with 'agree to disagree'.

'I'm not saying don't bring it up in the exam. It's just a question of how, and when. It's about the physical appearance of the uterus, remember?'

'How it's, like, purple because of haemorrhage infiltrating the muscle, yeah. I'm across that.'

'So if you can't see the uterus . . . What I'm saying is that it's an operative finding, because you can see the uterus then. It's not a clinical diagnosis because you can't see it from the outside. So if you've got a patient in the exam and you're dealing with a haemorrhage scenario, it's not a diagnosis you can make.'

'Righto. Well, I don't think I'd make it as a diagnosis, anyway. I think I'd be talking through the haemorrhage, looking at immediate management, and clinical features and investigations that'd help tell me what was going on. Then, I might mention it in the context of more extreme outcomes. That's when it'd come up, as the icing on the cake.'

'Which sounds fine. But earlier on it was sounding like it was the whole cake.'

'No, no. It was never that. But I might have said it a lot.

And that might have been influenced by the fact that I did like the sound of it. I've got to admit that.'

'And I might have overreacted to that a bit. But you do have a history there. Remember how, in your surgery exam last year, you were determined to bring up Fournier's idiopathic gangrene of scrotum?'

'Yeah, all right. But that was last year. And it was a bet. I had five bucks on that. People change, you know. I'm a much more mature person now.'

16

How dull must a town be when a twilight bat cruise is a highlight? Possible exception: Gotham City.

'A bat cruise, Philby'? my mother said when I told her. 'What on earth's a bat cruise?'

Why are you going on the bat cruise? That would have been another very reasonable question. Why when, only recently, it looked as though you might be getting a life? Friday night, ambling up the river on a decommissioned ferry to watch smelly winged rodents eat soft fruit. It makes dancing with girls look like a complete waste of time, doesn't it?

Agreeing to go was simply the least dramatic way to deal with it when it came up. I would have made a mess of any attempt to invent a prior arrangement. I was already packing a year's worth of lying into Wednesday night, and I couldn't have managed any more.

It used to be that a girlfriend I invented by accident was all I had to remember, then two that I'm 'juggling' (though I faked one and fumbled the other). Now that Frank's on with Zel my best lies are how I deal with most conversations. And that's not me. I'm not good at it. But the truth's not mine to go telling. Really, it isn't. But I feel like I have to do something. For Ron, for Sophie. It's almost like I have to hold the truth at bay and work to change it before they know. Somehow that's my job.

And on Friday that means it's up to me to make the bat cruise as normal as I can. To treat everyone the way I used to, pretend to a passing interest in bats if it's really necessary, hold back on the lying where possible and hope the evening ends with nothing gone wrong. Has Zel lined this up as a smokescreen? If she was having an affair with Frank, the last thing she'd do would be take him on a boat with Sophie and possibly Clinton.

I catch a bus into town, and my sense of unease grows at North Quay as I skulk past the *Paradise*. I hide on the bat-cruise side of one of the pillars holding up the freeway and I wait for the others. It's twilight. The *Paradise* won't be leaving for a while yet. Tonight their soundcheck music is Steely Dan, but that's not what I'll be listening to. I'm the guy who scores bats tonight, and can never set foot on the *Paradise* for the rest of his days.

Zel and Sophie arrive first. 'Before I forget,' Zel says, as more passengers start clustering, 'Ron says hello.'

'How's he going?'

'Oh, a little bit sorry for himself, but . . .' She's distracted by something over near the boat. 'Someone I recognise. Don't go too far, you two.' She leaves us for a clump of people near the gangplank. They see her coming, and there's air-kissing all round.

Sophie looks as if she's bored already. Her mood is set to be more lank than her hair. She's been trapped by these events before, I can tell.

I ask her if Clinton's coming and she says, 'We're not joined at the hip, you know.'

'So, I take it that's a No.'

'Yeah, it's a No. And what about you? No Phoebe? No Jacinta? No back-up option?'

'I didn't think of inviting them. Or anyone.'

'Really?' Said in the way you'd say it to a liar, not to a friend.

'It didn't seem like it was up to me to invite people. I know your mother said it was okay. But, look, I haven't been totally straight with you about Phoebe . . .'

'Hey kids,' Frank calls out, coming up beside us. 'Ship ahoy. Rum anybody?' He pulls a flask out of his sock. 'They've got a monopoly on these boats. Better to bring your own. Now, are we getting aboard?'

He puts an arm around each of our shoulders, steering us across to Zel and the boat. I don't know how straight I was going to be about Phoebe. Or Jacinta, or the absolute lack of back-up options, or anything else. There are too many lies open here, and some of them need closing. I would have invented an end to Phoebe, probably one that happened weeks ago, but that I hadn't felt like talking about till now. It would have been mutual, one of those things. Perhaps she was moving interstate. Phoebe's been applying for jobs since she finished her journalism degree, and now she's got one with a paper in Sydney.

There's not a truthful bone in my body. Sophie, Phoebe's someone I made up in the heat of the moment. An imaginary girlfriend that I never even imagined well enough to lie about consistently. Let's forget there ever was a Phoebe. Because there wasn't. Jacinta on the other hand – not that it's safe to use an expression involving the word hand where Jacinta's involved – Jacinta and me? That was another one of those things. There was definitely a Jacinta. You see the boat moored just along the wharf from here? I can never ever go on board it again. For the rest of my life, and I'm only twenty-one. And that's because of the second-best time I ever had with Jacinta. Disastrous dates? Don't get me started.

When we go on board Frank takes me aside and says,

'Had a few mouthfuls of the rum in the car park. So you take the keys, hey? You're driving back to my place.'

'So this is your plan? This is how you deal with the four of us being together for an evening? This is how you deal with me being dragged onto a fucking bat cruise? I don't even get to drink?'

'Yep. I play the fool, you play Mister Serious and keep me in line. That way we've each got a job that we're good at and no-one makes a mistake with the ladies. If I'm pissed, we've all got another issue to deal with. See? So don't go easy on me. Be a complete prick if you want. I reckon you could cover that.'

'One day, just one day, could we talk these things through before we do them?'

He sucks air down his oesophagus and lets out a big burp. 'Excellent start, my friend,' he says. 'All the personality of my grade-ten maths teacher.'

'Thanks.'

Frank and plans. Oil and water. They don't mix.

'Frank's nervous on boats,' I find myself telling the others as he roams the deck like a naughty chimp, clowning around and trying to bum lollies from kids – something that works for him, since he charms several of their mothers in a very temporary way.

Zel watches, but tries not to. I try to distract Sophie by asking open-ended questions about media studies. I manage to make it sound like a job interview. She gives me a look that says, 'Is it any wonder your girlfriends move out of town?'

We chug up river, past the malt smells from the biscuit factory and towards the setting sun and the bat colonies. A man with a beard and khaki ranger-type clothes comes up to the small podium and blows into the microphone a couple of times. He welcomes us, and tells us he thinks we're 'in for a good one tonight'. He starts giving us khaki ranger-type background information on the bats, and interrupts himself excitedly with a 'Hey kids' to report the first sighting, a lone bat flapping through the indigo sky above. The adults on the boat 'Ooh' and 'Aah' to start manufacturing a mood, pointing so that the children don't miss it.

'Is there something I'm not getting here?' I say to Sophie.

'Looks like a bat to me.'

'As in, the kind of things that fly over this city all the time, take bites out of your pawpaws, fry themselves on power lines and leave brown unremovable shit on your car?'

'Keep reminding yourself it's for charity. I'm sure Mum'll buy you a drink if you want one.' She sucks at the straw in her Coke. 'She's giving me money to be here tonight. That's how much she knows I like these things.'

Frank turns up again, just as I'm wondering if I'm the only one of us who's here in an amateur capacity. 'Philby, I think I missed the first bat.'

'I'm sure there'll be more.'

'Hey, why don't we go to the bar? That's a rule now. You miss a bat, you go to the bar. But you can come and help me, mate.' On the short walk there he half sobers up, and he says,' How do you reckon we're doing?'

'Baffling. No-one could have any idea what's going on.'

'Good.'

'Now, I'm guessing you'll be buying me a drink with that hooker money of yours, since I didn't bring supplies in my sock, and there'd be something very wrong happening if I was the only person who ended up going home out of pocket.'

'Hey, that Mister Serious thing? You don't have to do it when it's just the two of us, okay?'

'What? You can't think I want to be here. What's happening with our lives? We could be at the Underground, striking out with a series of maybe half-interesting girls. It's Friday night. And this is a charity bat cruise. Kids and old people. It's not where I want my life to be.'

'All right,' he says, as if I could be about to get boring. 'I'll get you your drink then. Jeez you hate paying for stuff, don't you?'

He orders a white wine for me and two Cokes for himself, and he scuttles off to the side to add a large dash of rum. If a wave came along now and rocked the boat and rolled him over the edge, it's quite possible I wouldn't say a word.

The ranger person is now talking about habitats, then diet, then breeding cycles. The kids are looking up at the sky, getting restless. They've been promised bats, and surely that means more than just an occasional one flapping overhead.

We pass Saint Lucia and the uni campus, where the brightly lit tennis courts stand out from everything else and the grand sandstone buildings are indistinct in the growing dark. I think I hear music drifting down from the Rec Club or the Refec on the breeze, but I might be imagining it.

No, it's there. Bass and drums, guitar chords firing off, vocals turning into something indistinct as they overcrowd the room they're in and make their way out through all the open doors, clattering off among the sandstone walls. A live band — Ups and Downs, the Riptides, someone else yet to leave this place completely and try their luck in a place where there might be luck.

'Now we're getting to the business end of the trip,' our narrator says, and the trees grow dense and the band noise ebbs away. 'Long Pocket and Indooroopilly Island will be coming up ahead on the right. And that's when I can promise you bats, kids.'

A bat cruise. There are bands out there tonight with the

slimmest chance of making it, bars, dance floors, lives going on and I'm just a passenger, here to keep the peace, to stop a lie from stumbling on a bat cruise. Frank owes me for this, and Zel does too.

'Now, here's what we're going to do. First, what did I say fruit bats ate?' There's silence. No-one told the kids the presentation was interactive. 'Right,' he says, though I'm sure no-one's cared enough to say a thing. 'It's got to be fruit, hasn't it? So are we ready to have some fun? Okay. I'd like you to take a look at the cage at the stern of the boat – that's the back end, kids. Here's what we do. And don't worry, the bats are ready for it. They'll come to the party and they'll be on their best behaviour. What we're going to get you to do is all crawl through that little opening into the cage. And the bats'll come and sit on the top of the cage, and you can poke the fruit up through the cage to them. And don't worry. They might snatch, but they won't scratch. It's only the fruit they'll want for tea. We only have the cage because they get a bit excited and they'd be everywhere if we didn't have it. Okay, so let's have the kids to the back, shall we? Tell 'em it's okay, mums. This is the bit we're all here for.'

The children don't move. No-one wants to be first in the cage. Some of them fight not to be pushed forward, despite stern parental talk of the 'you were the one who wanted to come' variety.

'Bugger this,' Frank says. 'I haven't come all this way not to play with the bats.'

'Kids. He said *kids*.'

'Have I been behaving like a grown-up? Anyway, look at them. Look how scared they are. Mum takes you up the river at nightfall and throws you in a cage up the back of the boat. Do they look happy with that idea? Nuh. Leave it to Uncle Frankie.'

He strides down to the cage, sticks his head in and takes a look around.

'And we'd strongly recommend that the parents hold back at this point,' the ranger says, 'and that we only have children in the cage.'

Frank pulls his head out of the cage and shrugs his shoulders as if to say, 'well, where are they then?' He pats the top of the cage like someone who's gone out for bats a thousand times, he looks at some nearby children and he smiles and nods. He goes over to them and crouches down, talking and pointing to the buckets of fruit and up at the sky. They start nodding too. One of them takes his hand. Frank leads six children, pied-piper-like, to the cage. He squeezes his way in first and sits in the back corner. The children follow, and so do a couple of others who were standing near them, then more from different parts of the boat until the cage is full.

Frank, it could be said, has saved the bat cruise.

'And now,' the ranger says, 'if we could have that gentleman out of there . . .'

But there's a murmur of disapproval from the passengers, particularly the parents. Frank's the big man on bat deck tonight, and the authorities can't touch him. He leans a hand out of the side of the cage and subtly shows the ranger the finger. There's a quiet cheer from anyone who notices.

The river bank to the right is now dark. The crew passes the fruit buckets into the cage.

'Look closely at the trees,' the ranger says, 'and what do you see?'

And the answer, finally, is bats. Nothing but bats. Against the almost-dark sky, the bats are waking, unfolding like umbrellas picked up by the wind and lifting from the trees. Bats in their thousands, thousands upon thousands, blowing in waves from the trees, like litter.

The boat swings around, the engines cut out. And there's a whir of slapping leather in the air, a strange musty sour smell, the sound of the last of our bow waves lapping invisibly against the darkened river bank, bats sweeping by above between us and the moon.

'Ready, kids,' the ranger says. 'Here they come.'

The first bat drops onto the cage, and the second is just behind it. They look as though they're sniffing, smelling out the cut, open fruit. The children duck down. Frank lifts a big piece of pawpaw out of a bucket and posts it up through the cage. A bat takes it and starts slurping at one end. The kids laugh. There are four bats now, then five, then seven, then the cage is covered with bats. Squealing bats above squealing children, all involved sounding as though they couldn't be having a better time as the feeding turns into a frenzy.

New bats arrive and fight with the old bats for position, and the children pass fruit up with both hands until it starts to run out.

'And now,' the ranger says, 'we're about to discover something else about bats. Remember how I said their diet was fruit? Well this makes their bowels very loose. And a good feed of fruit triggers something – and it's a thing they share with humans – called a gastro-colic reflex.'

Frank looks up at me over the busy bodies of the bat-feeding children, alarm on his face.

'And that gastro-colic reflex means . . .'

A bat shits, and it splashes from the side of the cage.

'Oops, there we go. They aren't even waiting for their cue tonight.' Another shit, this time *in* the cage and a child squeals, louder than before. 'Everybody out. They're going early on us. Let's get you out of there.'

Another bat shits, and another. The kids stampede, Frank gets trampled. Worse, he gets stuck. Drunk and panicking, he snags his shirt on the cage. The kids escape, but he's there to stay. And the top of the cage is black with loaded bats, shitting on Frank, splattering loose brown bat shit across his pale shirt and through his hair, and all he can do is go to ground, hide his face, and moan.

'And that's why,' the ranger continues, 'we actively discourage adults from going in the cage.'

There's spontaneous applause. Frank has unwittingly engineered a far greater highlight than he expected. The bats shit themselves hollow and squawk and screech and, one by one, lift off and fly. Franks shrugs his shoulders, basted with bat shit, and finally disentangles himself. In years to come, when the children tell this story, they'll never quite be sure whether he was just a man who didn't know boundaries or a hired clown.

In the car on the way to Sunnybank Hills, Frank's hair is scrubbed and spiky and he's wearing a spare khaki ranger shirt, but he still smells strongly of fruit that's passed through a bat.

'At least,' I tell him, 'you've finally turned the expression "boring as bat shit" on its head.'

'You were supposed to stop me, weren't you? Wasn't that the plan?'

'Oh, right, so it's my fault? No, the glory's all yours. You saved it, Uncle Frankie. Those kids weren't going in there without you.'

'And you've got to admit it worked. It certainly took the attention away from . . . other matters.'

'And I wasn't making a lot of headway with conversation, so someone had to do the job.'

'Thanks. Thanks, anyway. I didn't think you'd do it.'

'Do what?'

'Get involved.'

'I don't want to get involved. The only part of the night I was happy with was when the bats shitted on you. I want it to stop, but that's up to you. You and her. I think it's totally wrong. You know I do, and I don't really enjoy being part of the deceit. But I'm not going to blow it out into the open, am I? That's not up to me, either.'

'Look . . .'

'Don't give me that shit about needs. I don't really care about yours at the moment. I'm thinking more about Ron's – and I don't even particularly like Ron – and Sophie's. And don't say anything about Sophie. And don't tell me there's nothing left between Ron and Zel, because that's just wrong. And where did you get that lie about genitalia?'

'What do you mean?' It sounds like he's smiling, but we're on the freeway and I don't want to look away from the cars in front of us.

'That bullshit line about Vietnam. I mentioned it to Sophie and . . .'

'I didn't think you'd be repeating it to anybody. You idiot.' He laughs, but out of amazement more than anything.

'It was in context. And it's sorted out. I put it down to rumours from the Mowers people, plus his glass eye and his limp. I said the story going round was that he'd sustained multiple injuries in combat. Your name never came up. Is there anything else I should know about? Anything else you've made up that I shouldn't be dropping into conversation?'

'No, I think that's it. You just caught me by surprise on Monday, that's all. When the Zel stuff came out, you kind of went for me and I had to do something to hold you back. Anyway, I think there is something going on. I did wonder if it was to do with Vietnam, honestly, but I've never talked about it with her. It's not the kind of question you can ask.'

'Don't you see how risky this is? Don't you see how bad this is all going to get if you don't stop it?'

'Yeah, thanks Mum.'

'Great. You totally earn your place in the kids' cage right now, don't you?'

I didn't think it'd come to this, sitting in the car on the way back to Frank's, saying that and then saying nothing. But I didn't think he'd do this kind of thing, as though the consequences don't count. His judgment's never great, but usually it's only him who comes to harm. But, more than that, I've no idea what he's getting out of it. It's Zel Todd, after all. I know that's not the issue, but . . .

Frank and I began life in different worlds, and it's only chance that brought us to the same uni course at the same time. There are still issues that come along and make us look as different as two people could be, and I still don't often pick them. As far as I'm concerned – to add it up using some Frank Green maths – I couldn't find Zel Todd appealing if she were a single millionaire who came with a booklet of pizza vouchers and a carton of Staminade. But in Frank's eyes she's practically majestic. Mature and corporate and connected, cruising the gatherings of the ladies who lunch, and interested in him. Zel Todd dazzles him, and it's not just all that gold. So she makes the decisions, and Frank was left with no moral boundary to cross.

I spend the night on the sofa again – the same sofa I slept on nearly three weeks ago in my post-*Paradise* pants. I can hear Frank snoring through the wall, but at least there are no sounds yet resembling 'Eye of the Tiger'.

A car drives round the bend in the road, and its lights come in and glint from the collector plates. I've got a life ban for being caught, while employed, in the later stages of a sexual act on a floating nightclub. In the right company, there's nothing about me that would enhance my credibility more than that. But I could really do without it.

I try to get comfortable, but it's not that kind of sofa. Whatever position you settle for on this thing, your arms don't stop being in the way.

A steel ladder clangs against a tree in the front yard, and it's barely light.

It's Vanessa. She sees me when I look out through the sliding doors, and she waves. I put my shoes on and I go outside.

'What kind of seven o'clock do you call this then, Missy?' I say to her in my best Big Artie voice.

'That's for under the house. This is in the yard. Sounds like I get off on a technicality.'

'You might need some help, though. If you're about to start climbing, you should get someone to hold that ladder for you.'

'Okay. How about you?'

'Good choice. But first you have to tell me what's up there.'

'Nothing yet, but . . .' She signals for me to follow, and leads me under the house. 'Tah dah,' she says, making the quietest fanfare possible so as not to wake anyone above. 'The bird house. What do you reckon?'

'It's, well . . . it's amazing, actually.'

It's the Green house in miniature, but precisely the house in miniature, other than the enlarged front-door space to let the birds in. She's made guttering and painted on windows and a corrugated iron roof. There's even a butterfly hairclip next to the door, and it's been painted to match the real thing as well.

'I'd know that place anywhere,' I tell her. 'I can't believe what you've done with it.'

'Take a look inside,' she says, with the tone of someone who quietly knows that the best is yet to come.

On the internal walls, she's painted collector plates in miniature – a rabbit, a squirrel, the Princess of Wales in her Lady Di days. Rows of plates on each wall, with brown lines running along under them, like shelves.

'I had to use the tiniest brush, hey? And the little tins of paint you get for model planes. It's not that hard to make a bird house, but you don't see a lot of people kitting the inside out properly, do you?'

'Ness, it's like a Fabergé egg.'

'Yep.' She looks pleased, but puzzled. 'Except it's a bird house. I thought they were perfume or make-up. Fabergé . . .'

'Different Fabergé. Years ago. Very artistic. Fabergé eggs are pretty amazing. Collectibles in the multi-million-dollar range. What I meant was you've taken something small and simple, and turned it into something different by giving it an amazing amount of detail. This is art, this bird house.'

'Bullshit. You're kidding me.'

'No, really.'

'Hah. Art.' A smile stifles itself on her irregular teeth. 'Do you want to help me get it up the tree then, let the birds take a look at it?'

'Don't you want the people on the ground to take a look at it first?'

'No, not really. The main thing is getting it up there. That's what it's for.'

She straps on a tool belt and picks up a hammer and

some nails. As well as making the bird house she's made a stand for it that she can fix to the tree, and she finds a way of tucking that into the belt too. She takes the bird house in one hand and climbs with the other, first up the ladder, then onto the branches themselves. I'd worry about her falling, but it never looks dangerous. She climbs to where she wants to, high in the tree canopy, fixes the stand with nails and clips the bird house into place. She's back on the grass less than a minute later.

'I reckon they'll find it,' she says, looking back up into the tree.

'That was impressive work up there.'

'Just climbing. Some people can do it and some can't.'

'Well, you're definitely one of the ones who can, aren't you? Plus, you didn't just climb. You actually did something while you were up there. You sorted out the bird house. That's the kind of thing that takes balance and upper-body work.'

'Yeah. I've been doing those weights, you know. AJ's weights.'

'You wouldn't get a lot of use for some of your talents in the florist shop, would you?'

'No.' She passes the hammer handle back through its leather loop on the belt, and she leaves her hand resting on the steel head.

'If you could be anything in the world, what would you be?'

'Anything?'

'Anything.'

'Okay, I know that one already. Jessie's girl. I'd be Jessie's girl, and that way I could dump Jessie and go out with Rick Springfield.'

'Okay, and second to that?'

'Second to that. Well . . . Maybe something outside?

Involving trees? And machinery . . . Whatever. Whatever comes up. You've got to keep an open mind.'

'I've got an idea, and it's just an idea, but tell me what you think of it. I was talking to the boss from World of Chickens the other day and we were talking about how we needed new signs, and maybe a few other things for getting attention, but he doesn't have much of a budget for it.'

'I could do signs.'

'That's what I was thinking.'

'I could do whatever kind of signs, I reckon. I'm best with timber, but I can do other stuff, if you need it. And lights. You should get more lights. They get attention. You do that chicken thing out the front, right?'

'Yeah.'

'Well, lights for that.'

'Lights for that? Good.'

'Hey, what about a strobe? AJ could get a cheap strobe and I could rig it up. And you could have the chicken out there changing signs. Flicking through them.'

'Like that Bob Dylan film clip? The one where he . . .'

'The one where he changes the signs, yeah.' She's right into it now. 'But colour. I've seen it a couple of times. The clip's black and white. But yeah.'

'How about I call Ron later. I think these are great ideas. No promises, okay, but I'll give him a call. And if it doesn't work out, that's just because it's not in the budget. All right? But I'll be pushing for it.'

Fonzie the sheep ambles round the side of the house, and Vanessa tells him she might be doing signs – doing a sign job for a company across town. She swings her leg over him and they walk around like a six-legged creature, Fonzie grazing and Vanessa talking away.

Big Artie's at the door now, wrapped in an old dressing

gown. He's pointing high in the tree, showing Dorothy where Vanessa's put the bird house.

'She's a funny one,' he says to me when I go back up the stairs and inside. 'What a piece of work. It looks just like the house. Half that high would have done the job, though.'

'Maybe, but I think she likes the climbing. I could never do that. Like she said to me just before, some people are climbers and some aren't. I'd swear she was up and down inside three minutes, and most of that was spent fixing the bird house up there. I don't know about your balance, but mine wouldn't be up to that. I think a land-based job suits me pretty well.'

'Yeah,' he says. 'Yeah.' Looking from the bird house, to the ground, to the bird house again. 'That'd be fifty feet. I hope the birds work out they've got to look that high.' He laughs. 'Look at her now with the sheep. She's a funny one, isn't she? Where did we get her, Mother?'

17

'We had a queue once,' Frank says. 'I remember it well. It was a special time for the World. You got excited and spilled stuff, I kept my nerve.'

'There were hundreds of them. I went down fighting. Splitting chickens, humping bags of fries. We weren't all going to make it through to the other side.'

Monday's quiet. Too quiet.

But in an anticlimactic way, a way dominated by the threat of nothing continuing to happen. Sophie's out there putting in a lot of wing work, and the closest we have to an ominous soundtrack is Frank, with 'Disco Inferno' stuck in his head and sometimes making its way out of his mouth. Usually falsetto. Thanks for that, Frank.

'Hey,' he says, struck from nowhere by another unconsidered idea. 'Have you read the print on the window?'

'Plenty of times. I get to spend half these shifts on the other side of the glass, remember?'

'No, from this side. Have you read it? Ron Todd. Ddotnor.' Then again, with an accent – something deep and guttural, from somewhere intense but nonspecific. 'Ddotnor. Sounds kind of *Lord of the Rings*, hey? The Evil Ddotnor.'

'The Evil Ddotnor. Poor bastard. Give him a break. He's got one eye and no teeth, he keeps dozens of people in work, he gives your sister a chance to make some signs, and what is he? Evil. The Evil Frank Green more like, whatever that is backwards. What would the rest of the sign be? The World of Chickens bit.'

Frank looks, thinks, goes 'Snek . . . snek . . . Some of them just don't make sense at all, do they?' He picks up a pencil and writes his name on the bench in capitals. Then he writes it in reverse below, and stares at it. 'What do you reckon?'

'I think the K'd be silent.'

'Yeah. Good idea. So that'd be Neergnarf. Neergnarf versus the Evil Ddotnor,' he says, the last part of it in an ancient terminal groan.

'And what a titanic struggle that'd be.'

'Shit, yeah.'

'You're a bit bored again, aren't you?'

'Baby . . . Bored's not the word. Sirrah Lihp.'

'Sirrah Lihp. Why do I score such a loser reverse name?'

'Neergnarf versus the Evil Ddotnor.'

'It always has to be versus with you, doesn't it? It's like you're taking on some bad king. A struggle of oedipal proportions, toppling the paternalistic Ddotnor to win the hand of the mother-figure Queen Lez.'

'Do you have to make it sound like that? Do you have to make it all dirty, when I was thinking it was just sexual?'

'You and Queen Lez must be really glad all that Freudian stuff's out of fashion.'

Sophie comes in from the road and we go to change, leaving the nimble gnome-king Neergnarf defending the counter, tongs in hand.

'I don't seem to be having a lot of impact out there tonight,' she says while I'm unzipping her.

'I don't think it's anything to do with you.' She goes into the toilet to take the costume off. 'Mondays aren't our best days. But I was talking to your father yesterday about some ideas – some new signs.'

'So that's why you were calling . . .'

'Yeah. It's not much, but it's a start. It's Frank's sister who'll be doing them. I think she'll be good. And then I thought of something else. If you wanted to do the media stuff, the PR, for this place, how would you go about it?'

'I've actually thought about that already. I've got an assignment where you have to plan the media strategy for a local small business.'

'You should do it. Really do it, I mean. For this place, not just as an assignment.'

'I don't know that Dad'd like that.'

'We should talk to him. He doesn't have time to come up with a media strategy. I don't know if he's got the expertise, either.'

'But I don't have the expertise.'

'You've got more than some of us.'

'At least it'd get one assignment done that way. I can't believe how much work I've got to do. It gets depressing.'

'This'd be good then. And you'd not only get to plan it, you'd get to do it.'

I'm out at the lights again in a few minutes, and these shifts seemed so different a week or two ago. Were we getting on much better then, or is that just how I recall it? We'd talk about anything, we'd have a good time out the back, and that's what was saving this job for me. But it's the twenty-seventh of May. Exams are closing in for the people who work regular semesters, and Sophie's starting to feel it.

Ron calls when I'm next at the counter with Frank. I'm worried he might have changed his mind about the signs, but he's calling to invite me to the movies. His convalescence done, he's ready for the world again and all he missed was the bat cruise.

'Just on a work matter . . .' I try to jump in before the movie momentum gets too great . . . 'I've had an idea. To do with the new signs. I thought it might be a good chance to rethink the approach to the rest of the publicity. Media even. Nothing major, just get some fresh ideas.'

'Yes. Yes, I suppose we'll have to look at that. We don't want to just slap the signs up there. We do want a plan. Yeah . . . But you've got one, haven't you? You've got a plan already. I can tell.'

'Not a plan as such. It's not my area. But I know whose area it is. And I thought it could be a good time to have a media strategy meeting. Maybe you, me and the third-year media studies student on the team.'

'Really, we've got one of . . . ? Oh, Sophie? Do you think she'd want to?'

'Yeah, I do. And she can use it for an assignment as well, so it won't get in the way of uni.'

'Right. Even better. We should do this soon. We should definitely do this soon.' He's gone from movie talk to motivated in under a minute, but that's Ron. 'We should do this tomorrow. How's tomorrow? Dinner tomorrow?'

'Dinner tomorrow?'

'Make sure you catch a cab here and I'll fix you up. We'll be marking down the hours too, of course. I'd like to pay you a more executive rate for this kind of thing . . .'

'That's okay. Let's just get the customers in the door for now.'

'I'm tracking your time. This'll figure in your pay packet, even if it's only at counter rates. Now, do you want to brief Sophie? And I'll make sure I've got the *Courier-Mail* handy so we can pick a movie for Wednesday. Wednesday afternoon usually suits your schedule, doesn't it?'

'Yeah.'

So, I'm off again to the Dale, and throwing myself into the web of the Todds without a fight.

I explain the plan to Frank in the car on the way home, and he takes it entirely the wrong way.

'An assignment topic?' he says. 'You're getting my sister to do the signs and you're letting Sophie turn this place into an assignment topic? What is this? Bloody amateur hour? Some kind of experiment? What do you think you're doing?'

'What do you mean? It's a way of building up customer numbers without spending a lot.'

'It's marginal here already.'

'Exactly. What have we got to lose?'

'What have we got to lose? You don't know what I'm up against. This is camera money for you. Big Artie can't go up trees any more and he won't admit it. So Green Loppers is going to shit. This place has to keep working. I can't lose this job, and that includes the box of burgers you've got on your lap. Your family has always had money, right? Well, I pretty much come from a long line of tong jockeys, broom pushers and the occasional self-made man. It's a much more tenuous hold on things, okay? So we've got to make this place work.'

'I know, dickhead. That's what this is about. It's about someone doing something to make this place work. As opposed to standing there all evening with your mouth open catching flies, for example. It's about trying new ideas, and I don't mean pronouncing names backwards. It's about everyone getting involved. That's what I'm doing, and I don't notice everyone doing it. And it's about not sleeping with people we shouldn't, and being on the same team instead.'

From that point, things deteriorate.

Frank starts in Labour Ward at eight-thirty in the morning, as far as I know. Perhaps it's busier than usual. We don't see him all day. The way I recall the night before, he's the one who owes me the apology, not the other way round. So I don't go looking for him.

I hang around at the Mater after the last tute, still shitted off with him and with the turn of events, and I try to get some study done. This year was supposed to be better than it's been so far. No-one seems happy right now, not even Frank. He's plunged himself deep into a big mistake, he refuses to accept that and he doesn't even seem to be enjoying it. Not that I'm letting him any time I'm around. But he shouldn't push me. He shouldn't be the laziest bastard possible at work, and then criticise me when I try to improve things. It's for him, too, that I'm doing it, to keep him in a job.

It's not that I was expecting a glorious year, but I was hoping for better than this. The video camera, the trip to America maybe. I haven't given that a thought for weeks. The paperwork is sitting there at home and it still seems like an issue too big to deal with. I've got enough to deal with. I need to clear some space in my head some time, and work out what I'm going to do about UCLA. After this term, maybe, if the offer hasn't expired by then.

UCLA. I can't believe they said they'd take me. UCLA is like a place on TV – glamorous, gifted students all working hard, noise and guns and drugs on the streets, every bit of it several levels of intensity more than I can handle. Too big, too wild, too fast. And even if it's not like that, every frame of every movie, every minute of every TV show, every word of every article I've ever come across that has anything to do with LA tells me it is like that. So some of it must be true, and how do I take my place in it all, just me?

But I should stop thinking about UCLA for now.

It's pay day on Wednesday. I'd forgotten that. And my maths tells me this might be the Wednesday that gets me there, takes me to the grand total I need for half a video camera.

I could walk away from it all then. It's a real possibility. I'm gazing at chapter twenty-four, 'Foetal-Placental Dysfunction'. I'm there for the money, I could take the money now. I could spend time learning to use my video camera, instead of working at World of Chickens and dealing with Ron, and the unhappy Sophie who used to like me more (or fake better), and Frank who shits me, and the disastrous revelations that may not be far off.

That's what I could do.

I finish the chapter and, just after six, I walk down to the cab rank outside the hospital, I get into the first cab in line and I tell the driver 'Carindale'.

I pull out the World of Chickens notes I made at lunchtime and read through them. I could stay a couple more weeks, see how things go. That'd buy me some blank tapes.

Sophie answers the door when I get to the Todds, and she goes to pay the cabbie. Ron leads me to the sunken lounge, where three new pads of paper and three pens are waiting for us on the coffee table.

'Let's get some Diet Cokes happening,' he says, and goes to the kitchen, coming back with a large bowl of peanuts and three Diet Cokes on a tray. 'Thinking food. Grab yourself a handful.'

Sophie fetches a couple of old assignments from her room and joins us.

'All right then,' Ron says, realising it's up to him to start it. 'Philip's called this meeting.' He turns to me. 'So how do you think we should proceed?'

'Well, I've got some ideas but they're mainly about how

the place works, and things that might be selling points, so maybe we could go to Sophie first and get her thoughts on the prospects of media interest.'

'Soph?'

'No worries. Okay, it's a tough one, I've got to tell you that. If it was, like, U2 arriving in the country for a concert tour, it'd be a lot easier. But it's not. So don't expect miracles from me. Sure, it's good – it's a good place – but it's a chicken shop in the suburbs.' She's looking my way, as if there might be high expectations – three pads and three pens in front of us – and it's all because of me.

'So what you're saying is that we have to be realistic.'

'Realistic, and start small, but I think there are things we can try. Suburban newspapers first. They're not bad with local businesses, and maybe they'll go for something involving the chicken. Or maybe Dad – local guy making a go of it in the face of the multinationals. They hate multinationals. Also student papers. We're near the uni campus and there are lots of students in the area. Plus, they'd be a big part of our market. So maybe even sponsoring some student things at uni.'

'Okay, okay,' Ron says, his eyes almost closed he's giving it such thought. 'Would that be financial sponsorship, or in-kind?'

'Depends on the event, and on what you're looking for in return. Also special offers. Handbills out at the uni campus, mailbox drops. Special student discounts on Mondays, since they're pretty flat.' She flips the first page over and runs her pen down the next one. She stops and clears her throat. 'Is this okay?'

'It's great. It's great, isn't it, Ron? If we're being quiet it's only because we're waiting for what's next.'

'Yeah, that's right, mate. Didn't want to interrupt.'

'Oh, okay. Moving right along then, it'd be good to look at radio station promotions. We could at least give them a call. I don't know if they'd take us. We'd have to offer some free stuff to listeners – probably food for people who turn up – but it'd give us a good plug if it worked. And then the dream'd be coming up with a feature angle or news angle for the *Courier-Mail* – I don't know what that'd be yet – or a quirky look at it all for a filler story at the end of the TV news.'

'TV news?'

'Hey, no promises Dad, remember? That's big time. We don't start off shooting for that. I reckon this week I might put in some calls to the suburban and student papers, and maybe see what the radio stations think.'

'Good,' Ron says, nodding. 'Great.' Nodding and smiling. 'Bloody genius, if you want to know what I think.'

'No promises, but,' she says, and her cheeks start to flush. 'Got to give it a shot though. You don't get TV if you don't try for TV.' Then she smiles too, at the way she's sounding. As though TV might be big time, but it's not so big really. 'Of course, TV'd give us our best shot at targeting the Jean-Paul Sartre end of the market.'

'Yes . . .' Ron says warily.

'It's a media studies joke, Dad. Hey, Phil?'

'Kind of literary/media studies crossover. One of Sophie's ideas that we've been talking through at work. It's a niche market. I think that's what they'd call it.'

Then it's my turn. I tell them we've got a lot going for us with technique, for a start, and maybe we could be doing more with that. Most people deep fry, but we cook our chicken breast on a hot steel plate.

'So what are you thinking?' Ron says.

'I'm wondering if we can use that. Instead of just calling it "chicken", maybe call it "hotplate chicken".'

'And that . . .'

'That's a point of difference,' Sophie says. 'You've got to go for those. Hey, how about this? "*Famous* hotplate chicken".'

'*Famous?*' Ron's looking troubled. 'Can we say famous?'

'Define famous,' Sophie says defiantly. 'Of course we can say famous. It's like "ever popular" or "bestseller" or "cult classic". You say it first, and then it becomes true.' She takes a mouthful of Diet Coke. 'We can say famous, can't we Phil?'

'Yeah, it's a great idea. I'd buy it. "Famous hotplate chicken". Irresistible. Look what this degree is turning you into. And you always seem like such a nice honest person when you're in the chicken suit.'

'Hey, chicken suits'll do that. You should never make assumptions about people in chicken suits. What else have you got?'

'Okay, spices. What I'm thinking is that we're already the only takeaway place in the western suburbs doing five sauces – I'm pretty sure of that – and I wondered if there was an easy way of adding something more. And I thought, spices. Get some commercial spice mixes, like Cajun and oriental five-spice, and put them on the chicken fillets before we cook them. It wouldn't be hard, and it'd add to the "World" idea. Most of them would go with the sauces we've already got. You'd probably only have to add soy.'

'It's very gourmet.' Ron's wary again. 'Very top-end.'

'No, it's good, Dad. And it doesn't stop us doing anything else we do, including the whole and half chickens and the regular burgers without spices.'

'Which,' Ron says, clicking his fingers, 'we can call "classic". Your basic burger becomes "classic hotplate". Are we writing all this down? Is someone writing all this down? Famous? We can call this famous. It's going to be bloody famous. Hey love,' he says, and turns to Sophie with his chin on his hand, 'which'd be my best side for TV?'

On Wednesday, I meet Ron in town. He said he wanted to see a serious film, so I've chosen *The Killing Fields*. I asked him if he'd be okay with a film with some southeast Asian war content and he said he'd manage. That was all years ago now.

Plus, I wanted to say, you were never there. But that's a place we don't go.

It'd be an understatement to say that Sophie's performance last night exceeded my expectations. There I was thinking, I bet Ron's underestimating her, and I was underestimating her too. At least I'd thought about involving her. Why hadn't she involved herself already? There must have been times over the past few months when she saw opportunities going by.

Ron's in the foyer of the cinema, tickets in his hand, when I arrive. He asks if I want popcorn – his shout – and I tell him I don't eat in movies.

'I don't eat,' I tell him, 'and I don't talk. I should be clear about that up front.'

'Ah,' he says. 'An aficionado.'

'I just figure I'm there for the movie experience. I don't go to a restaurant expecting a video, so I don't go to a cinema and buy popcorn.'

'Exactly, exactly. The movie experience . . .'

'Plus, food noises. Food noises drive me crazy in there. Don't they get to you too? It's like, some important character's got a gun to their head, munch, munch, munch. Two people are breaking up, hand in the chip bag, fistle, fistle, crunch, crunch. Atmosphere. It counts for something.

The beauty of the cinema is that it's not like TV. You get to immerse yourself.'

'Good. This'll be good, then. I like the way you're thinking. This is absolutely what we're here for. Just one thing – could I get myself an ice cream if I promise to eat it before the film starts? There'd be ads, wouldn't there? I've kind of got my heart set on it.'

He buys a choc top and slurps his way through it during the ads and the previews. But he got my message. I made it as clear as I could that he wasn't going to be doing what he likes. It would have been family-size popcorn if I hadn't spoken up. Somehow I just know he's the kind of guy who tongues the chocolate off Maltesars, keeps his drink ice so that he can suck at it periodically and steps on all his old wrappers exactly when dramatic tension's essential. With some people you can tell. They never eat this stuff the rest of their lives, in cinemas they go mental. It's as though if you eat shit food in the dark, it doesn't count.

Ron flinches often during *The Killing Fields* and there isn't one long jolly musical number to break the tension, but he did say he wanted a serious film.

'Jesus,' he says when the closing credits roll. 'Holy bloody Jesus. Makes you grateful to be an Australian.'

'Quite a film, wasn't it?'

'Mate, it was awesome. Leaves you feeling pretty rough, though.'

'Exactly. And that's the point sometimes. It's got to be. That's why we picked it. I'm not against entertainment, but sometimes you've got to shake people.'

On the way out of the cinema, Ron's limp is more pronounced than usual. He's had to battle his way through the last two hours.

'Ah, daylight,' he says. 'Beautiful Brisbane daylight.'

He pulls his wallet from his pocket while we're standing in the foyer, and tells me he wants to fix me up for the movie now, before he forgets. He leafs through some notes and pulls out a twenty, and I tell him it's okay. I really don't need to be paid to go to a movie.

I particularly don't need to be paid the same amount that Frank gets from Zel for sex, but that's one point that's better left unmade.

He pushes the note into my hand and tells me I should step back sometimes and take a look at what I'm doing. He's off to buy gourmet spice mixes after this, the first new signs should be out at World of Chickens as early as this evening and he thinks things could be about to turn around. Plus, he would never have seen a movie like *The Killing Fields* if it hadn't been for me. And it's not the kind of film you'd like to see every day, but every once in a while you've got to go there. It's socially responsible.

'Quite a change for me,' he says. 'I'm used to films where, if they've got a problem, there's a song in it for sure.'

'It's a genre thing. There are plenty of films where the girls wear big skirts and fall for guys because of the cars they drive, but you can't have every film like that.'

'Not that there's not meaning in them.'

'No, of course not.'

'Take "Beauty School Dropout" in *Grease*, for example. Quite clearly a song about the importance of education. But you want to get into this game, the film game. What have you got in mind? If you were going to make a movie here and now, what would it be?'

'Here and now? I don't know. I don't know what kind of movie you'd make here. I think the way Woody Allen does things is really interesting, but there's something very Manhattan about it. People don't talk like that here. People don't go out on balconies above all that traffic and have those conversations here.'

'Conversations like what? If I wanted to see what Woody Allen was about, what's one I could get out on video?'

'There'd be a few. *Annie Hall*?'

'*Annie Hall*.' He takes a pen from his pocket and writes the name on his palm. He reads it and laughs. 'Better be careful going around with some woman's name on my hand.' He writes the word 'video' underneath, which either fixes the problem or makes it look like Annie Hall's a porn star. 'It's not . . . um, it's not like *The Killing Fields*, is it?'

'No. Not at all.'

'Good, 'cause . . . that was excellent, but something a little different'd be fine too.'

'No wars, but there's a lot of talking. Be ready for character stuff.'

'Character stuff. Good.' He nods.

'And, for something a bit edgier but also great film-making and some amazing acting, *Taxi Driver*. Robert de Niro in *Taxi Driver*. You've got to see that.'

'*Taxi Driver*.' The pen comes out again and, with the extra two words, his palm is full. 'So, um, same time next week, hey?'

'That'd be good, but it might be a bit close to the end of term next week. Maybe in a couple of weeks.'

'Oh, sure, sure. And your pick again of course but, if I could just put in a word for one I've been wanting to see for a little while, I think there's a film out with Madonna that's supposed to be rather good. Entertaining but thoughtful. And every young person these days loves Madonna, don't they? What's it called? *Desperately Seeking Susan*?'

I try ignoring the phone when it rings but, since I'm watching TV, I know I'm expected to answer it. My mother's still reading *Your Child in Trouble*, so she's in one of her strange distract-me-at-your-peril head-in-a-book moods. TV, around here, is seen as occupying one of the lower rungs on the cultural ladder. But my parents are pre-baby-boomer. It's not their fault.

It's Frank.

'I'm calling,' he says in a creepy, husky voice, 'from the lair of the Evil Ddotnor.'

'You can't be serious.'

'Yes, I can.' The husky voice again. 'I'd recognise the purple heart-shaped bed and the ceiling mirrors anywhere.'

'No, surely not.'

'I thought you'd had the tour.' Back to his normal voice again. 'Didn't they show you upstairs? Didn't they tell you they bought the place from a guy in the magazine business?' He says magazine business as though it's definitely in inverted commas. 'He bought it when it was a display home and he had the master bedroom fitted out with the gear and then he moved interstate or went bankrupt or something. And it's all fixtures. You can't interfere with the bed without buggering up the jacuzzi.'

'Frank, I'm okay about not having had the upstairs tour.'

'Mate, it's a fucking palace. I'm serious. I feel like Hugh Hefner in here. There's even gold bits on the phone.'

'Good. I'm happy for you.'

'Listen, I need to talk to you. Seriously. I didn't quite get what you were on about the other night. Monday, in the car. You were lining up Vanessa and Sophie to do things . . .'

'Because there's no budget.'

'Yeah, and I wasn't thinking. It was kind of a reminder that the place isn't doing so well, and I need that job.'

'I think it's doing better than it was. It's just . . . for various people's states of mind, yours included, I thought it'd be good if we could get it to do a bit better.'

'Yeah. I know. You should see Vanessa's signs. She's done a great job. It's practically all she's been doing since you gave her the go-ahead. We're borrowing the truck to take them over there tonight, actually, and she was thinking we might come by your place and pick you up. I think she wants you to see them first, since you lined her up for it. How would that be? Would six o'clock get us there by six-thirty?'

'Yeah, it probably would.'

'Righto then. Well . . .' There's a noise in the background, perhaps a voice. His hand moves over the mouthpiece and, for a few seconds, every sound is muffled. When he lifts it off again there's a new noise, something industrial, like a powerful vacuum cleaner or a pool filter. Then a sound that might be the frenzied quacking of a nearby rubber duck. 'Listen mate,' he says. 'Got to go. Six o'clock, hey?'

And, with that, his Carindale adventure continues.

Vanessa tells me she's come up with something 'a bit tricky', but she's determined to make it work. She says she took the Dylan clip as her inspiration, but she figured we couldn't go tossing the signs away one word at a time.

'Just wait,' she says, sitting between Frank and me on the bench seat of the Green Loppers truck. 'Just wait.'

We drive across town and the cab smells of sweat, fuel and mulched vegetation. Frank drives like he knows the truck well. Well enough that, to him, it probably doesn't even smell.

'Have you seen Frank's hands?' Vanessa says. 'Have

you seen how wrinkly his fingers are? He's been in water most of the afternoon. He's got this lady . . .'

'Ness.' Frank stops her. 'We're not talking about that tonight, remember. Not at all tonight, okay? You're part of the team this evening, and we've got a no-smutty-talk-at-work rule.'

'Okay.' She looks straight ahead, as if nonchalantly accepting what he's said, and then she turns back to me. 'Frank reckons he's been riding the skin train to . . .'

'Ness.'

'But we're not at work yet. I'm just trying to fit it all in before we get there.' Suddenly, she's less nonchalant. 'It's not fair. I don't get to say that stuff at home, but this is the Loppers truck. This is where Dad and Nev and that sit and swear all day. And you told me I'd be part of the team tonight, with the signs. I'm part of the team, I'm in the truck, I get to talk the talk. I get to say skin train to tuna town if I want to.'

'You don't even know . . .'

'It's a fish, Frank, it's a fish. You're not catching me out, pal. I'm part of the bloody team now.'

'Oh, so it's a bloody team now?'

'It is if I want it to be,' she says, and laughs.

'Ness and her bloody team, driving around town in the bloody Loppers truck.'

'Yep,' she says. 'Bloody yep.'

She turns the radio up. There's a Creedence double-play beginning, and she sings along to most of 'Lookin' Out My Back Door', and makes us join in on the choruses. If Jackson Browne's next, I know she'll have me doing oooos to 'Running on Empty'. They're that kind of family.

When we get to World of Chickens, we stop in the driveway to unload. The individual signs are light, but my muscles need every bit of their sporadic bullworking when Frank passes something large, timber and chickeny out of the back of the truck. It's the board that the signs will hang on, with its rooster's head on top and chicken legs. Four chicken legs – two for the front view and two for the back – with the pieces of wood joined by hinges at the top and ropes around knee level. Do chickens have knees? Surely everything has knees.

'I'll just take the truck down the back and get to the counter with Sophie, hey?' Frank says. 'You two should be right setting this up. And, Ness, you've got to be careful with Sophie. She's a devout Christian. So we all watch our mouths around here. Language and content, okay? You get what I mean? For Sophie's sake, we pretend all that sexual stuff doesn't exist. Including wrinkly fingertips, right? And we don't even mention god, 'cause her religion's very private. So you have to pretend I didn't tell you.'

Vanessa looks as though that's almost too much to remember, as though she came here for the signs, not for all this work politics and being careful with people.

'Honestly,' she says when he's back in the truck and she's picking the signboard up more easily than I'd like her to. 'That florist I work with, they don't come much more Christian than her, and we get on okay. I've got to go easy on the blasphemy, obviously . . .'

'Blasphemy?'

'Blasphemy. The god words, used for swearing purposes. First couple of times I cut my finger or spiked myself, she went nuts about the blasphemy. Of course, I kept doing it till she told me what it was. Now we're fine. There's plenty more words you can use.' The signboard slips from her hands and lands on her toe. 'Fuck. Fuck.' She scrunches her face up, in genuine pain. 'Ah, my fucking toe.'

'It's heavy, isn't it?'

'Nah, it's just the new paint. It's slippery.'

We open the board out and stand it by the roadside. There are runners on the front where all the signs go, one behind the other like files in a filing cabinet. To keep it interesting for the traffic, the chicken every so often has to pull up the front sign and move it to the back, displaying a new message. She starts to show me how it works, and tells me it'll really kick arse when she plugs the strobe in.

The board is white like a chicken's front and the writing on the signs is in bright primary colours, like T-shirt slogans for the chicken to wear. She says she got a bit artistic with the chicken features, and she hopes that's okay. We start racking the signs, with Vanessa reading them aloud as we put them up – 'eat me $4.95' (with a picture of a half-chicken meal), 'I am your burger – $1.95', 'it's your World', 'burger meister' and 'real meal deal'.

'So there we are,' she says, 'just like you wanted, I hope. And then there's the one Frank got me to do, which goes 'how good is slaw?' And, finally, the one I did today, 'famous hotplate chicken'. I didn't know this place was famous until Mister Todd called about that sign. Maybe Sunnybank's just too far away.'

The chicken suit is waiting inside and, by the time I'm wearing it, she's run an extension cord through the doorway and she's plugged the strobe light in. She gives it a test flicker across the sign, then turns it off until we're ready. The last thing she pulls out of her bag before we get started is a massive pair of pretend sunglasses.

'I got these in a showbag last year,' she says. 'I just thought, there'd be all that strobe action, and you said you were changing the image, you know? I would have preferred Ray-Bans, but . . .'

'But in the end you're not going to find a two-foot pair of Ray-Bans, and a chicken's never quite going to look like Tom Cruise. This . . . this is the look we need. Ness, things are about to change around here.'

She's gives a crumpled, embarrassed kind of smile. 'Well, get 'em on then.'

From there, the evening doesn't look back. Ness tapes the sunglasses to my head, and turns the strobe on. Suddenly, movement comes more easily out here. The strobe is very forgiving of poor white-guy coordination and it makes the whole experience even more surreal than usual. Plus, I have signs. I have something to do. Signs to unveil – grandly, cheekily, flamboyantly and, sometimes, when people least expect it.

Ness goes back to her bag, and this time she produces a tape recorder. She says she couldn't find any Dylan at home, but would Boz Scaggs or Alice Cooper do? She plays *Silk Degrees* and I'm a dancing chicken in these wild flashing lights, flipping through signs with something that would approximate rhythm if the signs were any easier to handle.

She tells me to do the windmill guitar thing, like Pete Townshend, and I figure she must have watched a lot of TV with her brothers over the years.

I have no idea if this is getting us custom, but it must be getting noticed.

'It's all in the lights,' I tell Sophie when it's her turn and she's trying to persuade me that she might just do it the usual way. 'Nothing hides dorkiness like a strobe. It's a scientific fact, and I've put it to the test several times at the Underground myself.'

She's not convinced, so we go out to the road before

she puts the suit on. I introduce her to Vanessa and we show her how the signs work. They're not as heavy as she'd thought.

'And,' Vanessa says, 'you can have either Boz Scaggs or Alice Cooper. Sometimes I have Christian tapes, but not today. Evie Tornquist, or that nun with the guitar.'

'Boz Scaggs'll be fine. Speaking of which – the radio station stuff we talked about last night, you and me and Dad. I called 4BB and something's cancelled this Friday morning, so we can get a White Lightning car out here for breakfast.'

'Seriously? I didn't think you'd get it happening that quickly. That's great. Great promotion.'

'I've said we'd put something on. And I've lined up the *Westside Chronicle* for the same time.'

'You are famous,' Vanessa says. 'You are the famous hotplate chicken place. 4BB – home of the classic rock double play. Live crosses to the Breakfast Bar, with traffic reports on the quarter hour, and on Fridays White Lightning strikes in your neighbourhood with Freebie Friday giveaways and stickers and Richie the Rat. You'll be wanting another sign for Friday then, if you've got the Bs. "Freebie Fridays, seven to eight".'

That's when Ron turns up, just as Sophie's looking at Vanessa as if she's wondering where the off switch is. He pulls in from the road and opens the car door, and he shouts out something about going shopping. But he's reaching over to the passenger seat by then so most of it gets shouted in the wrong direction. He gets out of the car holding a cardboard box. He's bought several large bags of mixed spices and wooden grinders, with the grinders for appearance since we're repositioning ourselves as 'gourmet but not flashy'.

He pulls them out of the box one by one and shows us the spidery lettering burned into their midsections. He once did a course in poker-work, he tells us, and he's only used it for sketching bareback riders until now. Ron's excited.

'Let's go inside,' he says. 'Can't leave Frank out of this. And I've got your pay cheques, too. And look at those signs. It's a big night. A big night at the World.'

I'm not going to be the one to tell him there are no Is in Cajun.

'Bloody excellent,' Vanessa calls it in the truck on the way back to my place. 'What a night. Twenty bucks cash, plus expenses. Cash and expenses – that's the kind of deal Magnum PI would get. And twenty bucks. Who would have thought? I'm definitely coming back on Friday. Freebie Friday with my new sign and Double B and Richie the Rat.'

'I don't know if we're definitely getting Richie the Rat.' Not that I want to shatter the dream, but . . . 'He might stay back at the Breakfast Bar and just cross to the White Lightning at Taringa.'

'Nuh, I reckon he'll be there. And I'll be there, too. I'll get Dad to drop me over. Richie goes out with the White Lightnings if there's food on. Just wait. You should listen to Double B more.'

'Well, I'll get my chance on Friday.'

Double B. Sophie has gone to takeaway-chicken heartland in snaring Double B, home of the classic rock double play and the enduringly awful Richie the Rat, radio prankster, unfunny crank caller, renowned over-the-airwaves burper of 'Happy Birthday to You'. I don't have to respect someone simply because they can control a gullet full of air. It's not a skill, just a dumb misuse of an oesophagus.

Vanessa sits between us eating her burger (oriental five-spice, with soy) and sucking on her large Sprite, high above the night-time traffic in the truck cab. And tonight she actually believes there's a world beyond the florist shop. And I know that, having helped that belief along, I need to deliver more than the chance to make a few signs. I think I know what she really wants. But Big Artie has to work it out too.

I'm surprised how much the signs and Ron's boxful of innovations have changed World of Chickens already. By the time we closed, it smelled different in there with all the spices we'd fried. Frank was getting into it, giving people advice on spice and sauce combinations, as if we'd been running it that way all the time. He was even flipping the fillets with something that resembled enthusiasm. And the smell of tonight's take-home burger box extinguishes the tree-lopping man-work odour in the cab. It's almost a restaurant smell, and that's a new thing for our burgers.

Sophie seemed least comfortable of all of us, left behind a little by her father's excitement, uncertain about the strobe in particular and only matter-of-fact about Double B even though it's pretty big news. She's not even planning to come on Friday.

When I ask Frank what he thought of the way she was tonight, he says she seemed all right to him. 'But you are always saying I'm not perceptive. She's got a lot of assignment deadlines. That's what she told me. It only really needs Ron and a chicken anyway, and Ness with the gear. But don't worry, I'm sure she'll be listening at home. I'm sure she'll be able to tell you on Friday night just how clever you were.'

Vanessa sucks her Sprite down to the ice and says to me, 'Is she your girlfriend?'

'Who? Sophie? No. We just go halves in a chicken suit.'

'Phil actually goes out with Ron,' Frank tells her.

'You'll probably see them turn up together on Friday morning. I keep saying it's not always a wise move to go out with people connected with work – particularly the married ones – but if the two of them will keep going to the movies for their management retreats, what are people going to think?'

'Really?'

'No, not really. Frank's kidding. Ron hasn't been having the best time lately. There's a few shitty things happening in his life, and I think he deserves a better break. He's got to have someone on his side. And if it's not going to be anyone else, it might as well be me. So we went to the movies today. And I'm going along on Friday morning to be the chicken, even though I'm not rostered on. Ron specifically asked me. Anyway, I was part of the planning. It makes sense that I'd be there.'

'Oh, righto. Had me going for a second. Hey, did you like the way I mentioned the Christian tapes to Sophie? I don't have any. I just didn't want her to feel left out. We get enough of that at the shop. Kerry – Kerry from the shop – says a lot of modern music's offensive, so I wanted Sophie to know that I hadn't meant to be offensive with the music I'd brought.'

'That was good, Ness. I think it was pretty subtle, too. Natural.'

Frank looks over Vanessa's head at me, and I try to give him a signal that says it was no problem. Sophie was . . . well, she wasn't her usual self, but Vanessa's remark didn't come close to giving anything away. If I'm the only one who's noticed a change in her, it makes me wonder if it might be connected with something I've done. I can't think what. But that's paranoid. It's exams, it might be Clinton, it might be plenty of things I don't know her well enough to know. It shouldn't, as far as I can tell, be Frank and Zel or the state of World of Chickens. When we last spoke about that she seemed sure her parents' affluence wasn't in question, and that her only problem with it was living up to her family's self-made-man expectations. Perhaps all I've noticed is how her mood contrasted with Vanessa's.

The lights are still on when we pull up at my place. My parents haven't gone to bed yet.

'Go on,' Frank says. 'Get in there and break that good news. Tell them you've done your bit and they have to cough up. Hey, have you even thought about what we can do when you get this camera?'

'No. Strangely, no. I think I've been too busy. It'll be good in the break though, won't it? When this term's done in a few weeks' time I can really get going. And, in case you're wondering, we won't be doing anything featuring your arse and biscuits. Ask him about that one the way home, Ness.'

Frank, not a person given to shyness, needs no asking and happily starts telling Vanessa the story as I'm climbing down from the cab. For her, the night will continue to be amazing all the way to its end, and her hope for some dirty truck talk will now be realised.

I pull my pay cheque out of my pocket on the way up the front steps, and the twenty dollars from earlier this afternoon comes out with it. There's no doubting I'm there now.

When I open the front door I can hear the TV. My mother is resting a mug of tea on the closed script in her lap and watching David Attenborough over the half-moons of her reading glasses, my father is sitting with a large novel and he's halfway through a glass of everyday brandy. 'It's Your World' one of those chicken signs said, and this is mine.

'I've got some news,' I tell them, and my mother looks over right away, as if it can only be bad.

'What?' she says, fiddling with the glasses as though she can't find my range easily. 'You can tell us.'

'Yes, that's the nature of news. You tell people. And sometimes it's good. Sometimes, also, you'd like it if people didn't assume it was bad, and let you tell them first.'

'Yes, sorry.' She corrects herself, starts again. 'What's your news?'

She mutes David Attenborough, and my father places his bookmark neatly into his book and closes it.

'This.' Said with the enthusiasm befitting a low-key triumph as I hold the cheque up for them to see. 'This is the pay cheque that pays for my half of the video camera.'

Or, it turns out, buys a person a rather awkward silence around these parts.

'Okay,' I tell them, 'we're going again on this one. Are you ready? Be happy for me. This is the pay cheque that gets me my half of the video camera. This, and the adjacent twenty-dollar note that you might have noticed, get me over the line.'

My father frowns, fiddles with his bookmark as if it's a bother, something needing straightening before new information can be processed.

'Tah dah,' I say, presenting the cheque again, as emphatically as I can. 'It's what we call "a good thing". Cheque, cash, many hours of noble toil. Equals video camera.'

'Right, well done lad,' my father says, staging a very average recovery from his state of complete non-excitement. 'Well done. Caught us a little unawares, but well done. We weren't thinking you'd get there quite this quickly. You are industrious, aren't you?'

'That's what a dollar-for-dollar incentive scheme'll do for a person.'

'All right. Yes, good work. When would you be looking at getting the camera then?'

'As soon as the cheques clear.'

'Right, the cheques. This one and my one, that'd be?'
'That's right.'
'Take a seat.'
'A seat? I'd rather have a video camera.' Boom boom.

I hate the things I say sometimes when I sense something's not right. But, no, perhaps I'm going to sit down and he's going to get his chequebook, and he's going to write the cheque for me now and hand it over here in the lounge room. He's not against a sense of ceremony when it comes to big transactions.

I sit. He doesn't move.

'Would you like a drink?'

'No thanks.' What am I supposed to say? The cash'll be fine? Even I know that's crass. Come on, come on. Make with the money.

'I might not be able to get the cheque to you right away.'
'Oh.'
'I was thinking it'd be taking you a bit longer.'
'That's okay.'
'And we might not actually have the money at the moment. You've lived up to your part of the bargain and by rights there should be a video camera in your hands within days, but I've been putting my bit away at a slightly different rate . . .'
'Oh. We sort of had a deal . . .'

My mother smiles a kind of it's-a-minor-hiccup smile, but they don't stop there. Usually they would, this time they don't.

My father looks over her way and she nods and says, 'Yes, Allan. It's time.'

He takes a deep breath – an unusually theatrical gesture for my father – and he says, 'Right, lad, there are a few things you should know.'

'Okay, first up . . .' I'm feeling nauseated already, feeling that my moment of low-key triumph has ricocheted to a bad place, but I don't know what kind of bad place. 'You are my parents, aren't you? Let's get that one out of the way straight up.'

'No, no. I mean, yes. We are your parents. Definitely. That's not it.'

'And no-one's really sick, or anything? Tell me no-one's really sick.'

'No, that's not it, either. Look, lad, it's money. Plain and simple. Don't worry.'

He tells me he wouldn't usually get to talking about the family finances, but I'm probably old enough to know and tonight seems as good a night as any. I'm twenty-one, and we did have a deal. He says he's not a man to renege on a deal but the thing I should know is that we aren't the kind of people who can just pull money out of nowhere. We've always been planners. Planners and, when we've needed to be, savers. And all that planning and saving should have things looking better than they do now, but there were a few investment decisions that went wrong in the seventies, and the mortgage had to take up the slack.

'So, we've got quite a bit of debt to deal with,' he says. 'A lot, actually. And I always like these dollar-for-dollar schemes when it's something important because it only happens if you really want it, and we've got time to get our half together. To get it together, without you having to worry. That's what this has been about, keeping all the worry from you.'

'But no, no it can't be like that.' Denial's been working for me as a defence mechanism lately, and I might as well get to it early in this conversation. 'It can't be.'

The way I feel right now, I'm going to keep saying it can't be until the problem goes away. Until he laughs and writes me the cheque. Until he tells me everything's fine, always has been, and this is just a cruel joke. But I don't let it end with denial. I have evidence, evidence in my favour that points out that we're completely okay financially. And I'm going to let him have it.

'But what about school? What about what that must have cost?'

'You got that scholarship. Certainly there were other expenses, but . . .'

'But you always said that the scholarship was a bonus. You said you were really glad I got it, but it was a bonus.'

'Well, what can you say when you're telling it to a young lad, when you're sending your little eleven-year-old out to do a big weekend of exams? "Remember boy, your entire future's riding on this"? Probably not a good idea. That's not to say we wouldn't have found the money somewhere. But we would have gone without other things.'

'But we've never gone without anything. That's not what we do. That's not what we have to do. Stop talking like that. That's other people.' Sophisticated defence mechanisms a smouldering ruin, all I've got are mad denial and nausea. Hate that.

'Well, there was that school trip to Africa that you wanted to go on.'

'Yes, but I couldn't go on that because I had to learn the value of money. It wasn't that we couldn't afford it. I just had to, you know, not take everything for granted.'

'Well done Mother is all I can say to that.'

'But that's why we do that thing where I raise half. The dollar-for-dollar thing. It's to teach me the value of money.'

'Right . . .'

'But I like taking things for granted. Some things, anyway. Or at least fifty per cent for granted. I'm always happy to raise half. I particularly want to take for granted ideas like us, you know, not being strapped for cash. I like that one a lot.'

'You were just a bit quick for us this time. And I wouldn't say strapped for cash, though we do try not to spend much, of course. Well, sometimes strapped for cash, sometimes just very careful. Why do you think we don't eat out or get takeaway a lot?'

'To teach me the value of home-cooked food.'

'Chalk another one up to Phoebe.'

'No.'

'Why don't you have a bicycle?'

'On these roads? Are you mad. You've always said how dangerous they are.' I look across to my mother for reassurance. She says nothing.

'And that computer-game package you wanted for the TV?'

'That would have been completely inappropriate. Think of the distraction from study.'

'And the time you wanted to go on holiday to Hawaii instead of the Sunshine Coast?'

'We've got some of the best beaches in the world here.'

'She's a genius, your mother.'

'I shouldn't have bought the new chairs for the dining room,' she says. 'That was my mistake, Philby. But I'd waited years to find some we could afford that actually went with the table. I put a deposit on them a while ago – when they were on sale – and I would have lost them if I hadn't paid them off. There's no drastic hurry for the camera, is there?'

'No, but . . . But you could have been a bit more honest with me all these years. There I am going around thinking everything's okay and we've got this sensible excellent dollar-for-dollar deal . . . I feel like an idiot now. Like I should have worked it out years ago.'

'There was no need for you to know. Really. You've never needed to know. Now, the camera,' she says, starting to look a little twitchy. 'I wanted to ask you a few things about it, anyway.' She wrings her hands together. 'Not about money. We wanted to . . . we were wondering, just, you know, wondering, what you were going to use it for.'

'Don't you listen? I want to be a film maker. I have for years. Should I have specified genre, or something? What do you think I'm going to use it for? Porn, of course. Nasty dirty porn. Can't work in a chicken shop forever, and someone's got to put this family back on its feet. What do you mean? What do you think I'm going to use it for? Frank's buttocks? Did I say I was saving up for the wide-angle lens?'

They've made me angry with this invented issue about the camera. This is about money, this conversation. Money and the system of lies that makes up my world. They're sitting back in their seats looking stunned. Why? Do they think Frank doesn't have buttocks?

Okay, time to pull this back in. My turn for the deep breath and the pause for consideration. I've ranted, it's been good, but I've ranted enough. I have to recant.

I tell them it's okay. They surprised me, and that only indicates what a good job they've done stopping me worrying about the money issue for the past twenty-one years. But they can't expect me to take it all on board in one go. And there's no hurry with the video camera. No hurry. And I'm staying on at World of Chickens. I'll be earning more there. I'll get the camera eventually, one way or another. And I'll do very normal, legal, hopefully clever things with it. No buttocks. And if money's ever a big problem, I'm sure there are things I can cut down on. From now on, they can talk to me.

'Good lad,' my father says. 'Very good of you. But

there's nothing to worry about, really. I think we're all glad to hear that Frank's bottom won't be involved when the camera eventually arrives, of course, but . . . I was just about to take a short walk to the drinks cabinet. Is there anything I can get you? Crème de Menthe perhaps? Drambuie?'

'No, thanks. I'll be fine. It's been a long day, actually. We were trying out some new ideas at work tonight, so I'm pretty tired. I might just go to bed.'

'Now, you're all right then?'

'I'm all right.'

'Don't be too worried about this.'

'I won't be.'

Liar, liar. The smell of burning pant must surely fill the air as I leave to clean my teeth. I look at the toothpaste on the brush, feel wasteful and try to scrape about a third of it back into the tube.

We had a deal going. On paper, it was a dollar-for-dollar deal, but that's not the real deal. The real deal was that we were okay. And maybe we still are okay, but my deal was that we were very okay. I just had to learn the value of money and home-cooked food, avoid distractions from study and the dangers on the road, and appreciate the nearby beaches. Which are, it has to be said, excellent. I can't help feeling that I could have been let in on the truth a little earlier, a little more gradually and not quite as close to the end of my obstetrics term.

Lying in the dark, I can't count the number of good and specific reasons we've had for not buying things over the years. I've listened to Frank's worries about his family and money and listened to Ron, and it felt easier to hear all that when I was only an observer. That seems rather smug now.

It's hard not to lie here, looking around the room at the shapes and outlines of things and wondering how much they cost, or how much they're worth. I don't know if it's the kind of issue I could ever have talked to Frank about but, right now, it's Sophie I want to talk to. I want to tell her what's going on in my world, and I want her to know what's really going on in hers, so that we could talk about it. Do I want that for me or for her? I'm not sure. Am I overreacting? Probably. But they took me by surprise, and they shouldn't have.

18

Okay, it rattled me, but by the next morning the world hasn't ended, there's still cereal and juice in the kitchen and my parents cope quite well when I query their choice to have the paper home-delivered every day.

I tell myself it's a sense of perspective that I need, and a day of true-life drama at the Mater Mothers' should be all it takes to give it to me. Think of baby Neil Armstrong up in Special Care, and financial comfort counts for less.

Telling myself that doesn't work perfectly, but at least it makes me remember I'll need to know some obstetrics soon, and it wouldn't be bad to give that most of my attention.

When I get home in the afternoon, there is no removal truck outside, the place isn't in the hands of the bailiffs – not that I'd know how it'd look if it was – and my mother's beef stroganoff smells like it always does.

I tell her I've worked out that I can earn what I need to buy the video camera myself in a few months, and then I ask her – okay, I have to fight off more nausea to manage it – what the hell they think they're doing, paying me an allowance when I'd regularly blow two thirds of the discretionary part of it on alcohol.

'You're a university student, Philby,' my mother says. 'What do you think we imagined you were spending it on? Antique clocks?'

On Friday morning, Ron turns up at six-thirty. My mother, confused by the early start, makes me a thermos of tea.

She's still in her dressing gown with her eyes mostly closed when she hands it to me, along with an old scarf in a plastic bag, and says, 'Now, you will be here for dinner tomorrow night?'

'I'll be back this evening. What do you think I'm doing? Going camping?'

'And tomorrow night?'

'Yes, I'll be here.'

She sees me to the door and waves me off as I walk down the path, thermos and bagged scarf in hand. She's said before that she isn't up to much mentally until she's got that first cup of tea in her.

Before I can explain to Ron what I'm carrying – if I can explain it – he's saying, 'I could go a cuppa. Very thoughtful, your mother,' and we're swapping seats so that I can drive while he drinks tea.

'Radio,' he says with a smile, and the tea laps against his moustache when I brake. 'Radio and a newspaper. That's two different communications media.'

Vanessa's new sign is already out when we get there, telling the passing traffic it's '4BB FREEBIE FRIDAY – free food 7–8 a.m.' And the passing traffic is paying attention – there's a queue at the door. Well, three people. For us, that's a queue.

'Look,' Ron says, 'One of them's wearing shoes. He might be back with cash some day.'

Vanessa's outside as well, and she's turned up looking like someone with a sense of occasion. There's blue eye shadow that she's borrowed from somewhere, a blue fluoro shirt (buttoned to the top, with a brooch at the neck), matching blue Swatch, big thick white belt, white jeans and boots. And her hair is all lace and volume. Vanessa's hair goes big when it needs to. Vanessa looks like the second daughter Zel Todd never quite managed to have.

The *Westside Chronicle* has a journalist and a photographer waiting.

'We were told there'd be a chicken,' the journalist says. 'A big chicken. No promises, but I think I can get you front page for a big chicken. What does it look like? Is it friendly? Could we get a pic with a kid?'

'Leave it to me,' I tell them. 'It'll only take a minute.'

They follow us inside where the day shift, who have come in hours early for this, are already at work. The hotplate is on and there's a tray of chicken breasts on its way from the fridge in the storeroom. I change out the back, and I can't help noticing the spice-grinder technique on display as I'm passing on my way to the road. These people are definitely not the A team.

I bounce out the front door, as friendly as a giant chicken with a moulded head can be. There are now people clustering outside. I pat the heads of a couple of children, and they shriek. Not a good idea. I lean over so that I can see them properly and say something human and reassuring.

A girl, who must be about four, looks right into my eyes and screams, 'Mummy it ate a man.'

We make do with a picture of me, Ron, Vanessa, the shopfront and a happy crowd of adult burger eaters.

Ron tells the *Chronicle*, 'We're aiming to bring the western suburbs a touch of class on a family budget,' and the journalist says, 'That's a quote for sure,' as she writes it down.

We talk about having quality in mind, and the customer. I tell them – and I can't believe I'm saying it – that Ron's a self-made man, you know, but I manage to stop myself getting into what he did for Australia in 'Nam.

The White Lightning car from Double B arrives, swinging into the driveway then swerving onto the pavement 'Miami Vice' style. But the man who steps out of the passenger seat is neither Crockett nor Tubbs. He's wearing all-over denim for a start, rather than pastel, and his walk is white-guy faux-funky rather than sincerely cool. He's a try-hard in Ray-Bans and red shoes, a black Rat Man T-shirt and a rat's tail hanging from the back of his messy hair and over his collar. It can only be the star of the Breakfast Bar, the much-anticipated Richie the Rat.

I'm about to turn to Vanessa to tell her these kinds of people are often disappointing in the flesh, but she's already plunging into some deep starry-eyed swoon, clutching one of my wings so the world doesn't drop out from under her.

Richie looks our way with an oily smirky grin and Vanessa goes, 'Oh god, oh god,' into my shoulder as he comes over. 'Could you get me a sticker, Phil?'

'Well,' Richie says, 'we've got the chicken and we've got the chicken's little helper.' He sizes Vanessa up from head to toe. 'How are you today, little helper?'

'I'm good, Richie,' she manages in a small voice that makes it clear she would have settled for a sticker. 'Love the show, mate.'

'That's the way, babe, that's what Richie likes to hear. Now, what's the drill? What have we got happening here today, darlin'?'

'Italian-style with mixed herbs and chunky tomato,' I hear Ron saying to my right, and he passes a chicken burger to Richie on a paper plate.

'Fancy.' He takes a bite. 'Fancy, but good. Not bullshit fancy. I like your style, mate. A plate of fries wouldn't go astray.' He turns to the White Lightning and shouts out, 'Hey lads, come and cop some of this.'

They set up and he does the first cross back to the studio, using the expression 'famous for their hotplate chicken' twice. He picks up comments from a few happy customers outside the store and he goes to a special World of Chickens double play – Mondo Rock's 'Cool World' and Status Quo's 'Rockin' All Over the World'.

'Mate,' he says to me while Status Quo's still playing, 'we've got a stack of "world" songs coming up. Not so many about chickens, but a stack of "world" songs. We've got some gun researchers on our show.'

Cars are driving past honking horns, people are waving, Status Quo is blaring from the speakers on top of the White Lightning. Richie the Rat and his crew stuff burgers into their faces.

'Back on air in ten,' he says as the chorus repeats. 'And we might just go with the chicken and the little lady, I think. No offence, Ron, it's just a question of the market. These kids look very Double B to me.' The chorus repeat tapers off, and he signals us to be ready. 'So,' he says dramatically, 'the Rat Man's out and about and back live at World of Chickens, Moggill Road, Taringa, home of the famous hotplate chicken burger, where they're giving it all away White-Lightning Freebie-Friday style for about another forty minutes. Come on down if you're in the neighbourhood. No, cross town for these burgers. Trust me, you won't regret it. And now, live here with me, I've got the big chook himself. And what's your name, mate?'

He trusts the microphone up into the beak. It's silver with a green foam end with two Bs on it. What's my name? What's my bloody bloody name? Do chickens even have them? Phil the chicken. Phil the chicken. Fill the chicken with what? And how would Sophie feel if I grabbed all the glory? What's my name? I've lost it again. What's my name in the real world even, not the chicken world? Starts with a P, sounds like an F. I want to go to the Mater now. My mouth is moving. There's no sound.

'I'm Vanessa, Richie,' a voice says next to me, and the mike vanishes. 'I'm Vanessa . . .' louder all of a sudden, booming from the top of the White Lightning . . . 'and I'm nearly seventeen, I'm a Gemini and I'm in charge of the signs and that around here. And I've got to tell you there's no-one else does famous hotplate chicken like these guys, and there's no-one else does classic rock like the Bs.'

'Little lady, you're playing my song. Why don't you tell us some more about you.'

'Well, it's early days yet, Richie, but I've got plans. I would have liked to have done hydraulics – like, a platform, with the chicken going up and down – but I can't really do hydraulics yet. But at night-time we've got a strobe. That's cool. I got it from my brother, the oldest. Hi, AJ.'

'And how do you think it's going here?'

'Mate, it's ripping along. Take a look.'

'And where to for you after this Vanessa?'

'Like, right now?'

'No, your future. Tell us more about those plans. Is there a guy on the scene, maybe? Where does a bright young thing like you see herself going from here?'

'Well, Richie, I'd be happy doing any of this kind of stuff, maybe even lopping trees. I'm a pretty fair climber and I've been working on the upper-body strength. I want something outside, anyway. I like it outside.'

'That's great, Vanessa. Don't you go away now.'

'No way. Hey, could you play some Alice Cooper for me? "You and Me" by Alice Cooper? That's a pretty special song. And could I say a cheerio to the guys at Green

Loppers, 'cause they always listen to Double B and they dropped me off here on their way to a job this morning.'

'No problem. We've got a few more world songs coming up first, but I'm sure we can find some Alice Cooper for you, Vanessa. But right now, an oldie but a goldie, Engelbert Humperdinck and "Winter World of Love".'

The song begins, the overblown strings rising from the car and drifting across Taringa. I'm still stuck wondering if the chicken has its own name, wondering why the hell we hadn't sorted that out earlier, when Richie the Rat says they'll be on their way shortly, and how would the little lady feel about a bit of a tour of the back of the White Lightning?

'We've got to get her on her way to work, unfortunately.' Suddenly, I come across a voice when it's really needed. 'But I'm sure she'd love a couple of stickers.'

When they're gone, Vanessa – laden with stickers, a Double B jeans patch and cap and a Rat Man T-shirt – says, 'I can't believe you did that for me. Just stood aside and let me do the talking.'

'No problem. I didn't actually know you'd be so good at it.'

'Sometimes,' she says philosophically, 'you only get one shot at things, hey? Mate, this has been great. Bloody excellent. Like, I'm a shithouse florist.'

Even Ron tells me it was good work, letting Vanessa have a turn, and he calls it 'a knack for spotting talent'.

We're in his car on the way to the Mater, and I'll be no more than a few minutes late for Antenatal Clinic. This morning was only a start but it was a good start, so we can perhaps relax a little. The sun's coming through the jacaranda trees on Coronation Drive and the day is warming up. Ron plays Herb Alpert and the Tijuana Brass and says, 'Do you mind?' before taking the scarf my mother gave me out of its bag and wrapping it round his neck. He pushes a couple of buttons and the windows and sun roof slide open. Cold air swirls around in the car and Ron – I can tell – pretends we're cruising the wide open road.

The scarf flaps around, Ron nods his head in time with the raucous horn section on one of the livelier tracks.

The wind slips through the open Merc, cool morning wind on your face. You could have done with some of that before the interviews. Next time, you decide, you'll be firm with them. There'll be no media commitments so early in the day. Or, at the very least, there'll be a couple of assistants plying you with strong coffee and croissants. No, bagels. What kind of life do they think you lead? What kind of time do they think you keep? You've never been a morning person, unless it was the morning after a long, unended night. Your parents are the only morning people you know, and they hardly understand you at all.

Yep, cutting chicken burgers, Ron and the Mater out of the story of this morning does improve it quite a lot. I'm sure it makes me sound at least a little like a movie guy who's hitting the breakfast media. While his head's still coming out of last night's party, of course.

'That was good,' Ron says. 'Wasn't it? Back there . . .'

'Yeah. It could really give us a kick along. It'll be interesting to see what Sophie's planning next.'

'So,' he says in a reflective way, 'there's a bit of hope for the World, the dental business is done . . .'

'Yep.'

'Okay, next issue . . . next issue. You don't mind do you?'

Do I mind? 'No.' Does that question have any other answer?

'I can tell you this,' he says, gripping the wheel firmly with both hands and turning instantly less reflective, 'because you're medical and you're a mate.' I think I could be about to mind. 'Actually, it's more of a query than an issue. And it mightn't be much . . .'

'Mmmm.' Minimal encourager. Damn. I should be ducking for cover, not mmmming.

'It's about this . . . situation, I suppose you'd call it. Just a question about this situation, and you can probably set me straight. It's not a big issue. Just wondering, you know. I've, um, how should I . . . it looks like I've, um, I've lost my edge.'

'Lost your edge? I don't think so. You backed everyone's plans this morning and ended up with a winner on your hands. I don't think you have to come up with every good idea yourself.'

'Yeah, not that edge. This'd be the other edge.'

'The other edge?'

'Mate, I'm talking about my edge as a man.'

'What?'

'The old fella, mate. He's behaving, well, like an old fella. Like the kind of fella who'd rather take it easy early on than come to the party. If you get me.'

'The party . . .' He's impotent. This is Ron Todd code for impotent, and it's me who's getting told about it. 'Oh. You mean . . .'

'Yeah. For a while, now. Quite a while. And it's not for want of trying.'

'Well, you know . . .'

'No, mate, *really* trying. I've picked up a few magazines and a video or two. Some mornings I work on it in the shower, just to see if I can get anywhere. But nothing.'

The reticence – the wheel-gripping and staring into the distance – that's all gone now. Replaced by a picture of a wet, nude Ron Todd, silently on the job alone in a Carindale ensuite. And I want to say, 'Ron, you and the shower, it's not my business,' but it's looking like I'm wrong.

'It happened round about the time we bumped up the loan to make a move on Max's Snax,' he says. 'I've never had a loan like this before. It was round about then, anyway. And I thought that, if I threw myself into the work, that'd take my mind off it and it'd settle itself.'

'And Zel? How's she responded, because . . .'

'Oh, no, I haven't talked about it with Zel. I can't tell her something like that. She means the world to me. I wouldn't want to upset her. I haven't even told her the business stuff, and it's driving me crazy. But why do both of us need to be crazy? That's why I wanted to fix it. I wanted to fix it before my masculinity was seriously on the line. If that's possible. But you can tell me – is it the kind of thing that, once it's gone, it's gone? Is that what I'm looking at here?'

'No, no that shouldn't be it at all.'

So here we are, in the Coronation Drive peak-hour traffic, and soon enough I'm taking a history of Ron's impotence. There's no choice. We go into the timing, into the details of his inability to achieve and maintain erections, into possible features of predisposing conditions. And I have the feeling that, if I didn't take an interest – a clinical kind of interest – Ron might not have talked about this again with anyone, and the problem would never come close to being fixed.

I get to discover, in Ron's own words, just how great a toll the stress of business and the recurrent dental abscesses have been taking on him. More than enough, I suspect, to be causing a whole range of problems. I tell him that sometimes that's all it takes and, whether it is that or not, his stress problems need dealing with, anyway. And not just by playing his tapes more, or buying a new self-help book. He should get this looked at, all of it, properly looked at, and in the meantime he should assume that something will be able to be done.

'It doesn't look any different, I don't think,' he says when we're stopped at a red light.

He starts undoing his belt buckle and shuffling around with his pants.

'Not my area,' I tell him as quickly as I can, but not before the driver of the big yellow brewery truck next to us has started taking an interest. 'A good GP'd be the first person to talk to about this.'

So he keeps his pants on, and we manage to merely blur the boundary a little more than usual, rather than completely obliterating it.

Meanwhile, Ron doesn't know it but, as we're sorting out World of Chickens, his private life might be slipping away. The problems might be bigger and more urgent than he realises. I'm angry with Frank, and I'm angry with Zel. Frank and his dumb speculation about a war injury and his general recklessness, Zel for not doing her part to sort this out. And I'm in the middle. Only me. It's up to me.

The lights change, and the road follows the curve of the river around to the right. On the freeway, the cold air comes in fiercely but Ron keeps the windows open.

Should I talk to Frank? Go back to Frank again and tell him what it is that might be going on? Impress upon him that Ron and Zel have a problem that should be fixable. Frank, whose fingertips wrinkle regularly from jacuzzi water, who has worn two new ties this week. Who can't, I realise, be trusted to do the right thing since, the way I look at it, he's been doing the wrong thing for weeks and hasn't seen the problem. Or do I have to go over his head? Do I have to go in boots and all and do I have to do it now?

We change lanes and move onto the Stanley Street off ramp. We'll be there in minutes. I'll put my white coat on, I'll call in a patient, this'll all keep for another time. Another shot at Frank, another attempt to make him see sense.

If I say nothing now, that's my only option.

'My mother . . . she does some acting.'

'Yeah? I think I'd heard that.'

'She's about to be in *Pirates of Penzance* at the Arts Theatre. They're rehearsing it now. And I think she's at a point with it where she could really use some style advice, particularly hair – those things can be tricky when you're doing G&S, particularly bringing it up to date a bit – and I was wondering . . .'

'Zel, Zel's your girl.'

'That's what I thought. So what'd be the best way to get in touch with her? Her pager maybe? We've probably got to get her involved pretty quickly.'

We pull into the patient-drop-off zone outside the Mater Mothers' and he says, 'Yeah, that's probably the best way. She's hard to track down during the day otherwise. Here, I'll give you the number.' He writes it on the back of a business card. 'The first one's the number you call, then you ask for the other number. That's the actual pager.'

'Great. Thanks.'

'No problem. Thank you. About the other thing. You really think it can be sorted out?'

'Yes, I do. I think we should assume it can be sorted out, one way or another, and you should do whatever you can to make that happen. So you should make that call to your GP and go in and mention everything you've told me today. And we can't know for sure how it'll go, but you've got to do that.'

'Yeah. Yeah, right,' he says. 'I knew you were the one to talk to.'

'That's okay. Well, good luck.'

It sounds dumb when I say it, but I don't know what else to say. What do GPs say when they refer people to specialists? I should learn that some time.

As the car pulls away from the kerb, he gives a honk of the horn and his hand comes out the window and waves. He takes the first right after the hospital, a side street that'll bring him back to the main road, and maybe we both have calls to make today. I look down at the card. Zel's number. I have to do something.

The noise from Antenatal Clinic comes out of the open double doorway at the top of the steps. There's the usual crowd of people clustering round the entrance: a couple of smokers having their last before going in (and lying about giving up), a woman six months pregnant punching a vending machine as it fails to deliver whatever she's promised the two-year-old gripping her leg. Inside, someone's name is being called.

Smokers don't seem to know that, to a non-smoker, they just about always smell of smoke or its metabolites, and those lies about giving up don't stand a chance if you've smoked the last one just outside.

I have Ron's card in my hand, with Zel's numbers on the back. I've tried sorting this out with Frank. I've talked to him. I've done the best I can, and it isn't changing a thing. If I don't talk to Zel, this'll turn bad for everybody.

Frank's judgement is out, and I have to do something.

Frank's judgement is out. It sounds as though one of Frank's headlights is out and I've taken the car to get it fixed. It's not the same. Not the same as being straightforwardly helpful, or bailing him out of the usual trouble. Every time that's been my job – every other time in the past four years when Frank's judgement has been out – I've got involved with his consent. Even with the butt photos, my plan was to talk him out of it if they got developed. But this is a new situation. There's no precedent.

I've wandered away from Antenatal Clinic, downhill towards Mater Adults' and the on-call rooms. I can think there, and make phone calls if there are phone calls to make. But I don't have to do anything, unless I definitely decide to. Then I'd call switch, say she's a doctor and I need to page her. They'd give me an outside line and I'd call the paging service and she'd call me back direct on the number of the phone in the hall. It wouldn't surprise me if she's called it before.

I stop. I put the card in my pocket. I'll talk to Frank today. This morning. One last time.

Two men come out of the on-call rooms with large bags of used sheets and towels.

'Dirty buggers,' one of them says. 'What if someone had called? Isn't that what they're supposed to be doing in those rooms? Waiting for emergencies?'

The other one laughs, and heaves his load up and into the already overloaded laundry cart. 'Reckon we're done.'

One pushes, one pulls, and the cart moves up the camber of the road and down towards the opposite gutter. Exposing – right in front of me – the bins, Zel Todd's car and Zel and Frank. Zel and Frank, who are engaged in something that should be kept much more private. She's standing on the broken low wall, Frank's reclining against the car and Zel's taking to him in a way I haven't had to think about since I saw *Alien*. Any more tongue and she'll have his head slurped into a sticky cocoon within seconds. We might never need to have that talk, if Zel's using Frank to feed her young.

The noise that comes out of me is a genuine groan, and it's out before I realise it. Zel turns and, suddenly, I'm part of this. Suddenly, it's Zel and Frank again. It's not a movie and she's not an intergalactic predator looking at me as though I'm her next victim. She's horrified, just as she should be.

Her head jerks away from Frank's and she stumbles from the wall. Then he sees me, too.

'Fuck,' he says, taking some time over it.

I go at him. 'What do you mean "fuck"? How can you possibly be surprised? You're outside, you idiots. You're next to a road. In the Mater.'

'Yeah, um . . .'

'Oh, right, they came for the sheets, did they? So you figured you'd have sex against the car.'

'No, no,' Frank says. 'It's just a goodbye thing. Look . . .'

'I've looked. I've seen enough.'

'Um, yeah. Shit. Antenatal Clinic. Thanks for reminding me, mate. Lost track of time there.' He picks up his bag and pulls out his white coat. 'Um, see you,' he says to Zel, and he's off. Across the road, into Nursing Admin, his bag trailing on the ground, one arm stuffing itself down an inside-out coat sleeve.

'Philip,' Zel, says, in a tone of voice that tells me she's older and I'm to be talked into a respectful silence. Big mistake, Zel.

'What the fuck do you think you're doing? Are you insane?' Not silence, nothing like it. 'Not only is this a road in a hospital, but what the fuck are you doing with your life? Haven't you thought about your family at all? Have you thought about what you might be throwing away, about the people who are going to get hurt?'

'Um, I really do have to go,' she says in an infuriating pastel-lipped voice, and she rearranges her hair and starts looking in her bag for her keys.

'No. No. You can't go. You can't run away from this. Frank can behave like a complete child, but you can't.'

'You should just mind your own business. That's what you should do.'

'And you should sort yours out. I've got dragged into this, but I'm in it now. Right in it. So don't give that shit about "business". You're going to listen to me, and you're going to hear just how it really is. And then you're going to sort this out.'

'This is nothing to do with you,' she says, her voice low and hard and angry.

She turns to the car, unlocks the door. I drop my bag and I run between the bins.

'It is to do with me,' I tell her as I jump down into the parking bay. 'I know things you need to know.'

'What rubbish. I'm going.' She climbs into the car, swings the door shut and turns the engine on.

I pull the passenger door open, and I'm still shouting. 'Listen, just for one second.'

'Away, Philip, away.' She puts it in gear.

'It's Ron. It's Ron, fuck you. It's the stress. It's taking its toll.' I get my right leg into the car, she hits it with her bag. As she stamps on the accelerator, and just before the tyre screech drowns out all other sound, I shout, 'Ron's masculinity is on the line. It's medical.' The car jumps from the parking bay, and no-one hears me say, 'You mean the world to him.'

Something, some part of the car, thumps into my right thigh and tosses me to the ground, the door swings open and clangs against the branch of a frangipani tree, snapping a piece of it away, and Zel is off down the road. I'm left sitting on the concrete in the last of the blue exhaust smoke.

'Hey,' Frank says when he comes up to me between patients. 'Bit of a spin-out earlier. You, me and the lady. Hadn't been banking on that.'

'No, not much on the planning, are you?'

'You, um, wouldn't be up for a coffee, would you?'

'Coffee's shit here. Always has been. I don't know why you keep suggesting it.'

I walk away to pick up the next patient's file but he comes after me, like a dog that knows it's in trouble and wants to slink along showing contrition.

'So, um,' he says, as if there's still a conversation to be had. 'It's got a bit complicated all of this, hasn't it?'

'A bit complicated? I might have suggested that a while back.'

'Yeah.'

'Come on.' Said just like an instruction to a dog.

I walk past the waiting patients, across the lino floor to the door, and Frank follows me. We go out and up the steps and across the road, across a patch of grass, on our way to nowhere in particular.

'Hang on a sec,' he says, and we stop. I turn around and he looks at me and then past me. He smirks, he can't help himself. 'We wouldn't have done it up against the car.'

'Yeah, that's the issue, isn't it? Whether she was going to be happy just pushing her tongue out the back of your head, or whether she was up for more by the roadside.'

'So, um, what do you reckon then? What are you going to do?'

'What am I going to do? I don't know. What do I reckon? I reckon the two of you are behaving like fuckwits and you couldn't be more selfish. I reckon this is going to turn very bad. And I reckon I've tried to point that out and you haven't been particularly interested, and I've had enough. You're on your own.'

'Yeah,' he says, and rolls his eyes. 'But what do you really reckon? Quit holding back on me.'

'Okay, what you don't know is that I still am holding back on you. I just gave you the mild version of how I feel about this.'

'Okay.' This time no roll of the eyes. 'I'm getting the picture.'

'Really?'

'Really. So, how did it go down there after I left?'

'Well, there's a set of big fat tyre marks on the concrete in the parking bay. You're not exactly good at confronting issues are you, the two of you?'

'Who is? Who likes issues?' He shakes his head. 'This was supposed to be much more straightforward, you know. I only agreed to this on the grounds that there'd be no complications.'

'Because that's how life works, isn't it? Maybe we should just tell Ron and Sophie what you agreed, and everyone'll be fine.'

'It wasn't supposed to be like this.'

'Yeah, but it was always going to be like this. And that's why I've been telling you to fix it. Now, they'll be missing us in Antenatal Clinic, so we shouldn't hang around here. We can talk about this later, if you want to talk about it.'

He nods and says, 'Yeah,' and we go back across the grass and the road, and down the steps. The doors to the clinics slide open.

'Either of you guys Phil Harris?' the clerk on the desk says. 'I've got an urgent message for a Phil Harris, one of the med students.'

He tears the top sheet from his message pad and hands it to me. He's ticked the 'please call' box and written the name Zel Todd next to it.

Frank looks at it and says, 'That's the home number.'

'I know it's the home number.'

'So what are we going to do?'

'We? I'm going to go down to the end room and I'm going to call. You're going to take the next patient. And I'll tell you what I can later.'

He looks like he wants to say more, and then he lifts the next file from the desk and calls out the name.

Zel answers after the first ring.

'What's medical?' she says. 'What did you mean about masculinity?'

'It's something I found out, something I just found out today.'

'Yes.'

'You understand I don't want to be in this position? You understand that I know that all of this is none of my business, but I've found out some things you need to be aware of? Frank talks to me, and Ron talks to me, so I hear things.'

'Yes. And what's happening with masculinity?'

'It's Ron. It could be the stress. And I'm really not supposed to tell you this. I'm betraying a trust by telling you this.'

'Yes, I know.' And she says it as if she actually does know. Her voice couldn't be more different to the way it sounded earlier.

'I'm not supposed to tell you, but Ron doesn't know why I have to tell you. He doesn't know anything about

Frank. Ron's taken the business stress pretty hard, and there were a few problems he couldn't have guessed when he took on World of Chickens. The stress, like I said, has taken its toll on a few aspects of Ron. And he finds it hard to tell you because he doesn't want to worry you and he says you mean the world to him.'

'He said that?'

'This morning. In the car on the way here. Ron's invested a lot in what he's made of himself. He's too proud to want to admit to you that it's not all going perfectly.'

'But he could tell me. Why couldn't he tell me? What would he tell you instead?'

'Because what you think matters most. He could tell me because that's not such a big deal, and because it's not my business. And some of it has a medical side to it.'

'But all I see is him being in a bad mood at home, and not wanting to talk if I ask him about it. And getting toothache every night and now his hip problems have flared up whenever he lies down and . . .'

'And some of the medical stuff, that's the stuff he kind of feels is putting his masculinity on the line. And I don't mean the toothache and the hip problems.'

'What? What do you . . . masculinity . . .' There's a longer pause this time. 'Ah, that kind of problem.'

'Yes.'

'A physical problem? A performance problem?'

'That's right.'

'Why didn't he . . .'

'I didn't say he was a perfect communicator. There's a bit he could learn there, but he's not alone in that. And he's a good man. Stress can cause this, you know. So can other things, but something should be able to be done.'

'Oh shit. Shit. Are you for real?'

'For real? Why would I make any of it up?'
'Oh shit. Oh, Philip, shit.'

An hour later, it all comes out.

Zel ends the call after 'Oh, Philip, shit,' and says she wants to see me now. Has to see me now.

We've had a lecture rescheduled for eleven, so that's when I report back to Frank. He catches up with me just as we're making our early exit from Antenatal Clinic, and I tell him she's on her way.

'On her way . . .'

'Yeah. She'll be here any time. She wants to talk face-to-face. To me.'

'Could be trouble.'

'Could be anything. Take good notes.'

He rolls his white coat into a ball, stuffs it into his bag and follows the others up the path to the lecture room.

Five minutes later, Zel pulls into the patient-drop-off zone outside the hospital. There's a scratch on the passenger door from the frangipani tree, a scratch and a long shallow dent.

'Thank you,' is all she says as I get in.

She pulls out, with the charms on her gold bracelets tinkling across the steering wheel as she turns it. We park in a side street a few blocks away. She adjusts her sunglasses, and looks out the windscreen. A car drives by, looking for a parking space.

And Zel tells me about the affair she thought Ron was having. An affair with someone much younger. She tells me about the cheerleader videos he's got hidden at home, at least ten of them, and magazines. Men's magazines. And she did a test that she found in a magazine article – not one of his magazines – and it showed that he had six of the eight major warning signs of someone who was cheating. And they said six was high probability.

'And after that . . . after that . . .'

After that, the inaccuracy of her high-probability magazine-test result suddenly hit home, and the life she's been leading hit home harder. She pulled handfuls of tissues out of the glove box and wiped her face vigorously, until a lot of her tan came away and her cheeks went red and shiny instead of the usual dusky cinnamon.

We agreed to call it 'a case of very poor communication on both sides'. I told her Ron had mentioned the videos this morning, and it had been clear they'd been a homemade kind of therapy. Fortunately, she didn't ask for my views on why he'd needed ten of them to know that it wasn't working, or on why every one seemed to be about cheerleaders. I didn't even know cheerleader porn was its own genre, until today.

Zel told me she watched bits of a couple, hoping that there was a problem with the boxes and the videos were something else. But at the same time it was in the back of her mind that, if they were what they purported to be, she might watch them with Ron, and that might help. But she couldn't do it. For a start she found she couldn't mention to Ron that she'd seen them but, even if she'd been able to, the movies were just too bad. 'Busty girls with exploding bras who kept falling on their pom-pom handles, and it never made any sense,' she said, as if that meant that the storylines would have given the two of them very little to work with.

I told her that had always been my main problem with porn, cinematically, across all its sub-genres. They use up their imagination on the titles, and I can't abide the disrespect for narrative.

'I tried to change my hair,' she said. 'I even signed up

for jazz-ballet classes, but he never noticed and it just made me feel old. Then I did the cheating test. Then . . .'

She called herself an idiot. She punched the steering wheel. She asked me questions. How to talk to Ron, how much to tell. Questions that are too big, too important, for me to try to answer. But I told her I thought she should be careful breaking anything dramatic right now, and that the first step might not involve Ron at all. So it's not like I held back and didn't interfere.

'Frank,' she said. Another moment of grim realisation. 'What do I do about Frank?'

I told her that was up to her too. What was I supposed to say? 'Ten cheerleader videos would make an excellent parting gift? Pom-pom porn could get to be Frank's second-favourite movie genre without much problem at all?'

At the end, she thanked me and she tilted the rear-view mirror her way and filled in the gaps she'd rubbed in her make-up, repastelled her worn lips, smacked them together and dabbed them with a tissue. 'Better,' she said, though it wasn't much, and she drove me back to an obscure entrance to the Mater. She squeezed my hand and thanked me again, and I got out of the car and walked quickly away.

Frank explains that he did take notes, but it wasn't much of a lecture.

And I tell him that there's a lot of stuff going on between Zel and Ron, things they have to deal with that aren't about either of us. I tell him what I can, and he knows he can't ask for more.

He's quieter than usual at lunch. I want to tell him it'll be okay if things don't work out with Zel. It's always okay soon enough. Options don't take long to show themselves to Frank. But I still don't know what she'll do, what this means to her now that she's far from here, across town, back on her turf in Carindale.

'Hey,' he says. 'How was this morning? The breakfast giveaway at the World. Ness was up early getting ready.'

'It was good. She was good. She did some on-air stuff, and she was really good at it.'

Ness, who seized the day. I'd forgotten that, with all that's happened since. Ness who came out and said it for the first time on the top-rating breakfast radio show in town — she knows what she wants to be instead of a florist. I hope they were listening, and I hope Big Artie gets this one right.

After lunch, we attach ourselves to a ward round, then we have an amniocentesis tute at four.

I keep hearing the tinkle of bracelet charms as Zel put her hands up to cover her face in the car. To hide for a moment, since the outside world had grown too big to deal with. It was tough, facing all that, but she could find a kind of good news in there, too. Six out of eight signs say that Ron's having an affair, they're all wrong and I might have bought her some time to work with that.

The tute goes on a while, later than it's supposed to.

'Better go,' Frank says, taking a look at his watch when we come out. 'With all that business you and Ness and Richie the Rat will have stirred up for us this morning, we don't want to be late. The World awaits.'

It's the last day of May and the afternoons are ending noticeably earlier. It's dark when we walk to the car, the beginnings of a clear, starry night. We join the trail of brake lights that's strung along the edge of town on the sweep of the freeway. We cross the river and leave the city to our right, with Human League playing on Double B. Frank turns it up, humming along to the bits he knows and then just humming.

Sophie hasn't arrived when we get to World of Chickens, so I take the suit. The team that's finishing tells us business hasn't been bad. There have been a few cars pulling out of the traffic to pick up early dinners, and a couple of people have asked if this is the place where Richie the Rat had it Italian style for Freebie Friday this morning.

This morning, or last century. The days are long when you leave home with a thermos at six-thirty and get caught up counselling old people in the midst of a crisis. So it's good to be away from talk and out at the road. Or it would be, if we didn't have the strobe and all those signs. Just when I really feel like slacking off, we've turned the job into something busy.

And customers are turning up, not in huge numbers but enough to mean that Frank is missing Sophie's work at the counter. I catch his attention and he shrugs and shakes his head. I signal to ask him if he wants me in there helping, and he nods.

It's another fifteen minutes before Sophie comes in the back door.

'Sorry,' she says. 'Sorry.' Looking awful, red-faced and sniffing. 'I'll just get changed.'

And then she's gone again, down the corridor trying to look like someone making up for lost time.

'Chicks,' Frank says, sighing at their perpetual mystery as he flips the last fillet for now. 'I think you'd better get out there and sort her out.'

'Me?'

But it can only be me. Sophie's the only Todd I haven't put into therapy today, and I need to complete my set. What's she heard? What's happened?

She's sitting on the steps, with her forehead down on her arms and her arms folded across her knees, and she's sniffing.

'Sophie . . .'

'Go away. Just go away.'

'Does that mean . . .'

'Go away.'

'Okay, do you want to do the counter, or be the chicken?'

'Counter.'

'Are you sure? Are you . . .'

'Go away. Please.'

'Okay, I'll just change and then we'll see . . . I'll just change.'

I can still hear the sniffing while I'm in the toilet, and it's drowned out only briefly by a westbound train. And I'm not going to go away, am I?

'I have just been having a very bad day,' is how she puts it, each word angry, when I come out in costume and try to talk to her again. 'There's a whole lot of things . . . a whole lot of things, all happening at once. And you . . . I can't believe you think I have to tell you.' She sniffs. 'Ah, my nose.'

'What's wrong with your nose?'

'Exams. I'm going to fail. I am going to fail. I had one this afternoon, an early one. They sprung it on us. I only found out about it a couple of days ago. And I had to get out of it, right? So I did that toothpaste thing, that swallowing toothpaste thing, where you swallow a lot of it and put on a couple of jumpers and run around and it gives you a fever, and you go to the health service and get a certificate. Well, I threw it up instead and it came out my nose.'

'I didn't realise things were like that.'

'No, you didn't,' she says, and for the first time I notice the minty smell. 'I didn't tell you. That's me, okay? It's like, I don't freak out. I freak in . . . Shit this is bad in the nose. It's like my sinuses are really clear but my eyes are watering.'

'Yeah, I know what it's like. I had a bad experience with Créme de Menthe once. A few times.'

'What'll I do? It's really burning.'

'Um, I don't know. Maybe they don't cover management of toothpaste burns to nasal mucosa until sixth year. Other than wash it out, I don't know.'

'Don't you laugh at me.'

'I'm not laughing. It's one of the less common self-inflicted injuries, but . . .'

'Don't you laugh because I know you were with my mother this morning.' Okay, that does stop me. I'm not laughing. 'I wondered about what was going on, and I didn't want to, and now I know.'

'What?'

'You were with my mother. I heard her talking to you on the phone to organise it.'

'I don't think you understand.'

'Oh really? Really?'

'I had to talk to your mother about my mother. She's in a play, a musical, *Pirates of Penzance* at the Arts Theatre, remember? I got your mother's pager number from your father this morning. I wanted to arrange style advice for my mother. Costume and hair. Mainly hair.'

'Yeah, right. And that accounts for all the shit going on over the last month. Your mother and Gilbert and Sullivan. You want to know what I think? Since that's just a lie. Here's what I think. My mother is having an affair. That's what I think's happening. Things are totally strange at home and you know what? The two of you are singing the same songs. And even though that's not one of the eight classic signs of an affair – even though she's only showing five of them, which means moderate risk – it's good enough to be a ninth sign as far as I'm concerned. I heard you both doing "Eye of the Tiger" on the same night two weeks ago, and I don't know what that's about but I do know she's big on talkback. There's nothing she listens to that'd play eighties music. Nothing newer than Neil bloody Diamond – that's my mother. Phoebe, Jacinta, my mother – for god's sake, how many is enough for you? I don't understand you at all. And you were bizarre on the bat cruise and then you saw her this morning. You've started getting very clumsy. And you pretend to be Dad's friend and my friend. Well, I've had enough.' That's when she stops. Snaps to a stop as if there can be nothing more.

So I go to the back door, and I shut it. I shut it slowly and calmly. I don't usually get angry with people, but I'm angry now and I want to say something cool and sensible. And then I want to shout at Frank later, a lot.

It doesn't quite work out that way.

The first cool sensible thing I can manage is: 'When will you people stop reading those fucking trashy magazines?' And the 'fucking' echoes off the houses on the other side of the train tracks. 'When will you stop putting me in the middle of things? I'm going to tell you what's happening. I'm going to tell you, and you couldn't be more wrong.'

She looks up. 'Yeah?' She doesn't know what to say next, what to believe, what she most wants to hear or what she might hear. She thought she'd caught me out.

'Okay. Here's what's happening. This is what's happening. I'm not even getting into the Phoebe and Jacinta issue – for which, by the way, there is a totally straightforward explanation – but here's what's happening with your parents. It started with your father talking to me, then your mother. There have been a few issues with the business expansion – and I'm not supposed to be telling you this, so if you tell anyone . . .'

'I won't.'

'It's going to be okay. But your father's been quite depressed, and he hasn't been able to talk about it. That's been difficult for both of them. Then they both started talking to me. So that's why I saw your mother today. There are some problems and I'm fucking helping, so I don't need that from you. And you were the one who said "Eye of the Tiger" was getting played everywhere. I can't believe you'd assume anything based on the fact that your mother and I both know it. How could you be alive now and not know it? For someone who's talking about friendship, you could have behaved in a friendlier way. You could have asked me. You could have said something the first time this crossed your mind, rather than just getting angry with me and then hitting me with it weeks later.'

'Shit,' she says, and puts her forehead back down onto her arms. 'Shit, shit. Don't be angry with me back. You can't be angry with me when you're dressed like a chicken. It's just too silly. Please.'

I can't say anything. I'm angry and sad and relieved at the same time. Sad about all of this. Relieved that she's believing me, but it can't quite be enough. Angry with myself for lying to her right now and still angry with her for thinking what she's been thinking. But despite that, as I look down at her out of the beak slot, I'm finding it hard to stay as angry as I think I should, watching her there folded up on the steps, distraught and now smelling strongly of mint.

'Remember,' she says, 'when you told me your favourite film was *The Graduate*?'

'*The Graduate*?'

'Yeah. It was on TV a couple of weeks ago. Not long after you'd said it was so good. So I watched it. And that was around "Eye of the Tiger" time.'

'There is no "Eye of the Tiger" time. Move on, idiot.' She laughs, so that's good. 'Did you actually watch the film, or were you just trying to . . . Did you see those gestures, the expressions on Dustin Hoffman's face, the little noises he makes? It's a one-off. It's amazing. He is simply a great actor. You give him a regular character and he makes it amazing. He's not one of those guys who needs to put on a dress or play someone's psycho brother to stand out.'

'Yeah, but Mrs Robinson . . .'

'It's a great film. That's why I like it. And Mrs Robinson is sad. I'm not setting out to copy *The Graduate*, with your mother or with anyone. Films are supposed to be about life. Life isn't supposed to be about films. Get it?'

A train passes, slowing down. The inbound trains always come by a few minutes after the outbound. A cat meows, somewhere on the other side of the line.

Sophie lifts her head and says, 'Hey, have you ever thought that cats don't really go meow? They can't do Ws. Their lips don't do that. They don't even do Ms. They just go yaah and then shut their mouths, or something, towards the end.'

'Surprisingly, I hadn't ever thought that.'

'So there we go. One of life's mysteries.'

'And it's so full of them, isn't it? So much mystery that it's the sensible bits I seem to go days without. I used to have them, you know. Back before I started recommending films to people, and getting over-involved. Or whatever.'

The cat meows again. Or, more accurately, yaahs, shutting its mouth towards the end to draw the sound to a close that masquerades quite well as a W.

'I'm sorry about that,' she says. 'I wish I'd . . . been smarter. It's been a shit of a day in too many ways. We should get to work.' She holds her hand out for me to help her up. 'How do you think it'll go? Mum and Dad? Is it going to be all right?'

'I think so. But it's got to be up to them.'

'Them and the guy who nearly picked up that psych medal.'

'I should stop saying that.'

We walk into the shop together and Frank, dealing with a couple of customers, says, 'Ah, some help.'

It's lucky for him that I'm the chicken now, and heading for the street.

'Patched up another fallen soldier,' he says when I'm with him at the counter after the next swap. 'Where would they be without you? Clinton problems, was it?'

'What the fuck do you think it was?'

'She doesn't know . . .'

'No, she doesn't. And I didn't tell her.'

Tonight, every zit on his neck annoys me, every minute we work together. His snuffly sinusy breathing, his stupid remarks, his cockiness with the tongs. Plenty of tiny things that don't matter at all annoy me a lot. And so does Sophie, as I'm standing here watching her. I want to go up to her right now and tell her how hard I'm trying and how little she knows me, if she thought she could make those assumptions.

Towards the end of my time at the counter, long after I've made myself stop watching her but haven't stopped thinking about the whole mess, I go out the back for another bag of fries. She's sitting on the steps in the costume, sniffing and trying to sing Cyndi Lauper's 'Time After Time'. In very different circumstances, it'd make me laugh. She hears me, and turns.

'Oh. Concentration problem,' she says. 'Remember your idea of singing to keep concentrating?'

'That was for out at the road.'

'The strobe kept getting in my eyes. I had to stop. I'm re-concentrating now. And I'm really sorry, you know.'

'Yeah. I'm sure we'll get over it.'

19

When we're in the car, I tell Frank what happened with Sophie. The way she'd added it up, the way she'd blamed me. I make it clear that I took some shit for him, and I covered. But that's all I tell him, and it should be all I need to.

Frank doesn't say much.

He calls me on Saturday, not long before dinner. He tells me it's over with Zel, first making it sound as if it was all down to him, then admitting that she'd worked it out that way, too.

'It's been wild, you know?' he says, but almost dismissively, making it sound as though he's describing a better-than-average summer holiday. It's enough to make me angry all over again. 'But all good things must come to an end. It met a short-term need, I think. That's what I think it did for both of us. And it was starting to get a bit intense, to be honest. Particularly for you – not that I get how that works, but, you know . . . And, jeez, she'd make demands, I've got to say that. I was in danger of getting rich, the amount she was calling. If we break it off now, well, that's probably the way to do it.' And I want to shout at every bland sentence he speaks, but I don't. 'She said it made her realise what a good man Ron is, and how she wants to work things out.'

'Good.'

'Yeah. The shit was about to fly, wasn't it? How do you think things'll be between you and Sophie?'

'How many times have I told you, there is nothing between me and Sophie?'

'That's not what I meant, dickhead.'

'I've got to go. Things'll be what they'll be. Fine, I guess. She fucked up, not me. It's a nice change, at least. Anyway, I've got to go and set the table. We've got people coming over for dinner.'

'Yeah, okay. It's Ness's birthday next Friday night. Did I tell you that? Are you coming?'

'Are we working?'

'No. And she wants you to be there. She said. She wanted me to ask you.'

'Then I'll come.'

I check with my mother that I'm setting the table for five, and I get the silverware out of the sideboard. Silver – I thought that was another symbol of affluence. Not that I craved affluence, but it's where I thought we were – at the regular end of the affluent part of the spectrum (or the affluent end of the regular part of the spectrum). But the silverware was a wedding present given to my mother's grandmother in 1895. All it's cost in the twentieth century is the price of polish.

I'm glad Frank called. Finally, something's getting sorted out. For the first time in days, I feel myself relaxing.

And relaxing, it turns out, is a big mistake.

My mother's friend Celia is a psychologist and her husband Roger is a law lecturer. They're both in *Pirates*. We're calling it *Pirates* tonight. That's the kind of thing that happens once we're well into rehearsals. I don't know what parts they're playing, but Roger does carry himself like 'the very model of a modern major general'. Is that *Pirates*? Do I care? The evening's all very pleasant but I'm used to these dinners offering me little more than that, and I'm used to blending into the background. Actually, maybe it's not all very pleasant. Not at all unpleasant but stuck somewhere stiff and formal, waiting for someone to ease up and take the rest of us with them. With Roger and my father both here, there are too many major generals in the room.

Also, it's fondue, and Frank's not invited. That seems wrong for a start.

But it's my mother – my mother who's the problem, failing to relax. It's her fault for inviting cast members round less than two weeks before opening. We don't usually do that. So tonight we fake, rather than make, conversation. Obstetrics, gourmet chicken burgers. That's my share of the topics, and no-one should pretend it's interesting.

I clear the table when we're finished. My mother brings in a homemade apple pie, my father offers our guests an appalling range of coloured drinks from memory. 'She's a psychologist, you fool,' I want to say to him. 'At least don't recite them in alphabetical order.'

Sadly, I'm the one who triggers the conversation we've been on the fringes of all evening. And all of us knew that's where we were, except me.

Celia tutors part-time at uni. She's an adolescent psychologist. So I ask her if she's working on the new unit with my mother.

'New unit?' she says. 'Which . . .'

'Yes, the new unit.' My mother interrupts her. 'I hadn't really got into the details with Celia yet. I've been going through the book first before getting her help.'

'What's it about?' I'm being conversational, because I've been brought up well.

'The book?'

'The unit.'

'Well, um . . .' She glances at Celia, who nods. 'It's

about young people who become mixed up in undesirable things. Not that there aren't a very broad range of things that are desirable to some people and that are or should be perfectly acceptable as long as there's consent and no coercion or money changing hands . . .'

'Good. It's going to be tough trimming it down to a two-line course summary though, isn't it?'

'Money changing hands,' she says, in case the point wasn't made well enough the first time. Whatever the point is. 'That twenty dollars you had the other day, Wednesday . . .'

'I did say I was saving money. It's not surprising if I'm in possession of some, is it?'

'Yes, but that particular twenty dollars . . .'

That particular twenty dollars. The Ron Todd money. The money that changed hands in a cinema foyer in the middle of the city three days ago. This, I fear, could be going to a very bad place, and dragging me right there with it.

'Who gave you that money Philby?' my mother says, and the question comes at me like a mike in the beak. I'm stuck again. She looks strained. 'Was it Mister Todd?'

'I work for him . . .'

'Was it Mister Todd, in the foyer of a cinema, after a matinee?'

'What?'

'I have a friend who was at the Forum on Wednesday at lunchtime. She said she saw you there, with a man who I think might be Mister Todd, and I think he might have been . . . forcing some money on you. She called me that evening.'

'Well, I think there's been a misunderstanding. It was Ron . . .'

'So, you took the money from Mister Todd. Yes, there's been a misunderstanding, Philby, hasn't there?'

'What?'

'There's been a misunderstanding and it's all our fault. We tried to instil values in you. We tried to show you that a person has to work for their money, and we never talked about boundaries. It was all that infernal dollar-for-dollar deal.' She glares at my father.

'I'm sorry, lad,' he says.

'And I'm very sorry too, Philby. You so wanted that video camera and you came up with the money very quickly, and you were seen there that afternoon, and you came home that night so proud of yourself for having earned the money for the camera, and you pulled the cheque out of your pocket and out came that twenty dollar note. And my worst fears were confirmed.'

'Phoebe,' Celia says in an excessively calm therapist's voice that she's been saving until now. 'We talked about catastrophising.'

'And you've always been a good boy. You've always kept your money in your wallet, not loose in your pocket. Haven't you Philby? And that twenty dollars was loose in your pocket . . .'

'Yes, but . . .'

'Does he give you drugs, Philip?' Celia says. 'Does he buy you drugs?'

'Drugs?' Okay, that's got me. I'm annoyed. And I know it's proving easy to get me there these days, but Celia manages it in one move. 'Only to heighten the orgasm,' I tell her. 'He bought me a coffee once. So that'd mean caffeine. It's a drug.'

'You never wanted me to meet that girl, did you?' my mother says. 'You really wanted me out of the house for lunch. Was it a girl, Philby, or . . .'

'Or did Ron Todd take me from behind in your bed for

money? Is that the whole question? Correct me if I'm wrong, but that seems to be what we're talking about here, even though no-one's exactly coming out and saying it. I didn't want you to be here that day because of how totally ridiculous you can be. You want an example? Tonight's good.'

Celia, quiet most of the evening, can't stop herself butting in now. 'Would you like to tell us about the night when you got fifty dollars for dancing wearing a glow-in-the-dark boa?'

'I didn't even get the . . . I was working on the bar. That was a drunk girl who looped it round my neck for a couple of minutes.' I turn back to my mother, since this started with her. 'I can't believe you. What's this about? I happen to get twenty bucks from Ron, I happen to get lassoed by a drunk girl, and this is how you add it up? Are you *insane*? How could you even think that way? How did those ideas even get in your head? You're going to have to do a lot better than that to back it up, if you're going to go round thinking that's what I'm into.'

So that's when the photos come out. The photos that I thought even the lab in Tweed Heads wouldn't develop. Celia has them, and she places them on the table in a row, in order. First, photos I'd forgotten about, the ones we took for our axed revue sketch. And, until now, it was no problem at all that they were photos of me in a dress with rosy cheeks and plaits, playing with dolls. Then there's Frank and the Tim Tam, all slightly out of focus but his face clear enough in one, others just arse and biscuit, as required. And Celia puts each of the doll photos down with a decisive snap, like a blackjack dealer, but she handles the Frank shots only by the edges.

'You don't understand,' I tell them. 'The dress photos

with the dolls are for a revue sketch that we decided not to do, the ones with the Tim Tams . . .'

'Tim Tams?' Celia says, and looks more closely at one of the photos. 'That's not a Tim Tam. That's a young man in the midst of a bowel movement, I'd swear it.'

'What kind of dirty perverted photos are you used to looking at? It's a Tim Tam, for god's sake. It was a prank. There was this surgery tutor . . .'

'There's always a story,' Celia says, with a voice so calm it's sinister. 'You're quick on your feet Philip, but there's acting in the family, isn't there? You can tell us how it really adds up. Remember, we're all on your side here. Whether that's a biscuit, or something very different.'

'And what about . . .' my father says hesitantly, 'I've been meaning to ask you about that music you were taping a few weeks ago. That song about touching and heat that you were taping over and over.'

'Oh, *et tu*, Allan? That was an idea of Frank's. It . . . oh, what's the use?'

'Does Frank give you money too?' my mother says, fear on her face now like a permanent stain. 'Or is that a matter of affection?'

'Frank can't afford me. He's always telling me how poor he is. Some days he can't even afford enough roughage to make it worth carrying a camera. You could not be more wrong with this. I'm a fumbling hopeless heterosexual who doesn't even use his bullworker enough to change his lot. I have chosen the Charles Atlas way, but I have fallen. I haven't had sex for fourteen months and that was with someone you never liked, and the closest I've got this year was when I went off early in my own pants and therefore didn't get paid for my job on the *Paradise*. Bad timing in all sorts of ways, but that's my life. And it was with a girl, and in the amateur capacity that I so richly deserve. And when I got another chance with the same girl and she came over here, I cut myself shaving, I got a bit tense, I played my tape, I bled in her drink, I accidentally gave her the impression that I'd slept with you and she ran away. Is that the kind of thing you want to know? Because I'm sorry for not keeping you up to date, and accidentally giving you the impression that I was a prostitute and a pornographer and at least some kind of success at something. Not that there'd be anything wrong with me being a prostitute, blah, blah, blah. I don't know about the pornographer bit, but most of my friends pick up some hooker money here and there and everyone goes home happy as long as safe sexual practices are observed.'

And just when it looks as though things can't get any worse, Celia says, 'Now, setting aside all that for a moment, why don't you tell me about Mister Wilson?'

My mother interrupts. 'Perhaps this isn't the best time . . .'

'No, I'm doing this properly or not at all,' she says. 'Why don't you tell me about Mister Wilson, Philip?'

'Mister who? There's no Mister Wilson?'

She fixes me with a look that works the way a pin works when it attaches a butterfly to a board. Mister Wilson. Oh no.

'Mister Wilson didn't even have genitals, damn you,' I shout at her. 'He was more like Buddha.' My mother looks down at her plate, at the last crumbs of apple pie. 'But I made him up, anyway. I copied from one of my friends at preschool. I'm like that. I even cheated when it came to imaginary friends. I've got no fucking life at all, so I had to cheat to imagine one. How about that?'

'Oh yes. And what was the preschool friend's name?'

Name? What was the bloody name? I look down at the table. I'm being done in by that name business again. My hand has a tight grip on my water glass and I'm stuck again on a name. And the whole Mister Wilson thing is about to turn ugly – even uglier – and he really was just a nice old imaginary friend who deserves much better than this, and was gone, anyway, by the time I'd turned six.

'George,' I tell her. 'George Glass.'

I look up at my mother. She knows the look I'm giving her. It could best be described as imploring. And when your only child implores, you should go with it. You really should. Or you will probably go to hell when you die. Bear that in mind, Mother. Bear it in mind now.

'Oh, George, yes,' she says in a spindly lying voice. 'I remember George. He always was quite a strange boy. He'd hide behind the geraniums whenever the dogs barked.'

Was it too much, after our guests had left, to end the evening by screaming at her, 'You've violated Mister Wilson forever,' and demanding a written apology? It was one of those rare moments when you decide, I can either go formal now, or maybe cry. And crying sucks, if you ask me. I think I also screamed, 'You were the one who introduced hand puppets to bath time,' even as my mother was already realising this whole disastrous evening was down to her.

Once I'd implored, she was broken. She knew she'd done wrong. But the evening was far too many allegations past saving.

I spend most of the next day in my room with the door shut, trying to study Beischer and Mackay, but mainly just sitting there being angry about still living at home. And everything else. Frank and Zel and Sophie, and my whole collapsed pathetically nonsexual life.

Surely there's a rule that one thing you don't tell people

about your adult offspring is the imaginary friends they might have had when they were four. My mother knows that now, but she knew it a little too late last night. She went with the fictional George Glass and his imaginary friend Marcia without even knowing where I'd got them from. She knew she'd done wrong.

My mother started doing puppet shows at bathtime when I was two or three. I hated how the shampoo stung when it got in my eyes, so she had to do something. And I got involved in the puppet shows, so it was only natural that, eventually, my imaginary bathing buddy Mister Wilson would arrive. Mister Wilson was a fat jolly old man who would come through the wall at bath times and make the whole unwelcome experience a little closer to bearable. He was, in his own chubby, crusty, totally invented way, a hell of a guy. Like my life, he was not sexual. And nor was my wearing of a dress (and a little make-up) for the purposes of a revue sketch, nor my not entirely willing participation in the placement of a chocolate biscuit between Frank's buttocks, nor my reluctant acceptance of a cash consultancy fee from Ron Todd.

However these things might seem to add up, some things are simply not to be added up. And there are far too many people in my life who are a long way short of learning that.

20

I never thought I'd welcome a twenty-four-hour shift in Labour Ward, but that's what Monday brings me and I'm glad of it. I decide that if the evening's quiet I'll use it as a chance to study. Exams are a week and a half away, and another whipping at Scrabble looks like a very unproductive use of time at the moment. I wonder if I can claim special consideration for impaired exam performance due to family dysharmony caused by my mother thinking I was a prostitute.

The morning's quiet, so I go to the usual sessions and afterwards I have lunch with Frank.

I tell him about Saturday night, but I give him the abridged version. The part about my mother thinking I had something going with Ron, and for cash. And how she lined up therapist back-up. The irony of me being the one suspected of coming home with hooker money in my pocket is apparent to both of us.

'Your life,' he says. 'It's even dumber than mine.'

'Depending on what Zel tells Ron.'

'Don't remind me.'

'Actually, mine still might be dumber. Remember the photos? The ones for O'Hare? They got developed.'

'Yeah?'

'Yeah. They came out on Saturday. My mother thinks I'm having a much more interesting life than I am, sometimes involving your arse.'

'Hey, only once,' he says, and then gives his hur-hur-hur-hur laugh. 'Did she say what she thought of the arse?'

'Shit, you and people's mothers. Don't even joke about it. There was a problem though, with the photos. You'll like this. My technique did leave a bit to be desired that day. The photos were pretty blurry.'

'Yeah? So she couldn't tell it was me?'

'No, she could tell it was you. That wasn't the problem. Imagine this – a shot that shows your face clearly, your arse kind of clearly and the Tim Tam is blurry.'

'Blurry? Oh . . .' He laughs, laughs till he practically blows his nose. 'Jesus. Really, did it . . .'

'Oh, convincingly. If there was any doubt that the dollar-for-dollar deal had run me off the rails, it was the alleged turd shot that was the clincher. I think they'd had a pretty bad time leading up to Saturday night, wondering what else they might find out when the moment of confrontation arrived.'

'Shit, I wish I'd been there.'

'Like I said, it was a big event. There was a therapist in attendance. They were ready for the worst. What they weren't ready for, bugger them, was a series of really simple banal explanations. And a son with a few quiet ambitions, who otherwise happens to be a loser who helps people.'

'Yep, it's so wrong. It's so wrong, isn't it? They should be so glad they've got you.' Hur hur hur hur. 'The loser who helps people. And the people don't make it easy for you, do they?'

'Life was a lot easier when I was just a loser who minded his own business.'

'The Sophie bit would have come your way anyway – that scene on Friday. If she was thinking what she was thinking. That all happened because of me and Zel.'

'Yeah? I don't know. It's too tangled up for me to guess what might have happened and might not.'

'So what's happening with her now?'

'What do you mean? Sophie? I don't think we're getting on very well at all.'

'Come on, think like a movie maker and tell me what's happening with her now. And this time cut the crap. You know how the story goes. You've got your game-playing, and there was plenty of that. That was always cute. You've got arguments, and that's where you are now. Then you fall for each other. You have to get shitty with each other in the middle before things get hot and heavy at the end. It's *The Taming of the Shrew* formula.'

'What? How many times do I have to have this discussion with people about my life not being a movie? Lives don't work that way. With stories you can have that sort of formula with the game-playing and then the arguments and then people falling for each other, and everyone knows it's a formula but they're happy to go along for the ride. Make the ride good enough and they all want the happy ending, anyway. It's all about the journey. Life doesn't come with those endings. With life you get ragged messy endings instead of resolution. You get exactly the kind of bullshit I'm getting now. You get bits of different stories happening at the same time. You get things that just drift off into nothing, even if it might have crossed your mind occasionally a while back that they might have amounted to something. And, anyway, maybe I didn't pay enough attention at school, but where's the bit in *The Taming of the Shrew* where she thinks he's sleeping with her mother?'

'You've got to update it a bit. But fine. Don't if you don't want to. I might have a crack at her if you're not going to. Presumably you're okay with that.'

'You're so wrong for her.'
'Might leave that to her, hey?'
'Whatever. Fine. She can do what she likes, obviously.'
'Obviously,' he says, and laughs.

A few hours later, I'm sitting making small talk with a patient and her husband. She's in the early stages of labour, he's dabbing at her brow with a wet washer and giving her two fingers to squeeze during contractions. He breathes with her, and I do too because it's harder not to.

After a while, the contractions don't seem to be amounting to much.

She's Jeanne, a receptionist at a big caravan park on the southside. He's Col, he fits seats in cinemas. This'll be their first. And so it goes. Does their story fit a formula? I don't think so.

Frank's wrong with his *Taming of the Shrew* theory. If the last month or two conformed to any genre, it'd be one that'd see our story finishing on a high-point for World of Chickens. It'd be more sorted out than it is now, I'd be played by some boyish Mickey Rooney type and last Friday would have been the eighties suburban equivalent of stirring the kids up to put on a show. Michael J. Fox could play me, but not the Alex P. Keaton 'Family Ties' version. I'm casting myself as good-hearted, with a strong right part to my hair and a sense of purpose that real life (or my own slackness) is perhaps too erratic to allow.

I take a break for dinner, and I don't hurry. On my way back, I walk up the hill towards Mater Mothers' and some of the evening's visitors are coming out to go home – a third-time father (I'm guessing) with two small children, a couple in their fifties. It's close to eight o'clock, closing time.

When I get there I decide I'll take the stairs instead of the lift and I go all the way to the top, the floor with the Special Care Nursery. I go in and take a look at the board just inside the door. Baby Neil Armstrong has gone, but the RN looking after his humidicrib tonight is just back from leave and doesn't know if he's gone home or to a regular ward or not.

Well into the night, Jeanne's labour accelerates. The contractions become closer and stronger. We start to see the top of the baby's head, moist matted black hair. I call the midwife more than I'm supposed to, but I keep thinking the baby might come out any time.

We see head, we don't see head. We see head, we don't see head. Everything slips back between contractions, but Col and I start to convince ourselves we're seeing more with each one.

The midwife stays. She tells me to scrub and put on a gown and some new gloves. She tells me – tells us – it's all going according to plan. And so it does.

'Swab, and get your drapes up and get into position,' she says. 'Quickly.'

Jeanne grips her thighs with the next contraction, turns her fingers white with a surge of effort and the head is out, properly out and never going back. All that waiting, and it's happening before I'd expected it to. The contraction seemed just like the others, but for some reason this was the one.

'Now check for cord. Finger past the occiput and check for cord.'

No cord. Good. No cord, but the head of a baby, slick and mucousy, and then the rest, the shoulders and everything else, sliding out into my hands. The baby cries and writhes, but in a healthy way, and turns itself red.

'What now?' the midwife says. 'What now?'

And I remember. I've made a list (chapters forty-one and forty-two) and I remember most of it, or at least enough. Col cuts the cord, the baby is examined and I concentrate on the placenta.

When it's over, I'm the fourth wheel on the tricycle. Just like that. I'm at the end of my list of things to do and check, and Jeanne and Col are grateful but I suddenly feel superfluous, intrusive. Which is okay – I'm both those things. The midwife is already in another room. It's business as usual for her. And in here it's brand new for three of us, but the other two have suddenly got themselves a baby. It's 3 a.m.

When I leave the room, I walk out of Labour Ward through the big plastic doors and I put money in the vending machine for a Kit Kat, but it doesn't come out. What is it with vending machines in this place? When I hit it – and I don't hit it hard – Kit Kats tumble out like a jackpot from a poker machine. So I scoop them up in my arms and carry them back in, and hand them out to everyone I know who's over the age of nothing.

'Beats cigars,' Col says, pretending to smoke one.

The garbage truck wakes me when it empties the bins outside the on-call rooms. Jesus and Mary loom from my walls. The digital clock beside the bed says six-eleven. I've slept for two hours.

Even when the truck's gone there are sounds. A slamming door, a rattling trolley, two male voices talking as they pass on their way up the hill, cars in the distance on the other side of the hospital buildings.

The air in the room is cold on my face, but the water in the showers is always hot. I can't believe I'm getting up now. I feel like I've only just gone to bed, as though I've started a messy dream and left it not half done.

It's a perfect winter dawn outside on the way to breakfast

in the dining room. On my cheeks it's cool as a slap but it's bright, and soon that'll translate into warmth. Finally, I can cross delivery off the list of things I'm supposed to do this term. I'm supposed to have done two, but it's not compulsory and I did want to do at least one. I'm surprised how routine it was – how it followed the script – but each bit happened just as I was dealing with the last so, after all those hours of waiting, it was over quickly in the end.

I'm still not happy with my mother, springing her therapist friend on me on Saturday. Is being close to a birth supposed to fill me with some kind of positive, generous feelings and make that shit me less? Bad luck. Right at the moment I'm better off away from home and in the on-call rooms, even with all the statues. You'll never be alone in there, but you're alone enough. You've got Jesus and family in plaster and wood and, sure, they don't say a word and their eyes are just chipped paint, but they won't call their therapist friends over, bring out the butt shots.

In the dining room I get myself a bowl of Nutri-grain and a big plastic mug of tea. The coffee here is worse than the kiosk, just a vat of dark sour stain. I could sleep. I could sleep right now. I don't even like Nutri-grain, the plastic mugs annoy me and I'm not big on tea. This is a flagellant's breakfast, a breakfast chosen to turn a bad mood worse.

But there's no point in imagining that New York lives are immune to nights like Saturday, even though that was my first thought. Parents everywhere, I suppose, indoctrinate their children with the standard set of values, and then assume they've turned to pornography and prostitution when flimsy coincidences arise. I'm surprised drugs rated only a passing mention. Soon enough, my mother will forget she lectures about media, and will blame the media for putting all this in her head.

It's less of a Brisbane story, actually. I don't know if it's just Woody Allen and his characters, or if there really are millions of people on Manhattan entrenched in analysis, but the Attack of the Killer Therapist over fondue seems, if anything, more New York than Brisbane. I can see Woody Allen doing it: 'And there I was, concentrating on the process of fonduing – they had me cooking my own meal as a distraction, I'm sure of it – and, out of nowhere, this therapist . . .'

Or maybe in second person, in a different voice:

You're out of there now, and you know it's for the best. You remember the moment the first photograph came out, the instant you realised they weren't thinking Tim Tam. You wonder if Baby Neil Armstrong has flown from this place, and you hope he has. Out to the suburbs, to an unnoticed childhood that belies its beginnings.

Concise, but not bad.

When Frank turns up for our eight-thirty lecture, I tell him I finally delivered one last night and I give him a Kit Kat.

'They were handing these out.' It's easier to put it that way, and I'm sick of explanations that have to go beyond about ten words. 'It was their first and the dad got pretty excited.'

I stay Tuesday night at the Mater. I can't concentrate at home. Or anywhere, in fact, so I might as well book myself more time in a cell with Jesus on the wall. Jesus demonstrating the worst of his misericordiae. Or should it be Mary's misericordiae, since these are the Mater Misericordiae hospitals? She looks much more as though she's come to terms with it.

I'm too annoyed with my mother to talk sensibly with her, so I call and tell her I'm staying here to do more work. Study work, not money-for-sex work, in case she's wondering.

I scam free dinner in the dining room by claiming to be rostered on, then it's back to my cell.

I figure screening will come up in either the written exam or the clinical so I flowchart how to proceed from the heelprick blood test, making sure not to rush to big investigations or unlikely diagnoses too early.

I wash my Monday clothes in the shower, I wring as much water out as I can and I hang them in the room, on the back of the chair and from Mary's thoughtful hand. They'll do for Wednesday.

I'm still annoyed with Sophie sometimes. I'd rather not be, but I'm not used to this. I'm used to a life that just ticks over, without this recent burst of wild allegations. I'm used to being irritated by Frank, in all kinds of inconsequential ways, and otherwise just taking things as they come. How could she think I would do something like that?

I also want to fix things with her. Weeks ago, we had something going that I'd like to retrieve.

But she's not at World of Chickens on Wednesday. She's studying. Did I know that? I don't think so. I knew she had exams, but I thought she'd be here. Smelling of toothpaste and fear perhaps, but here.

Instead, Barb is back as the fill-in chicken, standing kerbside doing a stiff, fearful kind of pointing when we walk up from the car park. Someone needs to tell her that strobes work even better if you don't stand as still as possible.

Ron's behind the counter, trying to make a burger but putting more effort into an excitable version of his boss-with-the-common-touch act. 'Ron,' I want to say to him, 'you're as common at they come, you don't have to do that.' But I don't.

'Business is up,' he tells us, while Frank sorts out the burger. 'I know it's early days, but business is up and three people have come in in the last hour talking about famous hotplate chicken. You were onto something there, Phil. They're starting to want us.'

'Good. That's good news.'

'So I'm bringing the mid-year party forward.'

'There's a mid-year party?'

'Yep, always. And this year it'll be bigger than ever. World of Chickens meets World of Mowers, this Saturday afternoon at my place.'

'And the feathers'll fly.'

'What? No, it shouldn't get to that.'

'It was a joke. Chickens meeting mowers. Don't worry about it.'

'Oh, yeah. Yeah, that's good. We could save that up for next time and get a cartoon done and put it on a flyer. You'll be there won't you? You guys?'

'We've got exams next week, actually.'

Ron looks crestfallen, like a kid facing the prospect of a wrecked birthday party. 'There'll be pizza. And a keg.'

'We'll be there, mate,' Frank says. 'Don't worry.' What is this? Guilt? Some attempt at a fresh start? Frank making good for the Zel affair by accepting pizza and beer as some kind of peace offering? 'We just won't be able to make a big night of it. We'll have to leave and get back to the books at some point.'

'It'll be good, you know. Actually, there's more news as well. Some of those things we were discussing, Phil. Come out the back and I'll show you something. We'll take a look at the figures. You don't mind holding the fort do you, Frank?'

'Consider it held.'

Ron, a bad actor always, doesn't convince any of us it's to do with figures.

'I've talked to Zel,' he says when we're in the storeroom. 'I've talked to the doc, and I've talked to Zel, like you said I should. And things are looking up. Early days there too, but they're looking up. We haven't talked like that in ages. We started talking and then it was going so well we got a bottle of Mateus Rosé out of the fridge and fired up the jacuzzi.'

'Ron, it's okay, I . . .'

'No, no mate. It's all down to you. Credit where it's due, and all that. Just talking mind, but it's a lot better than not talking.' And he claps his hand on my shoulder and says, 'Mate, if this gets any better, I could start getting erections again,' just as Barb waddles in to change.

'Sorry,' her muffled voice says inside the chicken head as she turns awkwardly, thumps against the door frame and waddles straight back out.

'Leave it to me,' I tell Ron, before he can even guess what the problem might be.

I catch her at the end of the corridor.

'No. Not my business,' she says, and keeps going, straight to the toilet. Before I can stop her, she's in there with the door shut, and possibly locked. 'Let's just get on with the job.'

'But to get on with the job, the first thing we've got to do is straighten that out.'

'Whatever,' she says through the toilet door. 'You and Mr Todd, you know, whatever. Not my business.'

'You don't understand.'

'Listen, there's a lot of shit I don't understand. So what?' She opens the door to hand me the suit and, with a clear change-of-subject face, says, 'Hey, does your mother do things at the Arts Theatre? I think my mother might know her.'

'Right, that conversation with Mr Todd before, that was medical, okay? In confidence. It should have happened in a different environment, but it didn't and I'd be grateful if you could make sure it went no further.'

'Oh, yeah, of course. Not that I heard it anyway. Everything sounds fuzzy in this head.'

'Medical-in-confidence,' I tell her, rather too sternly. 'So it wouldn't even matter if you did hear it.'

She backs off, and I don't care if she's treating me like a mad person. There was a message there that I needed to get across.

Ron stays around for the next half hour while I'm chickening, bothering Frank and Barb at the counter and telling customers he's the owner. I'm not even inside the building and his performance works as a long-range mime.

Barb's still wary when we go to change again. I'm sure I hear the toilet door lock each time she goes in there now, and she's never anything but fully dressed.

The door opens, she shuffles out, I zip her up. I ask her if she knows why Ron's still here and she says, 'He was telling us he wants to talk to you about a video he watched last night. *Annie Hall*. I'm thinking man porn, some kind of trannie thing and – surprise – it's a penis in there under that skirt. But I don't want to know.'

'It's Woody Allen.'

'Knew it.'

'You've got no idea. You've got no idea about Woody Allen, have you?'

'Woody. That tells me all I need to know.'

'You should watch it.'

'Hey, I'm not part of that scene.'

'There's no scene.'

'Whatever.'

'Stop saying that. Okay, let's pretend this never

happened. Let's pretend I'm just turning up to work now, and we'll begin like normal people. How was your day, Barb?'

'Fine.'

'Good. Did I tell you I delivered a baby early yesterday morning?'

'Look, I should probably be up front with you. I've got a boyfriend and we do it the regular way. I don't know what you're into with your woody and Ron's problems and who you were delivering that baby to, but let's keep it strictly business here.'

Frank agrees not to hurry at the end of the shift. I want my parents to be asleep when I get home.

My mother isn't. She's waiting, sitting in her usual seat and dressed for bed but with an airline carry bag beside her. My life so long ago slipped its moorings that for a second I genuinely wonder if she's up for a go at the *Star Trek* drinking game.

'I shouldn't have talked to Celia,' she says, without even saying hello. 'I shouldn't have got my head so stuck in that book she gave me. I should have talked to you. It all started backstage at *Pirates*. You know how things do?'

'Not really.'

'It started hypothetically. Other people started talking hypothetically, and some of what they were saying started to sound familiar, so I mentioned a few things as well. Always from the perspective of contradicting them and giving examples of things that could be misinterpreted, but were probably quite all right really.'

'Rather ironic now.'

'Yes, I realise that. And I argued with them. I know

they thought I was naive, but I argued with them and I told them everything really was okay here.'

'So what you're saying to me is that it's fine that they ended up talking you round and that you completely changed your mind, because you put up a bit of a fight early on?'

'No. That's when the photos arrived. They gave me a bit of a surprise at first, but when your father and I took a closer look we were reasonably certain it was a . . . food product in Frank's bottom. Though we were thinking Polly Waffle or Picnic. But the feeling among the cast was that it might be something a little more . . . troubling. And suddenly all the conversation was about me, us. You. It wasn't very nice.'

'The feeling among the *cast*? You showed Frank's arse photos to the cast of *Pirates of Penzance*?'

'Only because they were a bit blurry and I couldn't work out . . .'

'Oh, so it's all down to bad technique? My fault? That's why you had to show them?'

'I know it doesn't sound very good now.'

'Very good now? Can you tell me one time, ever, when it would sound good?'

'You become close when you're putting something on, a show I mean. Oh, *mea culpa, mea culpa*, Philby. It's utterly indefensible, all of it. I know that, and all I can do now is apologise in the strongest terms. It won't stop you coming to the opening, will it?'

'You're insane aren't you? I've done psych. You're insane.'

'No, discreetly coming to the opening.'

'Discreetly? The son who took the poo shot and slept with his boss for money? You can't be serious.' Then I remember Barb. 'And if you hear something about tonight,

tonight at the World, from someone in the cast whose daughter works with me, it was medical-in-confidence, okay? Ron was telling me about progress with a medical problem when she walked in. You shouldn't hear about it but, if you do, that's what was going on. And if you dare call Celia back in on this one . . .'

'No, never, no. Never again. I'm sure I won't hear anything. And if I do I won't believe it. And it's your business anyway, whatever you were talking about tonight and whatever you do with your life. If you happened to be with Ron, or Frank and the biscuit, well, your choice would be your choice. It was the money side of it that gave me a little trouble. It's not a very nice world, that world. The money, and the possibility that it wasn't a chocolate biscuit, but I never believed that.'

'Oh good. Well, everything's okay then.'

'Really?'

'No. Not really. Not at all. Could you stop telling me about all the things it'd be all right for me to be and just let me be what I am. I couldn't care about what you think, and where you draw your lines, somewhere between biscuits and money. Give me a break.'

'Yes. Yes, you're right. I just . . . it doesn't matter.' She looks down, notices the bag beside her, as though she's forgotten it with the direction the conversation's taken. 'All right,' she says. 'Now, I know this doesn't fix things, but I can only do what I can. And it's only on loan, but I hope it's better than nothing. It's from someone I work with. He bought it to take on holiday and now he's back so he won't need it for a while.' She reaches into the bag, fits her hands around something heavy and lifts out a video camera. 'Just a loan,' she says again, 'but we are working towards our half of the real thing.'

21

'Get one of these into you, my friend,' Vanessa shouts over the party noise, before I'm even up the stairs. She's standing in the front doorway, ready to meet people with a tray of drinks – green and crusty drinks in plastic cocktail glasses. 'Frank made 'em. Brizgaritas, they're called. I'm only supposed to have one. And what kind of birthday's that, hey?'

She shrugs her shoulders and rolls her eyes at the injustices of the world and its mistreatment of seventeen-year-olds.

In the half-dark room behind her, Status Quo jumps into Suzi Quatro. The dancing in there is bouncing the needle all over a seventies compilation album, and I can't wait till everyone gets the seventies out of their systems.

Ness leads me out the back, and I realise she's taking me to the old people's bit of the party. Frank, AJ, the parents, the neighbours, a cousin or two, Kerry from work.

'I'll leave you to it, hey?' she says, as if my place has been found for me. 'But I'll be back later looking for you for a dance, all right?'

Ness has never seen me dance.

'She's a good one, that one,' Kerry says, as Ness rejoins the indoor, interesting non-old section of the party. 'A good-hearted girl.'

A good-hearted girl who, I now notice, is wearing exactly what she wore a week ago to Freebie Friday. It's reassuring to know that we had special-occasion status, but maybe that was mainly because of Richie the Rat. Kerry is like a younger, less extreme Zel Todd. At least that's how she seems to me, but Frank tells me, 'No way, wouldn't touch her.' I don't ask him why. If there's some desirability difference between them, it'll never mean much to me.

Small talk, small talk. That's the next hour, but at least there'll be none of last Saturday night's photos and I'm not going to have to stay up until three to deliver a baby. It shouldn't be called small talk, it should be called long talk. It's not the amplitude that's the problem, it's the duration. However long it goes, it seems to go too long. And however small it is when it starts, it can't get bigger. That's the rule. Small talk can only dwindle into talk that's even smaller. Unless it's calm-before-the-storm small talk, and you've got photos to bring out, featuring a slightly blurry biscuit. But, no, tonight's is much more like the talk I'm used to – small talk that's slowly, witlessly killing time, another Friday night caught in dull company. If only a hundred bats would come along right now and shit on Frank and liven things up a little.

Chris, the carpet layer who lives next door, says, 'Mate, I wouldn't even try blue couch if I were you. It'll never grow under your trees,' and Dorothy's brother Ted nods and hmmms, as if it's a tough serious truth that's only starting to sink in. Then Chris's wife Narelle has a go at him about how many lights he left on before he came over and he says, 'Yeah, sorry love. I didn't have a free hand because of the beers.'

'There'd be, what, six lights left on over there,' she says. 'What do you think this is – the bloody show?'

Six lights. And even if you scrunch your eyes up tight and block out all the words but let in the noise, you can't come close to convincing yourself it's any kind of substitute for one of those party scenes in a Woody Allen film. Witty, awkward balcony conversations, the view along the lights of Broadway. There isn't, as far as I'm aware, one Woody Allen film that features a discussion about trying to grow grass under a Moreton Bay fig.

In Woody Allen films, no-one is so suburban that they own a tree.

There are speeches, which is the Green family way. There are always toasts and speeches. Turn a little older, pass your exams, get a job – none of it goes unheralded. Big Artie asks for 'a bit of shoosh', and there's the rather silly sound of maybe a dozen people tapping on plastic cups to help him get it. Vanessa stands next to him, grinning.

'For those of you who don't know me,' Big Artie says, 'I'm Arthur Green senior, Vanessa's father. First, I'd like to thank you all for coming to wish my little girl a happy seventeenth. And I do hope you enjoy yourselves – and make sure you get your share of the dancing and eating and drinking. Now, we're pretty proud of our Nessie, here. As a lot of you would know, Ness and school didn't always see eye to eye, but we always knew she was a good'n. She's now in her second year at Garden City Blooms and her boss Kerry tells me she's a good worker and the customers have nothing but compliments for her. She's also blossomed . . .' pause for wry smile at own carefully planned corny pun . . . 'into a bit of a sign writer for the food business. So if you're out Taringa way and passing World of Chickens, that's our Ness too. And on top of that, she tunes young Frankie's car, 'cause he's a lazy bugger and never took much of an interest.' Pause for everyone to have a bit of a laugh at Frank, Frank to raise brizgarita glass in good-natured acknowledgment. 'But we've got a special presentation for her tonight, and this is more than just birthday. It comes with an announcement. And that is that we've had a talk and, starting tomorrow, on weekends and days off from Kerry's, Vanessa is now officially a member of the family firm, Green Loppers. That mightn't mean a lot to some of you, but it means a lot to Ness and me. Neville, the shirt please.'

Nev steps forward with a new black shirt, folded as neatly and solemnly as a flag on Anzac Day. Big Artie shakes it open and there, over the logo, is the name Vanessa. Ness's grin starts to quiver as she realises this is actually happening. She wipes her eyes and takes the shirt and gives Big Artie a hug.

'Hey, there's none of that bullshit in tree lopping, love,' he says, but at the same time clapping a Popeye forearm around her and grinning too.

She shakes his hand and clears her throat. 'Any chance of putting 'climber' under the logo?'

'Now then. Don't want you getting ahead of yourself. This is just weekends and days off, you know, for the moment. And we'll see how it goes. You might not like it.'

'Dad, watch out. I'm pretty sure I'm going to like it.' She looks down at her feet, clears her throat again and looks up. 'Well, this is the big one. Seventeen and a Loppers shirt, and both of them on the same day. You sure don't get a lot of days like that. Now, there's a lot of people to thank, but you know who you are. Like Dad said – school? Not my thing.' She smirks and a few of her ex-school friends laugh. 'Yeah, righto. Some of you knew that already. But Kerry helped out. She gave me a job and she's taught me a thing or two, and that's always good. There's been a lot of big stuff in the last couple of weeks though, hasn't there? So I'd like to thank Phil and his team from World of Chickens for giving me my big break and for backing me when I needed it. Which is Frank too, of course, the hotplate chicken chef. Sorry, *famous* hotplate chicken chef. But Phil's the one who goes on those management retreats to the movies with Ron, and gets the big ideas happening, so thanks for that. And I'd like to say this has just been the best day. And it's been the best for the whole day, apart from the middle eight hours when I was at work but even then it was pretty good. But before then, put it this way, guess who got the birthday call from Richie the Rat at the Bs this morning? Yep, it was me. I got the big burping birthday from the Rat Man himself. Thanks very much for that one, Frank. But most of all Dad. I'd like to thank Dad for tonight. Mum and Dad for tonight, but Dad for bringing me onto the team. And I won't let you down, mate.'

She pulls the black Loppers shirt on over her blue top and the brooch at her neck shows through the undone collar.

'Good on ya, Ness,' Nev calls out gruffly, his rollie cigarette still sticking to his dry lower lip.

He starts to beat his hard work-chipped hands together in applause, and everyone else joins in.

'All right, all right,' Ness says, looking embarrassed and proud, waving her hands to slow the clapping down. 'Let's kill the lights and get the music back on, hey? Remember, Dad said he wanted some dancing.'

I need a new drink, so I head for the table we're calling the bar. Before I get there, the main light in the lounge room goes off and Supertramp's *Breakfast in America* starts to play.

'Can I help you, sir?' Frank says, ready to pour.

'Anything other than one of those brizgaritas. Can't guess where they would have come up with an idea like that.'

'Oh really? I think they're quite the thing on riverboats this time of year. Not that you'd ever get to benefit from that, Speedy.'

'Better make it a Sprite. Don't want to loosen my iron-clad self-control.'

'Make mine one of those green ones,' Vanessa says, coming up beside me. She holds the shirt-front out proudly, to show it off. 'What do you reckon?'

'Looks good. Looks like something you'll be putting to good use.'

'That's right. I wanted you to be here for me getting this. This could be the start of something. I just get that feeling. Bloody flowers, hey? Things are looking up. Thanks, mate. Thanks for everything.' She reaches out and shakes my hand firmly, then turns back to Frank. 'Hey, where's the bloody drink, bozo?'

'Yeah, righto,' he says, and pours her one.

'Ta.' She takes a mouthful, and dances off.

'I thought she was only supposed to have one of those.'

'So parental,' he says. 'And where has it got you?'

'I'm beginning to wonder.'

'Hey, the shirt, Ness's shirt. The lopping stuff. You did that, didn't you?'

'I was something to do with it. But it's not like she was hiding her interest.'

'Well, thanks. I hope it works out. She doesn't need an awful lot of strength for it, I guess, but look at those skinny arms . . .' He shakes his head. 'No, she might just do it. And it beats me climbing for a few hours here and there, and Dad sitting on his arse most of the week. Things, to be honest, are marginal at best. Sometimes, you don't know what you've got right in front of your nose, do you? He's a dumb bugger. Not exactly like my seventeenth, though. I think, when I was about fourteen, Dad picked someone else's name off an old shirt with his fingernail and told me to get up the bloody tree.'

'Which didn't exactly fill you with excitement, I imagine. As opposed to this, which was more like the footage of Charles becoming Prince of Wales.'

'Sure. Got that on a plate somewhere. Can't complain, though. It got me the car, doing weekends and holidays the last two years of school, and it wasn't a question of saving for half the car either. Anyway, it's all Ness's now, if she wants it. Let's get out of here, away from this table. It's someone else's turn.'

He leads me through the party and out to the front balcony. It's not as noisy here. He takes a mouthful of his drink and looks out across the street.

He leans forward on the railing and says, almost as if it isn't to me, 'I've got to tell you straight. That money from Zel? I really wanted not to need it so much, but it was a relief to get it. You might have been calling it hooker money, but you've been drinking it tonight. My parents'd have to have a long conversation with the bank before splashing out on a bottle of tequila at the moment. And it got me a second-hand Beischer and Mackay.'

'I didn't know that. I didn't know things were like that.'

'No, well, it's not the kind of thing you go round talking about, is it? And me bringing in a bit of extra cash looked like a better option than them selling things, their plates and stuff. I couldn't make them do that. Anyway, It'll get us through to the holidays, and after that maybe things'll be working out with Ness and the lopping. She's never liked that florist job, has she?'

'No. And I think she's right. I think she's going to like this. I really think it's going to work for her. And, just seeing her in there, it does kind of put us cynical bastards in our place a bit.'

'You know something? Something about Zel, and all

that? Zel Todd is what my parents have never managed to be. Look at them. Look at them in there. Are you thinking style file? It'll never happen, will it? They're still battling, and right now it's worse than it used to be. I have to come home with a box of burgers every shift, and we pretend I don't. We don't say anything, but dad reheats them and has them for lunch the next day. And I wanted to be part of something better. Something less hard, that's all.' He shrugs, as if the story's now told. 'I know it didn't fit into your moral world, all the Zel stuff, but I never said I would, did I?'

'No. Would you do it again?' I'm asking it straight, just as a question, and he knows that.

He thinks about it for a while. 'I doubt it. Too much in the way of consequences. It was all too hard on you. You poor fragile thing.'

22

We'll never be the same, the two of us. I don't usually have to be nose-diving towards consequences before I'll notice them, and adjust my course. But, like anything else, it's much more complicated than that. And I think we're coming through the other side. We started off in different worlds and we're still living in them now, even if I forget that sometimes. And even if my family circumstances aren't quite as I'd once thought.

I didn't realise what it all meant to Frank. It seemed like simple bad behaviour, that's how he told it at the time. A romp without a conscience, without anything else to it, without a second thought. And now he's thinking of it as over, as if that means every part of it's finalised. What happens to Ron and Zel and Sophie? I don't know. But that's up to Zel. I don't know if she should tell and what she should tell, but I'm pretty sure that that bit of it isn't up to me. I'm not pushing into this one again.

My mother tells me to take the video camera to the party at the Todds, since I didn't take it to Ness's seventeenth. 'I know you're an avant-garde film-maker,' she says, as I'm wondering how to tell her that parties are exactly not what I want a video camera for, 'but why not have a practice with it? But don't make a party video. Make it a documentary to show me what these people you work with are like.'

And she's bought me two blank tapes and charged the

camera, so mid-afternoon I'm in town catching a Carindale bus with the airline carry bag over my shoulder.

At the Todd's house there are signs pointing round the side, and the front door is locked. We're all welcome via the tradesman's entrance today. Via a flagstone path that winds among fern enclaves and tan-bark garden beds to the side door of the downstairs bar.

There's half a besser block propping the door open, and it's the rise-and-fall crowd noise saying darts, near miss, that comes out to meet me.

It's the Mowers crowd versus one version of the Chickens crowd, a couple of members of the other A team. No Frank yet, and no Sophie, as far as I can see. No Zel, either. The sliding doors are open and there's a keg on the patio, with people lining up to refill jugs. Ron's standing there chatting to the queue, benevolently proprietorial, with a half-full jug – but no glass – and a foam-dipped moustache.

'I've got a plan,' he says when he comes over. 'Oh, wait, I should fix you up with a beer.' He looks around for a glass, but not particularly hard. 'I'll get you one soon. Anyway, the plan. TV ad. Not straight away, but it's something to work towards. You could star as the chicken and direct. It'd be like Woody Allen.'

'Yeah.' But, I'm thinking, not much like Woody Allen. There's more noise from the darts. Someone's just missed a triple twenty. 'I think,' I tell him while I work out what I think, 'it's a great idea, obviously. But I agree we shouldn't do it straight away. Walk before you run, that kind of thing. And think how the Mowers crowd'd feel.'

'Don't worry. It's a different market, different rules. And they're nowhere near as visual. Have you noticed that? I have. So, as an actor, how would you take that on? How would you be the chicken?'

'How would I be the chicken?'

'How would you make the transition from roadside to film?'

'We'd better get me that beer.'

Out on the patio there are glasses, and Ron pours us one each.

'I happen to have put a lot of time and thought into being the chicken,' I tell him. 'You're talking to the right person. There's a lot, I think, that would translate from one medium to the other.'

'Is it that chicken head-space issue? Getting into the chicken head space?'

'Partly. The problem is, it's a very small head space. It doesn't do to be too much like the chicken. There's a story about the movie *Marathon Man*. Dustin Hoffman was running himself ragged to get ready for his part, to get into the role, and he was talking to Laurence Olivier, who was his co-star. And he said, "I'm running myself ragged so that I can get into the head space for this part. What do you do?" And Olivier said, "I act".'

'Yes,' Ron says slowly, as if a mystery's revealed itself. And perhaps it has, but who knows which mystery? 'Yes, I see. I knew you were the one to talk to.'

It's worse than small talk, and it doesn't get better when Ron starts pressuring me about rounding up a newspaper to check session times for *Desperately Seeking Susan*. Or when he moves from that to a Zel update.

'Progress on a lot of fronts,' he says in a wink-wink, nudge-nudge kind of way that makes me long for small talk, or more on the subject of how an actor might be a chicken. 'She's at a hair expo right now, as a matter of fact. She's getting back into the hair caper. You should have heard her talking about it, mate – side-parted bobs, corkscrew perms –

buggered if I know what half of it's about, but it's good to see her enthusiastic. And then there's the other fronts too, of course . . .' Wink wink, nudge nudge. 'I've got a plan up my sleeve. A bit of a romantic weekend at the Gold Coast in a couple of weeks. I put in some fast talking, scored us an upgrade to the honeymoon suite. Might even push it to three nights.'

'Sounds great.'

'Yeah, doesn't it? Of course, you only get the complimentary bottle of sparkling wine on the first night but, still, pretty bloody good, hey? Sophie'll take charge of the various Worlds while we're away. Her exams'll be over by then. She might need to run a few things by you from time to time. That'd be okay, wouldn't it?'

'Sure.'

Some time-out is rapidly becoming essential. I'm beginning to miss those tedious hours alone in my room with Beischer and Mackay.

On the pretext of putting my bag out of the way – whatever that means – I escape the party and go upstairs into the house. Sophie's in the kitchen, by herself, leaning against a bench and drinking a glass of Diet Coke.

'Hi,' she says, obviously not expecting to be interrupted.

'Hi, I just . . . I just needed a break actually, so I said I had to find somewhere for this bag. No, wait, I think you've seen one of these before. I was looking for someone to play the *Star Trek* drinking game with.' She laughs, and that's something I haven't heard for a while. 'How are the exams going?'

'Pretty badly.'

'Is Clinton coming along today?'

'I don't expect so. How about Phoebe? Or Jacinta?'

I'm over lying, but I can't immediately come out with

anything better, so I make a kind of Hmmm noise, as if the whole thing is best left alone.

'Hmmm? What's hmmm?' Or, in this case, not left alone. 'What's the story with them, really?'

'Really? Okay, the last person I was involved with was Jacinta. We saw each other three times. Two of those times went so badly they'd make the *Star Trek* drinking game look like a night out you could have as a prize in a raffle. I crashed and burned weeks ago and it's definitely for the best.'

'Oh, right. And Phoebe? Where did she . . . ?' She looks at me, then looks away, at the bottles on the counter. 'Doesn't matter.' What am I supposed to say? I can't tell her I invented Phoebe. Imaginary friends haven't served me well lately. 'Do you want a drink? I've got rum in this Diet Coke. I can get you some.'

'No, I'm fine thanks. I've got a beer somewhere.'

'What do you really have in the bag? If it's *Star Trek* printouts don't tell me.' She takes another mouthful of her drink. 'Okay, tell me.'

'It's a video camera.'

'You got one?'

'Well, it's on loan. My mother had the idea that I might use it here, but I don't think so.'

'No. It doesn't really need to be recorded, does it? Your mother probably wasn't thinking of watching a lot of darts. I'd be happy never to go back down there, actually. I should get you a drink. No, you've got one. That's right. Sorry.' She starts spinning a tissue box on the granite bench top. There's an awkwardness right now that we didn't used to have. 'I should probably go,' she says. 'Serve some stuff. Food, you know?' She picks the box up and puts it on her head. 'Do you ever do this? Just to check if you can balance it?'

'I know someone who used to do something like that as a posture test, and I've never felt good about posture.'

'Right.' Suddenly, she looks as embarrassed as a person with a tissue box on their head might be, as though it must have been put there by someone else, but it's her problem now.

'But that was just my mother, with the posture test. And, um, you balance it pretty well. And on the subject of my mother, and, um, other people called Phoebe, well, I can't remember the first time we – you and I – talked about that but I'm pretty sure some wires got crossed . . .' At the moment, I might even settle for listening to Ron talking about having sex with Zel. It's a topic that'll come up some time in the next few weeks, after all, and it won't be worse than this.

'I could help you with that bag. You could put it in the pantry. It'll be safe there.'

'That'd be very useful. Thank you. And I was also going to look for a bathroom.'

'Oh, sure. Everything's upstairs. There's a toilet just off the bar downstairs, but if I were you I'd go upstairs. Mum's got this rule about people keeping to Dad's areas of the house at these parties but, for you, we can probably make an exception. It's the last door on the left.'

'Thank you.'

She puts down the tissue box and takes my bag. The transaction – since that's what it seems to have become – is done. She should have given me a ticket or a number, in case someone else was looking after bags when I came back for mine later. I want to get even more out of here than before. Hide and kill time and then go.

The stairs are near the front door and the corridor on the second floor runs the length of the house, ending in an arched window that overlooks the back garden. I try the handle of the last door on the left, but it's locked. Inside, someone clears their throat. Obviously I'm not the only one with upstairs toilet privileges.

From the window I can see the edge of the patio and therefore the edge of the party and, over to one side, a feature that was out of view before, a large rectangular area covered with gravel and displaying concrete renderings of several famous statues. It looks as though I haven't had the full tour after all.

I walk back along the corridor, towards the stairs. It's better to pace than to crowd whoever's in the bathroom. Through one half-open door – I'm guessing Sophie's – I can see a single bed with Holly Hobby sheets, a brown vinyl beanbag and clothes strewn everywhere.

I turn at the stairs and there's still no sign that the last door on the left might be about to open.

It's not a long corridor, so I'm back at the window quickly and turning again. Turning, and catching a glimpse of a very regal shade of purple through the door opposite the bathroom, which isn't quite closed. I give it a nudge and it opens, and there's a purple heart-shaped bed, with a jacuzzi fitted along the border of the right ventricle and mirrors on the ceiling above, also making the shape of a large heart. I'm sure the only sheets you can get for that bed come with a bunny logo.

It's eerie, being this close to the scene of Frank and Zel's encounters, the lair of the Evil Ddotnor. I can even see the phone Frank called me on, next to the bed. It's ceramic and brass, and the ceramic parts are decorated with little blue flowers.

I can also see the door to the ensuite. And that guy in the bathroom across the hall seems to have taken up permanent residence. Okay, no contest. I've waited enough. The ensuite is mine.

I'm just about to flush when I hear voices – completely unfamiliar voices – coming into the bedroom, and then the sound of water thundering into the empty jacuzzi. All I can do is close the lid as quietly as I can, and sit down. The tub fills noisily, and more slowly than I'd like it to, then the hum of the engine and whoosh of the jets drowns out the words but not the giggling. Giggling and, within minutes, moaning. Two types of moaning – sharp panting moaning and a kind of deep buffalo moaning and what am I doing that I keep getting stuck in toilets? First the *Paradise*, now this.

It's the detail I don't like. This'd make a great story on Monday, or after my exams. The 'who did what with whom in the jacuzzi at the party' story. I'm always up for those, but listening to the actual doing part is something I could really skip. I stick my fingers in my ears and think about amniotic fluid, but the sounds of cattle and panic will always win. Would you please get this dreadful bovine sex over with and leave?

One last moo and it's done.

I hear the slop of a large body coming out of the tub and the pad-pad of heavy feet on the floor. On their way, dammit, to the ensuite. The door swings open, and a big nude bald man from the Mowers darts team jolts to a halt.

I smile, shrug, as if it's just one of those things.

'Towels,' he mouths and does a jiggly demonstration of drying. In case I ever doubted it, there's the evidence: the international symbol for towels is best not done nude, at least by men. Not unless you also need to signal the international symbol for pendulum.

I open a cupboard and, fortunately, it does have towels in it. I pull out a couple and toss them over. He winks, and shuts the door. There's a different tone to the murmured talk now, and it's mainly him speaking. Then the jacuzzi is turned off.

How does this kind of scene happen? Who is it who goes, mid-party, 'Hey, why don't we go put one away in Ron and Zel's tub? That'd be a lark.' Or perhaps it's the darts victory ritual. The Chickens people were looking very much like the B team when I last saw the score.

They talk in whispers and I'm trying not to listen to their dressing noises. The towels hit the laundry basket, feet pad-pad away across the thick carpet, the door to the corridor clicks shut. The last of the water gurgles down the plughole.

I give them ten seconds, then another ten. I flush and I leave the ensuite. I cross the scene of the cliché and, when I open the bedroom door, the bathroom door on the other side of the corridor is open too.

Movement out of the window and down in the garden catches my eye. It's Frank. He's here. And he's with Sophie. He's chasing her off the patio, across the lawn and around to the sculpture garden. And he's holding my borrowed video camera up to his head as he runs.

I don't know what it is I'm seeing, but it looks like life passing me by again. They're too far away for sound, so it hardly even seems real. It's a silent movie of life passing me by, but it's real enough. I get to have a stupid conversation with her in the kitchen about bags and tissue boxes and toilets, Frank gets to chase her round the garden. And, since before he squeezed his first zit, Frank would have been chasing girls around gardens for one reason only.

Step away from the window, I tell myself. This is all getting much more depressing than it's supposed to be. It's yet another reminder I don't need that Frank's form is nauseatingly better than mine and his unpartnered intervals much shorter. It's easier, I guess, if you're prepared to go out serially with members of the same family, and not fussed about generational issues.

But nothing, no signal from Sophie in the kitchen, said 'chase me' as she slouched against the counter taking mouthfuls of rum and Diet Coke and getting our conversation over with.

I want Clinton to come along now and break this up. A Frank and Sophie combination would make work hard to bear. Frank gives me details. Zel excepted, he always keeps me up to date with his liaisons, and here's one I really don't want to know about.

I step away from the window, go back into the bedroom and stand there for a while feeling stupid. I'm tired and I've stopped caring about what people think, so I lie down on the bed. If anyone else wants to have sex at this party, they can do it in a fern enclave or wait till later. This room is for depressed single people who are no good at darts and should be home studying.

And I wish the ceiling didn't reflect that quite so honestly. There I am in the mirror on this big purple heart, my head in the left atrium, my body in the left ventricle, looking very unbullworked and very over this. In the sculpture garden, Frank kicks sand in my face and Charles Atlas tells him he won't stand in his way.

They can do whatever they want, of course. Of course they can. Frank will, given the chance, because that's what he does. He even told me he might do this, and Frank would call that considerate. 'What more do you want?' he'd say, and maybe he'd be right. But he doesn't understand. There are some things you don't admit to, even when provoked. People should sense them if they know you, and they should act accordingly. And they shouldn't make a move on Sophie and chase her round the garden. But that's never been Frank – sensing things – and I can't complain if it isn't Frank now.

With Sophie it's not the same. I deserved better. We were friends and then it all changed. She thought I was having an affair with her mother and she kept it to herself for weeks, turned cool and less friendly. And I behaved like an idiot for her and did every single thing Frank thought I might, because it was fun to do it but also because there was a chance she might have noticed.

And how does it work out? Frank has the affair with her mother, I don't tell her and he gets to chase her round the garden. How could she think that about me, and how could she think it for weeks and let it spoil things? I'm angry again. And that stupid conversation in the kitchen. She's shut me out. She's a bag handler and a giver of directions and we share a chicken suit and, after these past few months, that's what it's down to. All it's down to. And I'm angry because I let her get to know me, a lot of me, out the back of World of Chickens. I'm angry with me for doing that too, for putting quite a lot on the line without ever taking one actual risk.

'Phil,' she says. She's at the door. Standing in the doorway, her drink in her hand.

'What?' It's not friendly, the way it comes out. But that's fine. It's not supposed to be.

'What do you mean, "what"?'

'I'm having a break from the party. Remember?'

'I just wanted to talk to you. To talk to you about something.'

'Some other time, maybe. After the exams. That'd be better. If the timing of things in my life is any issue to anybody.'

As if I want to hear about her and Frank now. As if I'm

some loser who needs to have it broken to him that there's something going on. I should tell her I'd be happy just to watch the video highlights later. Next weekend, maybe. They can both come over. There'll be pizza. How about that?

'You should leave me alone,' I tell her instead. 'I've had enough of all this for now. And thanks for looking after the bag so well. Good to see no-one fucked around with the camera.'

'No, I . . .'

'I've got exams next week, and you know how that affects people's moods? Put it down to that.' I sit up. I stand. I wanted to keep lying down to look as if I didn't give a shit, but it doesn't work that way. 'I've had enough of this, right? You, Frank, every bloody Todd I've ever met, my parents, Gilbert, Sullivan and this whole stupid small-town life. You don't even know what life looks like anywhere else, anywhere that really counts. Have you read *Bright Lights, Big City*? It's about New York . . .'

'I've read it. And it didn't seem to be about New York to me. Not really. It seemed like it was about a guy . . .'

'Whatever. It would really be better if you left me alone now. We were friends, you thought I slept with your mother and you kept that to yourself for weeks. The fact that you even thought it . . .'

'I'm sorry. I'm sorry about that. Give me a break. I had a lot of things happening at that time, and . . .'

'Busy? You were busy? Busy, so therefore I was sleeping with your mother, and now I give you a break? Usually when I see people are busy, I sleep with their mothers.'

'That's not it.'

'I have had enough of hanging around with people who think that way.'

'You don't know how I'm thinking.'

'Well, that's fine, because I'm pretty much sick of how other people are thinking, and what I'm thinking is that I've had enough. All my life is at the moment is study, shit from everyone I know and time in a chicken suit. There's not a whole lot of fun. I think I could do better.'

'*Better*? What's that about? This gets so boring. Every time you shit on your life – which is pretty often – you're shitting on all of us. Me, Frank, whoever. If you've got a problem with all of us, line us up and tell us. Don't just leave it at having a go at me. If you've got a problem with yourself, deal with it. I made one mistake, one fucking mistake, and you've decided it's unforgivable. You think you could do better? You think you could have some better smarter life somewhere else? You don't even have the guts to try. You were born for that chicken suit. You'll never go to UCLA.'

And, with that, she hurls her drink at me and it's almost as though it has physical force, rum and Diet Coke cannoning into my chest and sending me backwards until I'm sitting on the bed.

'Fuck,' she says. 'Fuck. That was stupid. I didn't mean that. I . . . oh, fuck.'

She runs from the room and the rum and Diet Coke soaks through to my chest, cold and trickling down inside and showing up dark on the front of my shirt. A door slams. She's shut herself in her bedroom, and I can't believe the things I said. There are ice cubes on the carpet and brown streaks of drink in the off-white shag pile.

I go after her. I run down the hall and I knock on her door and she says, 'Go away.'

'Do you really . . .'

'Yes, I really want you to go away.'

I don't know what to say, I don't know what to do.

'Sophie . . .'

'I have several tubes of Colgate freshmint and I'm not afraid to use them.' She laughs at her own joke and, for a second, things aren't as bad as they were.

Frank appears at the top of the stairs, video camera slung casually over his shoulder.

'What's happening, kids?' he says.

'I want Phil to go away.'

Frank mouths the word 'winner' and comes up to the door. 'Okay, Soph, Philby wants to know, is this one of the times when it actually means go away, or does it mean you want him in there?'

'I'm so embarrassed,' she says, probably to herself. 'So embarrassed.' And that's followed by the sound of punches thumping into pillow.

'Looks like we should go,' Frank says. 'It sounds like she's beating the shit out of Holly Hobby in there.'

'Phil.' It's Ron's voice from halfway up the stairs. 'The chickens need you. Your World's falling apart at darts, mate, and I'm thinking only you can save them.'

'Go,' Frank says. 'Go. Do it for chickens everywhere.'

'But what about . . .'

'Don't worry. Just go.'

So I leave him outside Sophie's door, I go with Ron and my feet even make a sound something like 'trudge' in the shag pile. I am escaping from my escape from the party. I don't know what's going on now. I'm not used to fighting with people, and I'm not used to anything that ends with a door between us. And then walking away, leaving Frank in my place.

Ron points to my shirt front on the way downstairs and says, 'Bit of an accident with a drink, hey? We should all stand well back when you've got a dart in your hand, should we?'

'Standing well back could be a very good idea.'

Ron's behaving like the host with the most because people throw drinks at his parties. He thinks it's all going perfectly, and that there's nothing better than a lot of beer and a lot of darts. Party Central, and he's the station master. Ron, ugly people just fucked in your jacuzzi. I want to tell him that, but today he can have the contented smile and I'll play the darts and eventually this'll all be over.

'Hey, mate.' It's Frank's voice. He's up at the railings above, looking down at us. 'Sorry, Ron, but I might have to come and get Phil soon. We've got to head off and hit the books.'

'You guys really earn those degrees, don't you?' Ron shakes his head as though our dedication's something to marvel at and it'll kill us to leave. 'Still, can't go before you've had a game, can you?'

Darts. I expect that I'd be bad at darts, or at least not good, at the best of times. This is not the best of times.

Soon, I'm flinging the darts into the board with some force but no aim, and I'm working a few things out. Ron's cheering me on, unambiguously my buddy and, let's face it, I want his daughter so much that I've sent her to her room and left her punching her Holly Hobby pillow, with only Frank to help the situation. Sophie and I have had a conversation that I will never understand. Perhaps two conversations — one in the kitchen, one upstairs — fitting neatly together like the Titanic and a large iceberg, and ending in grinding and carnage.

I should never have invented Phoebe. Or all of the other things I've made up as I've gone along. I should stop being so full of shit and start being full of something else instead. Look at Vanessa Green. She wanted tree lopping in the same kind of way I want film making, but she made it happen. I should be making things happen. Or at least trying, instead of hiding out here, in fear of Los Angeles. Hanging around at parties at Sunnybank Hills and Carindale, silently seething about them not being New York. Seething about grass and darts and who left the lights on. And so what? Seething about Sophie, and all that.

Geography's not the problem. It is what it is, places are what they are. And so what if they can't all be Manhattan? So what if some people's map of the world is bounded by the Hudson and East Rivers? It happens that my map's bigger than that, even if it includes places where people argue about six lights, or grasses that'll grow under fig trees, or whether or not people have the guts to do certain things. And all of that has to be as real as anything else.

It feels real enough, when the drink hits you in the chest, when the chance is gone, when you've taken another conversation at some stupid angle and turned it all wrong.

Darts, the new tactic: death or glory. I fling ambitiously at the triple twenty every time. I miss every time. The poor form of World of Chickens slumps to an improbable new low. Barb is pushing me aside saying, 'Here, give me those,' when Frank comes down the steps.

'We should be off, I reckon,' he says. 'I'm guessing the team'll find a suitable replacement.'

And finally, my darts time served, Ron lets us go. 'Righto lads, good to see you. See you back at the World, then. Thanks for everything.'

'I can catch a bus,' I tell Frank when we're going through the kitchen on our way out. 'A bus into town, then another one home.'

'It's raining.'

'They still run them in the rain. They've got roofs on them now. Besides, waiting at the bus stop would give me a chance to rinse my shirt out. It's starting to get sticky.'

'It's dark, it's raining, it's very off-peak and you'll be

waiting ages. Sticky is the least of your worries. And anyway, your camera's in my car. For safe-keeping. People were really starting to dick around with it. Mainly me.'

In the car, before he gets the chance to speak about what happened upstairs, I tell him I don't want to discuss it. I know we had that talk where he checked if I had any kind of interest, and I know what I said and let's just leave it at that.

I'm going to go home, I'm going to study Beischer and Mackay, I'm going to pass obstetrics. Even though, right at the moment, I don't care about it at all. I don't care about anything, I don't want to talk about anything.

'You know,' Frank says, three songs later during an ad break on Double B, 'once you've rinsed out the shirt, I think this is going to be fine.'

'Yeah, right. It's such a special shirt, after all. If it's in good shape, I'm pretty much guaranteed to be okay.'

'You, and your special shirt, and your rum smell and your video camera.' He's trying not to laugh, but not trying hard. 'Party boy. You should play the tape when you get home.'

'Yeah? I really don't think I'm likely to.'

'Okay, here's what I'm saying. Play the tape. You get inside and you play the tape. After that, it's totally fine for you to be in whatever mood works for you.'

'If this involves your arse and anything you found in their kitchen . . .'

Now he lets the laugh out. 'I'm so easy to read, aren't I? Bugger. I always wanted to be complex and interesting like you, but the old arse joke – it's too tempting. How could you go past it? No Tim Tams though, not this time.'

'Oh, no. What did you use?'

'Watch it and see.'

My parents are out when I get home. I want to throw the tape in the bin or at the very least erase it without watching it, but I told Frank I wouldn't. So I stick it into the machine, and press play. I know my mother will come home from rehearsals right now, as soon as Frank's buttocks are gleaming from the screen.

The picture crackles, from black into trees, shuddering trees. Sophie running away shouting 'piss off', an invisible Frank laughing. He traps her among the statues, her back to the *Venus de Milo*. He's got her looking west, straight into the sun. She's holding her hand up and he's losing her eyes in a triangle of shadow.

```
EXT.    GARDEN.    LATE AFTERNOON
SOPHIE's back is to a statue, as though she's
pinned there, having been caught. She still
has her glass in one hand, but she's spilled at
least some of her drink during the chase.

    FRANK
So, how's it going today, Soph?

    SOPHIE
You're sure there's no tape in that thing?

    FRANK
Of course. But you can still look through it if
you press the button. It's like watching you on
TV. So, Sophie, tell everyone what you think of
the party so far.

    SOPHIE
It's as bad as I thought it'd be. Slightly worse.
```

FRANK
How about that Mowers crowd?

SOPHIE
Exactly. How about that Mowers crowd? Chickens rule, Frankie.

FRANK
And what do you think of Philby?

SOPHIE
Phil? Why?

FRANK
Just wondering.

SOPHIE
(She frowns, drinks) You're not lying to me about the tape, are you?

FRANK
There's no tape. It just looks like TV when I look through it. Like you're on TV. It's like a doco.

SOPHIE
So, what was the question?

FRANK
What do you think of Philby?

SOPHIE
What's it to you?

FRANK
Okay, how are things with Clinton?

SOPHIE
Clinton? (She pauses, drinks) Over. If you really want to know. Fucked up for ages, finally over a week ago. Friday of last week. Not one of my better days. For all kinds of reasons. Anyway, I think I have to go now. There's something I have to do. Something I have to fix.

INT. BEDROOM. LATE AFTERNOON
SOPHIE is sitting on her bed, propped up by her Holly Hobby pillow. There's a Madonna poster from about 1981 on the wall behind her, and various objects that suggest she transplanted her childhood bedroom here when they moved to the house about four years ago. She looks distraught.

FRANK
So, you're embarrassed, you were saying.

SOPHIE
Stop this stupid pretend TV thing.

FRANK
Sure. Just tell me what you think of Philby.

SOPHIE
I don't think that matters now. I think we just had a big fight. I threw my drink at him. I've

never done that kind of thing in my life. He's, like, practically my best friend, or he was until I did something really stupid. And I know it was stupid and I went in there, where he was — I'd been looking all over the house — I went in there to tell him things. Fix it, and stuff. And he shouted at me and I shouted at him and I threw a drink at him. And I don't know how we pretend I didn't and go back to going halves in a chicken suit.

    FRANK
Supposing I suggest you have an interest.

    SOPHIE
Supposing I suggest you turn that thing off.

    FRANK
And how long might you have been harbouring these feelings?

    SOPHIE
I'm not a feeling harbour. I'm not a harbour of any kind.

    FRANK
Anything to stop you making some kind of move?

    SOPHIE
No way.

    FRANK
No way?

SOPHIE
That's right. I don't know what he's thinking.
I don't know what he wants. He's got accepted
into UCLA. Why doesn't he send them the money
and go? I don't know what he wants. What would
I say? What would I say to him? Okay, there's
this bit on page two of *Bright Lights, Big City*
where the guy talks about the likelihood of
where you aren't being more fun than where you
are. I might say that to him. And then I'd say,
dickhead, have fun where you are. But that's
enough. Enough prose. Now I'm going to do a
poem. Are you ready for the poem?

FRANK
Yep. Always.

(There's a bad attempt at close-up, losing
half of SOPHIE's face, then a change of mind
and reversion to previous framing.)

SOPHIE
'Had we but world enough, and time, This coyness, Lady, were no crime. We would sit down,
and think which way To walk, and pass our long
love's day.' He said that once. It's from a
poem, but the poem's about time, so don't get
any big ideas, just because it's also from a coy
bastard. He said it a couple of times in the
chicken suit. On the back steps of the World.

FRANK
And you can remember it all.

SOPHIE
Well, yeah.

FRANK
What do you think that means?

SOPHIE
I don't know. What do *you* think it means?

FRANK
I didn't say it. What do you think it means?

SOPHIE
(This time like de Niro) No my friend, what do you think it means?

FRANK
Are you talking to me?

SOPHIE
Are you talking to me? We watch a bit of Scorsese round here now. Are you bullshitting me about having no tape in there?

FRANK
Why would I do that? I'm against bullshitting. You know that. There's not one tactic in me. That's what they say. All I've got's the direct approach. Ask Phil. So, trust me, I'm a three-quarters doctor. If I scrape through surgery.

SOPHIE
I know I've blown it. I accused him of sleeping

> with my mother. I'm guessing that's one of
> those automatic strike-out things.
>
>   FRANK
> He's not the kind of guy who'd do that. It's
> just not him.
>
>   SOPHIE
> Thanks for your support.
>
>   FRANK
> Hey, I'm just calling it how I see it. It doesn't
> mean you don't have my support. Some people are
> like that and some aren't. And, I figure, as long
> as you're up-front about things, there's not
> much to complain about.
>
>   SOPHIE
> Are you sure there's no tape in that? The red
> light's . . .
>
>   FRANK
> That's just because my finger's on the button.
>
> SOPHIE reaches out, the picture goes to crackles.

Frank's buttocks don't appear once. I rewind the tape, and I play it again. I take it out, I put in my room, and I rinse my shirt. I let another ten minutes pass, and I call the Greens. It's Frank who answers.

'It's Phil.'

'Figured it might be. Good timing. I just walked in.'

'I've watched the tape.'

'Which bit did you like best? The bit where I had Ron's spare wig coming out of my arse like a bear from a cave, or the bit where I clenched his spare dentures between my buttocks and made them talk?

'Well, they were good, but I preferred some of the quieter bits, actually. The character-based stuff.'

'Yeah, surprisingly subtle, wasn't it? I like the way you don't even see the argument scene but, if you're going with *The Taming of the Shrew* formula, it's pretty much understood to be inevitable now, so you can run it off camera.'

'Very clever.'

'Well, it's all down to characterisation, and having that understanding of the inner workings of people. I think that's the key to being a really good film-maker.'

'So do you reckon I should call Sophie?'

'I can't believe you're asking me for advice.'

'Yeah, sorry. I think it was just a reflex. What I meant was, I might give her a call and see what she's doing tomorrow. I will give her a call, now. And apologise for my share of all that. For my excellent work off camera. I hope Ron doesn't answer. I know he'd be a pushover for a trip to the movies, but it's just not the same.'

'Even if your mother thinks it is.'

'My mother . . . not a word of this to my mother.'

'Never. You can trust me. Anyway, I owe you. I owe you something. Even when you were really shitty with me, you didn't blow my cover. But, yeah, you should call Sophie. I'm sure I'm not the only person who's been thinking all along that that looked obvious. Not that that's a problem, is it? Not in terms of my movie. It's all about the journey, isn't it? Something like that. I think I can remember someone saying that.'

'Yeah, me too. Some loser in one of his many angry moments.'

'Hey, that's "loser who helps people", not just loser. There are plenty of losers around who are selfish pricks. Remember that. You should stop being shitty with us all for a second – however justifiable it is – and look at what you've done. Look at Ness, look at every single Todd, look at the World. Look at me. You could have done nothing, and you didn't. And it made some kind of difference, right?'

'Thanks. There's still a fair bit to sort out, but thanks. I should go. I've got some paperwork to take a look at.'

Back in my room and under a pile of other things – obstetrics notes, miscellaneous junk – I find my UCLA documentation. The offer is about to expire, and maybe I was going to let it. Maybe I was going to let it slip quietly away, rather than risking a few weeks somewhere very different. I've made a lot of noise about getting out of here, and I've probably never looked like doing it. But all that noise is probably not even about here. This place is just an easy thing to be dissatisfied with, a fall-guy for anything that isn't working the way I'd like it to.

'If you've got a problem with yourself, deal with it.' Sophie shouted that at me like a football coach who'd done a weekend counselling course. There's nothing lank about her when she's angry.

So maybe I'll go to LA for December and January. LA. As if I'm any closer to comfortable with the idea. LA and an emergency room – how can I be ready for that? How can I? Who knows? But the time and place to work that out is December in LA, not here and now. And if I go and I hide in my room there all my free time – if I get free time – no-one'll know but me. And in a couple of months, I'll be home. And maybe I'll go out of my room sometimes, and maybe it'll be good. I might meet people, do things.

Two or three shifts a week at World of Chickens

between now and then should get me there – the airfare and some spending money. Not a lot of spending money, but some.

My mother's car glides in under the house and I hear her coming up the steps. I don't know how you go about getting a bank cheque for thirty-five US dollars, but she will. It can't be hard. I'm sure there are people braver than I am who do it all the time.

I'm going to do this. I'm going to fix the paperwork up now, I'm going to call Sophie and tell her and then, in six months, I'm going to see how things work in LA. After that, who knows? But it's as good a place to start as any.

I'm going to do this. I might be a long, long way from a lot of the cities where the big decisions are made, but I'm going to travel wherever I have to travel and do whatever I have to do. And if it doesn't work out – if I never shoot a frame and end up as a GP or a medical specialist or selling cars – it won't be because I haven't given it my best shot. So, here goes.

ACKNOWLEDGEMENTS

Other than the non-attendance due to illness of Sir Joh Bjelke-Petersen at a University of Queensland graduation ceremony on 10 May 1985, this story and the characters in it are made up. So no-one should go looking for my father if they're a Santa short at Christmas, or my mother if they're casting *The Cherry Orchard*. Furthermore, the business enterprise World of Chickens is also fictitious, and any resemblance to any other Worlds (of any kind) or businesses involved in the retail of cooked chicken and/or chicken pieces is nothing more than coincidence.

That's not to say that there weren't instances when the real-world expertise of others had a bearing on the novel. For advice concerning tissue-box balancing, unanticipated superhero powers, misadventures with bats, glow in the dark hens' night aids and more, I'd like to thank Bec, Catherine, Bronwyn, Alison, Allison, Maureen, Clare and Anthony. For information concerning the abovementioned graduation ceremony, I'd like to thank the University of Queensland Archives.

For showing us how good first novels can be, I'm grateful to Jay McInerney for *Bright Lights, Big City* (even though Phil's reading of it was rather coloured by his own circumstances).

I'm also grateful to Matt Condon for triggering the invention of Phil and Frank several years ago, when he invited me to contribute to *Smashed: Australian Drinking Stories* after giving away all the obvious drinks to other people and compelling me to go Green. If you bump into him, please buy him a brizgarita from me. (If you bump into me, a beer would do nicely thanks.)

And I'd like to thank the large team of people in several countries who got behind this novel and helped it on its way, particularly Rachel who, among other things, put Heart into it just when it was called for. Finally, I'm grateful to everyone at home for the continuing unqualified support, and Liz for inventing the Sunny Garden website and keeping it in a shape other writers can only envy.

BACHELOR KISSES
NICK EARLS

Jon, Rick and Jen share takeaway food rituals, sporadic cocktail nights and the quest for love. Rick seems destined to long, lonely nights beneath his Porky Pig doona. Jen consumes men like chocolate bars. And Jon gets lucky in a way he's never expected – more women than he knows how to handle. A young doctor with grand plans for the hormone of darkness, he finds his life is spiralling way out of control.

Bachelor Kisses is the mess Jon Marshall makes of his life when it stops making sense. It's the story of one man's hilarious search for meaning: a chaotic comedy of misjudgements, misinformation and misguided intimacy.

'Cute, funny, sexy.'
Cleo

'A fast-paced comedy written with verve and intelligence.'
The Bulletin

'A chaotic comedy with hidden depths, it's a rollicking read.'
The Australian

'Buy a Nick Earls novel and you need never be sad again.'
Who Weekly

PERFECT SKIN

NICK EARLS

'This book is utterly adorable. It made me laugh out loud.'
The Big Issue

Ten years have passed since Jon Marshall's footloose bachelor days, and he's come a long way. He's a partner in his own practice, owns a nice house in a nice suburb and cruises town in a Beemer. And he has a six-month-old daughter, Lily, affectionately known as the Bean.

But life hasn't taken the path Jon guessed it would back in his twenties. Buddies George, Oscar and Wendy coax each other through the challenges – back hair, dating etiquette, and a clumsiness with domestic pets – and Ash breaks all the rules. But it's the Bean who shows him life's possibilities.

Perfect Skin is a witty, moving and highly original snapshot of what it is to be thirty-something in a post-Duran Duran world.

'One of the few Australian Generation X novels to have made me roll around laughing.'
The Bulletin

'Warm, funny and deeply moving.'
The Courier-Mail

HEADGAMES

NICK EARLS

Frank and Philby meet at uni. Frank is the king of cool and dysfunctionally libidinous. Philby is nervous, nerdy, and dysfunctionally insecure. Somehow, they form a team, and go about chasing girls, passing their degrees and surviving many a green drink experience.

The hilarious misadventures of Frank and Philby are just part of what lies between the covers of *Headgames*. There's also a difficult unicorn, a shampoo fetish, a cyber romance, a shopping mall that goes on forever, a fishing trip with Keanu Reeves and much, much more.

From the comic to the bizarre, *Headgames* is Nick Earls at his adventurous best.

'No one quite portrays the preoccupations of the twenty-something male with as much insight and humour as Nick Earls.'
The Age

'Unless you've just had an injection of Botox, keeping a straight face as you read Earls's [*Headgames*] is nothing short of impossible.'
Who Weekly

'Earls's writing is so likeable, it's like an old mate telling you fibs over a few drinks, drawing you in with an exciting story before delivering the sucker punch.'
Cleo